THE MISSION

Ava the Destroyer Series

Book 1

by

Catherine M. Clark

Wylde Publishing

CHAPTER 1

SAND: THE UNINVITED UNDERWEAR GUEST, AND OTHER OCCUPATIONAL HAZARDS

Have you ever experienced the profound, skin-crawling annoyance of getting sand in your underwear? If so, you can perhaps begin to relate to my current, gritty discomfort. Despite spending years deployed in sandy, hostile environments, immersed in grit and dust, I still haven't grown accustomed to the insidious way it invades every crevice. The heat prickles under my fatigues, sweat pasting the fine grains to my skin in a way that makes me want to scream. Nor have I ever figured out *how* the damn sand manages to infiltrate my underwear *every single time*, just like this time, even when there is limited sand in this region.

I've been lying here, prone, pressed belly-down into the coarse earth for the past three interminably long hours, barely twitching a muscle, yet the relentless sand still manages to get in. The chafing starts, a low burn beneath the edge of my knickers. To distract my mind from the persistent irritation, a task that requires considerable focus, I mentally rehearse the mission parameters, run through contingency plans, and visualise alternative scenarios should things deviate from the meticulously crafted plan. A cold knot of unease tightens in my stomach, though; my concern is growing as the designated time window when the target was supposed to appear has ticked past. Thirty minutes overdue now. The silence stretches, broken only by the faint buzz of insects and the whisper of the wind across the desolate landscape.

My mission, assigned with curt efficiency, is to neutralise the leader of a new, particularly vicious terrorist faction that calls itself 'The Scions of Dawn'. Intelligence, gleaned from whispers and intercepted comms, indicates that the group would likely disintegrate without his charismatic, brutal leadership. His name echoes in reports, Dominic Santiago. Thus, I find myself embedded deep within the unforgiving terrain of Colombia, the humid air thick with the scent of damp earth and decaying vegetation. I'm anticipating Santiago's arrival. According to our intel, precise and recently updated, he was due thirty – no, now pushing forty – minutes prior.

I arrived hours earlier than strictly necessary, needing the cover of pre-dawn darkness to approach stealthily from my insertion point, a jarring parachute drop five miles out. The long, tense walk and crawl through hostile territory is standard procedure, leaving muscles screaming and nerves frayed, but essential for maintaining the element of surprise. Now, the waiting gnaws at me. Yet, the anticipation provides its own unique, paradoxical rush – a familiar jolt of adrenaline that acts as an invigorating stimulant for both body and mind, sharpening my senses, honing my focus, and keeping my attention locked onto the task at hand, despite the sand.

Finally, a shimmer in the distance. Headlights pierce the gloom, twin beams cutting through the twilight haze. My heartbeat, previously slow and controlled, gives a brief, hard kick against my ribs as the lights approach the ramshackle camp I've had under surveillance. The collection of tents and temporary structures sits vulnerably in a small clearing, looking deceptively peaceful under the fading light.

I make a minute adjustment to my ELR-SR rifle, the cold metal familiar and comforting against my cheek. Many in my line of work favour the heavier M107 Barret, a beast renowned for its stopping power, but I prefer the ELR-SR. Its quick calibre change capability offers unparalleled adaptability across diverse operations, a versatility that has saved my skin more than once. I train the weapon, now fitted with a high-powered scope, onto the oncoming vehicle. Peering through the optic, I focus, but the glare from the headlights obscures the interior. I can't confirm my target is inside—frustration prickles. Still, the vehicle's silhouette and the distinct pattern of its headlights match the intel, it *should* be Dominic's car, a rugged, black 4x4 Toyota Land Cruiser.

I shift my rifle's aim back towards the camp's central area, near the largest tent where Santiago is expected to alight, readying myself mentally and physically for the shot. The crosshairs settle, unwavering. But just as I regulate my breathing, preparing to enter that zone of absolute stillness required for a long-range kill, the sharp, distinct *snap* of a breaking branch rips through the quiet air behind me.

My blood runs cold. I *believed* I was beyond their established patrol boundary. Had I miscalculated? It appears they've altered their pattern since my reconnaissance last week, when I meticulously observed this location and monitored the guards' predictable habits. A rookie mistake? Or just bad luck? Either way, I'm compromised.

Carefully, soundlessly, I lay my precious rifle on the sandy ground beside me. My hand snakes down my leg, fingers brushing against the familiar, reassuring shape of one of the many daggers sheathed there. I slip one free – perfectly balanced, lethally sharp – its grip cool and solid in my palm as I slowly, fluidly, raise myself from prone to a low crouch, every muscle taut and ready.

As I pivot silently towards the direction the sound originated from, another noise reaches me – the distinct crunch of a boot on dead leaves and brittle sticks, closer this time, almost on top of me. Then, the rustle of bushes being carelessly pushed aside. Whoever it is, they are *very* close now, dangerously close. They're clumsy, loud. Not standard patrol behaviour. I melt backwards, seeking cover behind a dense clump of bushes and a cluster of thin trees, preparing to neutralise the threat.

There can be no half-measures out here. It doesn't matter who they are; they represent an unacceptable risk to the mission. I must remove them from the equation, swiftly and silently. Anyone blundering around this far out, this close to Santiago's arrival, is no innocent bystander. My heart rate, which had spiked, deliberately slows as I take measured, steadying breaths, sinking into the practised calm I rely on during missions. It took years of brutal training, mental and physical, to master this state, to achieve this level of detached focus. It clears the noise, sharpens thought, and allows me to analyse and react instantly to any situation.

I hear them approach, the sound resolving into a single individual stumbling through the undergrowth. A quick, peripheral scan back towards the camp confirms my fears – Dominic's Land Cruiser is pulling up, almost at its destination. My window of opportunity is closing rapidly. I have to deal with this interloper *now*.

I lift my right hand, the dagger poised, balanced perfectly for a lethal strike. I can hear the man's laboured breathing even before he breaks through the foliage, ragged gasps that speak of exertion. He sounds like he's just run a marathon, wheezing and muttering curses to himself under his breath about being sent out here. This tells me he isn't in peak physical condition, possibly overweight, and definitely not expecting trouble. Just as I register this, the man stumbles out of the bushes, moving past my concealed position. My assessment was accurate; this man is far from combat-ready. A protruding stomach strains against his sweat-stained uniform, his face glistening with perspiration under the dim light.

I rise silently, instantly adjusting my stance to accommodate the man's anticipated extra weight. I cannot allow him to make a sound, cannot risk him accidentally discharging the battered AK-47 slung carelessly over his shoulder. There's only one viable, silent takedown in this scenario: in one fluid motion, I surge forward, clamping my left hand firmly over his mouth and nose, muffling any potential cry. Simultaneously, I hook my arm around his neck, pulling him sharply backwards off balance, using his momentum against him while, with my right hand, I drive the dagger with all my strength into the soft spot at the base of his skull, aiming to sever the spinal cord.

I feel the sickening scrape of the blade against bone, the tell-tale vibration travelling up the steel into the hilt, a grim confirmation of a solid hit. As the blade sinks deep, severing the vital connection, the man goes limp after a brief, reflexive struggle – mostly just random nerve impulses firing in protest. I release my hold, letting his dead weight drop forward to the ground, pushing his body away from me with a grimace of distaste. As he collapses, I swiftly withdraw my knife, wiping the blade clean on the back of his stained uniform before his body settles onto the leaf litter with a soft thud.

Sheathing my blade as I move, I return to my previous firing position as quickly and silently as the terrain allows. Lying back down, the gritty sand immediately resuming its irritating invasion, I snatch up my rifle. Training the scope back onto the camp, my heart gives another jump – Dominic's car has arrived, doors open. I scan the area frantically; Dominic Santiago is already out, walking briskly towards the main tent, flanked by two guards. I missed my initial window, but perhaps not entirely.

Taking a deep, centering breath, I hold it, stilling my body, steadying my grip. I adjust my aim fractionally, compensating for the slight breeze and the distance, leading him just a hair. Then, without conscious thought, muscle memory taking over, I squeeze the trigger.

The suppressor does its job, muffling the sharp crack of the shot into a dull cough. It's a common misconception that silencers render shots completely silent; they don't. They merely reduce the sound signature, making it difficult to recognise as gunfire amidst normal background noise. But tonight, in this heavy quiet, the muffled report is still audible, though its direction is harder to pinpoint, buying me precious seconds.

Dominic crumples to the ground before his guards can fully react. That's my cue. I don't wait to confirm the kill. I scramble into a crouch, melting back into the deeper woods behind me before rising and moving swiftly, expertly erasing any sign of my passage, heading towards the extraction point five miles away.

As I move through the dense undergrowth, the irritating sand shifts, becomes actively uncomfortable, chafing insistently between the fabric of my underwear and my skin. A frustrated groan escapes me, low and guttural. *How?* I want to scream the question into the indifferent night, but I can't. I even wore smaller, tighter knickers today, hoping the snug fit would finally defeat the microscopic invaders. Clearly, it didn't work. With a familiar sense of resignation, I have to ignore it, push the discomfort down, compartmentalise it like every other time.

It takes me almost two gruelling hours to reach the extraction zone, constantly checking my back trail, employing every trick I know to ensure no one followed me, before finally breaking cover into the designated open field. I click my radio transmitter twice, and the pre-arranged signal notifies the pilot I am approaching. The LZ is cold for now. As I reach the edge of the clearing, the familiar, welcome thwop-thwop-thwop of chopper blades slices through the night air. Just as I step out from the treeline, I see my ride, a sleek, black military helicopter, descending rapidly; I drop into a crouch, head down against the rotor wash, and sprint towards the open side door.

A private, face grim, rifle trained warily on the woods behind me, is waiting at the door; I haul myself aboard in one practised movement. As soon as my boots hit the deck plating of the rear seating area, the pilot starts ascending immediately, banking sharply to get us out of the hot zone and avoid any potential ground fire or pursuit.

I unslung my rifle from my back, securing it carefully in the weapon rack, before taking a seat on the bench, facing the rear of the chopper, watching the ground fall away rapidly. The flight back to the forward operating base is quiet, conducted in near silence, which suits me perfectly. I prefer the quiet decompression after the high-intensity focus of a mission. As I sit there, the rhythmic vibration of the helicopter is a familiar lullaby. I desperately wish the private wasn't here. The sand. Oh god, the sand. The urge to drop my trousers and underwear right here and attempt to brush the cursed grit out is almost overwhelming.

But that would be… inadvisable. He'd probably enjoy the show far too much, but the potential fallout for me wouldn't be worth it. My hard-earned, fearsome nickname could easily morph into something crude and unflattering. In this male-dominated world, it only takes one perceived misstep, one moment of perceived weakness or foolishness, for a woman to be saddled with a demeaning label that's impossible to shake. No, the sand stays.

Once we touch down back at base, the transition jarring, I make a beeline for my bunk, peeling off my sandy gear with relief, changing quickly into a fresh uniform, then report immediately to my commander. Inside his cramped command tent, the air thick with the smell of canvas and stale coffee, I see he's deep in discussion, poring over maps with some men from the team tasked with addressing the burgeoning drug trade in this volatile region. As I approach, he looks up, dismisses the others with a nod, and greets me. I snap a crisp salute, standing rigidly at attention.

"At ease, Captain," Colonel Hanson says, his voice gruff but fair.

"Thank you, sir," I reply, relaxing slightly.

"What's your mission report?" he asks, getting straight to the point.

"Primary target eliminated, sir. Santiago is down," I report, keeping my tone neutral, factual.

"Any issues?" he inquires, his sharp eyes assessing me.

"Nothing I couldn't handle, sir." A slight understatement, perhaps, but the patrol guard was a minor complication, dealt with efficiently. "What's my next mission, sir?" I ask, already anticipating the next challenge, eager to keep busy.

"You don't have one." He pauses, his expression unreadable. "You are being reassigned, Captain. And it's against my explicit wishes," he informs me, his tone clipped.

"What?" The word escapes me, sharp with bafflement. Reassigned? I was supposed to be here for another five months, a full eight-month tour. I've only completed three. This makes no sense.

"You have been reassigned," he repeats firmly. "Intel says you are heading home to join a special task force. You will be working directly for the CIA. Pack your things and be ready. The next transport plane is leaving in precisely one hour." He extends a hand. "It was a pleasure working with you, Captain. Your reputation is thoroughly justified. That nickname everyone whispers… it's well-deserved," Colonel Hanson says, a flicker of something almost like regret in his eyes.

"Thank you, Colonel." I shake his hand, my mind reeling. A CIA task force? Back home? "I'm not keen on the nickname myself, sir. I do my job," I murmur, still trying to process this sudden, unexpected change. Working *for* the CIA occasionally is one thing – short-term assignments, specific objectives. But being formally *assigned* to them, stateside? The CIA can't legally operate within US borders, can they? So why pull me back now? Usually, I'd meet a handler in the field, receive mission details discreetly. This feels… irregular. Significant.

"Nonetheless, 'Ava the Destroyer' suits you," Hanson insists, releasing my hand. "Believe me, I'm not happy to lose you this soon, but the orders came down from high command. You are to report to Langley as soon as possible. So, get moving, Captain. I hope our paths cross again soon," Colonel Hanson finishes, his tone leaving no room for argument.

"Yes, sir. I hope to work with you again, too," I reply automatically, giving another salute before turning and heading out of the tent, my thoughts a chaotic whirl. Back at my bunk, I pack swiftly. Years of transient deployments have taught me to travel light; sentimentality is a luxury I can't afford. Bag slung over one shoulder, rifle case in hand, I make my way towards the airstrip under the oppressive Colombian sun.

Only one aircraft sits on the dusty tarmac, a hulking C-17 transport plane, its rear ramp lowered invitingly. I head towards it, spotting the pilot, Captain Jones, doing his final checks near the cargo bay.

"Captain Bekke," he calls out, surprise evident in his voice. "I hear you are joining us for the trip back to the States? Didn't think your tour was up yet?" he inquires, wiping sweat from his brow.

"Apparently not, Captain Jones. Seems I've been reassigned. Heading for Langley, orders came down," I reply, trying to sound nonchalant despite the swirl of uncertainty inside me.

"Langley, huh?" Jones whistles softly. "Sounds like you're moving up in the world, Bekke. Movers and shakers. Good luck with whatever it is. You'll be missed around here, Destroyer," Captain Jones says with a friendly grin.

"Don't know about moving up," I counter, managing a small smile. "Frankly, I'm baffled about why they'd want someone with my particular skill set back in the States. But thanks anyway, Jones." My skills are honed for foreign soil, for taking down threats far from home. What use could they possibly have for me at CIA headquarters?

"It is intriguing," Jones concedes. "Unless it's all top secret, need-to-know stuff. You'll have to spill the beans next time I see you. Anyway," he gestures towards the cavernous interior of the plane, "make yourself comfortable anywhere you like. You're my only passenger today, so stretch out. Try to grab some sleep on the way back; it's a long haul. We'll be wheels up in ten," Captain Jones states, turning back to his pre-flight checks.

"Thanks, Jones." I nod my appreciation, then trudge up the heavy ramp into the dim cargo hold. I find a row of webbing seats along the right side, stow my bag securely under them, place my rifle case carefully beside it, and then strap myself in tightly, cinching the belts until they bite reassuringly into my shoulders. Only then do I allow myself to close my eyes, seeking the oblivion of sleep, determined not to worry about falling out of my seat or the enigma waiting for me at Langley.

CHAPTER 2

REASSIGNMENT, REUNIONS, AND RESISTING JONES'S
BOURBON-FUELLED ADVANCES

The jolt of the plane touching down startles me awake. Years of snatching sleep wherever and whenever possible have trained my body, but the sudden return to solid ground always takes a moment to process. The low thrum of the engines changes pitch as we taxi, the familiar vibration shifting beneath my boots. Finally, the whine of hydraulics signals the loading ramp lowering, and I hear the distinct footsteps of Captain Jones and his co-pilot approaching the rear of the C-17.

"Captain Bekke," Jones calls out, his voice slightly raised over the residual engine noise. "Hope you slept well. Checked on you at one point—you were completely out cold."

I unbuckle myself, stretching limbs stiff from the cramped seating. "Like a baby, Jones," I reply, my voice a little rough from sleep. "And you know you don't have to keep calling me Captain when we're off duty. Bekke is fine, or Ava. We've known each other... what, four years now, haven't we?"

His eyes light up, a familiar spark of mischief in them. "Four years? Has it really been that long? Feels like yesterday we were celebrating your last promotion. We should go out for a drink tonight to celebrate your return, right?." He angles his body slightly towards me, lowering his voice a fraction, a subtle shift I've seen him use before.

I raise an eyebrow, knowing exactly where this is heading. "So, just as friends? You, me, maybe rope in David and Simon if they're around? A proper reunion?."

He grins, that easy charm that probably works on most women. "Well, that's always a good night, Bekke, you know I love a rowdy night out with the rest. But I was thinking more along the lines of just you and me. Quiet corner, maybe share a bottle of that decent bourbon. What do you say?."

There it is. I let out a soft sigh. "Jones, I'm flattered, honestly. But I think keeping things strictly friends is best for both of us," I say gently but firmly. "Besides, I have no idea where this new assignment is taking me or for how long. Could be shipped out tomorrow for all I know." I offer a compromise, "But I *will* hold you to that bottle of bourbon tonight, *if* I'm free and if any of the usual crowd are actually stateside. Otherwise, rain check until this mission wraps up, deal?."

He doesn't push, thankfully accepting the boundary with a nod. "You know it, Bekke. Wouldn't miss a night out with the gang for the world. Hope to see you tonight; otherwise, good luck with whatever hush-hush mission they've got you on."

With a final nod, Captain Jones heads down the ramp. I sling my gear bag over one shoulder, my rifle case over the other, the familiar weight settling comfortably. Following him off the plane, the cool morning air feels crisp against my skin after the stale recycled air of the transport.

After reporting in with the base commander and receiving my orders – report to Langley, Agent Moore, 0800 tomorrow – I'm shown to transient quarters, a basic but clean bunk I can use for the night. I dump my gear, the clatter echoing slightly in the small room, and immediately pull out my phone. A quick text goes out to the usual suspects, including Jones, 'Back stateside unexpectedly. Free tonight. Bar?'.

Responses ping back almost instantly. A few are in, eager for a catch-up; others are deployed, scattered across the globe. With hours to kill before evening, restlessness gnaws at me. The familiar itch for exertion, for pushing my body, takes over. I head straight for the training centre.

Hours later, muscles pleasantly aching, sweat stinging my eyes, I finally feel centred again. A long, hot shower washes away the grime of travel and training. I pull on comfortable jeans and a simple dark top – civilian clothes feel strange after weeks in fatigues. Stepping out into the evening air, I make my way off base towards the familiar lights of the local town, heading straight for 'The Garrison', our usual haunt.

The low thrum of music and chatter hits me as I push through the door. My eyes scan the familiar dim interior, automatically seeking out friendly faces. It doesn't take long. Jones spots me from a crowded table near the back, a wide grin splitting his face. He disentangles himself and heads my way, meeting me halfway. He slings a casual arm over my shoulders, a familiar, brotherly gesture, steering me towards the group.

"Everyone, look who the cat dragged in! The Destroyer herself graces us with her presence!" Jones announces, his voice booming over the din, causing heads to turn and whispers to ripple through the nearby tables.

The faces at the table – David, Simon, Roy – turn, breaking into cheers as my unwelcome nickname echoes around them. They surge towards me, a flurry of back slaps and quick hugs. "Hey guys, it's good to see you! Been too long. How's life treating you?" I ask, trying to inject warmth into my voice despite the internal cringe at the nickname.

"Great, Destroyer!"

"Doing good, Destroyer!"

"Can't complain, Destroyer!"

David, Simon, and Roy chorus almost in unison, their voices laced with friendly teasing. I groan inwardly. Some nicknames stick, no matter how much you hate them.

"Hey, Destroyer! You owe me twenty bucks!" a sharp, familiar voice cuts through the noise from behind me.

I spin around, a genuine smile finally breaking across my face as I see Emma elbowing her way through the crowd towards us. We came up through training together, two women navigating a male-dominated world, forging a bond built on shared hardships and late-night study sessions. We haven't seen each other in ages, our paths diverging on different assignments, but whenever our orbits collide, it inevitably leads to a night of hard drinking and harder laughing. My head already aches pre-emptively. Tomorrow morning is going to be rough. I silently pray that Agent Moore isn't planning an intensive briefing.

After the initial chaos of greeting Emma dies down, the six of us manage to snag a larger booth, the worn leather cool against my back. Tradition dictates the first round, *shots*. The harsh burn of cheap tequila momentarily clears my head before the stories begin. We take turns, catching up on missions – the ones we can talk about, anyway – promotions, disastrous dates, and the general absurdity of military life.

For me, it's always a careful dance. Most of my operations are classified, far beyond the clearance level of my friends. They know the drill, accepting my vague answers and redirections without pushing. It's part of the reason the nickname 'Ava the Destroyer' sprouted in the first place – whispers and rumours filling the void left by classified reports, growing wilder with each retelling until the legend eclipsed the reality. If they knew the truth, the stark reality of severed spinal cords, calculated demolitions, the cold efficiency required of an assassin… they might not be so eager to share a drink. Sometimes, the weight of that secret feels heavier than my rifle.

The night blurs into a haze of laughter, shared memories, and far too much alcohol. Somehow, miraculously, we all manage to stumble back to base in one piece, the camaraderie a warm balm against the usual isolation of my work. It's rare for so many of us to be in the same place, at the same time, a fleeting constellation of familiar faces in a life defined by constant movement.

They inevitably ask about my sudden return, my new

assignment, but I deflect, offering vague platitudes about finding out in the morning. Mentioning the CIA would immediately trigger speculation, assumptions about my work that are probably closer to the truth than the wild rumours, but still truths I can't share. Jones, bless him, knows just enough to keep his mouth shut, his love of flying outweighing any desire to gossip – getting grounded is his worst nightmare. He knows my reputation, knows I'm one of the government's top marksmen, frequently tapped for missions others can't – or won't – handle. He knows, but he doesn't talk.

My alarm screeches far too early, slicing through the thick fog in my head. I fumble blindly for my phone, cursing the incessant noise.

"Bekke, turn that bloody thing off before I shoot it! Or you! Whichever I can focus on first!" a disgruntled female voice groans from a nearby bunk. My head pounds too much to identify the speaker, but they clearly know me.

I finally locate and silence the offending device, but the ringing persists inside my skull. Thankfully, foresight prevailed last night. I grope for the bottle of water and packet of Advil I left on the floor beside my bunk. Two pills popped, followed by nearly half the bottle of water gulped down in one go. Slowly, the edges of the hangover begin to soften. I drag myself out of the relative comfort of the narrow bunk and stumble towards the showers, the cool tiles a shock under my bare feet.

Twenty minutes later, feeling slightly more human, I dress in civvies for the trip to Langley – jeans, a plain shirt, boots. A glance at my watch confirms I'm running late—no time for the mess hall, which is annoyingly situated on the other side of the barracks. I grab my bag and head out, calling a taxi as I walk. "Need to make a quick stop at a bakery in town first," I tell the dispatcher. A sausage and bacon sandwich – greasy, salty, perfect hangover food – and a very large, very strong coffee are acquired en route. By the time I've devoured the sandwich and downed half the coffee, the world starts to regain its focus. "Thanks for the detour and for getting me here on time," I say to the driver as he pulls up to the imposing Langley security gate, so I give him a good tip.

I approach the reception desk – imposing glass and steel – feeling slightly out of place in my casual attire. I slide my military ID across the counter. "Captain Ava Bekke. I have an 0800 appointment with Agent Moore."

The man behind the desk, stone-faced and impassive, barely glances at me before picking up a phone. A moment of silence, then he murmurs my name into the receiver. Another pause, a curt nod, and he replaces the handset. "Someone will be down in a few minutes. Please take a seat," he instructs, his eyes briefly flicking over me, assessing.

This feels… different. Usually, assignments here involve a quick brief, a guest pass, and directions to the relevant floor. I've worked with Special Operations before, one of the few departments requiring an escort, along with Drone Control in its separate facility. But there's another rumoured department, one whispered about without a name. A prickle of unease runs down my spine as I sink onto one of the surprisingly plush couches in the waiting area. Which department does Agent Moore belong to?

The receptionist keeps glancing over, his scrutiny making my unease grow. Why am I really here? Did I screw up? Miss something? But surely any fallout from Colombia would have been handled by Colonel Hanson? I force my breathing to slow, consciously unclenching my fists, noticing my fingers tapping restlessly against my thigh. I quickly shove my hands under my legs, trying to appear calm. The wait isn't long. The elevator dings, and a man in a sharp suit steps out, heading directly towards me. I stand automatically as he approaches.

"Agent Moore?" I ask, hoping this is finally him.

He offers no smile. "Agent Fergaston. Agent Moore is expecting you, but at a different location." He hands me a plain, sealed envelope. "There's a vehicle waiting for you out front; keys," he adds, pressing a key fob into my palm. "It's kitted out in the back, special operational setup, just so you're aware. It'll be your assigned transport for your mission." His eyes meet mine, serious and direct. "Don't open the envelope until you are secured inside the vehicle. Memorise the address, enter it into the satnav immediately, and then destroy the paper. The satnav system automatically erases the last destination entered once a new one is inputted or after the vehicle has been parked for thirty minutes." Without waiting for a response, Agent Fergaston turns and strides back towards the elevators, leaving me standing there, envelope and keys in hand, utterly gobsmacked.

Okay. This is definitely not standard procedure. Intrigue wars with a rising sense of apprehension. What in the world have I been reassigned to? But years of training kick in, suppressing the unease. Follow orders. Adapt. Stay alert.

I turn and head back out of the building, the morning sun feeling unnaturally bright after the cool interior. The car park sprawls before me. I walk towards the nearest row and press the unlock button on the fob. A chirp sounds to my right, and the lights flash on a large, black SUV – a Chevy Tahoe.

I approach the vehicle, slide into the driver's seat, and immediately lock the doors. The scent of new leather fills the cabin. Tearing open the envelope, I find a single slip of paper inside with just an address typed on it. I turn the key in the ignition. For a split second, I think the battery's dead – the engine start is almost completely silent, barely a whisper, a faint vibration through the steering wheel, the only confirmation it's running. Impressive modifications.

I quickly tap the address into the satellite navigation system. The route appears on the screen, leading me… out into the middle of nowhere. Just in case, I study the slip of paper, committing the address to memory before meticulously tearing it into tiny pieces. I push in the dashboard cigarette lighter, waiting for the metallic click as it pops out, glowing red. Carefully, I press the hot coil into the pile of torn paper in the ashtray, watching intently as the fragments curl and blacken, turning to smoke and ash. It's a small piece; the smoke is minimal and quickly dissipates. Satisfied, I pull out of the parking space and follow the satnav's directions, heading away from the city and towards the unknown.

CHAPTER 3

THE 'PARANORMAL' PROBLEM: MY ELBOW'S OPENING STATEMENT, AND OTHER SURPRISES FROM THE NEW MANAGEMENT

The drive takes nearly two hours, the urban sprawl gradually giving way to countryside, then increasingly isolated roads. Finally, the satnav directs me off the main highway onto a bumpy dirt track that winds through dense woods. My senses heighten, scanning the trees, watching for any sign of surveillance or ambush. As I navigate a sharp bend, a farmhouse comes into view, nestled in a clearing. It looks utterly ordinary, the kind of rambling ranch house you see dotted across rural America, complete with a wraparound porch and slightly peeling paint.

I slow the Tahoe, my eyes sweeping the property. Another black Tahoe, identical to mine, is parked near the front porch. I pull up alongside it, studying the house for another moment – windows dark, no sign of movement – before switching off the engine and cautiously getting out. The silence here is profound, broken only by the crunch of gravel under my boots and the distant chirp of birds. As I slowly approach the front door, it swings open before I reach it.

A man steps out onto the porch, dressed in a standard black suit, though it looks slightly rumpled, like he's spent too long sitting. He smiles, a polite but professional expression. He's older, maybe early fifties, with touches of grey at his temples contrasting with the brown hair on top. He looks like he belongs behind a desk, maybe nearing the end of his career. Please let this finally be Agent Moore.

"Captain Bekke," he says, his voice calm and measured. "It's good to finally meet you in person. I'm Agent Moore. Apologies for all the cloak-and-dagger theatrics. Necessary precautions, I'm afraid. Please, come in. We have a lot to discuss."

I study him for a beat, assessing his demeanour – calm, controlled, but with an underlying intensity in his eyes. "Agent Moore. A pleasure," I reply, keeping my tone neutral despite the lingering questions swirling in my head. "This situation… it's certainly raised a few questions about what exactly you need me for." He holds out his hand, and I take it. His grip is firm, surprisingly strong for a man who looks desk-bound. He releases my hand quickly and turns, leading the way back into the house.

I follow him inside, my eyes automatically scanning the interior as the door closes behind me. The place smells faintly of dust and disuse. The furniture is sparse, functional, covered in white sheets in some places. This isn't a home; it's a stage set, cold and impersonal.

"It's a CIA safe house," Agent Moore confirms, noticing my appraisal as he shuts and locks the front door. "This way." He leads me down a short hallway towards a room on the left.

As we enter, the low murmur of conversation ceases abruptly. Three people – two men and a woman – look up, their eyes fixing on me the moment I cross the threshold. One man is dressed similarly to Moore, in a suit that screams 'agent'. However, the other man and the woman are in casual civilian clothes, much like myself. A wave of assessment washes over me from the trio.

Agent Moore steps further into the room, gesturing towards me. "Everyone, this is Captain Ava Bekke. Also known as 'The Destroyer'."

I fight back another internal cringe at the nickname, forcing a polite, neutral nod towards the group. Why is he using that name? Especially here, with strangers?

"Captain Bekke, allow me to introduce Agent Sam Miller," Moore says, indicating the man in the suit. Sam nods, a professional but guarded expression on his face, and extends his hand. His handshake is standard agent issue – firm, brief, businesslike. "Agent Miller," I acknowledge, my eyes doing a quick assessment. Good build, looks like he maintains his fitness, probably mid-thirties. Fair hair, cut regulation short. He seems capable, but perhaps lacks extensive field time.

Moore gestures towards the other man. "This is Luca Cole." I turn and offer my hand. His grip is startlingly firm, almost crushing, and his hand feels unusually warm against mine. My eyes widen slightly. This man… he doesn't fit the mould. He's tall, powerfully built, with shaggy dark hair falling casually across his forehead and intense, dark eyes. His skin has a natural light tan, and he carries himself with an unnerving confidence, almost a predatory grace. He looks less like an operative and more like someone who just stepped off a Milan runway. A purely physical, involuntary flicker of attraction sparks deep inside me, quickly extinguished by professional discipline and a healthy dose of suspicion. Facing him in combat would be… challenging. Please tell me I'm not working with *him*.

Finally, Moore indicates the woman. "And this is Rosemary Peyton"

My breath catches slightly as I turn to her. *Beautiful* doesn't quite cover it. Tall, maybe an inch taller than my 5'7", with long, wavy blonde hair cascading around her shoulders and the most stunning green eyes I've ever seen. Like Luca, she radiates an almost palpable confidence, but hers feels sharper, more opportunistic. As I place my hand in hers, a jolt, stronger than static electricity, shoots up my arm, making my pulse jump. Confused by the sensation, I instinctively tilt my head, forcing myself to maintain composure. Her hand is as warm as Luca's, her grip just as strong. My body reacts again, a different kind of spark this time, a warmth spreading through my chest, my pulse quickening further. I find myself strangely reluctant to let go of her hand.

Her green eyes assess me with an intensity that matches my own scrutiny, a flicker of something unreadable – confusion? – crossing her features. Then, her grip tightens slightly, almost painfully, testing me. I meet her gaze, refusing to show any reaction, refusing to be the first to break contact. It feels like a silent challenge, a power play I wasn't expecting but won't back down from. Oddly, despite the pressure, my gaze drifts down her arms. I expect defined muscles, similar to Luca's build, to account for that strength, but her physique is surprisingly feminine, lean rather than heavily muscled. Confusing. I probably look more muscular than she does.

"Rose," Luca's voice cuts through the tension, low and firm, a clear note of command.

Rosemary – Rose – instantly releases my hand, though her gaze lingers, that strange confusion still clouding her eyes. She doesn't step back immediately, holding her ground for another beat.

Trying to break the odd tension, Luca turns his attention back to me, a faint smirk playing on his lips. "The Destroyer, huh? Quite the reputation. How exactly does one earn a nickname like that?"

I force a tight smile, uncomfortable with the scrutiny. "Wasn't my choice. Just battlefield rumours and exaggerated stories that got out of hand. It's actually 'Ava the Destroyer', but that doesn't make it any better," I explain, wrinkling my nose in distaste. My gaze flicks back to Rose, who still hasn't moved away, her intense green eyes still fixed on me. A slow, knowing smirk spreads across her face, erasing the earlier confusion.

"I'm going to like you," she says finally, her voice smooth, confident, with a hint of challenge.

"Thanks… I think," I reply, turning back to Agent Moore, eager to move past the unsettling introductions.

Moore gestures towards the remaining empty chair. "Please, sit down, Captain… Ava. We have a great deal to discuss. And I should warn you, some of it… well, some of it you might find difficult to believe."

As I sit down – pointedly choosing the chair next to Rose, a small defiance against the unease she stirs in me – Moore's words only deepen my confusion. Difficult to believe? What could be more unbelievable than clandestine meetings in safe houses and introductions to models moonlighting as… what exactly? Suddenly, the straightforward danger of Colombia feels appealingly simple.

"Would it be alright if I call you Ava?" Agent Moore asks, his tone shifting slightly, becoming less formal.

"Yes, that's fine," I reply, trying to keep my focus despite the strange undercurrents in the room.

"Good. And you can call me Adam," he offers with a small smile. "So, Ava, have you managed to keep up with the news much while you were deployed?"

I rack my brain, filtering through the mission reports, the long hours of surveillance, the snatches of conversation overheard in the mess tent. News? Not really my priority. Then, a fragment surfaces – Jones arguing with someone last night about the state of things back home. "Are you referring to the rising crime rates? The ones hitting major cities particularly hard?" I ask, recalling the phrase 'crime wave'.

Adam nods, his expression turning grim. "Yes, exactly. It's become so severe that people are beginning to flee the cities. We've been monitoring a gradual increase for the past twenty-three years. It seems to correlate with… with certain events. Twenty-three years ago, there were mass killings in various locations worldwide, not just concentrated in the US, and since those incidents, the situation has steadily deteriorated."

Mass killings? Twenty-three years ago? That's news to me. How could something like that not be common knowledge? A cold knot forms in my stomach. "Alright," I say slowly, processing this new, disturbing piece of information. "Do you have any suspects? Any leads on who's behind these… attacks?"

Adam's gaze flickers towards Luca and Rose for a split second before returning to me, a subtle shift that doesn't go unnoticed. "We have… a general idea of the *type* of individuals responsible," he replies carefully, his choice of words deliberately vague. "But pinning down precise identities has proven… difficult."

I look from Adam to Luca, then to Rose. Why the glance? And what does he mean, the *type* of person? It makes no sense. I study Luca and Rose again, a little more closely this time. There's an unusual warmth radiating from them, particularly Rose, similar to the heat I felt in their handshakes. It's subtle, but noticeable in the close confines of the room. Are they running fevers? "I don't understand," I state plainly, turning back to Adam. "How can you know the *type* of person responsible but not *who* they are? That doesn't track."

Adam leans forward slightly, his voice lowering. "Yes, well… this is where things become… unconventional, Ava. Very few people, even within the intelligence community, are aware of this. Luca and Rose here… they've been instrumental in helping us understand a different reality, one hidden within our own world. They've provided context for what's been happening since those initial attacks twenty-three years ago. The situation is critical now, Ava. They've agreed to help us actively track down the groups involved and identify any potential allies. That's why we've formed this task force. We need someone to lead it, someone with your field experience, your specific skill set." He pauses, his eyes meeting mine intently. "Frankly, Ava, you're one of the only humans we believe possesses the adaptability and resilience to confront what you'll be facing… and hopefully survive it. Sam here," he gestures to Agent Miller, "has volunteered his considerable technical expertise and field skills. He's a decent marksman, highly skilled, though not quite at your level, admittedly. He can provide overwatch when needed – a role I understand you often prefer to handle yourself when operating with a team."

His words hang in the air, heavy with implication. But one word snags in my mind, jarring and out of place. "Wait," I interrupt, unable to stop myself. "Did you just say… *human*?" The word feels loaded, deliberate. "That's a very strange way to phrase it. What's next? Are you going to tell me this is some kind of alien hunt? Because if it is," I shake my head firmly, "I think I'll pass, if you don't mind."

A low chuckle escapes both Luca and Rose. It grates on my

nerves, the shared amusement at my expense. I shoot them both a look sharp enough to cut glass, and the chuckles die abruptly.

"No, Ava, rest assured, this isn't an alien hunt," Adam says, though his expression now holds a hint of concern, perhaps anticipating my reaction to the truth. "But what we *are* dealing with… well, to someone unfamiliar, it might sound just as outlandish."

I try to regain control, pushing down the irritation. "So, let me get this straight. You want me to run a task force hunting criminals, operating within the US, but under the CIA? That doesn't sound right. The CIA charter restricts domestic operations."

"Technically, this isn't a CIA operation," Adam clarifies quickly, "It's a joint task force operating under special provisions. The CIA is providing logistical and technical support, resources. But the operational command will be entirely yours. You'll be issued FBI credentials for field use." The explanation feels slippery, full of convenient loopholes and bureaucratic jargon. My suspicion deepens. This whole setup stinks.

My pulse quickens, a flutter of anxiety beneath the surface calm I project. "Sir… Adam… am I permitted to decline this assignment?"

Adam hesitates again, his gaze shifting once more to Luca and Rose before settling back on me. "You can, Ava. You have that right. But I sincerely hope you won't. You were specifically requested… highly recommended as the only candidate the brass felt confident could handle this. We genuinely need your expertise, Ava. We believe we're at a precipice. If we don't start pushing back, actively confronting this threat now… the loss of innocent life will be catastrophic."

I close my eyes for a brief moment, the weight of his words pressing down. Innocent lives lost… the phrase echoes hollowly, stirring unwelcome memories. I push them away. Focus. "Okay. If I were to accept… how big is this team? Just the four of us?" I ask, dreading the thought of managing a large, unwieldy group. "I typically work alone. Managing others isn't my preferred operational style."

Adam shifts uncomfortably in his chair, his nervousness

palpable. I brace myself for the answer I already suspect I won't like. "For now… yes. It will be just the four of you," he confirms, his eyes flicking again towards Luca and Rose. "The initial strategy requires a small footprint, minimising attention. However, finding others… allies… who are willing and able to help will be part of your objective."

His constant glances towards the enigmatic pair finally push my patience too far. "Adam, why do you keep looking at Luca and Rose every time you seem uncertain about mission parameters or personnel?" I demand, my voice sharper than intended. "Are you implying *I* also have to recruit people for this task force? On top of everything else?"

"Well…" Adam begins, clearly floundering, "Luca and Rose are… consultants. Experts in the field we're operating in. They will also be… essential for your survival, should you encounter hostile forces directly." He takes a breath. "And yes, part of the mission is identifying and recruiting others who can assist. The four of you alone may not be sufficient to handle every situation you encounter."

This is getting increasingly bizarre. I turn my attention directly to Rose, sitting beside me, radiating that strange warmth. The faint scent of… pine? Vanilla?… seems to cling to her. "What agency do you work for, Rose? What's your background?" I ask, frustration simmering beneath the surface.

Rose looks distinctly uncomfortable, glancing at Luca, who gives her a barely perceptible nod. She turns back to me, her green eyes meeting mine squarely. "I don't work for any agency, Captain Bekke," she replies, her tone flat initially, before that challenging smirk returns. "But trust me, I am exceptionally lethal in combat."

I shake my head slowly, incredulity washing over me. I turn back to Adam, my patience finally snapping. "Is this some kind of elaborate joke, sir? Because if it is, I'm really not finding it funny."

Adam turns to Luca, his expression bordering on desperate. "How… how do we explain this to her? When you first approached me? I confess, I didn't handle the revelation particularly well myself."

Luca lets out a long sigh, pushes himself out of his chair, and moves to stand directly in front of me. My muscles tense instinctively at his proximity, his sheer physical presence unsettling. *What is he going to do?* The absurd image of the Terminator peeling back his skin flashes through my mind. I almost chuckle, then suppress it as Luca kneels, bringing himself down to my eye level. The intensity in his dark eyes is captivating and slightly intimidating.

"Ava," he begins, his voice low and serious, "the world you know… it's not the whole picture. There are layers, hidden realities." Oh god, here it comes. Not the Terminator scene, but something equally unbelievable, I suspect. "Rose and I," he continues, holding my gaze, "we belong to one of those hidden worlds. A world you're currently unaware of. It's known… as the paranormal world."

He just stares, his face completely serious, waiting for my reaction. Paranormal? Ghosts? Big Foot? My brain struggles to process the word, the concept. Then, a bubble of laughter escapes me, quickly escalating into full-blown, uncontrollable mirth. It's absurd. This has to be a prank. Jones and the others must be behind this, filming from somewhere.

"Yeah, right!" I gasp between laughs, wiping tears from my eyes. "Okay, very funny. Where are they? Where are my friends hiding? Are you guys filming this? Seriously, who are you people? Ghost hunters playing a joke? Think some poltergeist is causing the crime wave?" I try to regain control, looking around for hidden cameras, for the familiar faces I expect to pop out yelling 'Surprise!' My understanding of 'paranormal' is fuzzy, linked to late-night Tv shows and campfire stories – ghosts, demons, things that go bump in the night. Is that what they mean?

I start to push myself up from the chair, intending to call their bluff, but I freeze. No one else is laughing. Adam looks worried, Sam looks stoic, and Luca… Luca's expression is deadly serious. He reaches out, his hand surprisingly strong, and pushes me firmly back down into the chair. The casual display of strength sends a jolt of alarm through me. Instinct takes over. I react without thinking, years of combat training overriding everything else. I grab his right arm, yanking it forward off-balance, simultaneously driving my elbow hard into the side of his head.

The impact sends him staggering sideways with a grunt of surprise. I surge out of the chair, landing lightly on my feet, body coiled, ready for the next attack, automatically turning to face Agent Moore, the perceived authority figure. But before I can fully orient myself, a sound rips through the room, so deep and menacing it vibrates through the floorboards, up through the soles of my boots, and into my very bones. A low, rumbling growl, impossibly loud, impossibly close. The air crackles, thickens. Goosebumps erupt across my skin, the hairs on my neck and arms standing rigid. It sounds like… like a predator. A very large cat, something fierce and wild, right here in this room.

My head snaps back towards where Luca and Rose were. And I freeze. Utterly. Completely. For the first time since that horrific night watching my parents die, raw, primal fear grips me, cold and suffocating.

CHAPTER 4

WHEN "PARANORMAL" MEANS YOUR NEW COLLEAGUE SHEDS MORE THAN JUST CLOTHES

In front of me, something impossible unfolds, shattering the reality I know. My eyes lock onto Rose, but it's *not* Rose anymore, not entirely. Her body contorts, twists, *grows*. The low, rumbling growl I heard vibrates not just through the floorboards but resonates deep within my own chest cavity, a primal sound of immense power. The air crackles, thickens. As I watch, frozen in a state beyond fear, her clothes begin to shred, ripping like paper as she lowers herself into a crouch, her limbs elongating unnaturally. The sickening sound of bones popping and grinding echoes in the sudden, dead silence of the room. Dark, sleek fur sprouts obscenely fast from her skin, erupting through the tearing fabric, covering her arms, her torso, even her face. Her beautiful blonde hair seems to retract, swallowed by the encroaching black fur as the very shape of her skull contorts, elongating. Her teeth lengthen into vicious fangs, her nose and mouth stretching, reshaping into a predatory muzzle.

Time distorts. What likely takes less than a minute stretches into an agonising eternity, each horrifying detail searing itself into my memory. Where Rose, the beautiful, confusing woman, stood moments ago, now looms a creature of nightmare – a huge, sleek black cat, muscles rippling beneath its dark pelt. A panther! Somehow, amidst the terror locking my muscles, my brain supplies the identification. It stands easily as high as my chest on all fours, a predator exuding raw power, its growl a continuous, deep thrumming that shakes the very air I breathe.

A strangled gasp escapes me. I stumble backwards reflexively, my legs turning to water, collapsing onto my backside on the dusty floorboards. Panic, raw and suffocating, claws its way up my throat – a feeling I haven't experienced with such intensity since that horrific night years ago, watching my parents die. I scramble backwards frantically, desperate to put distance between myself and the beast, the rough wood scraping against my palms.

Again, Luca speaks Rose's name. "Rose," he says, but the tone is entirely different now–deeper, imbued with an undeniable authority, underscored by a growl that mirrors the creature's own. The effect is instantaneous. The massive panther immediately ceases its growl, lowers itself onto its belly, rests its huge head on its front paws, and, disconcertingly, licks its lips, its stunning green eyes – impossibly, still Rose's eyes – fixed on me.

My back hits the wall of the room with a dull thud. Trapped. My eyes dart towards the door I entered through – is it clear? Can I make a run for it? My mind grasps at straws. This can't be real. Someone must have slipped something hallucinogenic into my drink last night at the bar. This has to be a nightmare, another vivid, stress-induced terror playing out in my subconscious.

I stare at the panther, my breath coming in short, shallow gasps, every muscle screaming at me to flee. God, I wish I had my weapons. Any of them. Even a single dagger. Then, Agent Fergaston's words back at Langley echo in my mind, *'it's kitted out in the back'*. The Tahoe. Does it have weapons? Could I possibly make it to the car before this creature decides to pounce? My heart hammers against my ribs like a trapped bird, sweat prickling my brow, my palms slick despite the cool air in the safe house. I feel simultaneously wired and frozen, trapped in a horrifying paralysis.

Then, a voice cuts through the fog of panic, repeating my name, insistent.

"Ava!"

"Ava!"

"Captain Bekke, look at me!" Someone bellows the order. The use of my rank, the sharp, commanding tone – it slices through the terror, years of ingrained military training kicking in reflexively. I wrench my gaze away from the panther and find Agent Moore kneeling beside me, his hand reaching for my shoulder. I flinch violently away from his touch, recoiling as if burned.

"It's okay, Ava," he says, his voice attempting a calm I can see he doesn't entirely feel. His own face is pale. "They aren't going to hurt you. They are… Shifters. Panther Shifters, specifically. They are here to help us, I promise." His words barely register. Shifters? Like in fantasy novels? My brain struggles to process the information, grappling with the impossible sight still dominating my vision. I feel numb, paralysed by disbelief.

A soft noise draws my attention instantly back towards the massive panther, my head whipping around so fast I almost give myself whiplash. The creature has begun meticulously cleaning one of its enormous paws with long, rasping licks of its tongue. Luca has moved to stand beside it, one hand stroking the thick fur on top of its head, seemingly unconcerned. The panther leans into his touch, rubbing its great head against Luca's chest with a low, rumbling sound that might almost be a purr. A primal urge screams at me to yell at him, to warn him away from the dangerous beast, but my voice remains trapped, my mind still reeling.

"Ava, it's truly okay. I promise you, she won't hurt you." Agent Moore's calming tone attempts to penetrate my shock again. "There simply was no easy way to tell you, or to show you, what they are," he explains, his gaze steady, trying to convey sincerity.

Slowly, as the panther makes no aggressive move, a semblance of control returns. The rigid terror loosens its grip fractionally. I look again at the creature that was once Rose, focusing on its eyes. They *are* Rose's eyes – that same stunning, intelligent green. The cognitive dissonance is staggering. Unable to stop myself, the question tumbling out before I can filter it, I ask Luca, my voice barely a croak, "Did Rose… did she just *turn into* this… panther?"

Luca turns towards me, and to my utter confusion, a wide, almost relieved beam spreads across his handsome face. "Yes, Ava," he confirms warmly. "She did. She turned into a truly beautiful panther, didn't she? Rose is my Beta, which means she's second in command to the Alpha."

His words trigger fragmented memories – books I'd read years ago, dismissed as pure fantasy, featuring werewolves and other shapeshifters. Alphas. Betas. Pack hierarchy. It starts to click into place, slotting uncomfortable puzzle pieces into my shattered worldview. "So… you're her Alpha?" I ask Luca, the words feeling absurd even as I speak them.

He simply nods in confirmation.

"Ava," Agent Moore recaptures my attention, his tone shifting back to official seriousness. "They are here to help us. Luca can explain the entire situation when you feel ready, of course. But I must remind you, what you see here, what you hear in this room, is classified information of the highest level. If you speak of this to anyone not explicitly authorised, you will find yourself incarcerated in the most isolated, secure facility we possess, for the rest of your natural life. Do you understand, Captain?" His voice takes on that familiar, steely CIA edge, the one they all use when asserting authority.

I turn my gaze slowly towards Agent Moore, my voice still slightly shaky. "I understand," I manage. "Though I doubt anyone would believe me anyway."

Agent Moore offers a hand, helping me to my feet. My legs tremble beneath me like a newborn foal's, but I quickly regain my footing, forcing steadiness through sheer will. Across the room, Sam is calmly righting the chairs that were knocked askew during Rose's sudden, violent transformation, seemingly unfazed by the monstrous creature now grooming itself nearby. Did he already know?

I sink back into one of the chairs, my eyes never leaving the panther, "Is she… not going to change back?" I ask Luca the question hanging awkwardly in the charged air.

"She can't, not straight away," Luca explains patiently. "Shifting takes a significant toll, physically drains you. She'll be able to shift back soon. Control improves with age and practice; eventually, seasoned shifters can manage the change much more quickly, almost instantaneously."

"Okay," is all I can manage in response. Words fail me as my brain continues its struggle to reconcile the impossible reality I've witnessed. Seeing the massive panther, *Rose*, lying there so calmly beside Luca, its intelligent green eyes watching me intently, is profoundly unsettling. As my initial terror begins to recede, replaced by a bewildering numbness, that strange sensation returns – that faint, inexplicable pull towards her. A bizarre urge surfaces, wanting to run my hands through her thick, dark fur, to feel its texture, its warmth. I resist forcefully, clenching my fists, refusing to move, disturbed by the illogical impulse.

"Ava, are you feeling composed enough to discuss the mission?" Agent Moore asks gently, sensing my internal struggle.

I tear my gaze away from the panther, turning slowly towards him. I give a jerky nod, then immediately look back towards Rose-Panther, unable to completely ignore the perceived threat. My instincts scream danger, demanding flight, while this baffling pull urges me closer. Confusion muddles my thoughts; I feel utterly disoriented, trapped in some surreal Twilight Zone episode.

"As I mentioned previously," Agent Moore resumes, his voice carefully neutral, "we want you to lead this task force. Your primary objective will be to search for other… paranormals… who might be willing and able to help us fight those responsible for the escalating attacks – attacks that are not only killing humans but also… changing them… and, in some horrific cases, using them as a food source."

His words hang in the air. *Changing them? Food source?* The implications hit me with the force of a physical blow, nausea churning in my stomach. My head jerks back towards him so fast my neck cracks. "What… what did you just say?" I demand, my voice tight with disbelief and rising horror.

"Some of the Paranormals active in our world are forcibly turning humans into creatures like… well, like vampires… and even other types of shifters, or worse, binding them into demonic servitude," Agent Moore explains, watching my reaction closely. "And yes, tragically, there are also entities, possibly from other planes of existence, that have arrived here and are quite literally preying on humans for sustenance."

Hearing him repeat it, confirming the grotesque reality, makes me feel physically sick. The thought of humans being hunted, *eaten*… My gaze unwillingly flicks back to the panther. Would *she* eat me, given the chance? The fear I'd begun to suppress surges back, stronger this time. But another question worms its way through the horror. "What do you mean… turn them into *other* shifters?" I ask, my voice weakening despite my efforts. I take a shallow, unsteady breath. "Does… does that mean they could turn *me* into… into a panther like her?" The fear escalates, threatening to consume me.

Agent Moore hesitates, glancing towards Luca as if seeking guidance on how to proceed. Luca takes charge, his expression serious. "We need her trust, Adam," he says quietly but firmly. "Total honesty is the only way forward now. Do you want me to explain?"

"Yes, please," Agent Moore agrees immediately, relief evident in his voice, though worry still clouds his features. "You're right, Luca. Best be completely upfront at this point."

I turn my full attention to Luca, bracing myself for whatever nightmare fuel they are about to unleash. I feel utterly out of my depth and am certain that whatever he says will only amplify my fear.

"Ava," Luca begins, his voice soft but intense, his dark eyes locking onto mine, conveying a desperate plea for belief, for understanding. My muscles tense; the urge to bolt, to run screaming from this impossible situation, is almost overwhelming. "My pack," he continues slowly, carefully, "would *never* bite anyone intentionally to change them against their will. Rose and I are *born* shifters. You can usually tell the difference – the animal form of a true-born shifter is typically larger, more powerful than that of a bitten shifter. We are also inherently stronger, faster, and only born shifters can hold the rank of Alpha." He pauses, gauging my reaction, letting the information sink in.

He keeps his tone gentle, almost soothing, like explaining something complex to a frightened child. "In my pack, and others who follow the old ways, the ethical path, we would never forcibly turn anyone. The only exception, the only circumstance under which we *might* consider turning someone, is if a chosen mate-a human mate–was dying from severe injuries or a terminal illness, and even then, *only* with their explicit consent."

"Um…" Confusion furrows my brow. "If you don't bite anyone… and you're born shifters… then I don't understand. Who are these people, these mates with injuries and illnesses?" I ask, feeling completely adrift in this new, terrifying reality.

"I was just getting to that," Luca clarifies patiently. "Sometimes, humans become integrated into our packs, either as friends or, occasionally, as mates to pack members. It doesn't always work out, of course – revealing the truth can be… difficult for humans to accept. But sometimes, they handle it well, embrace our world, and choose to join us. These integrated humans are the *only* ones we would ever consider turning, primarily because losing a mate can be utterly devastating for a shifter, a pain few humans can comprehend. And again, crucially, we would only ever perform the bite with their full permission. Unfortunately," his expression darkens slightly, "there are other packs out there, rogue packs, who don't adhere to these ethics. They actively force humans to join their ranks, biting them against their will. This forced turning allows the Alpha to exert control over the newly bitten, essentially enslaving them. They use these forcibly turned shifters to swell their numbers, often using them as disposable fodder in attacks against other packs, thereby minimising the risk to their valuable born shifters." He watches me closely, assessing my reaction to this grim information.

I process his words, running them over and over in my mind. Intellectually, I understand what he's saying, the grim logic of it. But emotionally? It does little to quell the visceral fear coiling in my stomach – the terrifying knowledge that just one bite from either Luca or Rose could irrevocably transform me into one of *them*.

"Ava, we desperately need your help to stop these… monsters," Agent Moore pleads, his voice regaining some urgency. His use of the word 'monsters' causes both Luca and the Rose-Panther to twitch almost imperceptibly, a reaction Moore clearly notices. He quickly backpedals, "Our friends here," he gestures towards Luca and the panther, *"aren't* the monsters. They are allies. We can trust them implicitly. We need *your* specific skills, Ava, to hunt down the *real* monsters out there – the ones who are killing and turning humans indiscriminately. We need to keep your initial team small, just the four of you for now, in the hope you can operate under the radar, stay undetected for as long as possible, and take out as many targets as you can identify. However," he adds grimly, "if you uncover evidence of a larger group, something the four of you can't handle alone, then we have a specialised tactical team on standby that can assist with the takedown. We're getting desperate, Ava. We are losing this hidden war. If the truth about the paranormal world gets out prematurely, it could trigger mass panic. Humans, driven by fear, would turn on each other, creating chaos. And then," his voice drops, heavy with foreboding, "the paranormals aligned with evil will win without lifting another claw."

What he says makes a terrifying kind of sense. But overriding the logic, my fear begins to curdle, transforming into a familiar, cold anger. The memory of my parents' helplessness, my own childhood terror, surges back with unexpected force. That night, I vowed never to be weak, never to be paralysed by fear again. For the first time in years, feeling that same vulnerability now ignites the same fierce determination I felt back then. If these monsters win, if the world falls into chaos, there's no hope left for anyone. The world I know, the world I fight to protect, would cease to exist anyway. Better to fight now, to stand against the encroaching darkness, and hope we can stem the tide before it becomes an unstoppable flood. The fragmented stories I've overheard from colleagues in bars, whispers about inexplicable attacks and rising crime waves, suggest it might already be dangerously close to being too late.

Before I consciously make the decision, before I fully weigh the impossible odds, I find myself nodding.

"Ava?" Agent Moore leans forward, his face etched with cautious hope. "Is that a yes? You'll help us?"

"Yes," I manage, my voice cracking slightly from a throat suddenly gone dry. I clear it and repeat, firmer this time, the decision solidifying within me, pushing the fear back down. "Yes, I will help."

Relief floods Agent Moore's face. Agent Miller beside him murmurs, 'Great,' while Luca offers a solemn nod of approval. I return Luca's nod curtly, though the fear of being turned, the proximity of these powerful, unpredictable beings, still lingers like a chill beneath my skin.

Before anyone can speak further, the panther's body gives a sudden, sharp jerk. Then, the impossible process begins to reverse. Her massive form starts to shrink, the sleek black fur receding rapidly, melting back into smooth skin. I watch, utterly transfixed, gaping like an idiot as the transformation unfolds, still struggling to accept the reality of what my eyes are showing me. The gruesome sound of bones popping and shifting echoes again, making me cringe despite myself. I hadn't noticed Luca getting up until he came back into my line of sight carrying a large, fluffy towel and a canvas bag. He quickly drapes the towel over Rose's shrinking form just as her body finishes reverting to its human state.

She's crouched on the floor before me, completely naked.

Overloaded and still processing the initial shock, my brain fails to engage the normal social protocols. I should look away, give her privacy, but the entire spectacle is so overwhelming, so fundamentally world-altering, that normal thought processes seem suspended. By the time my brain registers the impropriety, it's too late. Both agents, Moore and Miller, have tactfully averted their gazes.

Rose quickly wraps the towel around herself as she stands, then grabs the bag Luca dropped beside her. "Thanks, Luca," she says, her voice slightly strained. "I'll just be a second." She glances at me, a quick, almost challenging wink flashing in her green eyes, before disappearing into an adjoining room, presumably a bathroom, closing the door firmly behind her.

"I'm still finding it hard to believe any of this is real," I admit, my gaze fixed on the door Rose just vanished through. "Even after watching her… change… twice. It still feels like I'm trapped in some bizarre, vivid dream." I finally tear my eyes away and turn back to the others, a profound weariness settling over me, the adrenaline crash hitting hard after the intense stress.

"Yes, it is quite an… amazing process," Luca agrees, studying me intently. He probably thinks I'm about to completely lose it, bolt screaming from the room. I wouldn't blame him; I'm sure it's a reaction he's encountered before.

"So," I begin, my voice faltering slightly as I try to gather my scattered thoughts. What's the protocol here? What's the next step in hunting mythical creatures? I settle on the only practical thing I can think of. "Where do we start? What, exactly, are we up against? And how the hell do we kill them?" My training asserts itself, seeking concrete objectives, tactical data, pushing the sheer impossibility of it all aside momentarily.

Luca takes the lead, his earlier warmth replaced by a focused intensity. "We'll be facing a wide variety of creatures, Ava, likely too many to list exhaustively right now. But I can give you the major players we anticipate encountering, other shifters, who, naturally, are not all allies. Vampires, certainly. Demons, possibly angels – though they tend to keep to themselves. Witches, warlocks, and mages, definitely. And maybe even some Fae. The sheer diversity of enemies suggests something powerful is orchestrating this, forcing cooperation between groups that would normally be at each other's throats. We suspect a god might be behind these attacks; only a being of significant power could unite such disparate, often antagonistic, factions. That's why they've been so devastatingly effective in gaining ground – this unnatural alliance."

"Wait!" The word bursts out of me. "Gods? I thought gods were supposed to be the *good* guys? Seriously? Gods are real, too? Not to mention demons and angels?" My head spins with this latest bombshell, threatening to dislodge my already precarious grip on reality.

Just then, Rose re-enters the room, now dressed casually in jeans and a t-shirt, looking disconcertingly normal after her monstrous transformation. She sits down in the chair beside me again. "How's she taking it so far?" she asks Luca cheerfully, discussing me as if I'm not even present.

"She seems… stuck on the fact that gods are real," Luca whispers back, though his whisper is easily audible in the quiet room.

"Erm," I interrupt, feeling irritation rise. "I am *not* stuck on the fact that gods are real! It's just… incredibly hard to reconcile! Because if they *are* real, then why have they let the world descend into chaos? Why allow wars? Famine? Suffering? What about world hunger? Where the hell have they been while people suffer and die? Why let people dedicate their lives, build churches, worship them, when they clearly don't give a shit?" The unfairness, the sheer indifference implied, ignites my anger again, paradoxically making me defensive on behalf of the believers I've never been among.

Luca and Rose exchange another one of those loaded, meaningful glances before Luca takes it upon himself to explain, his tone becoming didactic. "You must understand, Ava, thousands of years ago, gods *did* walk among humans. But, as often happens with power, some became corrupted, power-hungry, and they raised armies of paranormals – shifters, vampires, and others – to wage war against rival gods. This devastating conflict became known as the God Wars. It nearly resulted in the annihilation of *all* life, paranormal and human alike. Eventually, a coalition of powerful gods from opposing factions, horrified by the destruction, decided to create new planes of existence – what humans now refer to as Heaven and Hell, or the Underworld and the Realm of the Angels – and banished their warring children to these separate realms. Another, later conflict decimated most of the remaining gods themselves. Those few who survived agreed to withdraw from this earthly realm, effectively gifting it to the burgeoning human race as a mark of respect for the original creator god who first brought humanity into being. Only the angels remained behind in significant numbers, acting as guardians between the different planes, alongside the Reapers, whose task it became to collect the souls of the dead. Are you following this history lesson so far?"

I manage a numb nod. It's all I can do. The scale of what he's describing, the casual mention of gods and realms and soul collectors, is utterly overwhelming, bordering on unbelievable despite the evidence currently sitting beside me.

"Great," Luca continues, seemingly satisfied with my stunned silence. "So, it was decided that the reapers would act as cosmic arbiters. Those who could traverse dimensions would collect the souls tainted by evil – murderers, thieves, betrayers, basically anyone whose actions darkened their soul – and escort them to the Underworld. Reapers aligned with the light, often depicted with white wings, would gather the pure souls and guide them to the Realm of the Angels. However, at some point in history, a particularly malevolent god discovered a way to manipulate these darkened souls dwelling in the Underworld, twisting them, mutating them into demons and various other foul creatures. We don't fully understand the process, only that proximity to the Underworld's dark energies causes souls to corrupt and change over time. We will undoubtedly face some of these corrupted souls, these demons, in various horrifying forms. Much like vampires, actually. Another god, one fascinated with necromancy and forbidden experimentation, reanimated corpses, twisting life and death to create the first vampires. Like shifters, there are two main types, born and made. Born vampires are ancient, powerful, often appearing unnaturally pale, almost albino, with unsettling pinkish eyes. Made vampires, those turned by others, look more human initially, though their eyes often betray them with a reddish hue. They are generally slower, weaker than the born variety. In terms of raw power, born shifters like Rose and I are considered a fairly even match for born vampires in strength and speed—."

Rose lets out an audible sneer at his last statement, clearly disagreeing with the assessment of parity between panthers and vampires. She looks poised to argue, but Luca subtly elbows her in the ribs, a sharp, quick movement. She clamps her mouth shut, though her glare remains. Luca offers her a swift, smug smirk before continuing. The casual intimacy of the gesture, the lack of formal deference despite him being her Alpha, shocks me. If I elbowed Colonel Hanson in the ribs, I'd likely be facing a court-martial, or at the very least, scrubbing latrines for a month.

"Anyway," Luca resumes smoothly, ignoring the interruption, "as for *killing* these various creatures… beheading is a reliable method for most, including vampires and shifters. For shifters specifically, silver bullets tipped with wolfsbane can be effective. Against bitten shifters, the wolfsbane is particularly lethal, while silver is less so. For born shifters like us, it's the reverse – silver is more damaging, wolfsbane less so, though still unpleasant. With vampires, aside from decapitation, stakes or bullets crafted from the wood of the Pennantia Baylisiana tree are highly effective. It's an extremely rare tree; the vampires attempted a worldwide eradication centuries ago and nearly succeeded. Fortunately, witches and some vigilant human groups managed to preserve enough specimens to ensure its survival." Luca pauses again, marshalling his thoughts.

He continues, his tone becoming more speculative, "There are persistent rumours… legends, really… that certain powerful demons can only be truly, permanently destroyed by Hellfire. Normally, when you 'kill' a demon, its essence is merely banished back to the Underworld, where it eventually reforms and heals over time. Similarly, ancient tales speak of some older gods whose only true vulnerability is Hellfire. We have no idea which god, if any, is behind the current chaos, but the truly ancient, powerful deities you might think of are long gone. The gods potentially remaining are significantly weaker than their progenitors, each generation diluting the power further. But *if* the entity orchestrating this is one of those susceptible only to Hellfire… well, we might be thoroughly screwed. As far as anyone knows, Hellfire hasn't been wielded on Earth since the time of Hecate, goddess of magic and crossroads. She's the last deity I'm aware of who possessed that ability. So, let's just hope we don't encounter anything that requires it for termination. If the ultimate mastermind *is* vulnerable only to Hellfire, we'll have to find an alternative solution – perhaps imprisonment, or banishment to a plane they can't return from."

Luca lets out a long breath, slumping slightly in his chair as if the recitation has drained him. "Did I cover the basics adequately? Or have I missed anything crucial?" he asks, turning to Rose.

"I think you've covered more than enough for now," Rose replies, glancing at me with a mixture of concern and amusement. "We don't want to overload Ava *too* much on her first day, or she might actually decide to bolt," she adds, offering me another playful wink and a confident smile.

Her comment, her accurate assessment of the flight instinct still simmering beneath my forced composure, strangely solidifies my resolve. She thinks I might run? Challenge accepted. "I am *not* going to bolt," I state, injecting as much confidence into my voice as I can muster, meeting her gaze directly. "It's just… going to take a minute for all of this to sink in fully." I take another steadying breath, pushing down the residual fear and disbelief. Time to get back on mission footing. "So," I repeat my earlier question, focusing on the tactical, "where do we start?"

CHAPTER 5

GODS, MONSTERS, AND WHY YOU SHOULD NEVER ASK
ABOUT OFFICE POLITICS IN OTHER REALMS

Agent Moore decides to take over again, his tone regaining its professional equilibrium. "We think it's best to begin by meticulously reviewing the case files for each major city exhibiting elevated or unusual crime patterns. Perhaps revisit some of the more perplexing crime scenes, talk to any surviving witnesses, and attempt to discern *what* type of entity might have committed the crime. From there, try to establish a pattern, see if you can track the movements of any specific paranormals, and then… neutralise them. It's possible some are repeat offenders, creatures of habit returning to familiar hunting grounds. You might be able to conduct surveillance on those spots, stake them out, and hopefully intercept them in the act. Additionally," he adds, nodding towards Luca, "we possess some intelligence Luca has managed to gather concerning attacks on *other* paranormals, potential allies who would likely have sided with us. Maybe you can locate survivors willing to provide intel, or even join your cause, helping us locate those responsible so you can deal with them decisively."

"Okay," I manage, but frustration bubbles beneath the surface. The sheer scale of this, the ambiguity… it feels insurmountable for just the four of us. A cold weight settles in my stomach. I force myself to voice my concerns, professionalism demanding I address the tactical reality, however daunting. "Do you genuinely believe the four of us can accomplish this? It seems… an exceptionally tall order, sir. Agent

Moore," I correct myself quickly. "I thrive on challenging missions; they've always been the ones I relish the most, pushing my limits. But this… this feels beyond even my capabilities, and consequently, beyond the capabilities of a four-person team."

"We intend to start with a small, agile group," Moore reiterates patiently, though I detect a hint of strain in his voice. "As I mentioned earlier, we believe a small team will allow you to investigate without drawing undue attention. Apart from certain pack-based shifters, most paranormals tend to operate solitarily or in very small groups. We believe this covert approach offers the best chance of initial success. And, as I stressed, I *do* have another, larger team ready to deploy when you identify a significant concentration of hostiles and require overwhelming firepower." He pauses, frowning slightly. "Frankly, I'm not entirely sure how we'll manage the clean-up or the cover story *after* they engage, but we'll cross that bridge when we come to it. Necessity, Captain Bekke. With Luca's invaluable expertise, we've assembled a specialised weapons cache for your use." He hesitates, a flicker of disbelief crossing his own features. "It includes… and I still find it hard to believe I'm saying this… blessed swords, silvered blades, wooden stakes, custom-loaded wooden and silver bullets, high-voltage tasers, electrified capture nets, along with other, more exotic items. You'll also have advanced tracking devices and newly developed night-vision optics for those on the team who… lack natural night vision."

My head snaps towards Luca and Rose at his last comment. "You have natural night vision?" I ask, a surge of pure, unadulterated envy washing over me.

"Yes," Luca responds, a lazy, confident smile touching his lips. It's unfairly attractive. "We can see perfectly well in near-total darkness, almost as clearly as we see during the day."

"Wow," I breathe, genuinely impressed and intensely jealous. "I prefer operating at night, it's my element, but having to rely on those cumbersome night-vision goggles can be a massive pain, restrictive and disorienting." As I study Luca, his confident posture, the easy grace in his movements, I truly notice him again, objectively, beyond the initial shock. He and Rose both. They possess an almost preternatural beauty, a striking physical presence that seems… more than human. The thought escapes my filter before I can stop it, driven by genuine curiosity and that lingering envy. "Are… are all shifters this good-looking?"

A shared chuckle ripples between Rose and Luca as they exchange an amused glance. Rose turns back to me, her green eyes sparkling with mirth. "No, definitely not all shifters," she replies easily. "I guess we just drew the lucky genetic straw. You're not exactly hard on the eyes yourself, Ava," she adds, delivering another one of those disconcerting, flirty winks, accompanied by a smile just as cocky as Luca's.

A nervous chuckle escapes me. Heat rushes to my cheeks – something I rarely, if ever, experience. I think I look… functional. Passable. But stunning? Not by a long shot, especially compared to these two. "Ladies, if we could refrain from the flirting, please," Agent Moore interjects dryly, shaking his head slightly as if dealing with unruly recruits. "We have a critical mission to focus on."

I blush deeper, mortified at being called out, and offer Moore a curt nod, dropping my gaze momentarily. He retrieves a thick file from the countertop behind him, one I hadn't registered amidst the earlier drama. "Right," he says, all business again. "Based on recent activity and proximity, I believe you should start your investigation in Richmond, Virginia. We've recorded a few disturbing incidents closer, in Washington D.C., but not enough to establish a reliable pattern yet. Richmond currently presents the highest concentration of… unusual attacks."

Agent Miller nods sharply in agreement, his expression serious. Luca considers it for a moment, then concurs, "Yeah, Richmond sounds like a logical starting point. I'm aware of a pack – *used* to be aware of a pack – located just outside the city limits. We could check their former territory, see if any evidence remains from when they were attacked and… wiped out." His voice hardens slightly on the last words. "I know it's been a significant amount of time, years perhaps, but you never know what traces might linger."

The casual mention of a pack being 'wiped out' sends another chill through me. My new reality presses down, heavy and suffocating. The first question that springs to mind feels absurdly mundane, yet vital in this context. "What… what type of pack are we talking about? You know… what animal did they turn into?"

Luca turns towards me, his dark eyes seeming to probe, trying to decipher the thoughts behind my question. "They were wolf shifters, Ava," he replies, his tone neutral but carrying an undercurrent I can't quite decipher. "Wolves are the most common type of shifter. Unfortunately, they also have a rather… bloody history. Wolf packs have instigated numerous wars between shifter factions. At one point, centuries ago, they nearly eradicated all other shifter types. They aren't generally well-liked, primarily because many wolf packs display a callous disregard for turning humans, forcibly adding 'the bitten' to their ranks without consent. *This* particular pack near Richmond, however, was different. They were respected, even liked by some, because their Alpha was actively trying to rehabilitate the wolves' tarnished image." Luca's expression tightens. "So, if we encounter any *other* wolf packs still standing… assume they are hostile. They won't be our friends; they won't offer assistance. When I say we're dealing with wolves, Ava, you attack first and ask questions later. No hesitation." He holds my gaze intently, judging my reaction, ensuring the warning sinks in.

"Got it," I reply, forcing a cheeky, slightly macabre smile and offering a mock salute. "Wolves bad. Must kill." The corner of Luca's mouth twitches, fighting a smile.

Rose, however, beams at me, her earlier tension seemingly forgotten. "I like you more and more, girl," she declares brightly.

"Thanks, I think," I retort, matching her smile, though a sliver of my earlier fear remains. "We'll have to see how you handle yourself in a real fight before I decide if I like *you*—or not." I'm starting to accept her, despite the lingering terror her transformation invoked. The sheer unpredictability of these beings, their raw power, makes my job infinitely more challenging. How do you even begin to fight something like Rose in her massive panther form? The image replays in my mind – the speed, the claws, the teeth. A cold sweat breaks out on my palms.

Then, something shifts. A subtle change in the air. I hear… wind? Rustling leaves? It sounds like a window has been opened nearby, letting in a breeze. But I haven't seen anyone move, haven't heard a window slide open. The sound grows subtly louder, a persistent soughing, like wind rushing through distant trees. It pulls my attention, distracting me from the conversation. Frowning, I glance towards the nearest window, searching for the source. Outside, the trees stand perfectly still; there's no breeze stirring the leaves. No windows are open in the room. Utterly bewildered, I miss whatever Agent Moore is saying about Richmond logistics. Searching for the source of this phantom wind proves futile, amplifying my confusion, making me feel strangely disoriented.

And then, woven within the rushing sound, almost subliminal at first, I detect a voice. Faint, indistinct, like a distant whisper carried on the non-existent wind. My eyes widen involuntarily. I scan the room, trying to pinpoint the source, my heart beginning to thud erratically against my ribs. I notice Luca watching me again, a concerned frown creasing his brow. The whispering intensifies, coalescing into discernible words, seeming to echo inside my own skull.

"Ava!"

"Ava!"

My head snaps to the sound, towards Agent Moore, who is staring at me with open concern. He must think I'm losing it, second-guessing his choice. "Ava?" he asks sharply. "Are we boring you? I was reviewing the initial intel regarding the Richmond attacks, but you seem… elsewhere. Have you perhaps reconsidered? Decided you don't wish to be part of this task force after all?" His tone carries a professional edge, demanding my attention.

I shake my head quickly, trying to clear the fog, trying to force focus. "No! No, sir. Adam," I correct myself hastily. The wind sound, the voice – they begin to fade, retreating like an outgoing tide, leaving behind a residue of profound unease. "Agent Moore… Adam… I want to be here, I accept the assignment, but… but I think…" What am I saying? "I think we need to adjust our initial trajectory. We need to plot a course that allows us to head towards… Chicago." The name hangs in the air, surprising even me. "I'm not sure I can explain *why*, but I have this… feeling. A strong intuition. It feels imperative that we go there."

"Ava," Adam repeats my name slowly, his confusion palpable, "I said first names are fine. But… Chicago? I don't understand. What's in Chicago?"

"I'm not sure, Adam," I admit, feeling foolish yet certain. My instincts, honed over years of survival, are screaming at me. "But I *know* it's where we need to head first." My mind races, trying to reconcile this internal directive with the mission parameters. "Are there any reports, any similar attacks, maybe in… Pittsburgh? Along the route towards Chicago?"

Adam studies me for a long, assessing moment, then turns to Sam. "Agent Miller, what do we have on Pittsburgh?"

Sam walks back to the counter where the files are stacked, crouching down. The rustle of papers fills the silence. He reappears moments later holding another file, walks back towards us, and hands it to Adam. Adam flips through the file quickly, scanning the contents. He looks back up, his expression thoughtful. "There have been several incidents there, yes. Not as numerous as Richmond, which is why we initially prioritised heading south. Can you offer any concrete reason why we should deviate from the established plan, Ava? This 'feeling'… it's not standard operating procedure." His gaze is sharp, questioning my judgment.

I stare back at Adam, my mind blank. How do I explain a disembodied voice whispering instructions? How do I justify derailing a CIA-backed operation based on… nothing tangible? My credibility, fragile as it is in this new context, feels like it's about to shatter. As I open my mouth, intending to stammer out some half-baked excuse, Luca intervenes smoothly, taking the pressure off me.

"I concur with Ava," Luca states confidently, surprising me. "Heading north first makes tactical sense. We know there are, or were, more established shifter packs in the northern states, particularly around the Great Lakes region, compared to the south. Given that rogue packs represent a significant known threat, gathering intelligence on their current status, their numbers, and potential alliances early on seems prudent. It will give us a clearer picture of the scale of opposition we might face and help determine how much additional support we truly need to recruit." He delivers the assessment with such conviction that even *I* almost believe it was his idea. I don't miss the flicker of confusion that crosses Rose's face before she quickly masks it with a neutral expression.

Adam looks momentarily perplexed by this unexpected consensus but ultimately nods. "Alright," he concedes. "If you both feel strongly… we'll adjust. Start in the North, work counter-clockwise around the country. Pittsburgh first, then towards Chicago. Unless, of course, we receive actionable intelligence regarding fresh attacks elsewhere that demand immediate attention." He shifts gear back to logistics. "So, now that we've determined your initial route, we need to cover some operational basics." He takes a breath. "Firstly, avoid cheap motels, backwater hotels, roadside inns. Some evidence suggests victims are being targeted specifically when leaving such establishments. Staying in those kinds of places will likely draw unwanted attention to you much faster. Not that I imagine you'd choose them deliberately, but circumstances might tempt you to use one as a last resort. Don't. Secondly, Agent Miller," he nods towards Sam, "will be the designated point of contact for any necessary media interaction or press conferences. Since he'll often be functioning as overwatch during operations, it makes sense for him to handle public-facing duties. However, should you wish to maintain a lower profile, you might try coordinating through local police departments to release statements, demonstrating progress without revealing yourselves – assuming you can trust the local PD not to hijack the spotlight. The longer all four of you can remain out of the media spotlight, the better your operational security will be." Adam nods to Sam again. Sam reaches into his inner suit pocket and produces four sleek, leather wallets, the kind agents use to carry credentials. He hands one to each of us.

I immediately flip mine open. My own photograph, lifted from my military ID, stares back at me from beneath the official seal of the FBI. *Special Agent Ava Bekke.* How long *has* this task force been in the planning stages for them to have procured authentic FBI credentials for me? Will they hold up under scrutiny? The implications are staggering.

As if reading my thoughts, Adam clarifies, "These are entirely authentic identification documents. You and Sam are now officially recognised, within the relevant systems, as FBI Special Agents. Sam also retains his CIA credentials, but those are for emergency use only, under specific circumstances. Luca and Rose will be operating under the guise of Deputy U.S. Marshals." He anticipates my next question. "We structured it this way deliberately. A multi-agency task force often appears less suspicious, more plausible, than a large contingent from a single agency descending on a location. And frankly," he adds, glancing at Luca and Rose, "no offence intended, but neither of you precisely fits the standard Fed profile. Marshals often operate with… a bit more flexibility in appearance and methodology." He's right. No one would easily mistake the strikingly unconventional Luca and Rose for by-the-book FBI agents. Marshals, however… they often possess a rougher, less polished image. They don't adhere to the same strict haircut regulations or dress codes. The cover could work.

"Ava," Adam continues, bringing my attention back, "Luca and Rose will provide you with an intensive crash course on paranormal lore, creature identification, weaknesses, and known factions while you're on the road. We simply don't have the luxury of time for formal training before you deploy. This is precisely why you were selected, Captain. Your file highlights your ability to learn rapidly under pressure, adapt quickly to changing circumstances, and operate effectively, lethally, in any situation. We acknowledge that what you're about to face is unlike anything in your previous experience, but frankly, you represent our best chance among available human assets."

I ponder his words, trying to process the magnitude of it all. Me, facing down actual monsters, vampires, demons, whatever else lurks in the shadows. Could I really confront beings wielding magic? That cold tendril of fear, the one I thought I'd buried permanently after my parents' murder, begins to stir again deep inside, a chilling premonition. It's been dormant for so long, locked away behind walls of training and discipline. But the sheer, overwhelming *otherness* of this new reality threatens to breach those defences. The traumatic memories from that night – the shattering glass, the screams, the metallic tang of blood in the air – flood back with unexpected, sickening clarity. I abruptly push my chair back, the legs scraping loudly on the floor, and stand up, an uncontrollable urge compelling me towards the exit.

"Ava? Where are you going?" Adam demands sharply, his voice laced with concern and perhaps a hint of censure.

"I… I just need some air," I stammer, not meeting his gaze. "I'll be right back. Sorry." I turn and stride quickly out of the room, out through the main entrance of the safe house, desperate for space, for solitude, needing to regain control before I shatter completely. Outside, the sun feels unnaturally bright. To the right of the house, nestled under a large oak tree, I spot an old, slightly rusty swing set. Drawn by an inexplicable impulse, I make my way towards it. Sinking onto one of the worn wooden swings, I push off gently with my feet, the chains creaking rhythmically as I sway back and forth, back and forth. I stare out at the peaceful-looking woods surrounding the property, trying desperately to suppress the rising tide of memory and emotion, forcing the images back down into the dark recesses where they belong, striving to reclaim the stoic, unafraid persona that has defined me for so long.

CHAPTER 6

THAT AWKWARD MOMENT WHEN YOUR ALPHA WANTS TO TALK ABOUT YOUR FEELINGS (AND PHANTOM VOICES)

I'm unsure how long I sit there, gently swinging, the rhythmic creak of the chains a counterpoint to the turmoil inside me. I focus on pushing back the memories, compartmentalising the emotions, trying to regain the self-composure that feels dangerously fractured. It's been a very long time since I allowed myself to consciously dwell on those past events, on the night that shattered my world. Usually, they only surface in sporadic, uncontrollable nightmares, vivid flashes of terror that occur less frequently these days yet seem more potent during periods of idleness or intense stress. It's precisely why I prefer constant assignments, the relentless demands of the mission leaving little room for introspection.

As I slowly wrestle those thoughts back into their cage, the soft crunch of footsteps on the gravel behind me cuts through my reverie. Without looking, I instinctively know it isn't Adam or Sam; the tread is too heavy, deliberate for Agent Moore, and too confident for Sam. And the presence… it lacks Rose's specific energy signature, that strange pull I feel around her. It must be Luca. As I lift my head slightly, my suspicions are confirmed. Luca walks towards me, his movements fluid and assured, stopping a few feet away, observing me in silence, his dark eyes unreadable.

"Can I help you?" I ask, my voice neutral, perhaps a touch colder than intended.

Luca continues to observe me for another beat before answering, his gaze disconcertingly perceptive. "I came out to see if I could help," he offers, his tone unexpectedly gentle. "Are you alright? I understand this… situation… might be somewhat overwhelming."

"It's not that," I sigh, deflecting automatically, turning my gaze back towards the distant woods. I contemplate my next words carefully. Discussing my past, exposing that vulnerability, isn't something I ever do. Aside from the mandatory psychological evaluations when I first enlisted, none of my friends, none of my colleagues, are privy to the full story of what happened to me, what drives me. And I prefer it that way; it's a wall I maintain for survival. Yet… strangely, something about Luca's quiet presence, and perhaps Rose's too, makes me feel an uncharacteristic inclination to open up, just a fraction, a sliver of the truth.

"Something… something from my past resurfaced unexpectedly," I admit, keeping my voice low, devoid of emotion. "Something I usually keep suppressed. I just needed a moment alone to clear my head, regain focus. I'm okay now," I state firmly, standing up from the swing, signalling my readiness to return, to put the moment behind me.

"Remember," Luca says quietly, his gaze still holding mine, "I'm here if you ever *do* want to talk about anything. Rose is also an excellent listener, surprisingly insightful." He pauses, a thoughtful expression crossing his features. "As shifters, we all carry our own burdens, our own struggles. Part of being an Alpha, leading a pack, involves learning that keeping things hidden, bottling them up, invariably causes friction, breeds mistrust, especially within the close confines of pack life. Over time, my pack members learned to open up, share their issues, their worries. Since then, we've rarely had internal conflicts. So," he concludes with a slight shrug, "what I'm getting at, perhaps clumsily, is that I genuinely believe talking helps. I probably sound like every therapist cliché right now, but in our experience, it works."

"I appreciate the offer, Luca," I reply, meeting his gaze directly now, my professional mask firmly back in place. "But as I said, I'm fine. We should probably get back inside before Adam changes his mind about my suitability for this assignment," I say briskly, turning and walking towards the house. "What else do we need to discuss before we deploy?"

"Not much left, really," Luca replies, falling into step beside me. "We primarily need to decide as a group whether we'll review the case files for Pittsburgh here, before we leave, or make the trip first and set up shop there to analyse the intel."

"We should make the trip to Pittsburgh first," I suggest decisively, slipping back into mission-focused mode. "Get eyes on the ground, establish a temporary base, then organize ourselves and proceed from there. Analyse the files with the local context fresh in mind."

"I'm on board with that plan," Luca agrees readily. "Adam, however, expressed some concern about your readiness after your… abrupt departure." He hesitates for a moment, then stops walking, prompting me to face him again. "Ava, I need to ask you something— and it might sound strange, perhaps intrusive—but I need your complete honesty," Luca insists, his tone shifting, becoming more serious, probing. His request immediately sparks my curiosity, mingled with a thread of apprehension. Please don't let this be about me needing air. That's a vulnerability I'm not prepared to dissect.

"You heard something earlier, didn't you?" he inquires unexpectedly, his gaze sharp, analytical. "Back in the safe house, just before you left the room?"

His question catches me completely off guard. Involuntarily, my body stiffens, a betraying reaction. Luca notices immediately, a slow, knowing smile touching his lips. "Ah. So, you *did* hear something," he acknowledges softly.

I just stare at him, momentarily speechless. He wants honesty, but every instinct screams caution. Admitting I heard a disembodied voice whispering in a non-existent wind? Right after learning, shifters are real? They'll think I've cracked, cart me off to the nearest psychiatric facility for evaluation. Luca must see the internal debate raging behind my eyes; his ability to read micro-expressions is unnervingly acute. He'll be difficult to work with if he can pick up on every flicker of doubt or deception. He gently repeats his request, emphasising the need for honesty between us.

I close my eyes briefly, take a deep, steadying breath, and blow it out in a resigned sigh. I hope I'm not making a colossal mistake. "Um… yes," I admit reluctantly, meeting his gaze again. "Yes, I did hear something."

Luca studies my face intently as I give my response, then nods slowly, as if confirming a suspicion. What he says next makes my jaw drop. "About a year ago," he begins, his voice low, confidential, "while the few remaining members of my pack and I were evading a large group of hostile wolves – far too numerous for us to engage directly – I experienced something similar. I heard what sounded like the wind picking up suddenly, intensely, even though the air was completely still. Then, a woman's voice emerged from the sound, whispering instructions. It was so distracting, so unexpected, that the pursuing wolves almost discovered us. But then, just as abruptly as it began, the voice vanished, allowing me to regain focus and lead my pack to safety."

My mind reels. He heard it, too? A voice? "Okay," I manage, my own experience feeling suddenly less like a hallucination. "So… what did the voice tell *you*?" I ask, leaning in slightly, intrigued despite myself.

"It told me," Luca says, his gaze serious, "that there existed specific, clandestine departments within both the CIA and the FBI that were aware of the paranormal world. It instructed me to locate a Senior Agent Adam Moore and convince him to collaborate, to team up with us before the situation deteriorated further – before winning the secret war that apparently began twenty-three years ago became an impossibility."

His revelation hits me hard. Twenty-three years. A secret war.

The sheer scale of what we're facing, the entrenched nature of the enemy… it's staggering.

"So, Ava," Luca prompts gently, bringing me back to the present. "What did the voice say to *you*? My guess is it has something to do with your sudden insistence on Chicago?"

I finally manage to close my mouth, the need for caution warring with the relief of shared experience. Given what he just told me, honesty seems the only path forward. After a brief hesitation, I confess, "The voice… *she*… said we will find crucial clues in Chicago—clues that will lead us to what we are ultimately searching for."

Luca processes this, his expression thoughtful. "Is that all it told you? Nothing more specific?"

"That's all," I confirm. "It wasn't much, but the voice… it sounded desperate, urgent. As if heading towards Chicago was imperative. And for some reason," I admit reluctantly, feeling awkward and exposed, "the instincts that have kept me alive this long, the ones that have never steered me wrong before, are screaming at me to listen to her, to do what she wants." A wave of mental exhaustion washes over me.

"Okay, then," Luca accepts it without further question. "So, your voice was female, just like mine." He crosses his arms over his chest, the movement causing the muscles in his biceps to bulge impressively against the fabric of his top. For a fleeting, unwelcome second, I imagine running my hands over them… and then, incongruously, Rose's smiling face flashes through my mind. Startled by the intrusive thought, I quickly refocus on what Luca is saying.

"Perhaps it's the same entity guiding us both," he muses. "Regardless, I'm glad you were honest with me, Ava. It tells me I can trust you moving forward." He gives a wry smile. "From my experience, humans have a proclivity for deception. It often makes trusting them… challenging. Especially when confronted with realities they struggle to comprehend, fear makes them lash out. But watching you process everything today, how you handled the revelation about us… it makes me believe we *can* trust you."

"Thanks… I think," I reply, shifting uncomfortably from one foot to the other. "I generally consider myself an honest person, but when I heard that voice… combined with finding out your world exists… I genuinely wondered if I was starting to lose my mind."

"Well," Luca says with a surprisingly warm smile, "you're no crazier than I am, apparently. Come on, let's get back inside and get this unconventional show on the road."

We head back into the safe house. After another hour spent reviewing basic operational details and security protocols, Adam provides us each with encrypted mobile phones – strictly for mission-related communication, contacting him for updates, or liaising with local law enforcement when absolutely necessary. He also emphasises the need to sanitise any kill sites, briefing us on a dedicated cleaning crew, partnered with our tactical backup team, who will shadow us at a distance. We need to keep them updated on our location, where we plan to stay each night, and our intended movements, ensuring they maintain sufficient distance to avoid accidental overlap but remain close enough to respond rapidly. When available, they'll utilise separate safe houses to minimise exposure.

Once Adam finishes running through the myriad details, we load the voluminous case files into the back of my assigned Tahoe. He gives us a tour of the vehicle's hidden compartments, revealing the impressive array of specialised weapons concealed within its unassuming frame. I'm particularly impressed by the hidden compartment where the spare wheel would normally reside, accessible only via a biometric keypad. Inside is where we find an array of lethal, outdated weapons. Most of the weapons are custom-made, designs I've never encountered before – modified firearms, strangely shaped blades, the aforementioned stakes and nets. I know I will need dedicated time to familiarise myself with their weight, balance, and firing mechanisms.

The swords, however, immediately capture my attention. Beautifully crafted, perfectly balanced, several glinting with what looks like inlaid silver, while a few others have a duller, heavier appearance – iron, perhaps? Luca promises to explain their specific properties later. As I scan the arsenal, my eyes land on a stash of throwing daggers. Without hesitation, I slip one from its sheath and tuck it securely into the waistband of my jeans at the small of my back. The familiar weight is instantly reassuring. I hate feeling unarmed, vulnerable, but showing up at CIA headquarters packing heat seemed… unwise.

With everything loaded, we pile into the Tahoe for the drive to Pittsburgh, but we make a quick stop at the base so I can grab my weapons. I opt for the back seat alongside Rose, while Luca takes the passenger seat and Sam drives. It's a habit; I avoid sitting shotgun whenever possible if there are others in the vehicle. It's harder to see an attack coming from the front, harder to react defensively. During the drive, Luca uses Sam's secure laptop to book us two rooms at a nondescript motel on the city's outskirts, making sure we stick to the better motels available that don't accommodate the local riffraff. I request a room for myself, needing the space, the privacy, but all three immediately veto the idea. Luca firmly states that both Sam and I *must* have one of the shifters rooming with us at all times, a necessary precaution against potential attacks, particularly from vampires who might try to take us out individually while we sleep. I huff, arguing I can handle myself, but Rose points out, reasonably, that vampires possess abilities – speed, silence, that could overcome human senses, especially during sleep. Their heightened shifter senses, however, would provide an early warning system. It seems Rose is destined to be my roommate for the foreseeable future. A prospect that fills me with a complicated mix of apprehension and… something else I'm not ready to analyse. Sleep is going to be difficult, sharing space with a being who can transform into a giant predator, until I know, truly know, I can trust her. And even then… trusting *anyone* fully goes against every instinct I possess. It's how I've stayed alive this long.

Feeling relatively secure cocooned within the moving vehicle with my… unusual new colleagues, I decide to rest my eyes for a while. The late night catching up with friends, combined with the day's revelations and the prospect of sharing a room, means seizing any opportunity for sleep seems prudent.

I wake sometime later as the Tahoe slows, pulling into the motel parking lot. Glancing towards the front, I realise Luca must have taken over driving duties at some point during the trip. The fact I slept through the switch, didn't stir at the change in drivers, is highly unusual, a testament to how deeply exhausted I truly was after my 'short' night out with my friends.

"Request rooms not on the ground floor, please," I say, my voice still thick with sleep. "Whatever room *I'm* in, I want one that isn't easily accessible from the outside but still offers a viable escape route. Needs a rear window, preferably overlooking something that hinders approach – dumpsters, a steep slope, anything," I specify, years of ingrained security protocols surfacing automatically. Everyone turns to look at me. Sam just smiles and nods.

"Already planned on it, Ava," he confirms. "Glad to see you remember your basic fieldcraft, even after spending most of your recent time sniping from remote hides. Guess you didn't have to worry about motel room security much out there," Sam remarks just before opening his door and getting out to check us in. We remain in the vehicle, waiting.

I watch Sam stride towards the brightly lit motel office, his posture confident, professional. Beside me, Luca and Rose are murmuring quietly to each other in voices too low for me to decipher, even if I strained. I try to stretch discreetly in the back seat, but the limited headroom prevents a full extension, leaving my muscles feeling cramped and tight.

"Have a nice nap?" Luca asks, turning slightly in his seat, their private conversation apparently concluded.

"Yeah, thanks," I reply. "Seems I needed it more than I realised. Late one last night, catching up with friends. Didn't exactly expect to be deploying on a new mission quite this quickly. Usually, there's at least a day or two for intel review, proper prep time."

"Understandable," Luca nods sympathetically. "While you were sleeping, Rose and I were discussing dinner options. Wondering if you'd prefer to eat out somewhere in the city first, get a feel for the place, then come back here to go through the case files? Or would you rather order food in and review the reports while we eat?"

"We should definitely head into town," I state immediately, my mind clicking back into mission mode. "Find somewhere to eat, yes, but use the opportunity to scout the area. Observe the streets, gauge the atmosphere, and see how people are behaving. Get a baseline reading of the city's current temperature before we dive into the files."

"See, Luca? I genuinely like her," Rose remarks, turning to beam at me with that wide, infectious grin. "I'm actually looking forward to this mission now. Can't wait to see her in action," she adds, giving me another one of her trademark winks.

"Likewise," I reply honestly, though my mind is already calculating threat assessments. "I'm eager to observe you two operate as well. Though frankly, my conventional combat skills feel rather… trivial… compared to what you two are potentially capable of, especially in battle." Images from nature documentaries flash through my mind – the sheer predatory power of big cats. How do you defend against *that*? How do you fight Rose's panther form?

"That's where you might be mistaken, Ava," Luca counters thoughtfully. "While we *are* somewhat stronger and faster than average humans, even in our human forms, neither Rose nor I possess your level of specialised combat training. In our shifted forms, our strength and speed are exponentially enhanced, but our methods of attack become more… instinctual, limited, albeit powerful. Our primary advantage lies in overwhelming force, targeting vulnerable areas like the throat or limbs. That's why *your* training, your tactical thinking, is crucial. Many shifters rely too heavily on their natural power, becoming predictable." His willingness to share their potential vulnerabilities is surprising and strategically vital. Essential knowledge if I ever find myself facing hostile shifters.

"We'll definitely need to go over the specific weaknesses of other creatures we might encounter," I state. "Because right now, my tactical brain is struggling to compute how to effectively engage your… altered state, should the need arise."

"We can certainly do that," Luca agrees. "But you need to understand, Ava, most shifters like us, those trying to maintain secrecy, *won't* willingly shift in front of potential adversaries if they can avoid it. The process itself leaves us vulnerable, momentarily incapacitated, especially for younger or less experienced shifters, where the shift takes longer. Our best chance is usually to engage them while they are still in human form, pressing the advantage before they can fully transform." As he speaks, he shifts slightly, his head tilting, his focus suddenly sharpening on something outside the car.

Instinctively, I turn, following his gaze, and see Sam walking out of the motel office door, heading back towards us. My brain connects the dots – Luca sensed Sam's approach before I even saw him. My mouth engages before I can stop it. "Just how good *is* your hearing?"

Rose chuckles beside me, deciding to answer this time. "Let's just say we could clearly hear him finalising the check-in, the swipe of the key cards on the counter, the click of the office door latch as he started walking back towards the car. So," she adds with another mischievous grin, "if you ever want to have a truly private conversation around us, you'll need significant distance, a whisper quiet enough to be swallowed by background noise, or a very noisy environment."

"Right," I reply, my eyes widening slightly at the implication. "I'll… try to keep that in mind." Another surge of envy hits me – senses like that would be an unbelievable asset in my line of work.

Sam reaches the car and slides back into the driver's seat, handing me a plastic key card. "Got us rooms on the first floor, end of the corridor, furthest from the stairs and main entrance," he confirms, clearly having followed my earlier security requests.

We drive the short distance to the designated section of the motel. It's noticeably empty compared to the other wings; no other vehicles are parked in this section, offering us a degree of isolation and a clear view of anyone approaching. We unload our luggage and the heavy box containing the case files, taking everything up to our adjoining rooms. I immediately propose keeping the main file box in my room – Rose's and my room – allowing me constant access for review whenever needed. After hauling everything inside, the first order of business is security. I meticulously check the locks on the doors and windows, ensuring they are functional, noting potential weaknesses or entry points. While I do that, Sam methodically sweeps both rooms with a handheld device, checking for any hidden listening devices or cameras—standard procedure, but more crucial than ever given the nature of our mission.

Once Sam gives the all-clear, confirming our privacy, we collectively decide to head out for dinner. It's getting dark, and exploring the city while grabbing a bite seems the most efficient use of time. Before leaving my room, however, I perform one last, habitual security measure. I tear off a minuscule corner from a piece of paper and carefully wedge it, almost invisibly, into the top corner of the doorjamb, between the door and the frame. A simple, low-tech trick, but effective. If anyone enters the room while we're gone, the paper will fall, alerting me upon our return. Old habits die hard, especially the ones designed to keep you alive.

CHAPTER 7

HOW TO INTERROGATE A WAITRESS AND INFLUENCE PEOPLE

(POORLY, IF YOU'RE ME)

We eventually locate a diner downtown that advertises itself online as being open late. The sign glows neon against the darkening sky, promising coffee and comfort. At least, the online listing *claimed* it stayed open late. As we park the Tahoe in their half-empty lot and approach the entrance, a hastily scrawled sign taped to the glass door tells a different story. '*Closing 10pm until further notice. Subject to change.*' Their usual closing time of 2am is another casualty of the city's fear.

Pushing through the door, a bell jingles overhead. Inside, the classic diner aesthetic feels slightly worn and tired. We slide into a cracked vinyl booth tucked away in a corner, affording us some privacy from the few other patrons scattered amongst the tables, their hushed conversations barely audible over the low thrum of the ancient ventilation system.

Once seated, I grab a laminated menu, its surface slightly sticky, and quickly scan the offerings, standard diner fare. The others follow suit. Moments later, a waitress approaches, notepad and pen poised.

"Can I get you anything to drink while you decide on your food?" she asks, her voice carrying a hint of weary professionalism. I glance at her name tag, *Mel*. She looks us over, her gaze lingering perhaps a fraction too long on Sam's G-man neatness. But when her eyes land on Luca, her jaw practically unhinges, her eyes widening almost comically. I can almost *smell* the sudden wave of lust rolling off her, thick and unsubtle. Beside me, Rose gives a low chuckle, leaning closer to whisper directly into my ear, her breath warm against my skin.

"He gets that reaction a lot," she murmurs, amusement lacing her tone. "Judging by the scent cloud she's putting out, she is *seriously* hot for him right now."

Her comment, combined with the unexpected intimacy of her whisper, catches me completely off guard. A sudden coughing fit seizes me, hacking on thin air as if I've inhaled my own non-existent drink. Everyone at the table turns to stare. Mel, the waitress, fixes me with a distinctly unimpressed, slightly dirty look. Crap.

"Sorry," I gasp, trying to regain composure, acutely aware of Mel's disapproval. "Rose just reminded me of an inside joke from earlier; I only just got the punchline." I force a plausible smile, hoping to smooth things over. I need this waitress to be cooperative; antagonising her isn't part of the plan. "Could I please just have a hot chocolate?"

The waitress scribbles down my order, her expression still frosty, then waits impatiently for the others. Luca and Sam give their orders quickly. Rose, however, is still visibly struggling to contain her laughter at my earlier reaction, taking a moment longer to order her own drink. Mel gives her a sharp look before finally stalking off towards the counter to fetch our drinks.

"Thanks a lot, Rose," I mutter under my breath, shooting her a pointed, disapproving glance across the table. "I specifically wanted to talk to her, gather some local intel. Now she probably thinks I'm an idiot and might clam up. It's precisely why I suggested a late-night diner – waitstaff hear *everything*."

"Sorry," Rose replies, though she doesn't sound particularly penitent, her eyes still dancing with mirth. "But your reaction was just priceless! I couldn't resist. You have to understand, we have incredibly sensitive noses; picking up on strong emotions like desire and lust is…

unavoidable sometimes," she explains. Her explanation does little to soothe me; instead, a fresh wave of anxiety washes over me. My thoughts instantly flash back to the safe house, to my own involuntary reactions when first meeting Luca and, yes, even Rose herself. Had *I* given off some embarrassing scent they'd picked up on? The thought is mortifying.

Luca frowns slightly, his gaze sharp as he studies me. I tense, anticipating his question, hoping he didn't sense my sudden discomfort. "Why, specifically, do you want to talk to the waitress, Ava?" he asks, his focus shifting back to the mission.

"Waitstaff, especially in late-night diners like this, especially in a city on edge… they overhear snippets of conversation, local gossip, rumours," I explain, forcing my mind back to strategy. "Patrons talk while they eat, often without thinking. She might have picked up on something useful, some detail the official reports missed."

Luca's frown slowly morphs into an expression of thoughtful consideration. "That's… actually a very astute approach," he concedes finally, nodding slowly. "I hadn't considered that angle."

"That's precisely why they tasked her with leading this operation," Sam interjects smoothly, ever the supportive agent. "From reviewing her mission reports, it's clear she possesses an exceptional talent for locating targets and extracting information, often from minimal or unconventional sources." His casual mention of having read my classified mission reports makes me vaguely uneasy. How much do these strangers really know about me, while I still know next to nothing concrete about them beyond the impossible?

Our conversation is interrupted by Mel's return with our drinks. Thankfully, she seems to have composed herself, offering no further death glares as she places the mugs and glasses on the table. "Are you ready to order food?" she asks, her professional mask back in place, though her eyes still occasionally flick towards Luca. We all nod and give her our orders – burgers, fries, the usual calorie-dense diner staples.

Just as she turns to leave, I stop her. "Mel," I begin, keeping my tone friendly but professional, "before you go, would it be possible to have a quick word with you once you've put our orders through to the kitchen?"

She pauses mid-stride, turning back slowly, suspicion clouding her features again. She eyes me warily for an uncomfortably long moment before replying, "What… what do you want to talk to me about?" She glances nervously around the sparsely populated diner, clearly trying to assess the situation, wondering what trouble might be brewing.

Time to deploy the new credentials. I subtly reach into my pocket, retrieve the leather wallet Sam gave me, and discreetly flash the FBI badge, shielding it from the view of other patrons but ensuring Mel gets a clear look. "I'm Special Agent Bekke," I state quietly but firmly. "These are my colleagues. We're investigating the recent attacks in the city, and we were hoping you might be able to share anything you've heard – rumours, unusual stories, anything out of the ordinary your customers might have mentioned."

Mel's eyes widen as she stares at the badge, her mouth falling slightly open. She darts another nervous look around the diner, then back at the badge, seemingly torn. After a moment's hesitation, she gives a jerky nod. "Okay. Yeah. I'll… I'll be right back," she murmurs, then hurries away towards the kitchen pass-through.

"You enjoyed that, didn't you?" Sam observes, a knowing smirk playing on his lips once Mel is out of earshot.

"Maybe a little," I admit, a small smile touching my own lips. "It certainly beats pointing a gun at someone or, heaven forbid, holding a knife to a guy's nether regions to encourage cooperation. Considerably less messy, too."

Rose bursts out laughing again at my blunt assessment, a genuine, unrestrained sound this time, though she quickly stifles it as Mel begins walking back towards our booth. "Oh, Luca, can we *please* keep her?" Rose pleads sotto voce, nudging him playfully while he just shakes his head, clearly amused by her antics. Sam manages a quiet chuckle, quickly schooling his features back into professional neutrality as Mel approaches. She looks even more nervous than before, wringing her hands slightly.

"So… what do you want to know?" she asks hesitantly, her gaze darting between the four of us.

"Why don't you sit down for a moment, Mel? Make yourself comfortable," I suggest gently, then add, "This shouldn't take long," tapping the vinyl seat beside me. She eyes the space, then glances back towards the counter, where presumably her boss might be watching. The internal debate is clear on her face – risk getting chewed out by her boss or cooperate with the Feds. After a moment, she makes her decision and slides awkwardly into the booth next to me, perching on the edge of the seat.

She repeats her question, eager to get this over with. I get straight to the point. "What have you heard, Mel? About the attacks specifically?"

She chews on her lower lip for a moment, gathering her thoughts. "Well," she begins slowly, "all I really know for sure is what's been on the news. At first, they were saying maybe some new serial killer was loose in the city. Then I heard it might be gang violence spilling over. But if what I heard early on is true… then maybe most major cities have a serial killer problem right now? It's why we don't stay open as late anymore," she confesses, her voice dropping slightly. "People are genuinely scared to be out on the streets after dark. Even the downtown clubs have shifted their hours – opening earlier, closing earlier. It's messing with everyone's routine."

"Why did you initially think it might be a serial killer?" Sam prompts gently.

"Well… I'm not sure if it's true," she hedges, looking increasingly uneasy. "But some of the early news reports, before they started talking about gangs… they mentioned that… that a lot of the bodies they found had similar, really gruesome injuries." Her face pales noticeably as she speaks, her hands twisting in her lap. She leans in slightly, lowering her voice even further, turning almost white as she relays the next part. "There are… rumours… whispers, you know? That some of the victims… they've been completely drained of blood." She shudders visibly. "It scares the hell out of me, thinking I could be serving coffee to the person responsible for something like that. I've tried asking my boss to switch me to the day shift, but it's not easy with my college schedule, and he said the day shift is already full anyway."

Watching her, seeing the genuine fear etched on her young face, I feel a pang of sympathy. This fear is real, palpable, poisoning the city. I make a mental note, ensure she gets home safely tonight. Her shift ends soon, given their new closing time, probably within the hour. Pushing her further on the gruesome details seems counterproductive. I try a different tack.

"I understand why you feel unsafe right now, Mel, and I'm truly sorry you have to deal with that fear," I say sincerely. "But please know, we are working diligently to resolve this situation. Have you heard anything else? Any other rumours people have been talking about? Maybe speculation about *who* might be doing this? Or has anyone mentioned seeing anything… strange? Out of the ordinary? People often talk more freely after a few drinks; I'm sure you must get customers coming in sometimes, telling stories that sound completely unbelievable?"

She gives me a slightly puzzled look at my last comment, tilting her head as she considers it. She starts to shake her head, dismissing the idea, but then stops abruptly. Her eyes widen slightly as a memory surfaces.

"Actually…" she begins slowly, the colour starting to return to her face now that the topic has shifted from drained bodies. "There *was* this one customer, maybe a few weeks back? He came in already a little drunk, meeting up with his buddies, started telling this wild story, he got pretty loud about it. Mike, my boss, had to tell him to keep it down." She pauses, recalling the details. "Mike got annoyed because this guy kept insisting, swearing up and down, that he saw another guy… jump straight up the side of a building. Like Superman, or Spiderman, or something. Said it happened over on the east side, near that old abandoned industrial site. You know, where those huge old factories are? There's talk about converting them into apartment complexes, lofts and stuff, but nothing's actually happened over there yet. It's pretty deserted."

"Thanks, Mel, that's actually very helpful. We appreciate you taking the time to talk to us. It's the cooperation from upstanding citizens like yourself that truly helps us do our job and make this country great," Sam interjects smoothly, deploying the standard agency platitude. Mel beams at him, clearly flattered by the praise and his earnest delivery. It makes *me* cringe internally. That kind of generic government bullshit always grates on me.

Mel excuses herself after that, heading back towards the kitchen. I fix Sam with a stern look, which he doesn't fail to notice. "What?" he asks defensively.

"Don't use that canned crap around me, Sam," I say quietly but firmly. "It might have been drummed into you during agent training, but we both know it's mostly bullshit designed to manipulate." I hold up a hand, cutting off his imminent protest. He looks ready to argue the point, his agent training kicking in. I understand his perspective, but I press on. "Yes, I acknowledge that what she told us *could* be useful, potentially giving us a new area to investigate. But spouting lines about 'upstanding citizens making the country great' is just ridiculous. A simple, genuine 'thank you for your help', like a normal human being would have, would have sufficed. When government employees trot out those pre-packaged statements, it always makes me suspect they're being insincere, deceitful, that they don't actually believe a word they're saying."

Sam looks genuinely affronted, clearly unhappy with my assessment. He decides he *is* going to give me a piece of his mind after all. "I'm sorry you feel that way, Ava," he says stiffly, "but I *was* being honest. I wanted her to feel appreciated, to know that she *did* help us. So, no, I don't think it's crap or bullshit."

I notice Luca watching me intently again, that analytical gaze trying to dissect my reaction. I have a sinking feeling I know where his thoughts are heading. He decides to voice them, cutting through the tension between Sam and me. "Ava," he asks quietly, "is your… intense dislike… of what people might call standard government platitudes perhaps related to what happened back at the safe house earlier? The reason you needed to step outside?"

Fucking fantastic. He just *had* to go there. My eyes narrow, trying to control the surge of anger his question ignites.

Sam immediately latches onto it, his agent's curiosity piqued. "What do you mean? What happened back at the ranch?" he asks, looking between Luca and me, sensing an underlying issue.

I glare daggers at Luca, who has the grace to look slightly apologetic. "Sorry," Luca murmurs, "I assumed Sam would already be aware, figured it would be documented in your personnel file."

This only makes Sam frown deeper, his gaze shifting back to me, assessing, trying to connect unseen dots. I let out an audible groan. Thanks to Luca's big mouth, I have no choice but to offer some explanation now. "When I was a teenager," I begin, my voice deliberately flat, devoid of inflexion, "my parents were murdered right in front of me during a home invasion. All I received from the responding Police… and later, the FBI agents involved… were those same, typical, hollow government lines about what a 'brave little soldier' or 'good citizen' I was being, even as they made me relive the entire horrific event over, and over, and *over* again, trying to extract every last usable detail from my traumatised memory. So, yes," my voice hardens, becoming grittier as the repressed anger surfaces, "I now despise hearing those same empty, trained platitudes with a passion. They're used to appease the public, to make officials sound empathetic when often they're just… procedural."

Hearing my blunt explanation, Sam looks down, chastened. He looks like he wants to say something, offer some kind of standard condolence, but he clearly recognises that anything he *could* say right now would likely fall into the very category I just condemned. For a moment, it seems like he's wisely chosen silence. But then, after a beat, he opens his mouth again. I brace myself, expecting some clumsy attempt at sympathy that will only irritate me further.

"I… I'll try not to say things like that around you again, Ava. I'm genuinely sorry," he says quietly, sincerity in his voice. His simple apology surprises me, disarming my anger slightly. Rose, sensing the shift in mood, gives my arm a brief, comforting squeeze under the table before quickly letting go. I take a large gulp of my now lukewarm hot chocolate, feeling suddenly awkward and exposed.

Mercifully, Mel returns with our food just then, placing the plates down quickly before retreating, breaking the heavy silence. We begin to eat, the initial moments still thick with unspoken tension. I hate having caused this awkwardness, but my reaction was visceral, uncontrollable. I've always been a straight shooter – sometimes brutally so, no pun intended.

Trying to ease the atmosphere, steer us back to the mission, I say neutrally, "Okay, plan for tomorrow, once we go through all the Pittsburgh files and collate the attacks, we can try to categorise them. See how many seem likely to be vampire-related, based on Mel's information about the blood draining. Then, we can investigate the specific area she mentioned, that abandoned industrial site on the east side. Reconvene tomorrow evening, perhaps? After we've had a chance to talk to any relevant witnesses from the files? Unless someone has a different approach, they think we should consider? I am, after all, completely new to hunting actual vampires."

Luca picks up the conversational thread, thankfully ignoring the earlier awkwardness, while Sam remains quiet, seemingly still processing. "That sounds like a solid plan, Ava. Based on Mel's account of blood loss and if the case files corroborate similar MOs, vampire activity seems the most likely explanation for the Pittsburgh incidents. Most vampires *prefer* to operate alone when hunting, but they almost always belong to a larger group, a nest. It's possible the ones active here have either been sent by a larger nest elsewhere to stake a new claim, or there's already an established nest within the city itself. If it's the latter," his expression becomes more serious, "then we might eventually have to contend with a vampire King or Queen – typically ancient, powerful individuals. The older a vampire gets, the stronger they become, often developing unique, dangerous abilities over time as well."

I gape at him, trying to absorb this new layer of complexity. *Kings and Queens?* Seriously? "Okay, wow. Ancient vampires with powers? I am *so* far behind the curve on all this stuff," I admit, feeling overwhelmed again. "You guys are definitely going to have to start bringing me up to speed on the paranormal hierarchy because, honestly, Kings and Queens? How does one even *become* a vampire royal in the first place?"

Rose and Luca share another small chuckle, this time seemingly at my bewildered expression. I can't help but fidget in my seat, feeling distinctly uncomfortable, inadequate. Why *did* they choose me, someone utterly ignorant of this hidden world, to hunt its monstrous inhabitants?

"We *will* get you caught up, Ava, don't worry," Luca assures me patiently. "But it will take time; the paranormal world is vast and complex. There are countless species, factions, and histories. For now, it's probably best if we focus specifically on the creatures we think we're likely to encounter first. To answer your question, though, a vampire typically ascends to the status of King or Queen of a nest simply by being the oldest, and therefore usually the strongest, vampire within that established group. If their nest grows large and powerful enough, their rule often goes unchallenged. It's exceedingly rare for a younger vampire to successfully overthrow an ancient one unless some external force – another powerful paranormal entity, perhaps – takes out the leader first. Only then might a younger vampire attempt to seize control, usually by creating a *new* nest comprised solely of those they personally turned, as they wouldn't inherently trust other, older vampires unless they were demonstrably much stronger."

I listen intently, trying to absorb the information, struggling to reconcile this talk of vampire politics and power struggles, discussed so casually in a brightly lit diner, with my previous reality. It feels utterly surreal, like debating gang territories, but with immortal, blood-drinking monsters. I need more data, more tactical understanding. "So, there are different types of vampires? variations, like with shifters?"

Rose takes this question. "Like us, there are essentially two main types of vampires, like we mentioned before, the born and the turned," she explains. "Born vampires are inherently much stronger and faster. If a born vampire turns a human, they typically retain a degree of power, a psychic link, over their progeny. If the born vampire is particularly ancient or powerful, they can sometimes even communicate through their newly turned fledgling, almost like a remote viewing ability, though there seems to be a limit to how many fledglings one vampire can effectively control or maintain a strong bond with. A newly turned vampire, a fledgling, lacks the strength and reserves to turn someone else themselves; the process is too draining. They'd essentially exsanguinate themselves in the attempt."

"Right," is all I manage, processing the disturbing implications. One crucial question remains. "How… how exactly *do* they turn humans into vampires?"

Rose and Luca exchange another one of their unreadable glances, a silent debate passing between them. This time, Luca decides to answer, his expression becoming guarded. "It's… not the glamorous, romantic process you might imagine, Ava. Many humans, influenced by films and Tv shows that portray vampires as alluring, powerful beings, foolishly think becoming one would be… cool."

I screw up my face in disgust at his implication. "Um… *no*. Definitely not thinking that. I have absolutely zero desire to become one of *them*. Don't be ridiculous."

"Good," Luca says, nodding slowly, seemingly satisfied with my vehement denial. "Sorry, just had to gauge your reaction."

"It's fine," I assure him curtly. "I happen to like who I am, flaws and all. Not interested in trading my humanity for… whatever that is."

Luca continues, his tone becoming clinical again. "Anyway, the process itself bears some resemblance to what you see in fiction, unfortunately. The vampire must first drain the human victim to the absolute brink of death, exsanguinating them almost completely. Then, crucially, the vampire must feed the dying human *their own* blood, and *only* their blood, over a period of, typically, a day or two. This allows the vampiric infection, or curse, depending on your viewpoint, to take hold, initiating the transformation. The success and speed of the turning often depend on the strength and age of the vampire performing the conversion. As Rose mentioned, a newly turned vampire simply doesn't possess the necessary vitality; they'd suffer fatal blood loss themselves. Unless," he adds thoughtfully, "they could trust another vampire to bring them a fresh human victim to feed on immediately after initiating the turning, but I've heard anecdotal accounts suggesting that introducing another humans blood into the process can sometimes sever or weaken the psychic bond between the sire and the fledgling."

I listen, horrified fascination warring with revulsion, absorbing the grim details of this unnatural creation process, trying to reconcile it with the mundane reality of the diner around us.

Luca carries on, adding another layer of complexity. "Actually, Rose, I should correct something you stated earlier. There *is*, theoretically, a *third* type of vampire, a kind of hybrid, though exceedingly rare. As far as ancient lore suggests, only a god, or perhaps an exceptionally powerful magical being wielding specific life-and-death energies, could create such a being. I haven't heard credible accounts of one existing for centuries; they were reputedly even more powerful than standard turned vampires, often capable of challenging even the born ones, depending on their creator's power and were consequently hunted relentlessly by both vampires and other factions who feared their potential."

Rose looks at Luca, clearly surprised. "A third type? I've never heard of that. Do they have a specific name?" Her curiosity mirrors my own; it's oddly comforting to know even she doesn't possess all the answers about her own hidden world.

"They are called Dhampirs," Luca replies simply.

"Ooooooh!" Rose's eyes light up with recognition. "Dhampirs! I *have* heard that term, but I always assumed it was just some trendy, alternative name for vampires, you know, like something the goth kids came up with!" she says excitedly. Her sudden enthusiasm is infectious, breaking the grim tension momentarily. I can't help but chuckle, and even Sam cracks a small smile.

After we finish eating, we pay the bill, leaving a generous tip for Mel, both for her help and as silent compensation for the earlier awkwardness. Back in the relative anonymity of the Tahoe, just as Sam starts the engine, I stop him. "Hold on," I say, remembering an idea I wanted to do from earlier, which was prompted by our talk with Mel. "Before we return to the motel, I want to ensure Mel gets home safely."

"We don't really have time to be keeping tabs on individuals, Ava," Sam protests immediately, reverting to by-the-book agent mode, clearly getting on my nerves again.

"She talked to us, Sam. She helped us, despite being clearly terrificd," I counter firmly. "All I want to do is make sure she gets home safely tonight, just as a quiet thank you. Call it professional courtesy. Besides," I add, appealing to tactical logic, "you never know; we might just spot a vampire or even one of these shifters tailing her when she leaves work. It's also a good opportunity to observe more of the city at night, see how deserted the streets truly become. If there's absolutely no one out, it makes blending in, hunting these things ourselves, significantly more difficult."

"Fine," Sam concedes with a sigh, clearly unconvinced but unwilling to argue further. So, we sit there in the darkened car, parked across the street, waiting. Mel's shift should be ending any minute now; the diner clock visible through the window reads 9:55pm—five more minutes of surveillance in the quiet, watchful night.

CHAPTER 8

THE PERKS OF PAPER DOOR ALARMS, AND WHY MY ROOMMATE SLEEPS LIKE A LOG (LUCKY HER)

We trailed Mel home from the diner last night, maintaining a discreet distance, employing counter-surveillance driving techniques to ensure we weren't followed ourselves and, more importantly, that *she* didn't realise she was being shadowed. Luca took the wheel for this part; his enhanced night vision proved invaluable in the dimly lit streets, and he claimed, with unnerving casualness, that with the window slightly cracked, he could easily track her scent signature through the urban sprawl – a detail that immediately brought my own self-conscious worries about my scent back at the ranch flooding back. I shove the uncomfortable thought aside.

The city streets were eerily quiet, almost deserted. Not quite ominous, perhaps, but certainly devoid of the usual late-night foot traffic, save for a few small, huddled groups hurrying along under the jaundiced glow of the streetlights. A testament to the fear gripping the city. Mel reached her apartment building without incident, the only other movement being solitary cars passing occasionally. No sign of vampires, shifters, or anything else untoward. A dead end, it seems, but at least she's safe.

When we returned to our motel room, the tiny, almost invisible piece of paper I'd wedged in the doorjamb was still perfectly in place— untouched, unentered. This brought me a small measure of relief.

As anticipated, however, sharing a room with Rose significantly impacts my ability to sleep soundly. My ingrained need for solitude, for absolute control over my environment, wars with the forced proximity. Initially, she peppers me with questions, her curiosity apparently boundless. She seems fascinated by my history of solo missions, finding it alien to her ingrained pack mentality, where facing danger necessitates group cohesion and mutual support. The concept of deliberately operating alone, relying solely on oneself in hostile territory, appears genuinely baffling to her. She wants to know how I manage it, how I handle the fear, the isolation.

Fully detailing the brutal training, the years spent forging myself into a self-reliant weapon, the psychological conditioning required to suppress fear and operate with lethal detachment… that isn't an option. Explaining the raw, motivating fury born from witnessing my parents' murder, the vow I made to become strong enough that nothing could ever touch me like that again – that remains locked away. So, I offer her a simplified, sanitised version.

"While teamwork is a fundamental part of military training," I explain, keeping my tone carefully neutral, "I discovered early on that I have a particular aptitude, a preference perhaps, for solitary assignments. Especially in roles like… well, like mine," I hedge, avoiding the blunt term 'assassin'. "Relying on others introduces variables, potential points of failure. If your backup hesitates, if they make a mistake, it can compromise the entire mission, get you killed. So, I learned to plan meticulously, anticipate contingencies, ensuring I *don't* need backup. I've honed my senses, my situational awareness, to a razor's edge, constantly monitoring my surroundings." It sounds clinical, detached, failing to capture the hyper-vigilance, the constant low-level hum of adrenaline that defines my existence. "It's not easy to articulate," I finish lamely. "I'm just… adept at operating alone. It's how I function best. It's also, unfortunately, how I ended up with that ridiculous moniker, 'Ava the Destroyer'."

Rose listens intently, her green eyes wide with what looks

disturbingly like admiration. "Wow," she breathes. "That's… remarkable, Ava." Despite my discomfort with her intensity, a small, unfamiliar warmth flickers within me at her genuine, uncritical acceptance. It's… pleasant, being regarded as remarkable by someone like Rose, even if the reasons are rooted in darkness.

Eventually, Rose settles into her own bed across the small room, her breathing evening out into the slow, steady rhythm of sleep. Only then do I allow myself to move. Silently, I retrieve the heavy box of case files we brought from the car. Spreading them out carefully on the thin motel carpet under the dim glow of the bedside lamp, I begin the painstaking process of sifting through the reports, crime scene photos, witness statements.

Admittedly, exhaustion weighs heavily on me. Throughout the long, quiet hours of the night, fatigue claws at my concentration. I find myself nodding off periodically, my head jerking up just as sleep threatens to claim me completely, but I soldier on and wade through the files. Even with my professional desensitisation, honed over years of exposure to the worst humanity can inflict, some of the crime scene photographs are deeply disturbing. The sheer brutality, the specific nature of the wounds… they point conclusively, chillingly, towards vampiric assaults being the primary threat plaguing this city. Mutilated bodies, exsanguinated victims… the evidence aligns perfectly with Luca's earlier descriptions and Mel's fearful whispers. Also the number of missing person reports included in the files is significant, alarmingly higher than the statistical average reported twenty-three years prior, suggesting a terrifying escalation or a shift in tactics. Adding another layer of complexity, several reports detail dismemberments, attacks bearing the savage hallmarks of animalistic culprits – perhaps shifters, like Luca suggested, or possibly some other, unknown predatory entity lurking in the city's shadows.

Focusing solely on the confirmed or highly suspected vampire-related offences, I begin plotting the incident locations on a digital map overlay on my tablet. A discernible pattern emerges with startling clarity

– nearly all the attacks, the body discoveries, the blood-drained victims, occurred *away* from the city's east side. There are only two notable exceptions, outliers in an otherwise consistent distribution. The old adage springs instantly to mind, *'Don't shit where you eat'*. It reinforces the theory sparked by Mel's anecdote about the man seeing someone scale a building near the abandoned factories.

Therefore, I tentatively surmise, with growing certainty, that the vampires are likely harboured somewhere on the city's relatively untouched eastern side. Hiding in plain sight, perhaps, among the derelict factories and warehouses Mel mentioned.

I must have finally succumbed to exhaustion in the early hours, slumping over the files, because the next thing I know, someone is trying to wake me, their touch gentle but insistent on my shoulder. Years of ingrained reflexes, honed by countless hostile environments, take over instantly. Before conscious thought fully registers, I react. The knife I kept by my side during the night, tucked under my thigh, is suddenly in my hand, the cold steel pressing against warm skin.

I blink, my vision clearing rapidly, adrenaline flooding my system. Rose is kneeling beside my bed, her eyes wide with shock, the point of my dagger resting lightly against the pulse point in her throat. Realisation dawns. My brain registers it's Rose, not a threat. With a sharp intake of breath, I immediately pull the knife away, the adrenaline receding, leaving a faint tremor in my hand.

"Wow," Rose breathes, seemingly unfazed, a slow, cheeky grin spreading across her face. "That was… impressive. Incredibly fast. I might have to make a habit of waking you up, just to see if you're always that lethally responsive."

I groan, letting my head flop back against the side of the bed, the lingering adrenaline making me feel slightly nauseous. "I really wouldn't recommend it," I retort wearily. "Can't always promise my subconscious won't finish the attack sequence before my brain catches up. Waking up covered in your blood isn't high on my list of desirable experiences."

Rose just gives me a slow, deliberate, saucy wink before replying, her voice dropping to a low purr, "Oh, I can think of much better ways to wake up covered in me, Ava."

I force my eyes open again, finding her still grinning, looking entirely too pleased with herself, like the Cheshire cat from Alice in Wonderland contemplating a particularly plump mouse. "You," I declare, shaking my head, though a reluctant smile tugs at my lips despite my exhaustion, "are going to be trouble, aren't you?"

I decide, in that moment, not to rise to her flirtatious bait, not to be overly difficult about it. It's… surprisingly disarming. I haven't encountered many women I've felt even remotely attracted to. There was one brief relationship, years ago, during a long-term undercover mission where I was embedded in the same remote area for nearly a year. She was… beautiful, vibrant, showing interest in me first, catching me off guard during a rare moment of lonely vulnerability. I knew getting involved was stupid, unprofessional, a dangerous complication. But the mission dragged on, the isolation gnawed at me, and I needed… companionship. Needed some semblance of normalcy, however fleeting. I couldn't trust any of the local men; most were connected, directly or indirectly, to the cartel I was systematically dismantling. So, after meeting her, I did my due diligence – followed her discreetly, ran background checks on her and her family, ensuring they were clean, unconnected. As far as I could ascertain, she was just an ordinary civilian caught in the crossfire of a dirty war. So, when she continued her persistent, charming flirtation, I allowed myself, foolishly, to go along with it. Then, when my mission abruptly concluded, I simply vanished. Left without a word, without explanation. Severed the connection cleanly, ruthlessly. It was the only way. Sometimes, in the quiet moments between assignments, I still wonder where she is now, how she's doing. But since then, I've rigorously avoided any hint of romantic entanglement. Hookups, yes – brief, uncomplicated encounters with guys when I'm back stateside, purely physical transactions to scratch an itch, nothing more. Relationships? Too dangerous. Too complicated. Too distracting.

My thoughts are interrupted as I notice Rose is wearing only her underwear – a surprisingly delicate, lacy set that looks both expensive and incredibly appealing on her toned figure. I groan again, louder this time, mostly at my own reaction. "I really don't need this shit right now," I mutter, mostly to myself, but loud enough for her superhuman hearing to catch.

"I heard that," Rose replies smugly, her smirk widening.

"Good," I retort, closing my eyes again, feigning sleep I don't feel. "Then leave me alone and get dressed." I groan inwardly again at the absurdity of the situation – sharing a motel room with a stunningly beautiful shapeshifter who seems determined to flirt with me while I'm trying to process the fact that vampires are real.

Rose chuckles softly, apparently unfazed by my dismissal. I hear the rustle of clothing as she gets off my bed and starts pulling on a pair of jeans. Curiosity gets the better of me. I crack open one eye just a sliver, intending only a quick peek to see what she's doing. Big mistake. She must have sensed my gaze because she seems to be deliberately putting on a show. She swings her hips with exaggerated slowness as she pulls up her jeans, conveniently bending over deeply as she does so, offering me an unobstructed, frankly spectacular view of her very lovely, very firm backside. My breath catches. It's when she gives her bottom a final, deliberate little wiggle directly in my line of sight that I realise I've been staring far too long. I snap my eye shut immediately, heat flooding my face. Her soft chuckle confirms she knew I was watching the entire time. Damn her. Moments later, I hear the click of the bathroom door closing behind her.

With a sigh, I force myself to get off the floor, groaning as my back aches from sleeping in the stupid slumped-over position. I glance down at my own sleep attire – practical grey cotton shorts and a plain camisole top. Functional, comfortable, utterly boring. Especially compared to Rose's elegant lingerie. I quickly change into clean, equally boring underwear, then grab my standard black jeans and a dark grey Henley top, heading for the bathroom as soon as Rose emerges, towel-drying her damp blonde hair. She offers me a bright, knowing smile as I pass, but thankfully says nothing. I refuse to give her the satisfaction of messing with me anymore this morning. Though, technically, it's already past lunchtime. We'd agreed that late nights spent staking out potential vampire lairs would necessitate later starts to our operational days.

In the bathroom, I take a quick shower, brush my teeth rigorously, and scrape my hair back into a tight, practical ponytail. You'd think operating in my line of business would necessitate short, manageable hair, but I've never liked how it looks on me. Keeping it at least shoulder-length allows me the illusion of normalcy on those rare nights out, the chance to let my hair down, literally and figuratively, and pretend, just for a few hours, that I'm an ordinary woman.

When I emerge from the bathroom, feeling slightly more refreshed, I find we have company. Luca and Sam have joined Rose in our room, already reviewing the files I'd sorted, their heads bent together over the map I'd marked up. Noticing me, Luca looks up, his expression immediately concerned. "Did you manage to get any sleep at all last night, Ava? It looks like you've managed to categorise all the files for this entire area."

"Some," I reply evasively. "Enough. I figured I needed to play catch-up on the intel. And yes, based on the distribution pattern, what Mel told us last night seems accurate. There are only two reported incidents located on the east side; the vast majority are clustered elsewhere. My assessment is that our vampire, or vampires, are definitely operating out of that eastern industrial area she mentioned."

"Okay, then," Luca nods, accepting my assessment immediately.

"Let's grab some food first. We can refine our operational plan while we eat. Standard procedure dictates that we should check in with the main police headquarters first, get briefed on any new attacks reported overnight, before we proceed independently. We also need to formally notify the Police Chief of our presence in his jurisdiction," Sam adds pragmatically, looking over my marked map with a critical eye.

My stomach clenches slightly at the thought of dealing with local police forces. It's not my usual style. I'm accustomed to operating autonomously – slipping into an area, executing the objective, and extracting cleanly, leaving minimal trace. Bureaucracy, jurisdictional pissing contests… they just complicate things. But Sam's right; protocol demands it, especially if we want any chance of local cooperation down the line. We all agree, albeit reluctantly on my part, and head out to find some lunch before facing the local constabulary. This time, we find a different local diner, hoping to overhear any further discussions about the attacks. It's busy, bustling with the lunchtime crowd, the air thick with the smell of fried onions and coffee. We manage to find a booth, but the noise level makes detailed tactical discussion impossible. Over burgers and fries, Sam mentions he updated Agent Moore on our progress before we left the motel, letting him know we already had a potential lead and a geographical focus. This constant need for updates chafes; I prefer reporting *after* a mission is complete, success confirmed. But I understand the necessity in this fluid, high-stakes situation. I also notice, with some relief, that the tension from last night seems to have dissipated; Sam is acting normally around me again, his earlier stiffness gone.

Once we've finished eating and discussing what little we could amidst the diner's clamour, we head towards the city's main police headquarters, a large, imposing brick building downtown. As the designated task force leader, protocol dictates I take point. Striding towards the front desk, manned by a bored-looking Desk Sergeant, I pull out my FBI badge again, flashing it briefly but clearly.

"Hi, I'm Special Agent Bekke," I state clearly. "We're here to see the Chief of Police, please. He should have been notified yesterday that a federal task force would be operating in the area.”

“You don’t look much like a typical Fed, dressed like that,” the Sergeant observes dryly, eyeing my casual attire with open scepticism before picking up his phone and mumbling into the receiver. After a brief, one-sided conversation, he hangs up. “You’re just in time,” he informs us, his tone still bordering on insolent. “The Chief is about to head out himself. Seems there was another attack last night; a body was discovered less than an hour ago. Chief said he was on his way out to join you, anyway, figured he could show you the crime scene personally.”

“Thank you,” I reply tightly, already sensing this Chief is going to be problematic. His immediate focus on heading to the scene himself, rather than briefing us first, suggests territoriality. We step away from the desk while we wait, clustering together near the entrance. “I really hope this latest attack wasn’t anywhere near Mel’s route home last night,” I mutter under my breath, mostly to myself, “because that will just seriously piss me off.”

“We detected no discernible vampire scents anywhere near her apartment building or along the route we followed,” Luca confirms quietly, his senses ever alert. Just as he finishes speaking, a side door near the reception desk opens, and a large, imposing man strides out, heading directly towards us. He’s built like a former linebacker gone slightly to seed, his uniform straining slightly across his broad chest. This must be the Chief. He walks straight past me, making a beeline for Sam, clearly assuming the man in the suit is the one in charge. Predictable!

I intercept him smoothly, stepping forward and extending my hand before he reaches Sam. “Chief Thornton? I’m Special Agent Bekke, task force leader,” I state clearly, my grip firm when he reluctantly takes my hand. “This is Special Agent Miller,” I indicate Sam, “and these are Deputy Marshals Cole and Peyton.”

Chief Thornton pulls up short, his expression a mixture of

confusion and barely concealed annoyance. He looks me up and down, his gaze lingering dismissively on my casual clothes before flicking towards Luca and Rose with similar disdain. He shakes my hand briefly, then does the same with the others, though his attention keeps drifting back to Sam, as if he only wants to deal with the 'real' agent. "Apart from Agent Miller," he grunts, his voice gruff, "you're not quite what I expected. I'm Chief Thornton."

"Well, Chief," I reply coolly, refusing to be intimidated, "we find that maintaining a lower profile is often advantageous. We're trying *not* to draw excessive attention to our presence here. Agent Miller will serve as the public face of our task force when necessary, dealing with any media inquiries. However, we would prefer that official statements regarding our activities be channelled through your department's existing press conferences."

He clearly doesn't like that suggestion, his eyes narrowing slightly as he looks down at me – literally looks down, given his height advantage. "And why is that, Agent? The people of this city need reassurance. They need to *see* that something is being done about this violence plaguing *my* city." His emphasis on 'my city' grates.

"I understand that completely, Chief," I counter smoothly, keeping my voice level despite his confrontational tone. "However, our operational security relies on our ability to potentially infiltrate the gangs or track the individuals responsible for these attacks without revealing our identities prematurely. We need to identify not just the perpetrators, but who might be orchestrating this entire wave of violence, because it's highly unlikely these disparate groups all spontaneously decided to terrorise the country simultaneously. We simply cannot achieve that objective if our faces are plastered across the evening news after our first day in town." I inject just enough firmness into my tone to convey that this isn't negotiable, hoping not to escalate things further. Losing his cooperation entirely, however grudging, would hinder our investigation. But his condescending sneer tells me it might be unavoidable.

"I see," he replies tightly. "Fine. But speaking of crime scenes, we have a fresh one, as I'm sure my sergeant mentioned. How exactly do you intend to investigate it if you're so determined to avoid media attention?" he snaps back, clearly spotting a flaw in my stated approach. He has a point. We hadn't actually discussed the practicalities of crime scene analysis over lunch. Damn it. I don't want to appear unprepared or indecisive on our very first interaction, but I'm momentarily unsure how to answer without compromising our cover or revealing our true concerns.

As I rapidly cycle through potential responses, trying to formulate a plausible strategy on the fly, I realise the answer lies in the very premise I just established. "As I stated, Chief," I reply confidently, recovering quickly, "Agent Miller is the designated public face *and* our primary crime scene specialist. He possesses the most experience amongst us in processing conventional crime scenes. Therefore, *he* will initially be the only member of our team who will attend active scenes. He will then report his findings back to the rest of us for analysis. Our purpose in coming here today was primarily to introduce ourselves formally and to receive any updates on recent incidents, such as the one you're heading to now." It sounds plausible, hopefully plausible enough.

"Fine," Thornton concedes grudgingly, though his expression remains sceptical. He turns towards the Desk Sergeant. "Johnson, get someone to make copies of all reports related to the recent spate of violent attacks and missing persons cases from the last six months. Give them to Agent Bekke here." He gestures towards me. "Once those are ready, provide them with whatever procedural assistance they require while I'm out at the new scene."

"Yes, sir," the Sergeant replies dutifully.

"Agent Miller," Thornton says, turning back to Sam, "if you'll come with me." He then offers me a curt nod. "Agent Bekke, Marshals. A pleasure." The words are rote, devoid of warmth. He turns and walks back through the side door, Sam falling into step behind him. Not for one second do I believe he was actually pleased to meet us.

"Wow, Ava," Rose murmurs beside me once they're gone, keeping her voice low. "For someone who isn't *actually* an FBI Agent, you certainly sound convincing. I'm impressed." She gives me a subtle thumbs-up, hidden from the view of the Desk Sergeant. Luca nods in silent agreement beside her.

It takes nearly thirty minutes for the requested copies of the recent case files to materialise. A young officer hands over a surprisingly thick stack of folders. We take them, offer a polite thank you, and head back towards our motel. We spread the files across the beds and floor in Rose's and my room, the air filling with the dry scent of paper and cheap ink. We begin the grim task of reviewing the city's recent horrors.

The pattern is sickeningly familiar. All the recent attacks bear the hallmarks of vampires – exsanguinated victims, severe neck trauma, defensive wounds often accompanied by deep claw marks inconsistent with human fingernails. Several of the recent missing persons reports also fit the profile – individuals vanishing without a trace, often near known attack sites. It seems overwhelmingly likely that vampires are our primary problem here, possibly responsible for both the killings *and* the disappearances. All the attacks also adhere to the geographical pattern we observed earlier – concentrated away from the east side industrial zone. After nearly two hours immersed in the grim details, Sam calls. He's finished at the crime scene. We head out to collect him.

We find him waiting in the building's parking lot as arranged. He slides into the back seat with Luca this time, Rose having claimed shotgun for this leg. As I drive, Sam confirms our assessment. "Definitely another vampire attack," he states grimly, pulling out his agency-issued tablet. "But this one… it was far more vicious than the others detailed in the files. The victim was badly mauled, torn apart almost. If I didn't know better, I'd have suspected a bear attack." He pulls up the crime scene photos, the graphic images stark even on the small screen.

He's right. The level of violence is significantly escalated. Luca leans forward from the back seat, peering at the screen, his expression instantly hardening. "They've turned someone recently," he says definitively, his voice tight. "This level of frenzied violence… it's characteristic of a newly turned vampire. Fledglings often lack control, especially during their first feeds. It's like they're trying to claw their way *into* the body to get at the blood, driven purely by insatiable hunger and instinct." He sighs heavily, shaking his head.

"Okay," I say, my knuckles whitening on the steering wheel, dreading the implication. "What does that mean for us, tactically?" Rose has already explained that only older, stronger vampires typically possess the ability to turn others.

"It strongly suggests we might be dealing with an older, more established vampire here," Luca explains, his face etched with concern. "Not necessarily ancient, perhaps, otherwise they'd likely exert more control over their fledglings'… excesses, but certainly old enough, powerful enough, to sire others. It likely confirms the presence of a small nest, not just lone hunters." He meets my eyes in the rearview mirror. "Ava, I was hoping we could ease you into this world a bit more gradually. But this development… it means we need to accelerate your practical training. Specifically, focusing on vampire combat tactics. We need to do some training *today*, before we even consider going out tonight." His gaze is intense, unsettling.

From the moment Moore mentioned the paranormal, I knew this mission would be unlike anything I'd ever faced. The most challenging, the most dangerous. And yet… a part of me, the part forged in fire and loss, the part that thrives on impossible odds, feels a grim thrill, a surge of focused determination. Overcoming insurmountable challenges… that's the fuel that keeps me going. That's what Ava the Destroyer does.

"I was considering doing some initial reconnaissance of that eastern industrial area before nightfall," I reply, my voice steady. "But I agree, practical training takes priority now. Where can we do that without attracting attention?"

"We don't need any specialised setup for basic vampire tactics," Luca replies calmly, shrugging slightly. "Any reasonably secluded public park should suffice. Unless you'd prefer the privacy of booking time at an indoor sports centre or maybe a martial arts dojo?"

"No, a park is fine," I decide quickly. "The weather's decent today. Let's grab some snacks and water first, then find a park on the outskirts of the city, somewhere less frequented, fewer potential onlookers for our… unusual training session." I glance at the others. "Sam, would you mind scouting for a suitable park location on your tablet? Rose, maybe you could navigate us to the nearest grocery store for supplies?"

Rose chuckles, clearly amused by my sudden, focused enthusiasm. Little does she know, my eagerness extends beyond the simple thrill of impending conflict. I'm desperate to learn, to master new fighting techniques specifically tailored for confronting vampires, while also gaining any insight I can into how beings like Luca and Rose move, how they fight, how they think in combat. Knowledge is survival, and survival is everything.

CHAPTER 9

WARDROBE MALFUNCTIONS AND WHY MY FLIRTING SKILLS ARE APPARENTLY "CUTE"

After swinging by a convenience store to grab some bottled water and energy bars, Sam directs me via the satnav to a moderately sized park he found near our motel. We decided to stop back at the motel first, allowing everyone a chance to change into more suitable attire for a physically demanding training session.

Back in the slightly musty-smelling motel room, I pull on my standard training gear – worn, comfortable grey sweats and a plain grey t-shirt. Functional, familiar, designed for movement, not style. Emerging from the bathroom, I find the others ready. And promptly feel… inadequate. They look like they've stepped out of a high-end sportswear catalogue photoshoot. Luca and Sam are in fitted athletic tops that showcase their builds, paired with sleek training trousers. Rose is wearing stylish, coordinated workout gear that looks both practical and incredibly flattering. Again, I glance down at my own drab, functional outfit and internally debate the necessity of a serious wardrobe update if I'm going to be spending significant time around these three distractingly attractive individuals.

Rose must notice the direction of my gaze, my slight frown, because she approaches me, casually slinging an arm around my shoulders and pulling me into a brief, warm side hug. The contact sends a faint, unexpected jolt through me, similar to the handshake back at the safe house. "Hey, you look cute in what you're wearing," she says reassuringly, though her eyes hold a knowing glint. "I guess in your line of work, practicality trumps fashion, right? Things probably get ruined pretty quickly." She squeezes my shoulder gently. "Listen, maybe we can ditch the boys at some point, hit the mall? It doesn't have to be all hunt, kill, and destroy, you know. We could actually have some fun."

I manage a small chuckle, turning to face her fully. Suddenly, her proximity feels… intense. Overwhelming. That faint jolt I felt intensifies, sparking along my nerves. I can't help it; my gaze drops involuntarily to her lips, full and inviting. She notices immediately, of course, that damn perceptive smirk returning, making me flush hotly. Oh God. Kill me now. I *never* get flustered. My composure feels like it's fracturing, which only worsens when I try to reply.

"S-sure," I stammer, inwardly cringing as my voice comes out weak, embarrassingly high-pitched. I bloody *squeak*. "Yeah, we… we could pick up some new things for me. It's definitely been… quite some time… since I've had the chance." As I speak, I experience that odd, magnetic pull again, a physical sensation drawing me almost imperceptibly closer to Rose. Simultaneously, that same perplexed, troubled expression flickers across *her* face again, mirroring my own internal confusion. She abruptly steps back, breaking the contact, and the warmth vanishes, leaving me feeling strangely cold, adrift, like I'm suddenly missing something vital. What the hell is wrong with me? Rose looks equally unsettled, troubled by whatever just passed between us. Without another word, she turns and makes her way quickly towards the waiting Tahoe, where Luca and Sam are just climbing in. Rose bypasses the front passenger seat, hopping directly into the back alongside Luca without hesitation, effectively ousting Sam from his intended spot. Sam pauses, looking momentarily puzzled by her abruptness, then shrugs and settles into the front passenger seat.

A wave of confusion washes over me about what just transpired, the undercurrents thick and unreadable. Shaking my head slightly, trying to regain my equilibrium, I slide into the driver's seat, the new leather cool beneath my hands. I fire up the engine, the near-silent hum a stark contrast to the awkward tension now filling the vehicle. I follow the satnav's directions towards the park, the drive completed in a strained, uncomfortable silence.

When we arrive at the designated park – a sprawling green space dotted with trees, blessedly empty on this weekday afternoon – the awkwardness persists. As we get out, Rose immediately tells Sam she'll work through the basic shifter combat stances with him, but first, she pulls Luca aside, her expression still clouded with confusion and worry. Did I do something? Say something wrong? My mind races, replaying the brief interaction, searching for a misstep. If I did offend her, I have absolutely no idea how. But whatever it is, it must be significant, because as she speaks quietly but urgently to Luca, I see his expression shift, mirroring her confusion as he glances towards me. Rose's voice rises slightly in frustration, sharp enough for me to catch a few distinct words carried on the breeze: "...*can't be a prime... Luca, what is going on?*"

Prime? What does that mean? Before I can process it, Luca says something low and placating to her. Rose nods curtly, then walks off towards Sam, who has already started his warm-up stretches near a cluster of trees. Luca hesitates for a moment, watching Rose walk away, then approaches me, his own brow furrowed. As he gets closer, the questions bubble up, demanding answers.

"Okay, what is happening?" I ask, unable to keep the frustration out of my voice. This emotional rollercoaster is exhausting. "Have I upset her somehow? Done something wrong?" Simultaneously, despite the confusion, I feel an increasing intrigue about Rose, my gaze drifting towards her again, noticing she's stealing quick glances back at me before quickly averting her eyes. This push and pull, this strange awareness… it's deeply unsettling.

Luca places his hands gently on my shoulders, presumably attempting to calm my obvious agitation, although the gesture does little to soothe the unease churning inside me. "You haven't done anything wrong, Ava, okay?" he assures me, his voice calm, steady. "Put that thought completely out of your mind right now. Rose… she just needs some time to process some unexpected… feelings. Sort through her thoughts. She'll likely come around and talk to you when she's ready."

"Why can't *you* just tell me what's going on now?" I press, needing clarity, hating the feeling of being kept in the dark. "Rose and I… we seemed to be getting on great, which, honestly, is unusual for me. I don't normally connect with new people this quickly. But there's something about both of you… something that makes me feel… surprisingly comfortable."

"That's good to hear, Ava," Luca replies softly, "and I'm glad you feel that way, especially since we'll be spending a significant amount of time in close quarters. But this particular issue… it's not my place to explain. It's something Rose needs to discuss with you herself. It relates to… shifter lore, deep-seated beliefs. Let's just say the situation has presented her with something she never believed possible, especially for her. It's thrown her completely. She's understandably perplexed. Frankly," he admits, "I am too. But once Rose has spoken to you, then perhaps the three of us can have a broader discussion about shifter culture, traditions… lore."

His vague explanation only deepens my confusion, and now, a spark of anger ignites. He could tell me, but he won't. Fine. If he won't talk, I'll train. "Right," I say curtly, stepping back from his touch, shifting fully into professional mode. "Let's just get on with the training then, before I lose my cool completely."

For the next few hours, Luca drills me relentlessly on vampire combat tactics. He explains their typical attack patterns – favouring surprise attacks from behind, targeting the neck for a quick incapacitation. He details the insidious nature of their bite, how it slowly releases a paralytic or sedative agent into the victim's bloodstream, diminishing their ability to fight back. Then, paradoxically, as the sedative starts to break down, it induces a euphoric high, making the victim passively compliant, even welcoming the feeding if it continues long enough. A terrifyingly effective predatory mechanism.

"So," I ask, thinking tactically, "is there anything we could potentially wear? Some kind of reinforced collar, maybe, to protect the neck if they manage to bypass our initial defences?"

"Smart thinking, Ava," Luca acknowledges. "But unfortunately, we haven't yet found a material or design that offers sufficient protection without significantly impairing movement and flexibility. Sam experimented with a Kevlar-based neck guard, but it proved too restrictive, hindering head movement and peripheral vision. The idea was ultimately scrapped." He pauses, then adds thoughtfully, "Did you know Agent Moore actually tried to recruit you for this task force much earlier? Months ago, in fact. But he was denied access, told you were deep undercover, completely out of contact until you initiated pickup yourself."

A reinforced collar… the idea has merit, but I understand the drawbacks. Impeded movement is a death sentence against opponents this fast. I push the thought aside for now. "Yes, I was out of contact," I confirm. "Deep recon for target acquisition, then setting up the optimal kill zone. Standard procedure. They wouldn't have interrupted me at that critical stage. Still," I admit, a trace of frustration creeping back, "it would have been beneficial to have had more time to train specifically for *this*, to be better clued in, more prepared before deploying."

"I understand," Luca says sympathetically. "It's a shame the timing worked out this way. But you're a fast learner, Ava; you'll catch up quickly. Honestly, I wish we were easing you in against a few lone, newly turned vampires instead of potentially facing an established nest right off the bat. But," he adds with quiet confidence, "don't worry too much yet. Between Rose and I, we can handle most vampire threats we're likely to encounter initially." His certainty is somewhat reassuring.

We spend another intense two hours sparring, Luca demonstrating defensive manoeuvres, parries, counters designed specifically against vampiric speed and attack vectors. We break only briefly for water. By the end of it, I'm drenched in sweat, muscles burning, lungs aching, but my mind is sharp, focused. At one point, towards the end of the session, Luca decides to up the ante, utilising a fraction of his enhanced shifter strength and speed against me, forcing me to adapt, react faster, anticipate moves that seem impossibly quick. It's a brutal, humbling lesson, driving home exactly what I'm up against, the sheer physical disparity between human limitations and paranormal power. Despite my years of training, my honed reflexes, I can only hold my own against his controlled assault for so long. In the end, his superior speed and immense strength inevitably overwhelm my defences, pinning me effectively. It's a stark reminder of my vulnerability.

Exhausted but strangely exhilarated, we head back towards the motel to clean up. As we walk, a sense of dread begins to creep back in. I'm not looking forward to sharing the confined space of the motel room with Rose while this strange tension, this awkwardness stemming from whatever happened earlier, hangs heavy and unspoken between us.

When we enter our room, the silence is immediate, thick enough to cut with a knife. Rose is sitting quietly on her bed, avoiding my gaze. My earlier frustration, momentarily forgotten during the intensity of training, bubbles back to the surface, simmering alongside a confusing mix of hurt and anger. I let her have the first shower, needing a few minutes alone to try and process the situation, to decide how to handle this unexpected complication. Stewing in silence probably isn't the most productive approach, but it's my default setting.

When she emerges from the bathroom, wrapped in a towel, her hair damp, I shoot into the bathroom myself, hoping a scalding shower might wash away some of the tension, hoping she might leave, perhaps join the guys next door, giving me more time to avoid dealing with… whatever this is. No such luck, apparently. Thankfully, I remembered to grab a change of clothes before going in, so at least I won't have to linger once I'm dressed. My plan is simple, get dressed, grab my keycard, and go for a long walk, try to clear my head, calm the storm brewing inside me before I say something I regret.

CHAPTER 10

THE PRIME MATE PREDICAMENT: MY LIPS' UNSOLICITED
TESTIMONIAL, AND OTHER CRITICAL FAILURES IN MAINTAINING
PROFESSIONAL DISTANCE

Exiting the bathroom, dressed again in jeans and a t-shirt, I snatch my keycard from the nightstand and head purposefully towards the door. Just as my hand reaches for the handle, just as I'm about to announce my intention to go for a walk, Rose speaks, her voice cutting through the silence, stopping me in my tracks.

"Ava… there's something I… I need to discuss with you," she begins, her voice unexpectedly soft, hesitant, tinged with a vulnerability, a fear, that sounds utterly alien coming from her. It's so jarringly out of character that it halts my intended escape instantly. "It's… it's not going to be easy to explain, especially for someone from outside my world. You… you might also find it upsetting," she finishes, her voice barely a whisper.

"Well, telling me *something* is definitely better than this silent treatment," I snap back, turning to face her, unable to keep the anger, the frustration, from colouring my tone. My carefully constructed walls are crumbling. "Because right now, all I feel is frustrated by how you've been acting, and angry because I actually thought we were… getting on. Which, as I told Luca, is strange for me. I normally keep *everyone* at arm's length." I move towards the end of my bed and perch on the edge, needing the physical distance. Doing so, however, puts me closer to Rose again. As I turn my head to look at her properly, I feel it again –

that same weird, inexplicable internal tug, pulling me towards her. I shake my head slightly, trying to dismiss the sensation, clenching my hands into fists at my sides, fighting for control over my own reactions.

"You feel it too, don't you?" Rose whispers, her voice barely audible, her green eyes searching mine.

"Feel *what*?" I retort sharply, though my anger is momentarily eclipsed by confusion. "All I feel right now is pissed off with this entire situation! I'm completely lost as to what is going on with you, Rose!"

Rose drops her head, letting out a shaky sigh, and mumbles something under her breath. It's too low for normal human hearing, but somehow, I catch fragments: "*...maybe because human... can't feel it as strongly....*" Then she asks, her voice laced with a strange mixture of hope and desperation, "Do you... do you feel a pull? Towards me? Like something is drawing you closer?" Her eyes plead with me, hoping for confirmation.

Her question, her apparent awareness of the very sensation I'm struggling with, throws me completely. How could she possibly know? Instead of answering, I look down at my boots, unable to meet her intense gaze, trying desperately to rein in my temper, to avoid saying something that will make working together, living together, utterly impossible. But when she repeats my name, softly this time, "Ava?", my head snaps back up. The raw misery etched on her beautiful face, the unshed tears glistening in her eyes – it extinguishes my anger instantly, replaced by a confusing surge of protectiveness. Without conscious thought, without considering the implications, I'm suddenly on my feet, crossing the small space between us in two strides, wrapping my arms around her, pulling her close. It's an instinctive reaction, completely counter to my usual guarded behaviour, driven solely by the sight of her distress.

She looks briefly shocked by my embrace, stiffening, starting to pull away, but I hold her firm. I know, logically, after witnessing Luca's strength during training, that she could easily break my hold if she truly wanted to. But she doesn't. She remains still, tense, within my arms.

"To answer your question," I admit quietly, my voice muffled against her hair, "yes. Yes, I feel… something. I guess you could describe it as a pull. It's… subtle, most of the time, but it's there. What does it mean, Rose? Please, just talk to me."

"Oh, Ava," she whispers brokenly, burying her face against my shoulder, "you are going to hate me for this."

"How can I possibly hate you unless you tell me *what* is happening?" I reason, stroking her back awkwardly, trying to offer comfort I rarely give. "I can't hate you for something I don't understand. But," I add, a touch of firmness returning, "if you keep avoiding the subject, keep acting… like you have been… then yes, maybe I *will* start to hate you." As I hold her, a strange realisation dawns, the internal conflict, the push and pull I've been feeling… it vanishes completely when I'm this close to her. Holding her feels… right. It feels like coming home after being lost for a very long time. The thought is so foreign, so unexpected, it scares me. Instinctively, I start to pull away – I'm not a hugger, not like this. As I loosen my grip, the pulling sensation immediately returns, stronger this time, urging me back towards her.

"You just realised you're not acting like yourself, didn't you?" Rose states quietly, her voice still muffled, somehow sensing my internal shift. "That's why you just pulled away."

Her perception unnerves me, snapping some of my frustration back into place. I continue to withdraw my arms, stepping back slightly, even though that internal magnet tries to resist. "Rose," I say, my voice sharp now, demanding, "tell me what the hell is going on, right now. Or I swear, I *am* getting myself a separate room, because this emotional manipulation, whatever it is, is getting ridiculous."

She sighs again, a long, shuddering breath, then slowly lifts her head to look at me. The profound sadness swimming in her stunning green eyes hits me with unexpected force, making my resolve waver, melting the anger away again. God, those eyes are beautiful. I find myself fleetingly lost in their depths. Shaking my head slightly to clear it, I manage a quiet shout, my voice tight with contained emotion, "Rose!"

"I… I still can't quite believe this is real," she begins, her voice trembling slightly. "We… shifters… we were always told that… outcasts like me… would never find their Primes. Not that *anyone* has supposedly found a Prime in hundreds, maybe thousands of years, as far as anyone knows. It's become… legend. Myth. But… but here you are." Her gaze drops again. "And what makes it even stranger, even more impossible… is that you aren't even one of us. You're human."

"What's a Prime?" I ask immediately, seizing on the word I overheard her say earlier in the park. The word hangs in the air, heavy with unspoken meaning. "What does it mean? And what do you mean, you're an outcast? If Luca is mistreating you in any way, I swear I'll—" Anger flares again, protectiveness surging, ready to confront Luca.

"That's… that's one of the side effects," Rose interrupts me with a strained, watery chuckle. "Becoming fiercely protective."

I stare at her, ignoring the comment. "I am *done* with you avoiding the question, Rose. Stop messing around and give me straight answers!" I start to move away again, intending to retreat to my bed, perhaps even walk out the door this time. I need space to process this. I choose my bed for now, needing a barrier.

Rose takes another deep breath, squaring her shoulders as if preparing for battle. Then, she begins to speak, the words sounding almost rehearsed, as if she's been practising this explanation since our training session ended. "First," she clarifies, her voice gaining a little strength, "Luca has done absolutely nothing wrong. Quite the opposite. He took me in, gave me a home, a purpose, when my own pack, my own *family*, cast me out. Shifters like me… we aren't tolerated in most traditional packs. Because I refused to 'toe the line', refused to conform. They told me to leave, or face death." The raw heartbreak in her voice as she says the last words is palpable, twisting something deep inside me.

The revelation shocks me to the core. Cast out? Facing death?

"What?" I whisper, stunned. "What could possibly be so bad that your own family would threaten to kill you?" She takes another deep, steadying breath before continuing, her gaze finally meeting mine, defiant now.

"I'm gay, Ava," she states simply, boldly. "I'm only attracted to women. That lifestyle… it isn't tolerated in most traditional packs. They see it as a dereliction of duty, a refusal to contribute to the pack's future, to continue the bloodline. They tried to force me into a mating with a male shifter, but I… resisted. Violently. I almost killed him. So, they forced me to leave. Banishment. Normally, they would have simply executed me for defiance, but the pack leaders… they were my parents. My mother was the Alpha. So, they granted me the 'mercy' of exile, allowing me to leave with my life, on the condition I never return. If I ever set foot on their territory again, they vowed they would kill me on sight." The strength in her voice wavers slightly at the end, but her eyes hold a fierce pride. She watches me closely now, clearly gauging my reaction to her confession.

Without a second thought, I move back towards her, closing the distance again, pulling her into another hug, holding her tightly. My anger returns, white-hot this time, but directed solely at her monstrous parents. What kind of creatures, parent or not, Alpha or not, would do that to their own daughter? Just because of who she loves? "That's… that's barbaric," I manage, my voice thick with disbelief. "How can they act like that? Especially now, in this day and age? Rose, I am so incredibly sorry you had to endure that."

"It's okay," she murmurs against my shoulder, though her body remains tense. "Eventually, after… a difficult time… living on the streets, completely lost… Luca found me. At first, I fought his help, trusted no one. But he was persistent, kind. Eventually, I gave in, let him help me get back on my feet so I joined his pack. Under his guidance, his acceptance… I thrived. I became myself again. I rose through his pack ranks quickly because, for the very first time, I felt like I was truly *home*. Luca doesn't care who you love, or even what kind of shifter you are – or if you're a shifter at all. His pack, even when his father was Alpha, always welcomed diversity. What's left of our pack now… it's a mixed group, fiercely loyal to each other." The strength returns fully to her voice as she speaks of her found family, but a weariness still lingers in her eyes.

"Well," I say softly, pulling back slightly so I can see her face, "I'm glad you managed to find a real home, Rose. And I'm relieved I don't have to kick Luca in the balls after all." My attempt at levity works; a small, genuine chuckle escapes her, and some of the light returns to her beautiful eyes. Those eyes… God, they are captivating. I shake my head slightly, trying to focus. What is *wrong* with me? Rose is pouring her heart out, sharing deep trauma, something I *never* allow others to do with me, and here I am, getting lost in the colour of her eyes again. Rose must notice my momentary distraction because she chuckles again, louder this time.

"What?" I ask, curious about what gave me away.

"You lost concentration for a second there, didn't you?" she teases gently.

My eyes widen; my jaw drops slightly. How the hell did she *know* that? "Rose," I demand, seriousness returning, "what is going on? Why am I acting so out of character around you? Because honestly, it's starting to become more than a little concerning."

The sadness immediately returns to her eyes, extinguishing the brief spark of amusement. It confuses me, this rapid shift in her emotions. She squares her shoulders again, gently removing herself from my loose embrace, the action leaving me feeling oddly rejected, cold again. Her next words utterly shatter my already fractured understanding of reality, blowing the revelation about shifters and vampires completely out of the water.

"Within the lore of shifter communities, Ava," she begins, her voice taking on a formal, almost recited quality, "there exists a fundamental concept known as the Prime Mate bond. It's… it's a cornerstone belief in our existence, reflecting the idea that the universe itself, or the gods, predetermines two specific shifters to be perfect partners, destined soulmates. This magical element is deeply ingrained in our very being, passed down through generations. It can also lead to… significant complications… due to its extreme rarity and the perceived value placed upon it. Although all shifters retain the freedom to choose their own relationships, encountering one's true Prime Mate is universally acknowledged by all involved, as the mutual attraction is said to be irresistible. It physically and emotionally affects both individuals involved. Tradition, ancient shifter law, maintains that this sacred connection is specifically destined to produce offspring possessing superior strength, speed, and senses – the next generation of powerful pack leaders." She pauses, taking a shaky breath. "Severance of this bond *is* possible, though difficult and rarely undertaken willingly. It requires deliberate, prolonged distancing, or," her voice drops to a near whisper, "as the legends claim, a direct, verbal rejection spoken while looking directly into the Prime Mate's eyes will instantly, irrevocably dissolve the connection." She finally looks up at me, her green eyes filled with a tumultuous mix of hope, fear, and confusion.

Her words hang in the air between us. She's hinting at something monumental, something impossible, but my brain feels sluggish, unable to grasp the final, crucial piece. I feel like I'm missing an obvious clue, or maybe I'm just being deliberately dense, unwilling to accept the implication. Why is she telling *me* all this ancient shifter lore? I'm not a shifter. And even if we *were* together, biologically, we couldn't produce offspring. There has to be something else going on here, some other explanation.

Rose watches me intently, likely gauging my reaction, waiting for the inevitable freak-out. But all I feel is a profound, bewildered confusion, layered with a dawning, terrifying suspicion. My mouth engages before my brain can fully process the implications. "I… I still don't understand, Rose," I stammer. "I'm not a shifter. And… we could never have kids together, not biologically. So, this… this Prime bond… it must be something else affecting us. Maybe… maybe some kind of spell? Cast by an enemy to distract us, sow confusion?" It's a desperate grasp for a rational explanation in an irrational situation.

Rose just shakes her head slowly, a look of pained resignation settling on her features. "It's not that kind of spell, Ava, though it *is* a form of powerful, ancient magic. When I spoke to Luca earlier, in the park, I practically demanded he explain what was happening, because everything we've *ever* been told insists the bond can only form between a male and a female shifter, destined to propagate the species. Yet… here we are. Two females. And you… you're human, as far as we know." Her voice trembles slightly. "We honestly don't know *how* this is possible. But… if this *is* the true Prime Mate bond of our legends… then, Ava… I… I can't bring myself to reject it. I can't look you in the eyes and say the words that would dissolve it. To me, to any shifter who understands its significance… receiving this bond is… it's the most precious, sacred gift imaginable." She looks away, struggling for composure. "Before you start to panic," she adds quickly, her voice regaining some control, "Luca is already prepared to send me back to what remains of his pack. He'll have Elijah, his other Beta, come and join the task force instead. Luca originally chose me to accompany him specifically *because* he thought having another female on the team would make *you* more comfortable, so you wouldn't have to deal with too much testosterone."

Before she even finishes speaking, I'm shaking my head vehemently. "No," I state firmly, surprised by the fierce determination in my own voice. "Absolutely not. You're not going anywhere."

"Ava, I *have* to leave," Rose insists, dropping her head again, her voice thick with emotion. "Otherwise… we'll become too distracted. The bond… it will keep trying to pull us together, make it impossible to focus on the mission, impossible to stay away from each other. I'm leaving tonight, after we've finished our initial search of the city." Tears begin to trace paths down her cheeks. "I am so, so sorry I've done this to you, put you in this impossible position. When Adam first briefed us about you, when we reviewed the intelligence dossier he provided… it indicated you were… straight. That you typically hooked up with guys after missions." A flash of anger cuts through my confusion – Moore had me investigated? Watched? "Adam clearly went to considerable lengths selecting you, vetting you over months to ensure you were the right fit for this. This… this bond… it's unfair to you, it's wrong. So, I *have* to go." Her shoulders start to shake slightly as silent sobs wrack her body.

My mind is reeling, utterly overwhelmed. First, the revelation that Agent Moore had me under surveillance, gathering personal details about my private life – that intrusion ignites a cold fury I'll definitely address with him later. Also who the hell was good enough to tail me that I didn't even notice? Second, this Prime bond… designed to unite shifters, produce powerful offspring… none of which applies to us. It makes no logical sense. And yet… the thought of her leaving, of her being sent away because of this… it sparks a possessiveness, a fierce refusal I don't understand but cannot deny. There is absolutely no way I am letting her leave.

One crucial question cuts through the emotional chaos. "So," I ask carefully, needing to understand the core of this, "this bond… it isn't *real* feelings then? Not actual love? It's just… some biological imperative? Magic forcing two shifters together for breeding purposes?"

My blunt question seems to catch Rose completely off guard. She finally looks up at me, her beautiful green eyes red-rimmed and swimming with tears, with tear tracks glistening on her cheeks. The sight makes my own heart ache with an unfamiliar pang. I desperately want to pull her back into my arms, but I need this answer first. Rose starts to shake her head, managing to speak through her quiet sobs. "No… no, Ava, that's not quite right. Your *feelings*… they are entirely your own. The bond… its primary purpose is to bring the two destined souls *together* initially. It creates the pull, the awareness, the connection. You might not consciously *think* you have feelings for each other at first, you might even resist it. But the more time you spend together, drawn by the bond, the more you begin to realise the true, underlying feelings that were always there. As I said," her voice trembles, "the bond's function is to ensure the fated meeting happens, like… like destiny, ensuring you find the one you were always meant to be with." She starts to turn away again, overwhelmed, but I react instinctively, reaching out, my left hand gently cupping her chin, tilting her face back towards mine.

She tries to avert her gaze again, looking down, ashamed perhaps. "Rose, look at me," I demand softly but firmly. She just shakes her head, refusing. "Fine," I say, my voice hardening slightly, resorting to a different tactic. "Be like that then. I *wanted* you to look me in the eyes for what I'm about to say, but if you're determined to be a coward about this, then so be it."

My words hit their mark. Her eyes snap open, wide with anger and hurt at being called a coward. She opens her mouth, clearly about to unleash a furious retort, but I don't give her the chance. Seizing the opportunity, leveraging her anger-fuelled focus, I lean in quickly and plant my mouth firmly on hers.

CHAPTER 11

This Is Not A Drill: Kissing, Ripping, and The
Unexpected Permanence of Shifter Smooches

Rose freezes, utterly shocked by my sudden move, her lips parting in surprise as mine make contact. The instant our mouths touch, it feels like a high-voltage current surges through my entire system, a raw, electric shock that makes my nerve endings sing and my breath catch in my throat. It's overwhelming, consuming.

As that initial jolt passes, leaving behind a tingling awareness, I press the advantage, sliding my tongue tentatively past her momentarily unresponsive lips, seeking hers. My own lips move against hers, soft yet demanding, as I instinctively press my body closer, seeking more contact, more of that intoxicating energy.

It takes only a fraction of a second for her shock to vaporize, replaced by a reciprocal, consuming fire. Her hands come up, tangling in my hair, gripping my head almost painfully, pulling me tighter against her mouth. Her tongue meets mine, a fierce, possessive dance igniting between us. Pleasure, potent and unexpected, washes over me in dizzying waves as we sink deeper into the kiss, lost in the sudden, overwhelming connection. The greatest pleasure, however, isn't merely the contact of our mouths, the friction of lips and tongues; it's the almost searing heat radiating from her body, soaking into mine wherever we touch, sinking into my tongue, my lips, melding our skin together until the boundaries blur.

Rose breaks the kiss far sooner than I want, pulling back just enough for air, though her hands remain tangled in my hair, her eyes blazing with an intensity that mirrors my own racing pulse. I'd just started reaching up, intending to slide my arms around her neck, wanting to pull her even closer.

"Ava… are you absolutely sure about this?" she whispers, her voice husky, her breath warm against my face. "Because… the legends say… once we give into the bond like this… accept it fully… it becomes permanent. Irrevocable."

I feel like I've just sprinted a marathon; my breathing is shallow, ragged, sharp intakes struggling to draw enough air into my starved lungs. It's as if I've forgotten the basic mechanics of breathing. My heart hammers against my ribs, a frantic rhythm matching the thrumming energy between us. A natural high, intoxicating and fierce, floods my system. Talking feels impossible, an unnecessary interruption. I try to process her words, the gravity of them, through the haze of sensation. *Permanent.* The thought should scare me, but it doesn't. It feels… right. I give her words serious consideration for approximately three-point-four seconds before replying, my voice breathy, almost unrecognisable as my own.

"I'm… I'm so damn sure. Are you going to kiss me again, or not?." I'm not even certain if the sounds I make are actual words or just breathless gasps.

It must be coherent enough, because Rose doesn't hesitate. A predatory glint enters her eyes. Her fingers tighten their grip in my hair, tilting my head back slightly as she pulls me towards her again. Our lips crash together once more, hungry, demanding, and a low groan of pure pleasure escapes me, vibrating deep in my chest. Our tongues resume their desperate, searching dance as I finally succeed in wrapping my arms around her neck, pulling myself flush against her warmth. And in that moment, pressed against her, lost in the kiss, a profound sense of belonging washes over me. For the first time in my life, since the night my world ended, I finally feel… home. Like I've stopped running, stopped hiding behind the walls I so carefully constructed within the military.

I lose track of time, lost in the kiss, the embrace. I want more. Need more. Testing the boundaries, driven by an instinct I don't recognise, I slowly slide my left leg over her lap, planting my foot on the bed on her other side, straddling her now, increasing the points of contact, needing to feel her closer. Simultaneously, she responds, her other arm snaking around my waist, pulling me impossibly harder against her body. A sharp sting of pain registers as her grip tightens – she doesn't know her own strength – but it's instantly subsumed by the overwhelming pleasure, the raw intensity of the moment.

My hands begin to roam, driven by a need to touch, to explore. I reach for the hem of her t-shirt, intending to slide it over her head, needing to feel her skin against mine. But Rose surprises me again. With a sudden, swift movement, she grabs the back of my own t-shirt and rips it clean off my body, the sound of tearing fabric sharp in the charged air. I gasp at the sudden exposure, the cool air hitting my heated skin, the sheer unexpectedness sending another jolt of pleasure through me.

When my senses recalibrate, my own hands find the hem of her top again, sliding underneath, fingers tracing the smooth, burning skin of her stomach, her back. Her skin is unbelievably hot, radiating heat like a furnace. Goosebumps erupt under my touch as my hands roam upwards. Briefly breaking the kiss, needing both hands, I whip her top off over her head, tossing it aside without looking where it lands, then immediately reclaim her mouth, taking a deep, necessary breath in that fleeting moment. Rose retaliates instantly, her fingers finding the clasp of my bra, tearing it off with the same startling strength she used on my shirt. At this rate, I really *am* going to need that shopping trip she mentioned.

A low chuckle rumbles in my chest, and I feel Rose's mouth curve into a smile against mine. Since I lack her supernatural strength to simply rip *her* bra off, I opt for a different strategy. Pushing away from her slightly, ignoring her soft sound of protest, I stand up beside the bed and begin fumbling with the button on my own jeans.

"Get your clothes off," I command breathlessly, my voice husky. "Now. And hurry. I don't possess your impressive ripping skills, and frankly, I can't wait much longer." I chuckle again as Rose, accepting the challenge, tears her own bra off with a sharp *snap* of elastic, then practically busts the button off her jeans in her haste to shove them down her legs.

Somehow, fuelled by adrenaline and mutual urgency, I manage to shed my own jeans just a fraction of a second before she does. Standing there naked, impatient, desire coiling hot and low in my belly, I watch as she kicks her discarded jeans aside. I waste no time. Pushing her backwards onto the bed with some force, she willingly goes, landing on her back. She instinctively drags herself further up the bed until her head rests against the pillows. I crawl onto the bed after her, positioning myself over her body, straddling her thighs, pinning her gently beneath my weight.

Leaning down, I begin a slow assault, tracing patterns on her flat stomach with gentle kisses, my lips brushing softly against her heated skin. I pull back slightly, hovering just above her, letting the tip of my tongue trace the path my lips just took, tasting the faint saltiness of her skin. Her hands come up, exploring the sides of my body, fingers brushing tentatively against the curve of my breasts, sending shivers down my spine. Her body trembles almost imperceptibly beneath mine. I continue my slow ascent, moving upwards, feather-light kisses interspersed with delicate licks, until I reach the space between her breasts. I pause there, savouring the way her breath hitches, before moving higher, trailing kisses along the column of her throat. I take her hands, gently pinning them above her head as I move up further still, my lips brushing against the sensitive skin just beneath her jawline, teasing, licking softly.

Her body feels incandescent beneath me, the heat intensifying with every touch, every second. That heat radiates outwards, pushing the pleasure coursing through my own veins towards an almost unbearable peak. Her soft groans, the involuntary twitches of her body under my exploration, fuel my own escalating desire. Just as my lips reach the exquisitely sensitive spot just behind her ear, I feel her body lift slightly beneath me, arching instinctively towards my touch, a deeper, longer groan vibrating from her chest. Her hands escape my light hold, fingers digging into my waist with surprising force, the pressure sharp but electrifying, sending another wave of pleasure crashing through me, making me gasp. It feels like her fingertips are igniting my nerve endings.

I run my tongue lightly along the delicate shell of her ear, then let my body sink fully against hers, pressing my weight down, maximizing the skin-to-skin contact. The heat is astonishing, unlike anything I've ever felt from another human being. My body seems to soak it in greedily, tingling from head to toe. Losing control for a moment, driven purely by sensation, I capture her mouth again, sinking into another deep, searing kiss. Our bodies meld, moving together instinctively, feeling less like two separate entities and more like a single, unified being consumed by rising heat and need.

As our tongues engage in a slower, more sensual dance this time, my right hand begins to roam again, tracing the curve of her hip, fingers exploring the dip of her waist. Rose retaliates, her hand closing over my left buttock, her grip tightening, fingers digging in so hard I know I'll have bruises tomorrow. But in this moment, the pain is just another layer of pleasure, sharp and focusing. My exploring hand slides lower, dipping inwards, angling my body slightly to grant myself better access. As my hand moves between her legs, she automatically parts them further for me.

I tease her at first, letting the tips of my fingers brush feather-light over her smooth skin. After a few agonizing seconds, I shift my hand, using my thumb now, pressing firmly into the crease where her leg meets her core, feeling the frantic pulse beneath my fingertip quicken as I increase the pressure. She gasps, her body shivering violently, jolting against mine several times before trying to arch upwards again, the movement futile against my weight but pressing us even closer together. I continue my ministrations around her neck and upper body with lips and tongue, creating a counterpoint of sensation. Then, I shift my hand, repeating the pressure point technique on her other side, feeling her pulse leap again, her body jerking more violently this time, the reaction pulling a reciprocal gasp from my own lips. In that shared moment of heightened pleasure, I take her completely by surprise, gently sliding two fingers inside her slick heat. Her body arches hard against mine, lifting me upwards as a strangled cry escapes her, then she falls silent, her body rigid, breath held captive for several long seconds. When the moment passes, her body slumps back against the mattress, boneless, her fingers digging even harder into my skin, making me gasp again, my head thrown back.

The intensity of the feedback loop, the pleasure ricocheting between us, forces me to momentarily pause, pulling my fingers back slightly. Rose immediately uses the opportunity, locking her mouth onto my right nipple, her tongue swirling around the peak, making it pebble instantly, impossibly harder than it already was. My body shivers uncontrollably in response. She moves to my neck, trailing hot, open-mouthed kisses while I, recovering, slide my fingers back inside her, resuming a slow, steady rhythm, in and out, while my thumb finds her clit, beginning small, insistent circles. Her body begins to tense beneath my touch, her breath coming in short, sharp pants. I feel her nearing the edge. Shifting my position again, I move down her body, settling between her thighs as she instinctively spreads her legs wider.

Lowering my head, I push my tongue against her, gliding it firmly over her clit while simultaneously resuming the steady in-and-out rhythm with my fingers. I increase the pace, feeling her nails dig sharply into my back, hearing her breath catch, her body trembling on the verge of release. Seeking to prolong the moment, to push her further, I move my mouth slightly, nipping gently at the sensitive skin of her inner thighs. Rose is panting now, a sound raw and primal, unlike anything I've ever heard. I think I see faint ripples, like heat haze, shimmering over her skin. My left hand slides down her leg; she moves it further aside for me. When I reach her knee, I slip my fingers behind it, gently stroking the sensitive skin there. Her leg twitches, not from being tickled, but from another sensitive spot discovered. I continue the caress.

A groan escapes my own lips as Rose drags her nails, not painfully but with exquisite pressure, across the skin of my back. The sensation is unlike anything I've ever experienced, pure, unexpected pleasure. It drives me upwards again, my mouth finding her neck. I don't know what possesses me, some primal instinct perhaps, but I sink my teeth into the soft flesh of her neck, biting down hard. The metallic tang of blood fills my mouth as I feel the skin break. Rose's entire body goes rigid beneath me, arching violently off the bed. She fumbles blindly for a pillow, shoving it hard against her face just as I pull my mouth away, shocked by my own action, momentarily concerned I've bitten too hard. Through the pillow, I hear her muffled scream of release, a long, keening sound as her body remains arched, trembling uncontrollably. I slowly slide my fingers out of her, moving back up her body, trailing kisses just below her breasts, running my hands soothingly over her quivering skin as the waves subside.

Once Rose regains some semblance of control, she moves with blurring speed. Before I can react, she grabs me, flipping me effortlessly onto my back, her strength astonishing. With a low growl, she crashes her mouth down onto mine again, the kiss fierce, possessive, like she's on a mission to devour me. Her hands roam my body urgently, igniting fires everywhere they touch. My skin feels hypersensitive, tingling, almost painfully aware, as the incredible heat radiating from her body seems to seep into my very bones, heating me from the inside out. Wherever our skin connects, it feels less like contact and more like fusion, like we're melting into one entity. The pleasure is overwhelming, building rapidly.

When she breaks the kiss to move to my neck, trailing fire, I manage to whisper, my voice rough, "You don't... have to be gentle with me, Rose."

A low, predatory growl rumbles in her chest. "Good," she

breathes against my skin. "Because for a human… the first time with a shifter… especially *this*… it's an experience you'll never feel quite as powerfully again. So, hold on tight, Ava." And then she bites. Not a nip, but a full, predatory bite on the side of my neck. I feel the shocking pressure of elongated teeth sinking deep into my flesh, a sharp, invasive pain instantly obliterated by an explosive wave of pure, unadulterated pleasure that washes over my entire body, so intense it steals my breath, making me climax instantly, violently.

The force of it takes me completely by surprise. I feel like I'm suffocating, unable to draw breath, my vision whiting out, but in that moment, coherent thought is impossible, irrelevant. All I can do is cling to her, anchoring myself as wave after wave of ecstasy pulses through me, my body convulsing uncontrollably. When the initial, overwhelming surge finally begins to subside, leaving me trembling and breathless, Rose slowly moves down my body, kissing every inch of skin, each touch sending fresh tremors of pleasure rippling across my hypersensitive flesh. I feel dangerously close to climaxing again already.

She continues her descent, her hands caressing my legs, tracing patterns on my inner thighs. She settles between my legs again, her tongue immediately finding its target. Then she starts biting, sharp little nips around the edges of my pussy, each one making my body jerk violently, unpredictably. What the hell is she *doing* to me? Why is my body reacting like this, so much more sensitive, so much more responsive than I ever thought possible? Everything she does sends electric pulses through my system. As her tongue continues its relentless work, I feel something sharp, impossibly sharp, scrape lightly across my skin – my stomach, my ribs, my thighs. Claws. I feel claws lightly tracing patterns over my body. Logically, it should hurt, or at least be unpleasant. Instead, my body responds perversely, the strange sensation ratcheting up the pressure building low in my belly, pushing me closer to the edge again.

Just as I feel the familiar tension coiling tight, ready to snap, she moves abruptly, shifting back up my body, her mouth finding my breasts again, teasing my nipples with teeth and tongue. The sudden change, the withdrawal of that intense focus below, holds the impending climax at bay, leaving me suspended, aching, waiting. She teases me mercilessly, mirroring my earlier exploration, but with an added shifter edge. When she kisses my skin now, she uses her elongated canines, running the sharp tips lightly over my flesh just before her lips press down. Then she bites, gently but firmly, holding a small fold of skin between her teeth before soothing the spot with a kiss. The contrast sends sparks along my nerves, each sensation intensifying the building pressure within me, pulling my core tighter and tighter.

Her right hand slides back down between my legs, fingers seeking entrance just as another powerful spasm makes my body arch off the bed. Rose shifts position again, leveraging her strength, dragging me upwards against her body until I'm almost in a sitting position, cradled against her chest, completely supported by her. I've lost all control over my own limbs; my body feels like jelly, pliant and boneless. She holds me securely with one arm wrapped around my back, while the fingers of her other hand move inside me, faster now, deeper. The pressure inside me builds relentlessly, unbearably. I feel like I might actually pass out from the sheer intensity. I don't know how the words form, why I say them, but they escape my lips in a desperate gasp, "It's… it's coming!."

Her pace increases instantly, her fingers moving with forceful precision, the friction making my body physically rock against hers. It doesn't take long. The pressure building inside reaches its zenith and then shatters, releasing in a cataclysmic wave, stronger, deeper, more profound than the first. Ecstasy floods my senses, blinding, deafening. And in that moment of absolute overload, Rose bites my neck again, hard, while her claws, sharper now, dig into the flesh of my back. My vision explodes into a kaleidoscope of blinding colours. My body convulses, jerking back and forth uncontrollably as wave after successive wave of pure pleasure washes over me, stiffening my limbs even as I continue to shudder. Rose holds me tight against her heat, anchoring me as I ride the overwhelming tide.

I can't do anything else. I simply float, suspended in a sea of vibrant colour, detached from my own body, almost as if I'm flying. Dimly, through the haze of sensation, I feel Rose shifting beneath me, lowering my limp body gently down onto the bed. I feel her adjust her position, so she's now lying underneath me, cradling me. My head comes to rest on her chest, the steady beat of her heart a grounding rhythm as I slowly drift back from the precipice, floating in a warm, dark current, flashes of what just happened mixing with the lingering colours behind my eyelids. I love this feeling, this peaceful, weightless suspension. Then, reluctantly, I feel myself being pulled back, dragged away from the pleasant floaty darkness as awareness, sensation, begins to return to my limbs.

"Mmm, want… want to go back… dark, floaty place… good memories…" The words slur out loud, surprising me. A soft chuckle answers me.

"You want to go back where?" Rose's voice is warm, laced with amusement, vibrating pleasantly against my ear. "Sorry to drag you away from your 'dark, floaty place', honey. But we probably need to get up soon. We're supposed to be heading out in a few hours, remember?." She pauses, her tone shifting slightly. "Thought you might need that time to… sort yourself out. And maybe decide if you hate me or not."

Her last words cut through the lingering bliss, jarring me fully awake. *Hate her?* How could I possibly hate her after… that? My eyes snap open. Rose's beautiful face fills my vision, her green eyes soft, watching me with gentle concern. "Hello, you," I manage, a massive, dopey grin spreading uncontrollably across my face.

Rose laughs at my greeting, the sound warm and genuine. "Hello to you too."

I'm lost for a moment, basking in the aftermath, her earlier words about hating her momentarily forgotten. Then they resurface. I try to sit up, intending to demand an explanation, but my body refuses to cooperate fully. A deep numbness still pervades my limbs, though underneath it, a pleasant tingling persists. I decide to stay put for now. "Um… what do you mean, decide if I hate you or not?" I ask, confusion clouding my thoughts. "What kind of crap is that? I thought we settled that whole issue when I kissed you?."

Rose chuckles again, still holding me close. "Well… we kind of completed the bond, Ava. Permanently sealed it." She hesitates, looking suddenly nervous again. "I… I was scared to tell you everything beforehand, specifically about the… biting part. In case it freaked you out completely. Especially after… well, after things progressed so… intensely. I didn't exactly expect *that* to happen quite like it did." She takes a shaky breath. "Honestly, I was already panicking when I was trying to explain the bond basics earlier. But, to be fair, you didn't really give me a chance to mention the one crucial element required to solidify the bond, make it unbreakable. Plus," she adds, looking sheepish, "I wasn't even sure if the final step *would* work, given that you're not actually a shifter. But… it seems to have worked. Which is good. I think." She trails off, babbling slightly, clearly still processing everything herself.

I frown, trying to make sense of her rambling. "Rose, slow down. What are you talking about? Biting? Solidifying?." And then, another thought occurs, a practical one this time. "Also, any idea how long my body is going to feel this… numb? Well, numb everywhere except… down there… which is definitely, acutely *throbbing* right now." I shift slightly, confirming the persistent ache. "Anyway, back to the point, I would really like to kiss you again, but I genuinely can't seem to move."

Rose stares at me, her expression shifting from nervous to concerned. "How numb, exactly, are we talking here, Ava?"

"Very," I confirm. "My whole body feels like it's buzzing, tingling all over."

"Okay… that's… good, actually," she says, though she grimaces slightly as she speaks. "It means I probably didn't damage you permanently."

My eyes narrow. "Rose. If you don't tell me exactly what is going on, right now, I swear I *will* find the strength to move, and I *will* kick your arse the moment I can."

Rose manages a weak grin at my threat, then her face falls again, mirroring the earlier sadness. Oh no, not this again. "Rose, just spit it out!"

"Okay, okay!" she relents, taking another deep breath. "Well… we had to bite each other. Which, technically, you did first, on my neck. Broke the skin. Drew blood." She pauses, clearly gathering courage. "And I… I got so lost in the moment, so overwhelmed by… everything… that I completely forgot I needed to explicitly tell you that to fully accept the bond, to make it permanent, we *both* needed to bite each other and draw blood. It's… it's the final step, the ritual sealing." Her voice drops again, becoming almost inaudible. "I got… a little carried away. Overexcited. And I… well, I bit you. Twice, actually. And I might have… lost control just a tiny bit more… because my claws definitely came out. And I… I may have scratched you. A bit. Okay," she corrects herself quickly, looking utterly miserable, "maybe… maybe a lot. I am *so* sorry, Ava." She looks like she's about to start crying again.

I process her confession, running the sequence of events back through my mind. The overwhelming urge *I* felt to bite her… it wasn't just random passion then; it was the bond prompting the action. Now I understand. A slow grin spreads across my face as flashes of the intensity, the raw pleasure, replay in my mind. Then the other part hits me. *She* bit *me*. Twice. "Yeah," I say slowly, recalling the explosive pleasure that followed. "Yeah, I remember now. You bit me. And my body basically went into nuclear meltdown. What the hell *was* that all about?."

"It's… it's partly a shifter thing," Rose explains hesitantly. "A physiological effect we can sometimes have on humans when we bite them during… intimacy. But combined with the actual bonding ritual… it amplifies everything exponentially. Makes it so much more powerful, overwhelming." She looks genuinely contrite. "Honestly, Ava, I didn't expect it to have quite *that* profound an effect on you. It clearly caught you off guard." She sighs. "In our oldest stories, the lore surrounding the Prime Mate bond states you *must* bite each other, draw blood, during sex for the bond to become truly permanent, unbreakable. Over time, some shifters started… incorporating biting more frequently into intimacy, you know, just in case they stumbled upon their Prime without realising it. Trying to force the issue, perhaps." She looks away again, clearly uncomfortable. "As I said, biting seals the bond irrevocably. There are all sorts of rumours, legends attached to it, things no one really knows are true anymore, because, as I mentioned, witnessing a true Prime bond hasn't happened in living memory, maybe not for centuries. It's why I tried to warn you earlier, told you there would be no turning back once we… crossed that line." She finishes sheepishly, still babbling slightly, looking incredibly worried about my reaction.

I consider everything she's said, replaying the entire encounter again in my mind, focusing on the sensations, the emotions, the sheer intensity of the connection I felt. Honestly? It doesn't bother me one bit. Not the biting, not the claws, not the permanence. "Okay," I say calmly. "So, what's the actual problem then? Why would any of that make me hate you?."

"Well…" Rose looks down again. "I wasn't sure you *really* understood what you were agreeing to, what permanence truly meant in this context. And… well, I hurt you. Physically. I damaged your body… possibly quite a lot." She gestures vaguely towards my back.

"Rose," I interrupt gently, "I believe I specifically recall saying 'don't go easy on me'. I don't mind things getting a bit rough; adds to the excitement. I'll heal." Then, a sudden, chilling thought strikes me, eclipsing everything else. "Wait a minute… if you *bit* me… drew blood… does that mean… am I going to turn? Become one of… the bitten?." The fear I thought I'd conquered surges back, cold and sharp. She never mentioned *I* would also have to change.

"No!" Rose answers quickly, vehemently shaking her head. "No, Ava, you won't become like me. That kind of turning, the forced or intentional bite to create another shifter… that can only happen under very specific circumstances, primarily involving the full moon." She pauses for a second, then adds, almost absentmindedly, a thoughtful frown creasing her brow, "Which reminds me… when *is* the full moon again?." She taps her chin lightly with a finger, momentarily lost in thought.

I manage to shake my head, relief washing over me, quickly followed by amusement at her slight derailment. "Okay, good. But you wait," I warn playfully, feeling more like myself again, "I am *still* going to kick your arse when I can move properly." Then, another thought occurs, practical this time. "But first… I'm starting to feel my body again. It feels… incredibly sensitive. Anyway… give me a kiss. I hate waiting."

Rose chuckles, the worry finally receding from her eyes, replaced by warmth and affection. She leans down, planting a soft, lingering kiss on my lips before settling back beside me, curling up against my side. As she gets comfortable, something else crosses my mind, making me cringe inwardly. "Rose?"

Rose rests her head back on my shoulder, her warm breath ghosting against my skin. When she replies, the vibration of her voice travels through my entire body. "Yes, Ava?."

God, I love the way she says my name. But I need to focus. "How… how good is your hearing, exactly?."

She shifts slightly, propping herself up on an elbow to look down at me, a curious expression on her face. "Why do you ask, Ava?."

I groan as the simple vibration of her voice against my skin sends another wave of pleasant tingling through my still hypersensitive body. How long *is* this going to last? Shouldn't the aftereffects be wearing off by now? "I… I was just wondering… hypothetically… how far away someone, say, Luca, would have to be… to *not* hear what… transpired… in here? You know… just out of intellectual curiosity, of course."

Rose chuckles again, the sound rich and knowing, and those

damned vibrations do strange, wonderful things to my equilibrium and my still throbbing lady bits. Images flash through my mind – claws, teeth, heat – making me shift uncomfortably. "Are you perhaps worried about what Luca might have overheard from next door?" she teases gently.

"Um… well… maybe," I admit reluctantly. "And whatever the hell you did to me during the… bonding… my body is ridiculously sensitive right now. Just the vibrations of your voice talking are… doing strange things to me. And definitely affecting my aforementioned throbbing parts."

Rose lifts her head fully, her green eyes sparkling with mischief as she looks directly into mine. "Really?" she purrs. "Just how sensitive are we talking here, Ava? Is this… something I could potentially tease you with? For a little while?." As she speaks, she rests her hand gently between my legs, cupping me softly, the warmth instantly soothing yet simultaneously provocative.

"Very, *very* sensitive," I confirm, my voice catching slightly. "And if you *do* tease me, then I reiterate my earlier threat, I *will* kick your arse so hard you'll have a bruise to match the one I can definitely feel forming on *my* arse right now." Her grip earlier was… impressive. "Anyway," I add quickly, trying to regain control of the conversation, "don't change the subject. Answer my question about Luca's hearing range." My voice hitches up slightly at the end, betraying my rising panic at the thought of Luca having overheard everything.

"Ooh, feisty. I'd like to see you *try* and kick my arse," Rose retorts playfully. "And sorry about the bruise. And the scratches. I promise I'll kiss them all better later." She gives my leg a reassuring squeeze. "But to answer your question… Luca *knew* I needed to talk to you. I wasn't sure how you'd react – whether you'd scream, or shout, or maybe even attack me. So, Luca thoughtfully took Sam out for an early dinner, gave us some privacy."

Relief washes over me, potent and immediate. I relax back against the pillows, the tension easing from my shoulders. Thank God.

They weren't next door. But then Rose drops another bombshell, dashing my relief instantly. "However… you *did* manage to scare the occupants of the room on the *other* side when you… vocalised your pleasure so enthusiastically. Then you promptly passed out. I had to quickly assure them through the door, when they came knocking concernedly, that everything was perfectly okay in here." She pauses, then adds with a mischievous glint, "Also… I *did* hear Luca and Sam return about halfway through our… conversation. I wasn't exactly anticipating the… outcome… we achieved, so I might have slightly underestimated the time I told Luca we needed. Sue me."

I manage to push myself up into a sitting position this time, albeit slowly. I gape at Rose, utterly mortified. "Please tell me you are joking right now," I plead. "Are you seriously telling me Luca *did* hear us? And by the way," I add defensively, feeling my face flush crimson, "I did *not* scream! *You* were the screamer, definitely not me!."

Rose shifts position, easily moving to straddle my lap like I did hers earlier, leaning down to give me a quick, teasing peck on the lips. "You are *so* unbelievably cute when you blush, Ava," she murmurs against my mouth.

"I never *used* to blush before I met you!" I protest, pointing accusingly at my own heated face. "This is entirely your fault!."

"And don't worry too much about the neighbours," Rose continues breezily, ignoring my accusation. "They were probably just jealous. They did mutter something about 'dirty perverts' as they walked away, though." She shrugs nonchalantly. "Also, I *did* hear Luca tactfully take Sam back out again almost immediately after they returned; I think he realised you were being rather… expressive."

"They WHAT!?" I exclaim, torn between mortification and amusement. "Right, forget kicking *your* arse. Let's go find the neighbours and kick *their* arses instead!." Then I shake my head, starting to laugh despite myself. The entire situation, the past twenty-four hours… it's just completely, utterly unreal.

"Ava…" Rose whispers, leaning closer again, her voice

dropping to a suggestive purr. "Fancy sharing a shower with me? Considering how sensitive our bodies apparently are right now… it could prove to be a very… fun… experience," she finishes, winking slowly, making me chuckle despite my embarrassment.

I consider her offer for precisely two seconds. "Why the hell not?" I reply, managing a weak wink back. "But fair warning… you might actually have to help keep me on my feet."

Before I can process what's happening, she scoops me effortlessly up into her arms, bridal style, her strength still surprising me. And in seconds, we're in the bathroom, the door clicking shut behind us.

CHAPTER 12

THE MORNING AFTER THE BITE BEFORE
(AND OTHER EXPLANATIONS FOR EXCESSIVE NUMBNESS)

After a shower that felt intensely stimulating and deeply relaxing, leaving me simultaneously energised and feeling like I could sleep for a week straight, I find myself buzzing with a strange, unfamiliar energy. It starkly contrasts the profound exhaustion that usually follows intense physical exertion or adrenaline dumps. My primary, most pressing issue right now, however, is a gnawing hunger. Standing in the steamy bathroom, I study my reflection critically in the mirror, tilting my shoulders to examine my back. A network of fine, red scratches criss-cross my skin, souvenirs from Rose's unrestrained passion. Surprisingly, they don't sting or itch as much as they look like they should. I also instinctively check my neck, half-expecting to see nasty bite marks, vivid purple bruises blooming where her teeth sank in. But there's nothing—just smooth, unmarked skin.

"Rose?" I call out, puzzled. "Why don't I have bite marks on my neck? Or maybe just one really impressive hickey?"

Her voice comes from the other room, laced with amusement. "Ah, that. It's… another side effect, I believe. Something specific to the bonding process. When our… souls… melded, just for that moment, it triggers accelerated healing in both partners. Part of the magic, I suppose. The scratches on your back were definitely much worse immediately after… well, *after*. They've already partially faded. Just like where *you* bit *me*," she adds pointedly, "that's completely healed for me already." Her explanation makes me relax slightly, though the concept of souls melding still feels disconcertingly intimate, alien! Then my stomach interrupts with a loud, demanding growl, reminding me of its emptiness. Rose chuckles from the bedroom.

"We'd better get you something substantial to eat before we head out," she calls back. "Otherwise, that rumbling stomach of yours is going to give our position away to any vampires lurking nearby."

I place a hand protectively over my offending stomach, glaring down at it as if that might silence it. "Yes, well," I retort playfully, catching her eye as she appears in the bathroom doorway, already mostly dressed, "I think it's entirely *your* fault I'm this ravenous." I offer her a slow wink.

"Come on then, hungry girl," Rose replies, grabbing my hand and pulling me towards the bedroom. "Let's get you fed quickly, before the boys come knocking, wondering what's taking us so long." We're too late. Just as Rose reaches for the handle to our door, she lets out a soft groan, as there's a sharp knock on our door.

I quickly pull my hand free from hers just as she opens the door to reveal Sam standing there, looking distinctly uncomfortable, his gaze shifting awkwardly between us.

"Are... are you two ready to head out?" he asks, his eyes flicking quickly over our state of partial dress, then settling somewhere near my shoulder, avoiding direct eye contact. He seems to be trying to assess the atmosphere, perhaps expecting lingering tension or some continuing problem between Rose and me after the training session, where there was clear tension between us.

"We are," Rose confirms briskly, her tone all business now, masking any trace of our earlier intimacy. "But we'd definitely like to grab something to eat on the way. Ava's practically starving." Sam just nods, still looking slightly flustered, while clearly eager to escape the charged atmosphere of our room. I silently chuckle to myself as I quickly finish dressing. The last thing I need is for Sam, despite his reassurances earlier, to develop further suspicions about Rose and me. I know agency regulations; relationships between team members are strictly frowned upon, seen as potential distractions, liabilities. And I know Sam, despite his recent defiance towards the Chief, still possesses a core adherence to protocol. He *would* report concerns to Agent Moore if he believed our relationship compromised the mission.

As I pass Luca on my way out, leaning casually against the wall near their door, he catches my eye. The corner of his mouth lifts in a knowing smirk, and he gives me a subtle, almost imperceptible wink. *Great*, I think, *just great*. So, *he* definitely knows, or at least strongly suspects, how our 'talk' concluded. I feel an embarrassed flush creep up my neck again. Perfect. Just bloody perfect.

I stride past him towards the rear of the Tahoe, needing to focus on prepping for the night's operation. As I pass, I whisper under my breath, low enough that Sam, walking ahead, won't hear, "Keep your mouth shut about this, Luca. If Sam gets confirmation, he *will* cause problems." I don't need Luca's enhanced hearing to know he caught every word. Hopefully, Rose, following close behind, heard it too. It saves me the awkwardness of trying to pull her aside for a hushed, suspicious-looking conversation.

Reaching the back of the Tahoe, I swing open the trunk, the familiar scent of oiled metal and cleaning solvent hitting me. Time to gear up. As I begin selecting weapons, I risk a quick glance back towards Rose. Relief washes over me as I see her usual bright smile is back in place. Catching my eye from behind Sam's back, she offers another quick, conspiratorial wink. My own lips curve upwards in response, a warmth spreading through my chest that has nothing to do with the evening air and everything to do with the woman walking towards me. God, I really am turning into a teenage girl again, emotionally speaking, instead of the cold, hard operative I've always been.

Luca joins me at the open trunk as I start laying out my preferred loadout. "Standard sidearm, definitely," he advises, his voice low, professional again. "And take one of the custom pieces chambered for the wooden-tipped rounds. Might be wise to leave the silver/wolfsbane one for now, unless we get intel suggesting shifter involvement later." He points towards a complex-looking tactical holster lying amongst the gear. "This rig should work for you – designed to carry up to three sidearms, plus a stake and multiple blades. Though," he adds thoughtfully, "I wouldn't personally recommend relying on a stake. Unless you possess the reflexes and improbable luck of that fictional vampire slayer, you're likely too slow for it to be truly effective against a seasoned vamp." His casual mention of Buffy is jarringly surreal. "I'd also suggest a couple of flash-bangs, standard fragmentation grenades just in case, and your usual complement of daggers," he concludes, laying out the suggested items neatly in front of me.

I strip off my light jacket, then pull the intricate holster rig over my head, settling the weight onto my shoulders. It feels lighter than my usual military-grade setup, the leather straps softer, more pliable, yet somehow more complex, like something designed for... well, bondage came disconcertingly to mind as I started tightening the straps across my chest and waist. I briefly worry the straps might irritate the still-healing scratches on my back, but as the leather settles against my skin, there's no pain, no discomfort. Another unexpected side effect of the bond, perhaps? This accelerated healing is definitely a perk I could get used to.

Rose walks up silently behind me, reaching out as if to help adjust the holster straps. Despite myself, despite knowing it's her, I flinch, jerking away instinctively. Old habits, ingrained distrust. She immediately looks hurt again by my involuntary reaction. I groan inwardly. We really *do* need to talk properly about boundaries, about how we navigate this around Sam. Trying to smooth it over without raising Sam's suspicions further, I say quickly, "Sorry, Rose. Just... not used to anyone helping me gear up. Force of habit. When I start prepping for a mission, I tend to... zone out, run through tactical scenarios in my head." It's a half-truth, plausible enough, hopefully. It seems to work; the hurt fades slightly from her eyes, replaced by understanding, though the need for a real conversation hangs unspoken between us.

This time, I allow her to help adjust the straps, her fingers brushing occasionally against my skin, sending little sparks along my nerves despite the layers of clothing and leather. I try to ignore it, focusing on securing my weapons, but I notice Sam watching us intently from the front seat, his expression unreadable. Just as I clip the last dagger into place, we all jump, startled, as a female voice, smooth as velvet, emerges seemingly from the oppressive darkness just beyond the Tahoe's ambient light.

"I assure you, I mean you no harm… *shifters*."

Instinct takes over. In less than a heartbeat, I have one of the wooden-bullet pistols drawn, spinning towards the sound, weapon up, seeking a target. Beside me, Luca and Rose react simultaneously, emitting low, guttural growls, their hands blurring for a split second, morphing into large, dark paws tipped with wickedly long, razor-sharp claws. The image flashes through my mind – those same claws scraping, not unpleasantly, across my skin earlier. Heat rushes to my face again. *Perfect*, I think sarcastically, *bloody perfect*. Things just can't possibly get any more awkward or complicated tonight. Is this some kind of cosmic balancing act? Experience the best orgasms of my life, then immediately get thrown into mortal danger while blushing like a schoolgirl?

I forcefully shake the distracting memories away, sharpening my focus back onto the immediate threat. A threat who apparently knows what Luca and Rose are. Why would they out themselves like that in front of a potential human? And more importantly, how did this woman approach us so silently? Even Luca and Rose, with their enhanced senses, didn't seem to detect her until she spoke.

Before I can demand identification, Luca voices the conclusion his senses have already reached, the single word laced with menace, "Demon."

A literal cold chill washes over my body, prickling my skin despite the warm night air. My focus narrows instantly, every sense straining, listening, watching for any sign of movement from the direction of the voice. A demon. If she's a demon, she *must* be an enemy, especially given Luca and Rose's visceral reaction. Although I have to admit, Rose's growl… it sounds strangely… sexy? Resonating through my body almost like… like a recognition? *Kill me now, please*, my brain screams silently. What the hell has happened to me? This bond thing is seriously messing with my operational effectiveness.

A low, throaty chuckle echoes from the darkness, followed by that same breathy, sultry whisper, deliberately seductive, designed to lure and disarm. "Relax. I am here solely for *Ava*. I am not your enemy tonight… shifters."

Rose visibly bristles, her jaw clenching, the growl deepening in her chest. "You are not going anywhere *near* Ava," she snarls, her voice dangerously low, promising swift retribution. "You'll lose your head before you take another step closer."

Luca addresses her in an equally uncompromising tone, "Demons are *no* friends of ours. Leave now or face the consequences."

An unnerving silence descends, stretching for several tense heartbeats. Then, a distinct, leathery *fwhump-fwhump* sound breaks the stillness – the sound of large wings beating the air. Briefly, my mind scrambles, trying to conjure images of demons based on fragmented mythology and B-movie horror flicks. Monsters with leathery wings, horns, maybe? My thoughts drift unwillingly to images of the Devil from catechism classes long ago. The cold chill intensifies.

"As I stated," the unseen visitor repeats patiently, her voice retaining its seductive edge, "I am here as a friend. My Master sent me personally to bring Ava a gift. A token, he hopes, that will aid in protecting her as she confronts our mutual enemies."

I whisper urgently to Rose beside me, "Can you see her?" She gives the barest perceptible nod, her eyes fixed on the darkness. Damn my inadequate human eyesight.

No one speaks. The standoff continues. I refuse to just stand here, waiting to be attacked. Time to take control. "Come out into the light where I can see you," I call out, my voice steady, authoritative, "Then you can explain exactly why we should believe a single word you say."

"Do you take me for an idiot, Ava?" the demon retorts, her voice laced with amusement. "The moment I reveal myself, your... *attack dogs*... will be upon me." Luca and Rose simultaneously deepen their growls at the insult, their bodies tensing, looking poised to launch themselves into the darkness.

"If you truly come as a friend," I counter sharply, "perhaps insulting my colleagues isn't the wisest opening gambit? And for the record, only my *friends* get to use my first name. Until I know who you are and what you want, it's Agent Bekke to you." I pray Luca and Rose hold their positions, give me a chance to get answers before resorting to violence.

"Apologies," the voice replies, though the amusement remains evident. "No insult intended. Perhaps I should have said... your attack *cats*?" A light chuckle follows. Okay, now she's deliberately pissing me off.

"If you continue with the insults, I *will* let them deal with you," I warn, my own anger rising. "But frankly, I'd prefer answers first. Espccially if there's even a remote possibility any part of your story is true."

"Fine," the voice sighs dramatically, as if humouring a petulant child. "Have it your way. I shall approach and explain. As I said, I am here as a friend. You are not the only ones fighting this war, you know."

"Let her approach," I say firmly, glancing towards Luca and Rose, hoping they'll acquiesce. "I need answers. I can't keep negotiating with shadows."

Luca hesitates for only a fraction of a second, his initial anger visibly receding slightly, replaced by cautious calculation. He gives a single, curt nod. "Fine."

Rose instantly turns to Luca, glaring, clearly disagreeing vehemently, but she remains silent, respecting his authority as Alpha.

Luca addresses her glare anyway, his voice low but firm. "Ava is leading this task force, Rose. If she requires answers, I will allow her the opportunity to obtain them. However," his eyes narrow again, fixed on the darkness, "if our… guest… makes a single hostile move, she will not survive the encounter." His determination is absolute, leaving no doubt he means it.

Rose turns back to me, her expression pleading, silently begging me to reconsider, to prioritise safety over information. I meet her gaze steadily and give a slight shake of my head. Then, raising my voice slightly, I address our unseen visitor, "You can come out now."

I hear the leathery beat of wings again, closer this time, followed by a subtle shift in the shadows just ahead of us. Rose tenses beside me, her body radiating unmistakable heat, enough that I can feel it even standing a foot away. I instinctively move slightly forward, positioning myself partially in front of her. The look she shoots me promises retribution later for putting myself between her and a potential threat. I reach back without looking, my fingers finding her furred paw, giving it a brief, reassuring squeeze – or as much of a squeeze as I can manage around something three times the size of my hand. It seems to work, marginally; her rigid posture eases fractionally. And then, a woman steps gracefully out of the deepest shadows. She's dressed entirely in black, form-fitting leather that accentuates a dangerous and alluring figure. It's the wings that steal my breath, huge, black, leathery wings, like those of a giant bat, unfurl from her back, easily spanning six feet or more from her back to tip. They glint dully in the ambient light spilling from the open trunk. She cocks her head to the side, observing us, her eyes flicking down to where my hand briefly touched Rose's paw. I can't help but gape at the impossible sight of her, at the sheer tangible reality of those magnificent, terrifying wings.

Luca must notice my reaction, the direction of my stunned gaze. "Ava?" he asks quietly, his own eyes narrowed, focused on the demon. "Can you… can you actually see her clearly?"

The question seems odd. "Of course, I can," I reply, confused.

"Why wouldn't I be able to?"

"Ava," Luca explains patiently, never taking his eyes off the demon, "there are certain entities, certain beings within the paranormal world, that require… the Sight… to perceive accurately. Most shifters, for example, cannot clearly see certain types of Fae, or indeed, many forms of demons."

"Ah, I can answer that," the demon interjects smoothly, her voice regaining its sultry quality. "I am *allowing* Ava and you to perceive me. It is… one of my minor abilities."

I can't help myself. The sheer tactical advantage… "That's… incredibly cool," I admit, thinking aloud. "God, I wish I could do that in my line of work. The missions I could pull off…."

"Ava, NO!" The shout comes simultaneously from Luca, Rose, *and* Sam, sharp and filled with alarm.

I stare at them, bewildered by their unified, panicked reaction. "What?"

Our winged guest answers before they can, a predatory smile touching her lips. "You misunderstand, Ava. I am a Crossroads Demon. I *can* make wishes come true, grant abilities like selective invisibility… for a price, of course. The small, insignificant price of a tiny fragment of your soul. So small, you'd barely even miss it," she finishes, holding up her hand, thumb and forefinger pressed so closely together they almost touch, emphasising the supposed insignificance of the cost.

My throat goes instantly dry, a desert wasteland. Fear, cold and stark, grips me. *Crossroads Demon. Price of your soul.* Did I just inadvertently make a deal? Sell a piece of myself simply by wishing out loud for her ability?

"Don't worry yourself, Ava," the demon purrs, clearly enjoying my distress. "I am not here tonight to broker a deal, unless you have a particular desire you wish to discuss?" She raises a perfectly sculpted eyebrow. "As I stated, my Master sent me with a gift for you. No strings attached to *your* soul, I assure you."

Still deeply unsettled, I glance towards Luca and Rose, seeking their assessment. That's when I notice Sam, who has remained silently vigilant until now, staring intently not at the demon, but at where my hand had briefly held Rose's paw. He saw the exchange. Damn it. I immediately let go of Rose again, refocusing my attention entirely on the demon, trying to project professional calm.

"Ava, I don't believe you've inadvertently sold anything," Luca clarifies, his voice tight with suspicion, clearly not trusting the demon's assurances. "As far as my knowledge extends, deals with Crossroads Demons typically require a formal contract, usually signed in blood."

"So," I demand, forcing my voice to remain steady, addressing the demon directly, "what should we call you?"

Her dark eyes, unsettlingly ancient, flick back to mine. She seems to consider the question for a moment. As I hold her gaze, her eyes do something incredibly strange – they blink, but sideways, like a reptile's nictitating membrane, an inner eyelid flickering across the dark iris. It's unnerving, inhuman. "My given name is Madiya," she replies finally, her voice smooth again. "But you, Ava, may call me Madi, if it pleases you." Madi's gaze sweeps across us again, lingering on Luca, then Rose, then back to me. Her eyes do that weird sideways blink again. A slow, knowing smile spreads across her lips before she murmurs, almost to herself, "Interesting… very interesting."

"Can you please just get to the point?" I snap, my patience wearing thin. Her games, her cryptic pronouncements, are grating on my nerves. "Why are you *really* here? How do you even know who I am? What does your 'Master' truly want? And what, exactly, do you find so 'interesting'?"

Her smile widens at my sharp tone, revealing teeth just slightly too pointed to be entirely human. She gracefully folds her massive wings behind her back, tucking them neatly against her leather-clad form. "My Master's knowledge is vast; how he knows of you is not my concern. He commanded me to find you," she replies evasively. "Have you, perhaps, made any significant pacts or deals recently, Ava?"

"If you are indeed a Crossroads Demon, then you serve Papa Legba," Luca states flatly, recognition hardening his tone. The name resonates vaguely in my memory again, associated with voodoo lore, deals, crossroads… but the specifics remain frustratingly elusive.

"Nope. No deals," I confirm curtly. "Get. To. The. Point."

Madi sighs dramatically, as if our lack of engagement is ruining all her fun. She draws herself up slightly, her demeanour shifting, becoming marginally more direct, though still tinged with boredom. "My Master instructed me to bring you this ring," she says, holding out her hand. Resting in her palm is a simple, yet intricately crafted, silver ring. "He believes it will aid you in your current mission, offer a measure of protection against the enemies you face. He feels you… require assistance." Her tone shifts again, becoming genuinely curious, predatory. "And *what* I find interesting, Ava, is the nature of your intertwined auras."

Auras? What the hell is she talking about? Before I can question her further, Rose cuts in, her voice tight with hostility, "Ava will *not* be accepting any so-called 'gifts' from Papa Legba. Anything offered by him, or his servants, invariably comes at the cost of a soul."

My head jerks towards Rose, then back to Madi. *A soul!* That's it. Papa Legba. Guardian of the Crossroads in voodoo legend. Granter of wishes, collector of souls. The stories I'd dismissed as folklore suddenly feel chillingly real. Panic flares again, cold and sharp. "I'm not interested," I state firmly, shaking my head. "Not interested in any ring if it means forfeiting my soul." This new world, with its demons and soul bargains, is dredging up fears I thought long buried. This vulnerability, this *fear*… it isn't me. It's not who I trained myself to be.

Madi lets out another low chuckle, seemingly amused by my reaction. "As I assured you, Ava, there is no cost *to your soul* for this particular gift," she reiterates smoothly. "Your soul remains entirely your own. Unless, of course," she adds, her eyes glittering with dark amusement, "there *is* something else you desire? Some other ability, perhaps? I am always available to negotiate…." She smirks knowingly, eliciting another low growl from Rose.

"Stop trying to make things worse," I snap, cutting off her sales pitch. "I am *not* interested in making any deals. Period. Now, why should I believe *anything* you say about this ring being free?" My anger is rising again, mirroring Rose's, but as I focus on the feeling, I realise it's not entirely my own. It feels… shared. Echoed. Like Rose's fury is somehow bleeding into mine through that inexplicable bond. We *really* need to talk about this later, assuming we survive this encounter.

Madi's gaze flicks between Luca and me, then settles pointedly on Luca. "My Master anticipated your scepticism," she concedes. "He instructed me to provide… corroborating evidence… that this gift is genuine, not some elaborate trap." She pauses, then asks Luca directly, "Tell me, shifter Alpha, have you perhaps encountered any… instructive whispers carried upon the wind recently? The significance of the phrase eludes me personally, yet my Master assured me *you* would comprehend its meaning."

I exchange a startled glance with Luca. He's the only one I've told about the voice I heard back at the safe house. Had he shared his own experience with anyone else? I remain silent, waiting for his reaction, his lead on how to handle this unexpected, specific revelation. His expression shifts subtly, surprise giving way to wary consideration. Then, slowly, deliberately, I see his hands relax, the shifter claws retracting, melting back into human fingernails. His entire posture softens fractionally. The message is clear, he no longer perceives Madi as an immediate, unequivocal enemy, at least, not for this moment.

Luca's change in stance clearly throws Rose off balance. Confusion wars with suspicion on her face. Her confusion deepens when Luca asks Madi calmly, "What, precisely, does the ring *do*? How, specifically, will it help Ava?"

"Luca, you can't be serious!" Rose protests immediately, her voice sharp with disbelief. "We cannot trust her! Or her Master! Ava is *not* accepting, let alone *using*, whatever cursed object that is!" Her anger is now directed squarely at her Alpha.

Luca turns to Rose, his eyes flashing briefly with that intimidating crimson light around the edges – the assertion of Alpha authority. Rose flinches almost imperceptibly, lowering her head slightly in submission. "Sorry," she mutters, looking instantly contrite, though still clearly unhappy.

"Rose," Luca says, his voice firm but calm, "I believe this specific gift *is* genuine. Offered without the usual price attached to Papa Legba's bargains. Ultimately," he adds, glancing towards me, "it is *Ava's* decision whether she chooses to accept it, and whether she chooses to use it." I can feel Rose bristling beside me, radiating disapproval, but she remains silent.

Madi, however, decides to stir the pot again. "Well," she interjects smoothly, a sly smile playing on her lips, "I didn't say there were *no* strings attached whatsoever. Just none involving the forfeit of Ava's soul. My Master *would* appreciate… a favour. Perhaps. At some point in the future, should he ever find himself in dire need of assistance. And even then," she stresses, meeting my gaze directly, "that favour would not involve compromising Ava's soul in any way. He wishes *that* to remain entirely where it belongs." Rose looks like she's about to explode, but Madi continues speaking quickly, "Consider it an investment in a potential future ally. You are going to need allies in the war that's coming, shifters. Powerful ones. My Master hopes this gift will serve as a gesture of goodwill, convince you that *he* can be such an ally." She pauses, then adds significantly, "He is also aware of certain plans that have recently been set in motion. And he confirms… you *are* heading in the right direction."

"Fine," Luca concedes after a moment's consideration, clearly weighing the potential benefits against the inherent risks of associating with a being like Papa Legba. "But it remains Ava's decision whether she utilises the ring. And for now, consider your Master's offer of alliance… under advisement. That tentative trust," he warns Madi, his voice hardening again, "will be instantly revoked if he, or you, does anything to betray it."

A slow, satisfied smile spreads across Madi's face. She lifts her right hand gracefully and snaps her fingers sharply. There's a disorienting flash of purple and black energy, a final, echoing beat of powerful wings, and then… she's simply gone. Vanished into thin air.

In the same instant she disappears, I feel something solid materialise in my left hand, settling into my palm. I know, instinctively, what it is before I even look. Slowly, I raise my hand, unclenching my fist. Resting there, nestled in the centre of my palm, is the ring. It's even more beautiful up close – silver, intricately carved, embedded with tiny, multifaceted jewels that seem to shift and shimmer in the dim light, forming complex symbols I don't recognise, perhaps? It feels… strangely warm to the touch.

CHAPTER 13

RING AROUND THE ROSIE, POCKET FULL OF... MAGICAL
RETURNING JEWELLERY?

I stare down at the ring nestled in my palm, its intricate surface feels warm against my skin, the tiny, embedded jewels seeming to capture and refract the dim light spilling from the Tahoe's open trunk. Everyone else is still frozen, staring at the empty space where the winged demon, Madi, had stood moments before, their expressions a mixture of shock, confusion, and lingering hostility. Rose turns towards me first, her gaze immediately locking onto my outstretched hand. When she registers the ring resting there, raw panic flashes across her features. Before I can react, she lunges forward, swatting the ring violently out of my hand with a sharp cry. It flies through the air, hitting the gritty asphalt of the parking lot with a faint clink. But in the same instant it lands, it vanishes from the ground and reappears, impossibly, resting innocuously back in the centre of my open palm.

A low, frustrated growl rumbles in Rose's chest. The sound vibrates through the tense night air, a primal expression of fear and anger. It should make me nervous, but strangely, a part of me finds the sound... comforting? Protective? I shake the illogical thought away. Panic begins to take root in my chest now, cold and constricting. My eyes widen, my hand trembles uncontrollably, and I instinctively drop the ring again. Once more, it hits the ground, only to instantly rematerialise back in my hand. This time, Luca and Sam, drawn by Rose's reaction, witness the impossible phenomenon.

Seeking assistance, needing some kind of rational explanation in this utterly irrational situation. I turn my pleading gaze towards Luca, he seems to instantly recognise the rising distress in my expression and quickly moves to my side, gently taking my trembling hand in his, to examine the ring closely. He focuses intently on the intricate patterns formed by the tiny jewels and carved symbols, his brow furrowed in concentration.

Sam, ever the pragmatist, finally breaks his silence, his voice tight with concern. "Is she in danger from it, Luca? Is it… cursed? Possessed?"

Luca considers the ring for another long moment, his thumb brushing lightly over the strange symbols, before replying thoughtfully, "I don't believe so, Sam. Not inherently dangerous, anyway. The jewels… they're arranged in the patterns of ancient runes. Two distinct sets, actually, intertwined. Which suggests it likely possesses two primary functions, two different enchantments."

"Well, Madi conveniently vanished before explaining what those functions are!" Rose interjects vehemently, her voice laced with panic. "We can't trust it, Luca! We can't trust anything offered by Papa Legba! We need to find a way to get rid of it, destroy it somehow. It's too dangerous for Ava to possess!" She looks desperately between Luca and me, clearly terrified on my behalf.

"Ava," Luca suggests calmly, ignoring Rose's outburst for the moment, "try deliberately placing the ring down somewhere. In the back of the vehicle, perhaps."

I look at him incredulously. Did he not just witness the ring repeatedly refuse to be put down? But then he gives a subtle jerk of his head towards the rear of the Tahoe. Understanding dawns. Maybe intent matters? With my pistol still held loosely in my right hand, I use my left thumb to shuffle the ring towards my fingertips carefully. Taking a deep breath, I step towards the back of the vehicle and gingerly place the ring onto the surface of the trunk floor. I hesitate for a beat, bracing myself, then snatch my hand away quickly, fully expecting the ring to reappear instantly in my palm. I stare down at my empty hand, heart pounding. Nothing happens. I glance back at the trunk floor. The ring remains precisely where I placed it—a collective sigh of relief ripples through our small group.

"Okay," Luca says, visibly relaxing. "It seems the enchantment compels it to return to you only if it's involuntarily removed from your person – dropped accidentally, knocked away. If you choose to put it down, it stays put."

"Well, it can stay right there in the car then," Rose declares immediately, relief flooding her features, making her look years younger for a fleeting moment.

"I wouldn't risk leaving it behind entirely, Ava," Luca counters pragmatically. "Given its apparent connection to you, it's likely safer on your person, even if you choose not to wear it. I genuinely don't believe the ring itself will harm you. Based on Madi's words and Papa Legba's potential motivations in this conflict, I suspect it is a genuine gift, intended to aid and protect you." His assessment sounds logical, yet the unease lingers.

I remain hesitant, staring at the innocuous-looking ring resting on the trunk floor. Just as I reach for it, steeling myself, Rose's hand darts out, grabbing my wrist, stopping me.

"Rose," Luca says sharply, his voice dropping into that authoritative Alpha tone again, his eyes flashing crimson at the edges for a split second. "It is not your choice to make. You have no say in this matter, regardless of... recent developments." His meaning is clear, a stark reminder of pack hierarchy and the boundaries of our newly formed bond.

Rose clenches her jaw, defiance warring with ingrained submission, but after a tense moment, she releases my wrist, stepping back slightly, though her expression remains mutinous.

"It's okay, Rose," I murmur, offering her a small, reassuring smile I don't entirely feel. I pick up the ring. Its surface feels strangely inert now, lacking the warmth it seemed to possess earlier. I carefully slide it into the small, tight coin pocket of my jeans, pushing it deep down. There's no way it can accidentally fall out from there.

Just as I secure the ring, my stomach breaks the tense silence with another loud, embarrassing rumble. The sudden, mundane noise shatters the tension, and everyone, including me, lets out a surprised chuckle.

"Right," Luca says, clapping his hands together lightly, shifting back into mission mode. "Let's finish gearing up, get Ava some much-needed food before we have to contend with a different, more dangerous kind of monster tonight."

I focus on my loadout, standard sidearm – a reliable Glock 19 today, then the two custom pistols Luca indicated earlier, ensuring I know which is which by feel alone – one loaded with wooden-tipped rounds, the other with the silver/wolfsbane combination, just in case our intel is wrong or we encounter something unexpected. Then, a wide grin spreads across my face as Rose wordlessly hands me one of the short swords from the cache. God, I still can't get over how beautiful these blades are, especially knowing their potential paranormal origins rather than standard CIA issue. The balance feels perfect in my hand. I study its elegant lines for a moment, then slide it smoothly into the specially designed sheath integrated into the back of my tactical holster. Finally, I secure my preferred quartet of daggers – two in the sheath under the gun on my right thigh rig, one tucked securely inside my left boot, the last positioned horizontally at the small of my back. Ready.

Feeling considerably more prepared, if still slightly unnerved by the ring situation, I climb into the back seat of the Tahoe. Rose follows immediately, sliding in beside me without hesitation, reinforcing the unspoken decision that she's sticking close tonight. As she closes her door, sealing us in the relative quiet of the vehicle's interior, I seize the opportunity for a quick, private word before Sam gets in.

"Rose," I whisper urgently, keeping my voice low, "we need to be incredibly careful around Sam. If he gets concrete proof that something is happening between us, protocol dictates he has to report it to Agent Moore. They could easily pull me off the task force, or worse, demand Luca replace you."

"I wondered why you acted so strangely when Sam found us basically half-dressed in our room," she whispers back, a frown creasing her brow. "But why would they care? It's none of their damn business what happens between us privately."

"Agency policy," I explain tersely. "Strict rules against operatives on the same team forming relationships. They see it as a distraction, a compromise to operational security. Sam and Moore! They're typical agency men, drilled in the regulations. They will see us as a liability, demand one of us be reassigned. And given my specialised skills versus your… unique nature… I'm worried they'd demand it be you." I inject urgency into my tone, needing her to grasp the seriousness of the situation. "Haven't you noticed how Sam's been watching us? He suspects something already."

Rose considers my words, her expression turning thoughtful, then concerned. "Okay," she concedes just as the front doors open and the guys climb in. "Okay, I understand. I'll be… discreet… when we're around him. But," she adds, a mischievous glint returning to her eyes as she turns fully forward, "don't expect the same restraint when we're alone." She offers me a tiny, almost invisible wink just as Luca starts the engine.

I feel my face heat up and quickly look away, staring out the side window at the darkening streets, trying to ignore the unwelcome blush. Then to make things worse my stomach echo's around the interior of our car as it lets out another deep rumble. "We should hurry before Ava passes out from hunger," Luca replies to the sound of my stomach, glancing back at me in the rearview mirror with a cheeky smile.

Rose, naturally, decides to make things exponentially worse. "Yeah, I'm absolutely famished too," she chimes in brightly from next to me. "Had a really good, intense workout earlier this afternoon. Definitely need to sink my teeth into something substantial… before I start thinking one of you looks tasty enough to eat."

Luca bursts out laughing. I, on the other hand, choke on my own saliva, dissolving into an embarrassing coughing fit. Rose reaches out, patting me sympathetically on the back, while Sam, thankfully misinterpreting her comment completely, reprimands her.

"Try not to scare Ava too much, Rose," he advises seriously.

I manage to stifle my coughing, now I'm ready to throttle Rose. This woman is going to be the literal death of me, one way or another. I shake my head, exasperated, but can't suppress the small smile tugging at my lips. I lean to my side slightly, whispering again so low only Rose and Luca's enhanced hearing could possibly pick it up, "You. Are. In. So. Much. Trouble." I know she heard me; I hear her soft, throaty chuckle in response.

After grabbing food from a brightly lit drive-through – burgers, fries, milkshakes, fuel for the coming confrontation – we head east, towards the derelict industrial estate, towards the cluster of abandoned factories Mel mentioned. Luca finds a concealed spot amongst some crumbling outbuildings, tucked away in deep shadow, where we can observe the target buildings without being easily seen from the main access road. Rose and I quickly devour our food in the back seat – well, I eat normally; Rose inhales an amount that seems physically impossible for someone her size, prompting another round of internal calculations about shifter metabolisms.

"When it comes to fast food like this," she explains, noticing my bemused stare, "we have to consume a lot to get adequate energy. We're primarily carnivores by nature; a huge steak would satisfy us much better. This processed stuff… it hardly makes a dent, metabolically speaking."

"Sorry," I apologise, feeling suddenly guilty. "I didn't even think to ask what you guys might prefer. I just assumed everyone defaulted to drive-through for mission stakeouts." Another thing to learn about my unusual colleagues.

We settle into the uncomfortable silence of waiting, scanning the dark, silent factories. Two hours crawl by, marked only by the distant sounds of city traffic. Then, finally, movement. A lone figure detaches itself from the deepest shadows near one of the larger factory buildings, moving with an unnatural speed and grace across the rooftops, leaping gaps between buildings that would be impossible for any human.

"Target acquired," I murmur unnecessarily, adrenaline beginning its slow, familiar burn.

We all exit the Tahoe silently, melting into the shadows ourselves. We don't approach immediately, instead watching as the figure reaches a specific factory – the one Mel's contact mentioned seeing someone scale – and slips easily through a broken window high up near the roofline.

Luca turns to Rose, his voice low. "Rose, I think it's best if you shift for this initial entry. Your senses are sharper in panther form. I can stay human for now, guide Ava, relay your signals – she doesn't know our non-verbal cues yet. Sam knows a few, but until we establish better team synergy, it's safer this way. Besides," he adds grimly, "whoever, whatever, is inside will likely know we're approaching the moment we breach the perimeter anyway."

Rose nods curtly, without hesitation, and immediately begins stripping off her clothes right there in the darkness. Despite the tactical situation, despite everything, I can't help but watch, fascinated and slightly flustered again, as moonlight briefly illuminates her lean, athletic form before she begins the transformation. Sam, ever the gentleman, tactfully turns away, affording her privacy. He doesn't see the impossible beauty of the shift, the way muscle and bone rearrange, the way dark fur flows over smooth skin.

Once the transformation is complete, the magnificent black panther stands where Rose was moments before. She seems hesitant for a split second, her intelligent green eyes finding mine in the darkness, then she moves towards me, slowly, deliberately. I stand my ground, refusing to show fear. She butts her massive head gently against my chest, rubbing the side of her sleek face against my tactical vest, a gesture startlingly reminiscent of a domestic cat seeking affection. Instinctively, automatically, I place my hand on top of her head, sinking my fingers into the unbelievably soft, thick fur. The familiar, intense heat radiates from her body, soaking into my palm, grounding me. I lean down slightly, mirroring her gesture, rubbing the side of my face against hers. A deep, rumbling purr vibrates through her body, resonating against my chest. The sound, the contact, feels strangely intimate, profoundly calming.

I pull away reluctantly as I catch Sam glancing back out of the corner of my eye, likely wondering about the purring sound. Time to move. Luca gives a silent hand signal, and we follow as he melts into the deeper shadows, heading towards the target building. I draw the custom pistol loaded with wooden-tipped rounds, its weight solid and reassuring in my hand. Rose falls into step beside me, her movements utterly silent despite her size, a phantom predator padding through the urban decay, while Sam takes up position on Luca's other flank, his own weapon held at the ready. We move like ghosts towards the lion's den.

We approach a narrow, debris-strewn alleyway that runs between two of the hulking factory structures. Halfway down, almost swallowed by shadows, is a heavy-set door leading into the building our target had entered. Sam, taking point for a moment, tries the handle. It's locked solid, unyielding, he grunts in frustration. Luca steps forward, placing his hand on the tarnished metal. With a barely perceptible twist and a surge of what I can only assume is shifter strength, the handle groans, metal shrieking softly as the mechanism inside gives way. The door pops open with a reluctant creak. I'm half-surprised he didn't rip the entire handle off.

The moment we cross the threshold, we're plunged into an oppressive, inky blackness. The air is cold, stale, thick with the smell of damp concrete, rust, and something else… something faintly coppery and unsettling. I instinctively reach out, my hand finding the warm, reassuring presence of Rose's panther flank beside me. Simultaneously, I fumble for the night-vision sunglasses from my belt pouch. They look more like sleek wraparounds than actual military goggles, and I can't help a flicker of doubt about their efficacy.

"New tech, Ava," Sam murmurs from my other side, sensing my hesitation as I prepare to put them on. "Not quite as powerful as full military-grade goggles, but they're more than adequate for this kind of work. Significantly less cumbersome, much lighter, and they don't restrict your peripheral vision or slow you down as much. Trust me, they work."

Slipping them on, the world transforms into the familiar eerie landscape of greens and blacks. The interior of the factory floor swims into view – vast, cavernous, and filled with the skeletal remains of forgotten machinery. Sam dons his pair as well. With a silent nod from Luca, we begin to move deeper into the derelict structure, my hand remaining lightly on Rose's side, a silent connection in the disorienting gloom.

The ground floor is a labyrinth of decaying equipment and rubble, but yields no immediate sign of our quarry. Rose, however, seems unerringly focused, her great head held low as she sniffs the air, leading us towards a rusted metal staircase at the far end of the building. She moves with a fluid grace, silent as smoke, and I find myself relying on her senses as much as my own enhanced vision. As we ascend, the metallic tang in the air grows stronger.

When we reach the landing of the next floor, Rose doesn't even pause to sweep the area. Instead, she continues directly towards the next flight of stairs, her powerful form flowing upwards. I start to voice a question, to ask why we aren't clearing each level methodically, but Luca anticipates me. His hand shoots out, not ungently, covering my mouth, while his other finger presses to his lips in a clear signal for silence. My initial instinct is to protest, to pull away, but then understanding clicks – vampires, like shifters, likely possess acute hearing. Any unnecessary sound could betray our exact position. I bite back my question and nod, following Luca's lead.

The third floor. As we step onto this level, Rose freezes. Her body tenses, ears swivelling, and I see her nostrils flare as she tests the air. A low, almost inaudible growl rumbles deep in her chest, the fur along her spine bristling slightly. This is it. Our target is close. Luca taps my shoulder lightly, gesturing for me to follow him. We move off the stairwell and towards a doorway that leads onto the main factory floor of this level. The door itself is mostly gone, only the top half hanging precariously from a single hinge. Sam peels off to the other side of the broken doorway, creating a wider field of fire. Rose, with incredible stealth for her size, lowers her body and slips through the narrow opening, turning left once she's clear.

Luca signals for me to follow. We both duck beneath the jagged remains of the door. Instead of trailing directly behind Rose, Luca flattens himself against the interior wall, his weapon up, scanning. I mirror his actions, pressing my back to the cool, rough concrete. I notice Luca periodically checking our rear. This whole approach is alien to me. If I were operating solo, my entry would have been far more… explosive. Roof entry, or even a controlled demolition, to flush the target. This cautious, methodical infiltration is a discipline I only use when I have to. My preference for overwhelming force often deems infiltration too risky.

The corridor here is lined with what were once likely offices or smaller workshops. As we pass each doorway, Rose pauses momentarily, a quick sniff, a subtle shake of her head if it's clear, then she moves on. Despite her apparent certainty, Luca and Sam still perform quick visual sweeps of each room before we continue our slow advance. Finally, the corridor opens into a vast, high-ceilinged chamber, rows upon rows of towering metal shelving units dominating the space, interspersed with larger, unidentifiable pieces of machinery. It's a perfect ambush site.

Luca gestures to the right, indicating that he and I will take that flank. Sam begins to move slowly along the left. Rose, however, to my sudden, sharp alarm, pads silently into the centre of the open space, positioning herself directly between the rows of shelving, completely exposed. My protective instincts flare, a visceral urge to pull her back, to shield her. I make a move towards her, but Luca's hand on my arm stops me, his grip firm. When I meet his gaze, he curtly shakes his head, then holds up his palm in a clear 'stay' signal. Reluctantly, I hold my position, my unease coiling tighter in my gut. Taking orders in the field, especially when I disagree with the tactical decision, is a rusty skill, one I haven't had to exercise in years. It chafes.

Rose stands utterly still in the open, a living statue of black fur and coiled muscle, for what feels like an eternity. The silence in the vast room is absolute, broken only by the drip-drip-drip of water somewhere in the darkness. Rose was right, damn her. I *have* become protective. The thought is an unwelcome distraction when a voice suddenly slices through the silence, making me jump, just as Madi's had done earlier. The sound is smooth, cultured, but laced with an undeniable undercurrent of malice, and it seems to emanate from the darkness somewhere above us.

"Well, well. Come to play, have we? Shouldn't you be scuttling around in Michigan, or some other dreary hole your kind prefers to inhabit?"

Rose lets out a low, warning growl in response, a sound that vibrates through the floor.

The voice continues, dripping with sadistic amusement, "Or perhaps you've brought me offerings? Am I to turn one while I drain the other? A delightful dilemma. Though I would have thought you'd turn them yourselves, add them to your dwindling pack?"

The vampire clearly knows Rose isn't the only non-human, and Sam and I may be her human lackeys or potential converts. He's also given us a nugget – confirmation of shifter presence, or at least vampire *belief* of shifter presence, in Michigan.

Luca decides to answer, his voice calm, projecting confidence. "We're merely passing through. I wanted to make you aware we'd be in the city for a night or two, just as a professional courtesy. We seek no trouble."

A deep, throaty laugh echoes from the shadows above, a chilling sound that makes Rose shift her stance almost imperceptibly to the left. It's so subtle, I almost miss it. But then it registers – one of the non-verbal cues Luca mentioned. Rose is pinpointing the target's location for us.

Sam, catching the signal too, begins a slow, almost imperceptible creep further along his left flank. Luca mirrors the movement on our side, easing towards the end of one of the towering shelving units, while Rose glides further to her left, still maintaining her position in the more open central aisle.

My dislike for her exposed position intensifies. I also wonder if our target is buying Luca's placid explanation. My answer comes swiftly.

"Passing through? I think not," the vampire sneers, his voice taking on a harder edge. "You're stragglers, aren't you? Somehow managed to evade the purge, and now you're sniffing around for payback. A shame, really. It just means I have to clean up the mess others left behind."

Suddenly, Rose explodes upwards, a black blur of fur and fury, snapping her powerful jaws at empty air just as a shadowy figure detaches itself from the top of one shelving unit and leaps with impossible agility to the next, disappearing again into the upper gloom. The vampire is fast, agile, and clearly comfortable in this three-dimensional hunting ground. I raise my pistol, aiming towards where I last saw the flicker of movement, but it's already too late. He's gone. Luca remains largely still, only the subtle shift of his stance and the way he raises the short sword he carries indicating his heightened readiness. His left hand, I notice, has subtly transformed, fingers elongating into wicked-looking claws.

The vampire's voice drifts down again, this time from a different section of the darkened ceiling. "Too slow, pussycat. Far too slow. Why don't you just surrender? Make it easy on yourselves. The last dregs of your kind will be eradicated soon enough. There aren't many of you left, are there? Once I deal with you, we'll be one step closer to our ultimate goal. No one will be left to oppose us. This world… this world is finally going to be ours. And all the humans? They'll learn their proper place in the new order – as the cattle they truly are." His tone is so smug, so utterly convinced of his superiority, that I find my grip tightening on my pistol, my free hand clenching into a fist.

"Who set this in motion?" Luca calls out, his voice still remarkably cool, attempting to bait the vampire. "If we're all going to die anyway, why not indulge our curiosity?" It's a classic interrogation tactic, but my nerves are frayed. This isn't like any hunt I've ever been on.

Another laugh, colder this time. "I'm not a fool, shifter. He has planned this for a very, very long time. I will not betray him. Your only choice is to join us or die. So, what will it be? Except, of course, for the humans you've brought with you. They will be fed upon. Or perhaps turned, for sport, tonight."

Rose unleashes a ferocious, guttural snarl and surges forward, disappearing into the narrow aisle between two towering rows of shelves. Luca immediately moves to follow, taking the adjacent aisle, while Sam swiftly positions himself at the end of Rose's row, effectively guarding her rear. I want to be the one covering her, a desperate urge, but Luca gestures sharply for me to stick with him as we track her progress through the metal labyrinth. He stops abruptly, and in the same instant, Rose's head whips around in our direction from the aisle she's in, her eyes wide, a silent warning. My blood runs cold. I know, instinctively, I'm in danger. I spin, raising my weapon, reacting to a sudden shift in air pressure beside me, a whisper of movement too fast to track.

I'm too late. A vice-like grip seizes my right arm, the one holding my wooden-bullet pistol. The strength is inhuman, crushing. My arm feels like it might snap. In the next instant, I'm airborne, yanked from the aisle, my back slamming hard against the concrete floor. The impact drives the air from my lungs. The vampire is dragging me, flinging me across the open space as if I weigh nothing. All I can do is try to curl inward, to brace for the inevitable collision. Simultaneously, a deafening crash echoes through the factory – the sound of metal shelving units toppling, a cascade of screeching, tearing metal. My first, panicked thought is for Rose – is she caught beneath it?

Then my world explodes in pain as I collide with a solid brick wall. I manage, just barely, to get my hands up to protect my head, but it means dropping my primary weapon. The force of the impact still rattles my skull. Before I can even try to reorient, he's on me, a heavyweight pressing me down. I hear Rose roar, a sound of pure, untamed fury, followed by the distinct slap of running footsteps – Luca and Sam, hopefully – and the heavier, pounding rhythm of paws, but they sound like they're heading *away* from me, towards the crashing shelves. Then, an intense pressure on my neck, pinning me, and an eerie, evil chuckle sounds right beside my ear.

Desperate, I try to push the vampire off, but he's impossibly strong. My free hand scrabbles for one of my backup weapons. My fingers close around the grip of the pistol holstered on my thigh – the one with silver-tipped bullets. I yank it free and fire twice, point-blank. I must have missed, or the bullets are ineffective, because the vampire doesn't release his hold. Instead, his grip tightens, and he hisses.

"Bitch! Shooting me? That was a very bad idea. Now, I'm going to make this hurt." His voice is pure malice.

I'm shocked. I thought I had hit him, it seems I did, but it made no difference. Then the horrifying realisation dawns – I grabbed the wrong gun. Silver bullets. Useless against this type. I dropped the only one with the specialised wooden rounds when he first grabbed me.

I'm flying through the air again, a ragdoll in his grasp. This time, there's no chance to protect myself. My head connects with another wall with sickening force. Stars erupt behind my eyelids. The pain is immediate, blinding, and a wave of dizzying blackness threatens to pull me under. I know, with a chilling certainty, that I'm about to lose consciousness. Just as the last vestiges of my awareness begin to wink out, a piercing scream rips through the factory, a sound so filled with agony and terror it sends an icy shard of fear straight through my fading consciousness. For one terrifying, lucid moment, I'm petrified it's Rose. Then, the darkness claims me completely.

CHAPTER 14

HOW TO ALIENATE A POLICE CHIEF AND INFLUENCE

PUBLIC OPINION, AVA BEKKE STYLE

I drift in a sea of darkness, blessedly free of dreams or nightmares. Utter blackness, then I heard the same voice again, again, whoever she is whispers, '*Get to Chicago,*' Then, slowly, reluctantly, I feel consciousness returning, pulling me back towards sensation. Fragmented memories start to assault me – the dark open expanse of the room, the chilling scream, the blinding pain in my neck, Luca fighting, Rose… Rose fighting. The fear, the helplessness. I gasp, trying to bolt upright, convinced for a disorienting second that I'm still in that room, surrounded by vampires.

A firm but gentle hand presses against my shoulder, stopping my panicked movement. "Easy, Ava," a familiar voice murmurs, soft and low. "It's okay. You're safe now."

The voice, the warmth radiating from the hand… it anchors me. Rose. My heart rate, already hammering from the returning memories, gradually begins to slow. I blink my eyes open, expecting the dim, dusty room. Instead, I see… the ceiling of our room. My head throbs violently with the small movement, making me wince and close my eyes again, instinctively trying to burrow my face into the heat source, which is solid, the radiating heat is all around me in my curled-up sitting position, which is comforting and feels achingly familiar. I shift slightly, trying unconsciously to get closer, wanting my whole body to feel that soothing warmth. A low groan escapes me as muscles I didn't know were injured protest the movement.

A soft chuckle sounds from above me. An arm tightens around my waist, pulling me closer still, pressing me firmly against the source of the heat. Confused, I force my eyes open again, slowly this time, just a fraction. My blurry vision focuses on… someone's shoulder? My head is resting on someone's shoulder. Disorientation mixes with alarm. Where am I? Who am I sitting on? I try to pull away, instinctively recoiling from the unknown intimacy, when the voice speaks again, closer now, right beside my ear, I realise Rose is sitting up in our bed, cradling me in her lap.

"You're not going anywhere just yet," Rose murmurs, her voice husky with sleep or concern, maybe both. "How are you feeling? Do you remember what happened?"

Rose. Relief washes over me, potent and immediate. I stop struggling, relaxing back against her warmth, tightening my own hold around her waist as I realise, I'm essentially lying draped across her body. I try to gather my scattered thoughts, pushing past the throbbing in my head. The scream. That final, chilling scream I heard before passing out. "Are *you* okay?" I ask urgently, my voice raspy. I crane my neck, ignoring the renewed stab of pain, needing to see her face, needing confirmation. "The last thing I remember… that scream… Was it you? Are the guys okay?"

"Shhh, easy," Rose soothes, gently tilting my head back down. "Everyone is fine, Ava. I promise. We're all okay." She pauses, then adds, a vicious little grin spreading across her face, visible even from my awkward angle, "The vampire who attacked you, though? Not so much."

"What happened?" I whisper, the effort making my head pound again. "After I passed out? My head… feels like someone used it for target practice."

"You took a nasty hit," Rose confirms gently. "When I saw you go down, saw that bastard feeding on you… I got so mad… I think I moved faster than I ever have before, but was attacked by a second vampire, who stopped me from getting to you. But I managed to catch him just before he could finish you off or escape." She hesitates, the grin fading. "Luca managed to deal with the other bitch so I could get to you. The one attacking you… he made a mistake trying to deal with me instead of finishing you quickly. He didn't stand a chance. I… uh… I made him pay. Ripped him to shreds, literally."

The graphic image makes me cringe, but a grim satisfaction follows. Good. "Okay. Good," I whisper, relieved, "I was… worried. Before I passed out, I panicked, thinking maybe… you had been hurt."

"I'm fine, Ava, really. Mostly superficial cuts. Don't worry about me," she reassures me. "*I* was the one panicking, though, when I smelled your blood spreading across the floor. I was so enraged, so focused on tearing him apart, that I couldn't shift back immediately afterwards to check on you properly. Had to wait for Luca to stabilise you first. God, Ava, I couldn't shift back until we were almost back here." Her face clouds over, remembering the fear.

A practical question surfaces through the haze of pain and relief. "How… how did you fit in the car? In panther form?" I try to picture the logistics and fail.

Rose actually chuckles, the sound a welcome relief. "Well," she admits sheepishly, "I may not have exactly helped the situation regarding Sam's suspicions. Luca carefully laid you across the back seat. Then I basically shoved past him and crawled right on top of you. I tried to keep my weight off you, but I held myself up as best I could, but there wasn't exactly a lot of space. So, yeah, I was pretty much lying on you until I finally calmed down enough to shift back, which happened just before we arrived here. Then I just… dropped onto you when I shifted back and pulled the blanket Luca had thrown over me around us both as I pulled you onto my lap."

I process this, imagining the scene. Sam must have loved that. Still, it was probably the only feasible option. "Okay, well, I guess it couldn't have happened any other way," I concede. "Unless we stayed at the scene until you shifted back, which wasn't an option, I assume?"

"Definitely not," Rose confirms. "Just as Luca was checking you over, we got an urgent call from Chief Thornton. Someone nearby must have heard the commotion, maybe the scream, called it in as shots fired or a disturbance at the abandoned factory. He said he was dispatching officers and wanted to know if *we* wanted to head over there too. He demanded to speak with you immediately. Obviously, with me still stuck as a panther and you unconscious, we had to clear out fast. Luca managed to fob him off with some story, but the Chief apparently wasn't happy about it."

I groan inwardly, pinching the bridge of my nose. Just what I needed. "What exactly did Luca tell him?"

"Standard procedure, basically," Rose shrugs. "Told him we'd tracked a high-priority suspect to the abandoned property, cornered him inside. Said the suspect resisted violently, attempted to escape, and in the ensuing struggle, you were injured when he shoved you against a wall, and the suspect… unfortunately… died." She grimaces slightly. "Luca implied our backup team handled the body disposal, citing jurisdictional protocols. Apparently, Thornton lost his temper completely at that point, started shouting about needing access to the body, demanding you report to his office first thing this morning." She relates the conversation, cringing slightly at the memory of the Chief's fury. I just bury my face against her shoulder again and groan louder this time.

"Why did he say *that*?" I lament. "Why not just say we were patrolling a different sector, didn't hear anything?"

"Sam insisted we needed to be seen making progress, taking suspects off the street," Rose explains. "And technically, we *did* take out a vampire, a couple actually. We *did* help the city, even if we couldn't exactly provide bodies or tell the truth about *what* we took out." Then, a sudden thought seems to strike me, cutting through the throbbing pain. A flicker of panic. "Rose," I ask urgently, "what did you do with the… the bodies? The vampires you killed?"

"Ava," Rose says gently, "there *are* no bodies."

"Wait… What?"

Rose gives a small, slightly weary chuckle. "Right. Guess we forgot to mention that particular detail amidst all the chaos. What happens when you kill a vampire?" She pauses for effect. "They turn to dust, Ava. Ash. Convenient, really. Means no evidence is left behind… apart from a small amount of your blood on the floor, which," she adds casually, "I took care of before we left."

I slump back against her, relief warring with revulsion. Ash. Okay. That simplifies things considerably. Then the implication of her last comment hits me. I pull back slightly, meeting her gaze. "How… how exactly did you 'take care of' my blood… if you were still a panther at the time?" I have a horrible suspicion, but I need to hear her say it.

Rose hesitates, then whispers the answer so low I can barely make it out, avoiding my eyes. "I… licked it up."

My nose wrinkles involuntarily in disgust. "Eew! Yuk! Seriously?"

Rose finally meets my gaze, chuckling softly at my reaction. "Hey, you're going to have to get accustomed to a few… unusual… things, being around shifters, honey," she teases gently.

We lie there quietly for what feels like a long time, maybe forty minutes, before I attempt to move again. My head protests vehemently, but I manage to swing my legs over the side of the bed, planting my feet on the cool floor. She moves to help me as I carefully stand, heading towards the bathroom. The thought of cleaning the dried blood out of my hair is suddenly paramount. Rose has to practically hold me upright under the shower spray, carefully washing my hair for me as I brace myself against the tiled wall, feeling weak and shaky. This time, despite the intimacy, there's no room for fun, only careful necessity. As I stand there, letting her minister to me, I realise the hypersensitivity I experienced after our bonding has faded completely. A small part of me feels a pang of regret that we didn't get to explore that heightened state for longer before the mission went sideways.

Once clean, getting dressed proves equally challenging. I feel feeble, useless, as Rose has to help me again. Any lingering awkwardness vanishes in the face of necessity as she kneels before me, patiently helping me into clean underwear, then carefully guiding my legs into fresh jeans. I'm immensely grateful, in this moment, for the bond we share, for the intimacy that makes this potentially humiliating situation feel… natural. Caring.

Back in the main room, Rose texts Luca, letting him know I'm awake and dressed. Moments later, Luca and Sam appear at the door, their faces etched with relief and concern when they see me upright. After confirming I'm okay, Luca repeats the story Rose told me about his tense phone call with Chief Thornton. It's already approaching lunchtime. I declare I can face the Chief, but only after I've eaten. Food first, bureaucracy later. We head out, going to the same diner we'd visited yesterday, hoping for a quiet meal before the inevitable confrontation.

About an hour and a half later, feeling marginally stronger after consuming a large breakfast, we head to the police headquarters. Sam immediately offers to handle the Chief, shield me from his likely tirade, but I shake my head. "No, Sam. If I'm supposed to be leading this task force, I need to face him myself. Can't hide behind my team." We briefly discussed Luca's cover story on the way over, refining the narrative. He was right; we *have* to be seen getting results, even if the details are… fabricated. Especially given the lack of bodies. We need to establish our authority now, set a precedent, hoping the message filters through to other jurisdictions. We also agree it's crucial to keep the news about neutralising the 'gang members' under wraps for now, preventing any potential surviving vampires – unlikely, but possible – from being alerted.

Walking into the station lobby, the same Desk Sergeant from before gives us a collective dirty look but says nothing as we head towards the rear offices. "The Chief is expecting you in his office," he calls after us sullenly. "You'd best head straight back there. Wouldn't want to keep him waiting any longer than you already have." His smarmy tone makes me want to punch him.

"Oh, I'm sure we have a few minutes to spare. Wouldn't want to seem *too* eager," I retort over my shoulder, unable to resist. His expression sours further. Good. We proceed towards the back.

As we walk through the main bullpen, the atmosphere is noticeably different from yesterday. Instead of hostile glares, several officers and detectives look up as we pass, offering nods, even quiet murmurs of "Good job." The news of last night's events, however sanitised, has clearly circulated. I ignore the unexpected show of support, focusing on the impending confrontation. Reaching the Chief's office door, I rap my knuckles sharply twice, then push it open and walk straight in without waiting for a reply. Time to set the tone.

Sam starts to protest beside me, "Ava, maybe we should…" I silence him with a quick finger to my lips.

"What in the hell do you think you're doing?!" Chief Thornton bellows, his voice booming across the office. He'd clearly been pacing, waiting for us. "I never gave you permission to enter my office!"

I ignore his outburst, calmly walking further into the room and deliberately sinking into one of the visitor chairs positioned in front of his large, imposing desk. "I was informed you wished to speak with me, Chief," I state coolly, meeting his furious gaze without flinching. "Here I am. However, I don't have a great deal of time, so perhaps we could get on with it? We *do* have actual work to do." My deliberate calmness seems to infuriate him even more. He huffs, puffs, his face turning an alarming shade of red, looking like he's about to explode. Finally, seeming to realise his bluster isn't working, he throws himself back down into his own chair with considerable force.

"What the hell happened last night?" he demands, leaning forward aggressively, trying to intimidate me with proximity and volume. "And why wasn't I notified *immediately* that you had identified suspects, let alone engaged them?"

"Firstly, Chief," I begin, keeping my voice steady and level, "I don't answer to you." I don't get any further. He flips completely.

"This is *MY* city, Agent!" he roars, slamming a fist on his desk. The volume makes my head throb painfully. "You damn well *do* answer to me while you're operating within my jurisdiction! Either that, or you can pack your bags and get the hell out, and you won't be welcomed back! I've looked into you, Bekke! Made some calls! What I found... I don't like it. I don't want *your kind* operating in my city!"

His words, the implication, send a jolt through me, but I keep my expression impassive, refusing to give him the satisfaction of a reaction, even though his mention of digging into my past makes my eyes widen fractionally in surprise. "And what *kind* would that be, precisely, Chief?" I ask, my voice soft, laced with ice.

"An assassin," he spits the word out like poison, a smug smirk spreading across his face now, clearly thinking he's gained the upper hand. "A trigger-happy mercenary hiding behind a government badge. That's what my contacts informed me. They can't fathom how someone like *you* ended up with FBI credentials."

"My *past*," I state evenly, meeting his smirk with a level gaze, "is precisely *why* I am suited for the *present* situation. The CIA sought out an individual with a very specific, highly specialised skill set, someone capable of getting the job done, no matter the cost, and they recruited *me*. I was granted FBI credentials specifically to lead this task force, because the threats our country – indeed, the entire world – currently face require someone... uniquely qualified... to deal with them effectively. The government *you* work for, Chief, established this task force and granted me operational autonomy to achieve its objectives, neutralising these threats and keeping the people of *our* country safe." I lean forward slightly myself now, matching his earlier aggression. "I was *assured* I would have the full cooperation of local law enforcement agencies when necessary. Last night, we didn't *require* your assistance. We planned a capture operation, hoping to gain vital intelligence. That plan went sideways when the primary suspect resisted violently. Yes, I sustained an injury during the attempt to subdue him.

And yes, unfortunately, the suspect ultimately died during the ensuing fight. But," I add pointedly, "he is now permanently off your streets. And before he expired, he *did* confirm his involvement in several recent killings here in your city, even boasted about them." I wasn't going to mention that there were actually two of them in the end.

I take another slow, deliberate breath, holding his furious gaze, pressing my advantage before he can interrupt again. "We have been operational in your city for less than three full days, Chief, and we have already successfully neutralised a dangerous killer responsible for multiple deaths. Remind me… what significant progress have *you* made on this case prior to our arrival?" The question hangs heavy in the air. I watch his face flush an even deeper shade of crimson. I expect another bellowing outburst, but instead, he takes a different, far more contemptible tack, clearly trying to get under my skin personally. The attempt instantly evaporates any lingering shred of respect I might have had for the man.

With another nasty smirk, he leans back in his chair and says condescendingly, "So, it *was* you screaming like a frightened girl last night, then? The one the passerby reported hearing before they called 9-1-1?"

I maintain my composure, refusing to let his pathetic attempt at provocation land. Leaning forward again, continuing my calm composure, I reply firmly, "Chief, I assure you, I *never* scream. Not even," I add pointedly, letting the implication hang heavy, "when subjected to enhanced interrogation techniques." From behind me, I hear Rose let out a distinct snort of amusement, but I ignore it, knowing exactly what she finds funny. As far as I'm concerned, I have no memory of screaming, therefore, it never happened. End of discussion. "The *suspect* screamed when apprehended," I continue smoothly. "Now, do you have any further childish insults or jurisdictional games you wish to play? Or may I get back to my actual job of making *your* city safer?"

The smirk finally drops from the Chief's face, replaced by impotent fury. "I don't like you, Bekke," he snarls. "And I don't like your methods. Fine. If you require assistance, my officers *will* provide it, as mandated. We all want our citizens to be safe. But make no mistake," he leans forward again, his voice low and threatening, "I *will* be escalating my concerns about your conduct, your entire task force, up the chain of command. So don't get too comfortable in your position. I doubt you'll be keeping it for long."

I rise slowly from the chair, deliberately looking down at him. The gesture isn't lost on him; he flinches almost imperceptibly. "Don't *ever* threaten me, Chief Thornton," I state calmly, each word precise, sharp. "You do whatever you feel you must. But I assure you, I am not going anywhere." I turn towards the door, pausing at the entrance to his office, ensuring my voice carries clearly out into the silent bullpen. "And just so we're clear, you will *not* be holding any press conferences today regarding my team or the events of last night. We need to ensure that if this… *gang member*… has any associates still operating in the city, they aren't tipped off prematurely that we're onto them." I catch myself just before saying 'vampire'. *Need to be more careful.* "If you are asked for a statement by the media, you will defer, citing the ongoing federal investigation under the Domestic Terrorism Act. You will *not* mention our involvement at this time. Furthermore," I add, turning back slightly to meet his incredulous gaze, "I trust I won't hear about you attempting to take credit for *our* work either. Because if I do, *I* will make calls, look into your service record, and seek *your* removal from command. When *we* decide the time is right to hold a press conference, *Agent Miller* will be conducting it. You," I offer magnanimously, "may stand beside him, *if* you choose to cooperate fully with us going forward, not obstruct us. We are supposed to be on the same team here, Chief. We have enough real enemies out there; don't make the mistake of creating more."

The Chief surges to his feet, his face contorted with rage. "You cannot stop me!" he sputters, spittle flying. "You cannot dictate how I run *my* department or handle the press in *my* city! *I* will be the only one addressing the media regarding this! He speaks through gritted teeth, radiating fury.

"So be it," I reply calmly, turning my back on him and walking out of his office, leaving him fuming in my wake. I stride purposefully through the bullpen, ignoring the stunned faces of the officers, heading straight for the main exit. We anticipated this potential outcome, this level of resistance, during our planning session. We have a contingency. Time to activate it. As we pass the desk Sergeant, who quickly looks away, pretending not to notice the simmering tension, I murmur quietly to Sam beside me, "Alright, Sam. You know what to do."

"Ready when you are, Ava," he replies, his voice grim but resolute. "See you after."

Luca, Rose, and I exit the station, stepping out into the now bright afternoon sunlight. Across the street, in the small park area, the press corps is already gathering, cameras jostling for position like hungry vultures. Dressed in our unassuming civvies, we blend easily into the background, drawing no attention as we walk past the assembling media scrum. We head around the corner towards where our Tahoe is parked, ensuring we're out of sight before they see us entering a government vehicle.

Sam gives us just enough time to clear the area. Then, as planned, he steps out of the main entrance of the police station and confidently approaches the waiting reporters. We watch the live feed on my encrypted phone as he begins the press conference, not in front of the station as the Chief clearly intended, but across the street, in the public park. He introduces himself, outlines the formation of the new federal task force dedicated to combating the rising wave of violent crime, and assures the public that everything possible is being done to ensure their safety. Then comes the masterstroke. Sam states, calmly but firmly, that regrettably, the task force is currently operating *without* the full cooperation of Chief Thornton, who has actively obstructed our initial efforts. He expresses hope that individual officers within the city's police department, dedicated public servants committed to protecting their community, might choose to assist the federal task force directly, even if it means going against the Chief's uncooperative stance.

We watch, captivated, as chaos erupts. Chief Thornton comes storming out of the station moments later, stumbling down the steps, red-faced and blustering, shouting denials, trying desperately to regain control of the narrative. But the reporters, smelling blood, turn on him, peppering him with aggressive questions about his lack of results, his alleged obstructionism. Through it all, Sam stands calmly nearby, fielding questions coolly, subtly reinforcing the narrative, the Chief is hindering the investigation, prioritising ego over public safety, perhaps even trying to get the effective federal task force disbanded simply because their early success highlights his failures.

Sam initially baulked at this aggressive tactic, citing inter-agency protocols and potential long-term repercussions. But I'd insisted. We needed to send a clear, unequivocal message, not just to Thornton, but to every police chief, every sheriff, in every city we might visit going forward. We are in charge. We will not be bullied, obstructed, or walked over. If local authorities work against us, they will be publicly exposed and made to look incompetent, just like Chief Thornton does now, squirming under the media spotlight. In the end, Sam reluctantly agreed; establishing dominance early was crucial for the mission's success. Otherwise, word would spread that we were weak, easily manipulated, and securing cooperation elsewhere would become impossible. Sometimes, scorched earth is the only language bullies understand.

CHAPTER 15

Chief Complaints, Sword Retorts, and Surprisingly

Sappy Confessions

Once Sam rejoins us in the Tahoe, the adrenaline from the confrontation with the Chief still buzzing faintly under my skin, we head back towards the relative anonymity of our motel. The mood in the vehicle is subdued, contemplative. Sam seems relieved the press conference went relatively smoothly, despite the Chief's predictable theatrics. He relays that Thornton, after his initial bluster, eventually backed down when faced with Sam's calm counter-narrative and the reporters' aggressive questioning. Apparently, the Chief even managed a grudging, "Well played," directed at Sam before retreating back into the station. We share a brief, weary chuckle at that small victory, though a part of me worries about potential repercussions down the line. Making enemies, especially powerful ones like a city Police Chief, is rarely strategically sound, no matter how satisfying it feels in the moment.

Back in the slightly stale air of the motel corridor, we bundle into Rose's and my room, needing to debrief and decide our next move. The adrenaline crash leaves me feeling drained, the dull throb in my neck a persistent reminder of last night's encounter. We find places to sit – Rose and I automatically gravitate towards the bed, while Luca and Sam take the two uncomfortable-looking chairs near the window.

Once settled, the silence stretches for a moment before I feel compelled to address the elephant in the room – my performance, or lack thereof, during the vampire fight. "Sorry about last night," I begin, keeping my gaze fixed somewhere on the patterned motel carpet. "My reaction time… it wasn't good enough. I've only ever failed twice in my life, truly failed when it mattered. That," I force myself to meet their eyes, "was the second time. The night vision sunglasses helped, they definitely cut through the darkness, but that vampire… he was just too damn fast, too unpredictable for me to track effectively in close quarters. There was no way I could reliably use a firearm on him, even though I did manage to land a couple of shots – with the wrong damn gun, of course, after dropping the one loaded with wooden rounds." Frustration bubbles up again. "I simply can't react quickly enough with projectile weapons in that kind of chaotic, close-quarters engagement against something that fast. From now on," I declare, making the decision as I speak, "I'm relying on the sword primarily in those situations. At least with a blade, even a near miss, an imprecise strike, might create an opening, hinder them long enough for a more effective follow-up attack."

"It's okay, Ava," Luca replies immediately, his tone reassuring, non-judgmental. "It was your first real encounter with a hostile vampire in close combat. Honestly, I'd hoped for a slightly… less intense introduction for you. But I agree, utilising the sword makes tactical sense. As you say, even a glancing blow could disrupt their rhythm, create an opportunity."

"That's easy enough for Ava to say," Sam interjects, sounding slightly glum. "She clearly has sword training. I, on the other hand, have had precisely zero training with swords. I experienced the exact same issues last night – reacting too slowly, unable to get a clean shot off."

"I can help teach you, Sam, if you want," I offer sincerely, surprised by my own willingness to take on a training role. I'm happy to run through the basics, share what I know."

"I can also assist with your training," Luca adds, nodding towards Sam. "I may not possess Ava's level of formal swordsmanship, but I'm proficient enough to get you started with fundamentals, stances, basic parries."

"Count me out," Rose chimes in emphatically, flexing one of

her hands, the subtle shift hinting at the claws beneath the skin. "Zero sword training here either. I'll stick to what I know best," she finishes with a predatory grin. Seeing the momentary flash of her potential weaponry sends an unexpected, unwelcome jolt of heat through my system, my mind instantly recalling the feel of those claws against my skin. My cheeks flush slightly. Damn it. Rose catches my reaction, her grin widening into a knowing smile. I quickly look away, focusing back on Sam, determined to ignore her teasing.

"If you don't mind, Ava," Sam says thoughtfully, "perhaps I could start my training with Luca? Get the absolute basics down first? Then maybe transition to working with you for more advanced techniques?"

"Sure, Sam," I agree readily. "Sounds like a plan. Just let me know whenever you're ready."

Luca then steers the conversation back towards the immediate mission objectives. "Considering the learning curve, especially with Ava and Sam adjusting to facing vampires directly… and given that we've potentially stirred the nest by taking out two of them now… I believe our best course of action might be to conduct our next reconnaissance during daylight hours. Vampires may prefer the night – sunlight significantly weakens the born ones and is lethal to the turned, but neither type actually sleeps in the traditional sense. If they are using the surrounding abandoned buildings as a lair, we might still be able to find evidence, perhaps even catch them in a vulnerable state, if we approach cautiously while the sun is up."

"Wait, what?" The words burst out of me again, disbelief warring with ingrained pop-culture knowledge. Everyone turns to look at me. "What's up, Ava?" Rose asks, deliberately adding that breathy undertone to my name again, her eyes dancing with mischief. *Oh, I am so going to get her back for this later.*

"Well," I begin, feeling slightly foolish, "aren't vampires supposed to, you know… burn up in direct sunlight? Like, poof," I emphasise the word, raising my hands in front of me and then flinging my fingers outwards dramatically, mimicking an explosion.

Rose chuckles openly at my animated display, while Luca and Sam share amused smirks. "Sorry, Ava," Luca says, his smile kind, "not all of them go 'poof' quite so dramatically." He elaborates, "As I mentioned, born vampires, the ancient ones, merely become significantly weaker in direct sunlight – reduced to roughly human levels of strength and speed. Though," he adds thoughtfully, "there are persistent rumours that vampires over a thousand years old develop a greater tolerance, finding sunlight merely… uncomfortable. However, for turned vampires, yes, direct sunlight is lethal. They begin to disintegrate, turning to ash quite rapidly if exposed for more than a few seconds. So, I suppose, in the end, they do kind of go 'poof', as you put it."

"Huh. That's… disappointing," I admit, a surprising flicker of childish regret passing through me. "I was kind of hoping to witness one actually go 'poof', you know, like in that old show, *Buffy the Vampire Slayer*." I shake my head, refocusing. "Anyway, your point about daylight recon is sound. It might be advantageous to find their lair during the day. If we return to the factory where we encountered the first one, maybe we can find some clue he left behind, something indicating why he was there specifically. It could potentially lead us to the others." Then another thought occurs to me, connecting dots from the files. "The number of missing persons reported in this city has remained relatively steady over the years, hasn't it? If there was a large, active nest here, feeding regularly, wouldn't those numbers be higher? The fact that the vampires we encountered last night seemed to be operating alone, at least initially… it feels off. Maybe… maybe there's something else going on here besides just a simple nest?" My mind races, considering possibilities – are they transient? Part of a larger network? Using this city as a temporary base?

"You raise a valid point, Ava," Luca concedes, frowning thoughtfully. "It is unusual. We definitely need to ascertain the scope of the threat we're facing here. So, when should we head back out?

Conduct this daylight reconnaissance?”

“Perhaps we should head out before it gets dark?” Sam suggests pragmatically. “Give Ava some time to rest properly first? Her head injury….”

“My head is still throbbing slightly,” I admit reluctantly, “so resting for a few more hours before we head out again would be beneficial, especially if we do encounter more resistance. I need to be at peak operational capacity.” Saying it aloud makes me feel weak, vulnerable, and I hate it.

“That sounds agreeable to me,” Sam nods. “In the meantime, perhaps Luca and I could begin that sword training?” He looks towards Luca expectantly.

“Absolutely,” Luca agrees readily, rising from his chair. “No time like the present. Let’s do this.” He heads for the door, Sam following close behind. “Ava, Rose, let us know when you’re ready to head out later this afternoon.”

Once the guys had left, the door clicking shut behind them, I sat on the edge of the bed for a second in silence. Rose was looking at me, an unreadable expression on her face, and I waited, unsure if she’d look away. Finally, her gaze dropped. She seemed to be waiting for something, as if she wasn’t sure what to say or do. Seizing the moment, I launched myself at her, taking her completely by surprise. She toppled backwards from her seat on the edge of the bed, landing on her back with me straddling her, her arms playfully pinned to her sides. Looking into her wide, startled eyes, I leaned in. “You,” I whispered, “are in so much trouble.”

Rose laughed, the sound genuine and warm. “What did I do?” she asked, her voice laced with mock innocence.

“You know exactly what you did,” I retort, though my stern tone is failing. “You need to stop doing things like that around Sam.” I gave her a quick, soft peck on the lips before rolling off her to lie beside her, staring up at the bland motel ceiling. Rose shifts onto her side, snuggling close, resting her head on my shoulder. The simple contact is comforting.

"How's your head, honey?" Rose asks softly, her voice close to my ear, careful not to aggravate the throbbing.

"It's okay," I murmured. "It was getting better until that horrible man started to bellow. I so wanted to punch him to shut him up."

"Me too. He has a nerve, talking to you like that."

I closed my eyes, gripping Rose's arm, which she has wrapped around me, drawing comfort from her presence. A wave of exhaustion washed over me; I'm starting to feel overwhelmed with so much happening at once. For the first time since I watched my parents being killed, I felt my emotional control fraying. I'd kept those feelings locked away for so long, and I didn't like this vulnerability one bit. In the past, I've been called a cold-hearted bitch. I didn't want to be like that with Rose, even though this whole situation with her has hit me like a tidal wave, so fast it almost washed me away. I have to try to find a balance as I lie there with my eyes closed.

"Ava, what's wrong?" Rose's voice is gentle as she pulls herself up, repositioning herself to straddle me. She cups my face, her thumbs brushing my cheeks. Her green eyes, full of concern, search mine as I reopen them. That's when I realise a single tear has escaped, tracing a path down my cheek. Rose's thumb gently sweeps it away. I stare up at her, battling to keep my emotions in check.

"Honey, please talk to me," she urges, her expression pleading. "I can't help if you don't tell me. I know this has happened very quickly for you. I hope whatever is making you sad isn't anything to do with me." She looks desperate for reassurance.

I shake my head slightly, and a visible wave of relief washes over Rose's features. Gathering myself, I decide to tell her the truth. I'd been thinking about it since yesterday; if this thing between us, this bond, is going to work, I have to tell her everything. Since the first day I met them, I'd felt an unexpected level of comfort talking to both her and Luca. Maybe there's something about shifters that makes them easy to talk to.

So, I tell her about my parents, about how their murder had made me shut down emotionally. I explained why I'd enrolled in the military, seeking an outlet for my anger, vowing to never feel weak or helpless again, determined to bring down as many bad people in the world as possible. Then I describe how discovering the paranormal world, seeing her shift for the first time, had made me feel true fear for the first time since my parents' deaths.

Rose winces at that, her eyes closing briefly as if in pain, and she tries to pull away. I hold her gently but firmly, stopping her, needing her to hear all of it. "Then," I continue, my voice quieter, "as all of you told me more and more about your world, it just made me feel weaker." I take a deep breath. "Back at the ranch, when we were discussing which city to head to first, I heard a voice… And then again, after I got my head cracked open last night, I heard the same female voice, telling me to get to Chicago." I didn't mention Luca hearing a voice; that was his to share if he chose to.

"This world of yours," I admit, the words tasting like ash, "it makes me feel weak. And I was scared, for the first time, of failing. Last night… it didn't help. It just proved my weakness." The Police Chief's dismissive attitude replayed in my mind. "His reaction made me wonder if maybe I wasn't the right person for this task." I pause, then force out the last, most difficult part. "What's happening between us… that scares me too. Which is strange, because I've never been scared of a relationship before – not that I've had many. People have always called me a cold-hearted bitch because I never show my emotions. I don't want to be like that with you."

Rose stares at me for a long moment, her expression unreadable. I start to feel a knot of anxiety tighten in my chest, fearing I'd just screwed everything up. Then, her mouth is on mine, a firm, possessive kiss that takes my breath away. I hesitate for only a second before sinking into it, my eyes closing as I let myself feel. This time, tears escape from each eye, but these are tears of relief, of a happiness so intense it is almost painful.

When Rose finally breaks the kiss, a kiss charged with a storm of emotions, she rests her forehead against mine, staring down at me. "You stupid bitch," she murmurs, her voice thick with feeling. "You've impressed me since the moment we met. Not many people have ever done that in my life, especially not a human."

"Thanks… I think," I manage, unsure how to take her typically blunt compliment.

She shakes her head, a small smile playing on her lips. "Everything has been a lot for me to deal with, too. I technically lost my family as well, not in the same way you did, but I lost them. It feels like we're up against the world." Her smile fades. "Then I met this beautiful, infuriating woman I just knew I would get on with. But I never expected the ancient prime mate bond to appear between us. Our history, our lore, has always told us it can never happen between same-sex partners." Her voice drops, raw with remembered fear. "I was so scared to tell you about it, expecting you to shout and curse me. I even thought you might try to kill me, blaming me for the bond, thinking I was trying to force you into something. You didn't. You embraced it, shocking me to no end and making me a very, very happy woman. I'm still scared you'll change your mind at some point." Rose closed her eyes briefly, then opened them, her gaze locking with mine. "I'm so sorry about your parents, Ava. And… what's with the voice? Who is it? Or are you trying to gently tell me you're a bit crazy?"

"I'm not crazy," I say, a small smile touching my own lips. "I don't think I am, anyway. But I have no idea who it is or why they want me to go to Chicago." I examine Rose, her fierce loyalty, her vulnerability, and the unexpected depth of her feelings that mirror my own turmoil. Then it hit me, a moment of stark clarity. Rose and I are more alike than I realise. We both lost our parents, our original families, and ended up essentially on our own. I found a surrogate family in the military, rising through the ranks, becoming a top sniper, an assassin, even developing a taste for explosives. She found her family in Luca's pack, becoming one of his trusted betas. Both of us, damaged in our own ways, forged into weapons by our pasts, were now brought together by some ancient, inexplicable bond, destined to be together.

A fresh wave of emotion surges through me. I pull Rose back down to me, our mouths crashing together in a kiss fuelled by understanding, shared pain, and a desperate, hopeful passion. I pour every unspoken feeling into it, hoping it will tell her everything words couldn't. The kiss deepens, the world outside the circle of her arms fades away, promising not just solace, but a shared strength. Eventually, the storm of emotion gives way to a gentler current, leading to a few precious hours of shared warmth and much-needed sleep.

CHAPTER 16

WOKE UP WARM, GEARED UP WEIRD, AND FOUND GOD
(IN A CREEPY CULT FLYER)

We wake just before 5pm, the afternoon light slanting weakly through the gap in the cheap motel curtains. I surface slowly from a deep, dreamless sleep, finding myself plastered on top of Rose, my head comfortably pillowed between her breasts, her arm draped possessively around my waist. Well, this is definitely a new sleeping arrangement for me. All I recall before drifting off is the overwhelming urge to soak in as much of the incredible heat radiating from her as possible, a primal seeking of warmth and comfort. I guess that translated into unconsciously moulding myself onto her during our sleep. A low chuckle rumbles in Rose's chest as she stirs, clearly amused at finding me in this position.

"Morning, sleepyhead," she murmurs, her voice thick with sleep.

I manage a vague noise in response, nuzzling closer for a second before reality intrudes. Mission. Vampires. I give her a quick, sleepy kiss on the collarbone before reluctantly rolling off her, the cool air of the room a stark contrast to her warmth.

We share the cramped shower again… purely for efficiency, of course. Saving water. Time. Definitely just conserving resources, *honest*. We manage to keep things relatively focused this time, aware of the impending operation. Afterwards, while I pull on clean clothes, Rose texts Luca, letting him know we'll be ready to move in twenty minutes. He replies almost instantly, confirming they're already on their way back from their training session.

After we're both dressed, me back in functional jeans and a t-shirt, Rose looking effortlessly stylish even in casual wear, we then hear the faint, almost silent hum of the Tahoe pulling up outside. We head out, meeting Luca and Sam in the parking lot, so we climb into the back seats. "Are you feeling better, Ava?" Luca asks, glancing back at me, his dark eyes assessing, concerned.

"Much better, thanks," I confirm, feeling significantly more rested and clear-headed than after the previous night's ordeal. The throbbing in my neck has subsided to a dull ache. "How did your sword training session go, Sam?"

"Uh, interesting," Sam replies, looking slightly sheepish. "I think it went reasonably well, all things considered. Though I felt like a complete novice again, utterly clumsy. The last time I seriously held anything resembling a sword was probably when I was a kid, playing knights with a wooden one in the backyard." A faint smile touches his lips at the memory.

"Well, it takes time," I offer encouragingly. "I spent years actively seeking out instructors, anyone willing to teach me unconventional weapon skills, swords, knives, and various martial arts. People thought I was crazy, they couldn't understand why a modern soldier would want to train with archaic weapons. Seems almost prescient now, doesn't it? Like some part of me knew I needed to be prepared for... well, for *this*. For what we're up against now." The thought sends a strange shiver down my spine, destiny, or just a series of coincidences?

"Well, whatever the reason, it seems it was the best decision you ever made, Ava," Luca remarks thoughtfully, as he pulls the car smoothly out of the motel parking lot, heading back towards the eastern industrial sector, where we encountered the vampires. Well, I only saw one, kind of, more of a blur really, so I guess I still can't say I've seen a vampire.

The drive takes about thirty minutes, navigating through the late afternoon traffic. Luca finds a discreet parking spot again, tucked away amongst crumbling warehouses, offering good concealment but easy egress. Time to gear up for the daylight recon. Sam retrieves his gear first, opting to stick with his standard sidearm and a tactical shotgun for now, acknowledging his lack of sword proficiency. Luca selects one of the swords again, perhaps for its specific properties against certain entities, or maybe just to encourage Sam, I'm still not sure. Rose, interestingly, doesn't select any overt weapons, relying, I suppose, on her natural abilities. Given that it's still broad daylight, shifting into panther form is out of the question; it would draw far too much unwanted attention.

As the others prepare, ensuring comms are functional in case we get separated, I turn my attention to my own loadout. The routine is familiar, grounding. Pistols checked and secured, wood-tipped rounds in the primary custom piece, standard Glock as backup. Daggers positioned – thigh, boot, small of back. Then, the sword. The one that felt… right, after last night, this is what I'm going to stick with. It slides smoothly from the trunk compartment into my hand, the balance perfect, the edge gleaming almost like the blade's edge is sparkling like diamonds. Something about this particular blade resonates with me. I slide it carefully into the sheath across my back, the weight comfortable, familiar now.

My fingers brush against the coin pocket of my jeans. The ring. Madi's gift. Papa Legba's 'investment'. I transferred the ring from the jeans I had worn the previous night. I hesitate. Should I? I'm tempted to find out what it will do. But the lingering distrust, the unknown cost, the potential danger… I slide the ring out, holding it in my palm, studying its intricate runes, the tiny, glittering jewels. It feels cool to the touch, even though it's been against my body; it should be warm, shouldn't it? Is it safe? Is it a trick? Is it worth the risk?

Taking a deep, steadying breath, I make the decision to take a calculated risk. Potential benefits outweigh the unknown dangers, for now. Closing my eyes for a brief second, I slide the ring firmly onto the ring finger of my right hand.

For a moment, nothing happens. I almost sigh in relief, or maybe disappointment, I'm not sure which. Then, a peculiar sensation washes over me, starting from my hand, spreading upwards like a warm tide, moving rapidly to the top of my head, then cascading down to my toes. It's not unpleasant, just… strange. Disorienting. The world tilts slightly, a wave of dizziness making me sway for a second or two. Then, just as quickly as it began, the sensation passes, leaving me feeling… normal. Exactly the same as before. Except… I blink, shaking my head slightly. Everything seems… sharper. Brighter. The colours of the decaying buildings around us appear more vivid, the textures of the brickwork and rusted metal more defined. I dismiss it as a lingering effect of the dizziness, my senses perhaps momentarily heightened by the brief anxiety spike.

The Tahoe locks automatically as Luca closes the trunk. I draw the sword back out of the sheath and hold it loosely at my side, point down, hoping the blade might blend somewhat against the dark fabric of my jeans. I walk towards the others, who have already begun moving towards a different entrance to the same factory building we investigated previously. They glance towards the sword in my hand, then offer brief nods of acknowledgement.

"Okay, listen up," Luca says quietly as we gather near a broken-down service entrance. "Based on our observations, the vampires' lair could be somewhere within this cluster of buildings. Our objective today is daylight reconnaissance *only*. We locate their resting place if possible, assess numbers, identify entry and exit points, look for weaknesses. We only engage if we have the advantage. Understood?" We all nod. "And remember," he adds, his gaze sweeping over us, "assume they can hear better, smell better, maybe even *sense* better than we can anticipate. Move slow, stay quiet, stay alert."

This time, Luca takes point, slipping through the warped metal doorframe like a wraith. I follow, Rose close behind me, Sam bringing up the rear. The air inside is thick with the smell of dust, damp decay, and something else… a faint, cloying sweetness I didn't notice last night. My unease ratchets up a notch. We move cautiously through the ground floor, clearing rooms methodically, finding nothing but debris and shadows. Reaching the stairwell we used before, we ascend slowly, sticking close to the walls, avoiding the centre of the steps where they're most likely to creak. Rose takes the lead now, her movements utterly silent, her head constantly scanning, sniffing the air subtly. When we reach the floor where we encountered the vampire, we fan out slightly, maintaining visual contact, moving in pairs down the long corridors lined with empty, echoing rooms, past the rows of silent, rusting machinery. The silence is oppressive, amplifying every tiny sound, the scuff of a boot, the drip of water somewhere distant, my own heartbeat loud in my ears. We reach the far end of the large open room where the fight occurred. Nothing. No sign of recent activity, no lingering scent strong enough for Luca or Rose to comment on.

We proceed upwards again, towards the top floor, the one containing what looks like administrative offices. The light is slightly better up here, filtering through grimy windows. We adopt the same search pattern, moving in pairs, clearing room after room. Most are empty, stripped bare long ago, containing only dust and dereliction. We're nearing the end of the hallway, only a few closed doors remaining, when Sam suddenly calls out, his voice low but urgent.

"Luca, Ava… I think we might have found something."

Luca and I quickly converge on his position, joining Rose standing in the open doorway, so we know which room they are searching. Sam waves us in. Immediately, I notice the difference. This room… it feels *used*. The layer of dust is thinner here, disturbed. There are items on a large wooden desk that look incongruously new against the backdrop of decay. We move inside cautiously and join Sam, who is already standing by the desk, examining its contents. I walk up to the desk, my eyes scanning the desktop.

Spread across the dusty surface is a detailed map of Pittsburgh.

Certain areas are marked with rough circles drawn in red ink – specific neighbourhoods in the north, south, and west sections of the city. A handwritten note is scrawled across the top margin, '*Confine activities to these zones ONLY for now. Avoid East.*' The marked areas correspond precisely with the locations of the vampire attacks detailed in the files we reviewed.

"Does anyone recognise these specific areas? Know anything about the demographics, the typical activity levels?" I ask, looking at the others, hoping for insight.

Sam leans closer, studying the map. "Based on my general knowledge of the city layout… I believe these are primarily the poorer sections of Pittsburgh. Lower-income neighbourhoods, areas with maybe higher rates of unemployment, less consistent police presence. I could be wrong, but that's my initial assessment."

"That would fit their pattern," I muse aloud, tapping a finger against my lips. "Target the more vulnerable areas, areas where disappearances or unexplained deaths might attract less immediate attention, less public outcry. If they started hitting affluent neighbourhoods first, the political pressure, the media scrutiny, would bring down intense heat much faster." It's a cold, calculating, but effective strategy for predators wishing to remain hidden.

"I think you're right, Ava," Luca agrees, his expression grim. "It makes perfect sense. I didn't specifically cross-reference victim addresses with socioeconomic data when reviewing the files earlier. A critical oversight. We need to incorporate that analysis moving forward." He looks annoyed with himself for missing the correlation. I share his frustration; it seems obvious in retrospect.

"It could be their standard operating procedure in every city they infiltrate," Sam speculates, his voice tight with anger. "The way the attacks have escalated so gradually over the past twenty-three years… it suggests a long-term, deliberate strategy. They've managed to operate largely undetected for decades, slowly growing their numbers, expanding their influence, hiding their activities beneath the background noise of urban crime. And now… now it's finally reaching a level where it *is* being noticed, but things are already so bad, so widespread… it might genuinely be too late to easily contain it."

"We're on the job *now*, Sam," I state firmly, placing a hand briefly on his shoulder, trying to project confidence I don't entirely feel. "And we *will* make a difference. We'll reduce their numbers, disrupt their operations, hunt down the leaders who initiated this nightmare."

Luca carefully folds the map and hands it to Sam, who slips it into a large evidence bag from the small backpack he carries, which apparently contains a basic crime scene investigation kit. We examine the other items on the desk – a cheap notepad, a couple of pens. Sam bags the notepad as well; I can guess he'll be trying pencil rubbings later to see if any impressions remain from previous pages. The other miscellaneous items – an empty coffee cup, a discarded newspaper, seem irrelevant.

I'm about to turn away, concluding the room has yielded all it can, when something catches my eye – a small pile of pamphlets stacked on the corner of the desk, almost hidden beneath some scattered papers. Curious, I pick one up. The cover depicts a quaint, modest-looking church building, identified by the small print as being located somewhere on the city's *east* side. But it's the bold text printed across the front that grabs my attention, sending another chill down my spine, *'The Dawning is Near! Join us now and SURVIVE the new world that is coming… or SUCCUMB to it.'* Inside, it lists standard Sunday service times and contact information. Survive the new world? Or succumb? It sounds less like a church invitation and more like a threat, or a recruitment drive.

CHAPTER 17

THE PHANTOM BLING: MY FINGER'S FREAKY NEW FEATURE (AND ROSE'S FULL-BLOWN FREAK-OUT FUEL), PLUS OTHER ODDITIES OF OUR EVENING DRIVE

My knowledge of conventional religion is rudimentary at best, limited mostly to mandatory school lessons. Personal experience has fostered a deep scepticism regarding the existence of any benevolent deity. Yet now, factoring in Luca and Rose's revelations – actual gods, warring factions, ancient betrayals, possible surviving entities orchestrating global chaos… The irony of vampires, creatures of darkness, potentially using a consecrated church as their haven, possibly as a deliberate insult, a final 'fuck you' to the absent gods… it's almost too perfect.

I share my thoughts with the others, holding up the pamphlet. "Given the location, east side, where we suspect they're based, and this… *message*… These might not be simple church flyers. Could they be using this place, this 'church', as a front? Luring unsuspecting humans in, either to be turned into more vampires or simply drained dry as convenient food sources?" I pass the pamphlet to Luca, watching his reaction as he reads it. Sam and Rose quickly grab copies for themselves from the stack.

"It certainly wouldn't hurt to investigate," Sam agrees immediately, his eyes narrowing thoughtfully as he reads the pamphlet. "If the vampires Rose and Luca neutralised *were* indeed operating out of this specific church… then what was this place used for? Unless they used this place for training or something, for those they turned?" He looks determined, ready to check out the church right *now*.

"We need to proceed with extreme caution," Luca warns, his gaze flicking between us. "We should definitely check out as many of these surrounding abandoned buildings as possible first, while we still have remaining daylight. Then, perhaps before heading back to the motel for the evening, we can do a preliminary drive-by of the church location. See if anything looks overtly suspicious. The major issue, however," he adds, looking pointedly at Rose and then back at me, "is that if this church *is* their primary lair, they *will* smell Rose and me long before we get close enough for effective surveillance."

"So," I state the obvious conclusion, "if we want to get eyes on the church itself without alerting them, it can only be Sam and me initially."

"I'm afraid so," Luca confirms grimly. He glances towards Rose again, a silent question passing between them. She fidgets slightly, clearly unhappy with the idea of me approaching a potential vampire nest without her immediate backup, but she doesn't voice an objection. "How do you feel about that approach, Ava?"

"We don't necessarily need to get out of the car initially," Sam suggests practically. "We could just do one or two slow drive-bys first. See if we spot anything overtly out of place. Or," he adds, tapping his backpack, "we utilize a few of these compact remote cameras I brought. If we can find a discreet location nearby, we could potentially place one without needing to physically approach the church building itself."

"Luca, you can't seriously consider letting them get out of the car to place cameras near a potential vampire nest!" Rose protests immediately, her earlier reticence vanishing, her gaze fixed fiercely on Luca. "If that *is* where they're holed up, it's far too dangerous for Ava and Sam alone!"

I quickly interject before a full argument erupts, offering my own compromise. "How about this, tonight, we *only* conduct one or two slow drive-bys, purely observational. If, based on that initial look, we still suspect it might be their hideout, then we return tomorrow, perhaps around lunchtime when there's likely to be more ambient pedestrian and vehicle traffic to provide cover. *Then*, we attempt to place a camera or two. I have workout clothes back at the motel; I could pretend to be out for a run, jog around the block a few times. Or Sam could do the jogging. The other provides overwatch from a nearby vantage point, just in case things go sideways."

They consider my proposal. Sam answers first. "I like that plan, Ava. Makes sense. I'll do the jogging; you take the overwatch position. Your skills are better suited for that role anyway."

Luca nods slowly in agreement. Even Rose looks somewhat placated by the revised plan, though her concern for my safety remains evident in her eyes.

We spend the next couple of hours methodically clearing the adjacent abandoned buildings, working our way through the derelict structures as the afternoon light begins to fade. We find nothing else of interest – just more dust, decay, and the lingering ghosts of industry. As dusk begins to settle, painting the sky in shades of orange and purple, we decide to call off the search for the day and head back towards the Tahoe. I jump into the front passenger seat this time, keeping the newly acquired sword unsheathed, resting across my lap, just in case our drive-by of the church attracts unwanted attention. Sam gets behind the wheel. We drop Luca and Rose off several blocks away from the church's location, a necessary precaution to avoid their shifter scent potentially alerting any vampires nearby. Then, just Sam and I, proceed towards the target address on the east side.

As we turn onto the street where the church is located, the change in atmosphere is immediate, palpable. This area is significantly more run-down than the other parts of the city we've seen, characterised by neglected buildings, cracked sidewalks, and an air of quiet desperation. Exactly the kind of place predators might choose to hide, where disappearances might go unnoticed or unreported for longer. The perfect hunting ground.

Sam maintains a slow, steady speed, crawling along the street as my eyes scan everything – windows, doorways, rooftops, the few people shuffling along the sidewalk. They all seem to be deliberately walking on the opposite side of the street from the church, giving the building a wide berth. Interesting. Then, as we draw level with the church itself – a modest, slightly dilapidated stone building – I spot him. A figure lurking deep in the shadows near the main entrance, partially obscured by the church's large wooden sign and the overhanging branches of nearby trees. He's trying to remain unseen, but doing a poor job of it. He's wearing a long, dark trench coat despite the relatively warm evening, the hood pulled up, concealing his face entirely.

"Got a lookout," I murmur quietly to Sam, nodding towards the shadowed doorway. "Hiding in the shadows over there. Definitely trying not to be seen." Sam quickly glances in the indicated direction, then back at the road. I wait for his confirmation, but when he doesn't say anything, I turn to look at him. He's frowning, glancing back towards the church again with a puzzled expression.

"What?" I ask.

"It's practically pitch black over there, Ava," he replies, confused. "The streetlights on that side of the road seem to be out. How could you possibly see anyone standing in those shadows?"

We've driven past the church now, the figure lost to view behind us. I frown, perplexed by Sam's statement. Pitch black? No, it's not. We still have decent ambient light, the lingering twilight of late dusk. I look around us – I can see the details of the buildings, the cracks in the road, perfectly clearly. It feels like… well, like twilight out. Then I glance at the clock on the Tahoe's dashboard. My own frown deepens. 9:42pm. At this time of year, true darkness should have fallen at least an hour ago. It *should* be properly dark by now. Very dark. Which means… I shouldn't have been able to see that figure standing so clearly in deep shadow. What the hell…?

Lost in thought, trying to understand the discrepancy, I barely register us pulling over to pick up Luca and Rose. They slide into the back seat, immediately questioning us about what we observed. I remain silent, still grappling with the impossibility of my own vision, the strange persistence of twilight only I seem to perceive. Sam relays our findings.

"Area around the church is definitely suspicious," he reports. "All the streetlights on that block are out, looks deliberate. Pitch black right in front of the building, like they've created their own pocket of darkness. It's definitely worth a closer look tomorrow. Might need to deploy a camera with good night-vision capabilities." He pauses, then adds, glancing towards me with a puzzled expression, "Ava claims she saw a guy hiding in the shadows near the door, acting as a lookout. But honestly, I don't see how that's possible. It was way too dark to make anything out over there."

His words, confirming the darkness only he experienced, send another jolt through me. Too dark for Sam, but perfectly visible to me? It's not twilight. It's the ring. It *has* to be the ring Madi gave me. The realisation hits me with the force of a physical blow. The ring I slid onto my finger back at the industrial site. I look down at my right hand resting on my lap, expecting to see the glint of silver, the sparkle of jewels. But... my finger is bare. The ring is gone. Vanished.

Panic, cold and immediate, grips me again. It's not there. I run the fingers of my left hand frantically over my right ring finger, searching for the familiar cool metal band. Nothing. Just smooth skin. It's not just invisible; I can't even *feel* it anymore. My breath catches in my throat, anxiety tightening its icy grip.

"Ava? What did *you* think you saw?" Luca asks, his voice pulling me back from the brink of panic, though my eyes remain fixed on my empty finger.

Someone touches my shoulder gently. I jump violently, letting out a small, startled gasp, my head snapping up. "What?!" I exclaim, my voice shaky, my heart hammering against my ribs.

"Whoa, Ava, easy," Luca says softly, his expression concerned. "Are you okay? We asked what you saw back there, but you didn't answer. You seem... a little panicked, to be honest. What's wrong?"

"You almost jumped out of your skin when I touched you," Rose adds, her voice laced with worry, her hand still resting lightly on my shoulder.

I look between them, their concerned faces blurring slightly as my anxiety spikes again. Sam looks equally perplexed from the driver's seat. "Well…" I begin hesitantly, not sure how to explain.

"Ava, what's wrong?" Rose prompts again, her grip tightening slightly on my shoulder, her tone demanding an answer now.

"Well…" I take a shaky breath. "I… I can see perfectly fine right now. It's not dark for me at all. For example," I say, pointing across the street from where we're now parked, "there's a man walking a Rottweiler over there. He's wearing a blue jacket, black jeans, and has brown hair." I describe the scene clearly visible to *me*, then wait for their reactions, bracing myself for the inevitable explosion of questions.

"What the fuck, Ava?" Sam exclaims, twisting in his seat to stare out the window in the direction I pointed. He squints into the darkness. "I… I can barely even *see* him from here, let alone make out colours!"

Luca's eyes narrow, his focus intense as he studies me. "Ava," he demands quietly but firmly, "tell me, right now, how you can possibly see that clearly in this light?"

Rose, however, seems to connect different dots, her eyes widening, though thankfully, she cuts herself off before revealing too much in front of Sam. "Do you think this has anything to do with… you know…?"

Sam, misinterpreting her veiled reference, his analytical agent brain working faster than the shifters' in this instance, suddenly exclaims, "The *ring*!" He looks pointedly at my hands, then frowns deeply when he sees nothing.

"The ring?" Luca and Rose echo simultaneously, their gazes snapping to my hands as well, searching for the object Madi bestowed upon me.

"But… you're not wearing it," Sam states, confused. "Ava,

what the hell is going on? You're starting to really worry me now."

"I *am* wearing the ring," I confess sheepishly, feeling incredibly foolish. "Well… I *was* wearing it. I put it on earlier."

"*What?*" all three exclaim in unison, their voices sharp with shock and concern.

Rose immediately grabs my right hand, turning it over, examining my ring finger closely, while Luca leans forward, peering intently. I lift my left hand as well, showing them both are bare. "Ava," Luca says again, his voice low, serious, "please explain what's happening. We're all extremely worried about you right now."

I turn in my seat so I can face all of them, holding up my right hand for inspection. "Okay," I take another deep breath, trying to remain calm despite the bizarre circumstances. "Before we left the industrial site earlier, I… I decided to put the ring on. The one Madi gave me. I slipped it onto my ring finger, right hand. At first, absolutely nothing happened. Then, I felt a weird… warmth sensation washing… pass… over me, got dizzy for just a second or two, and then… I felt completely fine. Normal. I honestly forgot all about it until just now, when Sam said it was too dark for him to see the lookout back at the church."

Luca and Rose both continue to examine my hand, probing the skin of my ring finger, searching for any trace, any irregularity. Finding nothing, Rose finally looks up, her expression a mixture of fear and fury. "Fucking demons!" she spits out. She turns to Luca, her voice tight with panic. "How the *fuck* do we get it off her finger now if we can't even see it, let alone feel it?!"

"I don't know, Rose," Luca admits grimly, still studying my hand thoughtfully. "But… it doesn't *appear* to be actively harming her. And Madi *did* explicitly state it would help her, protect her. And," he adds, looking significantly at me, "it *is* clearly helping her already, granting her enhanced vision."

"So, we're just… going to do *nothing*?" Rose demands incredulously, her fear palpable.

"No, Rose," Luca replies patiently but firmly. "Not nothing.

We remain vigilant. But until we have *any* indication that the ring is causing Ava harm, we proceed cautiously. If we manage to locate a trustworthy witch or mage during our travels, perhaps they can shed some light on its properties, maybe even determine how to safely remove it, if necessary. But for now," he concludes decisively, "it *is* aiding her, providing abilities perfectly suited to her needs in this fight. It's a shame Madi didn't bring one for Sam, too. My guess is it's likely one-of-a-kind, possibly some ancient, powerful relic." He seems lost in thought for a moment, considering the implications. Then, addressing Rose directly, his tone softening slightly, "Rose, if *anything* adverse happens, *anything* at all that suggests the ring is harmful, I promise you, we will immediately head straight for New Orleans. We'll find Papa Legba himself and demand answers, okay?"

Rose shakes her head, clearly unconvinced, unhappy, but she slumps back in her seat, lapsing into a tense silence. Sam, meanwhile, just looks at me, a mixture of awe and distinct jealousy visible on his face.

"Right," I say, trying to break the awkward tension, my stomach choosing that moment to rumble loudly again. "Can we please go get something to eat now? All this demonic jewellery drama is making me incredibly anxious, and I really need some food."

"Sam, let's get going," Luca instructs, turning back towards the front. "Can you find us somewhere to eat? Preferably in one of the areas marked on that map we found? Might as well combine dinner with some passive surveillance, keep an eye out while we eat."

"The diner we visited the first night, Mel's place, it's located within the western marked zone on the map," Sam reports, already consulting his tablet.

"Yeah, let's head back there then," Luca decides. "Good food, and who knows? If Mel's working again tonight, maybe she's picked up some fresh gossip for us since our last visit." He shifts back fully into his seat, ready to move.

As we pull away, I lean my head back against the seat, a sense of profound unease settling over me despite the ring's apparent benefits. I have a feeling I'm going to be dreading being alone in our room with Rose later tonight. I can already picture her, convinced the ring is demonic, trying every trick she knows to somehow pry the invisible, intangible object off my finger. Although… maybe, just maybe… I can turn her obsessive worry into a game of sorts? Use her frustration for something… considerably more fun. Or perhaps, optimistically, she'll have forgotten all about it by the time we've eaten. I immediately dismiss the thought with an inward chuckle. Like that's going to happen. She is *so* not going to forget.

CHAPTER 18

PAPA LEGBA'S DREAM BAR & GRILL: FAVOURS, FUTURES,
AND WHY YOU SHOULDN'T MAKE DEALS BEFORE COFFEE

Once we reach Mel's diner, Sam parks strategically near the front entrance, angling the Tahoe so it sits directly under the brightest parking lot light. The calculated placement ensures maximum visibility, anyone approaching the vehicle while we're inside will be clearly illuminated. Good tactical thinking. I appreciate the foresight, but a different, more immediate problem presents itself.

"Sam," I begin, glancing down at my own body, acutely aware of the arsenal I'm carrying, "are you perhaps forgetting something rather… conspicuous?"

He turns towards me, his expression blank, genuinely confused. "What? What have I forgotten?" he asks, looking around the vehicle's interior as if searching for a misplaced item.

"Um… *weapons*, Sam?" I reply, gesturing vaguely at myself. "My rather extensive collection of them? Or did you *want* me to stroll into a crowded diner looking like I'm preparing for urban warfare, potentially causing mass panic?"

Sam's eyes follow my gesture, widening slightly, but a concerned and then bewildered expression takes over. "Just… just leave the sword on the floor in the back. Tuck it under the seat. No one will notice it there," he suggests dismissively, then opens his door and gets out. Luca and Rose are already out, seemingly unconcerned, leaving me momentarily dumbfounded in the back seat. Seriously? Just leave it on the floor.

I watch them head towards the diner entrance, Rose pausing briefly to glance back, noticing my hesitation. She immediately changes course, walking back to my side of the car and opening my rear door. Wordlessly, she reaches across me, carefully takes the sword, and slides it onto the floor under the front passenger seat, ensuring it's completely hidden from view. As she leans back out, she risks a quick glance towards the diner door – Sam and Luca are already inside, not watching us. Seizing the opportunity, she leans in swiftly, pressing a quick, warm kiss to my lips before grabbing my left hand and tugging gently, urging me out of the car. I still don't move, held captive by worry while no one else seems worried at all.

"What's up now, honey?" she asks softly, looking at me with concern in her expression. "Is something else wrong? Something you haven't told us?"

I stare at her, incredulous. "Rose," I whisper urgently, "you seriously expect me to walk in there with *multiple firearms* and *four knives* strapped to my body?

Rose stares back at me, blinks several times, then slowly lets her gaze travel over my body, from my shoulders to my boots. I watch as confusion dawns on her face, quickly morphing into wide-eyed panic as the reality of what I'm saying sinks in. "Luca!" she calls out sharply, her voice higher pitched than usual, laced with sudden alarm. "Get back here! Right now!"

Luca, alerted by her panicked tone, rushes back out of the diner, immediately assuming a defensive posture, scanning the surroundings for threats. Seeing nothing obviously wrong, he approaches us, his expression shifting to annoyance. "Rose? What is it? What's going on?"

"Ava just casually informed me," Rose explains, her voice tight, her eyes still fixed on me as if I might spontaneously combust, "that she is currently carrying. As in, *fully* carrying. Like the other night. Guns, knives, the works!"

A deep frown creases Luca's brow as he looks me over again,

clearly perplexed. "Rose, what are you talking about? She only had the sword."

Deciding actions speak louder than words, I reach discreetly, unclipping the Glock from the holster on my left side. Keeping the weapon low, shielded by the car door, I pull it out just enough for them to see the grip. Both Luca and Rose swear simultaneously under their breath. By this time, Sam, alerted by Rose's shout and Luca rushing back out, has also reappeared, looking utterly bewildered.

"What the hell is happening now?" he demands, his gaze flicking between us. Then he spots the gun in my hand. "Ava! Why have you drawn your weapon to go get food?!"

"Because I *always* have it on me, Sam," I reply, exasperated. "Just like the other two pistols, the taser, and the four knives currently strapped to my body." My frustration is evident. Sam stares at me, then runs a hand through his hair, looking utterly baffled, clearly thinking I've finally lost my mind. To drive the point home, I holster the Glock and smoothly draw one of the daggers from my thigh sheath instead, the blade glinting faintly in the parking lot lights.

Now it's Sam's turn to swear, colour draining from his face. "What the... Ava? How? How are you *doing* that? We can't *see* any of it!"

"What! Are you serious, you can't see any of the weapons on me?" I say, looking down at them all, feeling a little panicked by this new realisation.

Luca, however, looks intrigued rather than panicked, his analytical mind clearly working. "Ah," he murmurs, a slow smile spreading across his face as understanding dawns. "I believe we may have just discovered the ring's *second* function. I suspected it might have two, given the dual sets of runes. Weapon concealment. Fascinating." He turns to me, his eyes alight with scientific curiosity. "Ava, are you willing to conduct a small field test? Go into the diner, fully armed as you are right now, and observe if anyone reacts. See if the concealment holds under scrutiny?"

I consider it for a moment. Honestly? I don't particularly care what random strangers think. Technically, as deputised federal agents, we *could* legally carry concealed weapons anyway, though perhaps not quite this extensive an arsenal, especially not including knives and potentially non-regulation firearms. I know Sam is carrying his standard issue sidearm discreetly. "Why not?" I shrug, holstering the dagger smoothly. "Let's see if Papa Legba's gift holds up." I step out of the car.

Rose, still processing, immediately reaches out again, her hands starting to run almost frantically all over my body – my sides, my back, my legs – clearly trying to physically locate the weapons she now knows I'm carrying but cannot see or feel. Any other time, under different circumstances, I might find her invasive search… stimulating, even nice. But right now, it's just awkward.

"Feel anything you particularly like there, Rose?" I quip dryly, raising an eyebrow, unable to resist the tease.

Rose jolts as if shocked, snatching her hands back as if burned, her cheeks flushing crimson as she glances sheepishly towards Luca and Sam. Seeing the stern disapproval on Sam's face, she turns back to me, cringing, and mouths a silent, "*Sorry.*"

"Relax, Rose," I say, offering her a reassuring smile and a subtle wink that Sam hopefully misses. "I'm not going to report you for sexual harassment. Might have done the same in your position." Luca laughs softly while Sam continues to look disapprovingly at Rose, clearly not appreciating the breach of professional decorum. "Alright then," I announce, turning towards the diner entrance, "Let's go see if I can clear the place out and maybe get another irate visit from the Chief, demanding to know if I've been screaming again." Rose chokes back another laugh at the reference, shaking her head.

I push open the diner door and walk in, deliberately moving slowly, casually, scanning the room, observing the patrons, waiting for any reaction – a gasp, a pointed finger, a panicked dive under a table. Nothing. No one bats an eye. They see a woman in jeans and a T-shirt, nothing more. The concealment is absolute. Impressive. And incredibly useful. I head towards the corner booth we occupied before, finding it miraculously free despite how unusually busy it is today. As I slide in, the others follow, their expressions ranging from Rose's relieved amusement to Luca's thoughtful intrigue to Sam's lingering bewilderment.

Mel, the waitress from our previous visit, spots us almost immediately and heads over, a genuine smile lighting up her face this time as she recognises us. She bypasses the rest of us, heading straight for Sam. "Agent Miller! I saw the press conference you gave! It was brilliant!" she gushes enthusiastically. "I was laughing so hard when that pompous ass of a Chief came storming out, looking like his head was about to explode! Serves him right." She lowers her voice slightly. "Anyway, seriously, thank you. Thank you all for coming here, for actually *doing* something to help our city."

Sam puffs out his chest almost imperceptibly at the praise, though he manages a modest smile. "Thank you, Mel. We're just doing our jobs, trying our best. Please, continue to be cautious when you're heading home or walking around the city, especially at night. Hopefully, we can make things truly safe for everyone again soon."

"Do… do you really think you can?" Mel asks, her earlier fear replaced by a fragile hope.

"We're certainly making progress," Sam replies reassuringly, his agent persona firmly back in place. "Keep an eye on the news for updates." She nods, seeming somewhat comforted, then remembers her duties. She efficiently takes our drink orders – coffees all around – and heads off to retrieve them.

"Well," Rose remarks quietly once Mel is out of earshot, "I guess that means she hasn't picked up any fresh gossip since last time, or she probably would have spilt it already."

"Maybe," Luca concedes, "but it might still be worth asking directly later, just in case." He glances towards me again, his eyes briefly scanning my torso and legs, then shakes his head slightly, a look of faint disbelief still on his face. "That ring, Ava… it's truly remarkable.

Incredibly handy. First, enhanced night vision, and now complete weapon concealment? It significantly increases your operational capabilities, makes you exceptionally versatile… and potentially very deadly."

"Having my weapons completely concealed *is* a massive tactical advantage," I agree, a slow, predatory grin spreading across my face as I consider the possibilities. "If no one can see I'm armed, potential adversaries might drop their guard, underestimate me. Think of the scenarios… I could act as bait, pretend to be a lost tourist, just some ordinary woman walking down the street… then spring the trap, take them out before they even realise I'm a threat."

"Okay, now I *am* officially worried," Rose murmurs, shaking her head slightly, though her eyes are gleaming with excitement. "The way you're smiling right now, Ava… it's terrifying."

"Oh, I'm just contemplating all the creative ways we can use this to catch our enemies completely off guard," I reply sweetly, unable to stop grinning. This ring changes everything.

"Now *that* is an excellent strategic possibility," Luca agrees immediately, his own mind clearly running through similar tactical scenarios, nodding slowly.

"Are you serious, Ava?" Sam interjects, looking slightly alarmed. "You actually *want* to deliberately walk into the metaphorical lion's den, looking like easy prey, and then try to take on potentially multiple paranormal targets entirely on your own?"

"It wouldn't exactly be the lion's den, Sam," I counter smoothly. "More like… tactical infiltration using unconventional camouflage. But yes, the principle holds. I could wander the known hunting grounds at night, appearing vulnerable, while you three remain hidden nearby, ready to provide backup or create a diversion. When they inevitably make their move on the 'easy target', you guys emerge, drawing their attention. In that moment of distraction, they forget about me, the 'harmless' civilian… and then," my grin widens, "I remove their heads."

I'm so engrossed in outlining my plan that I fail to notice Mel returning with our drinks until she's right beside the booth. Her face blanches visibly; she must have overheard the tail end of my comment about removing heads. Shit. Think fast.

"Sorry!" I exclaim quickly, forcing a bright, innocent smile. "Just talking about this incredibly violent new zombie video game, my cousin keeps making me play online. He's obsessed with beheading the zombies. It's ridiculously gory," I explain, trying to sound convincingly like a normal person discussing gaming, hoping she buys the flimsy cover story.

Luca and Rose manage to stifle their chuckles, turning them into coughs, while Sam looks utterly horrified that Mel overheard my grim tactical assessment. Thankfully, Mel seems to relax slightly, the colour returning to her face, though she still looks a little shaken. She quickly distributes our drinks and takes our food orders – Luca and Rose again ordering amounts that could feed a small army – before retreating hastily towards the kitchen.

Once she's gone, we quickly finalise our plan for setting up cameras at the church tomorrow, briefly discuss the potential risks and contingencies involved in approaching the church. I reiterate my desire to personally infiltrate the church during daylight hours, perhaps playing the role of a potential convert, but the others unanimously, emphatically shoot down the idea. 'Too reckless', 'unnecessary risk', 'insufficient intel'. They're probably right. Still, the prospect of playing possum, using the ring's concealment to lull an enemy into a false sense of security… it holds a certain professional appeal.

CHAPTER 19

DECAPITATIONS, DECONTAMINATION (MAGICAL AND OTHERWISE), AND
DELIVERING DIPLOMATIC DEVASTATION TO DIFFICULT DUNDERHEADS

After finishing our meal, during which Mel pointedly avoided our booth, sending another server over instead, we paid and left the diner. As we walked back towards the Tahoe, the relative quiet of the evening street was suddenly shattered by a piercing scream echoing off the nearby buildings. It sounds close—terrifyingly close.

We all freeze instantly, heads snapping up, listening intently. Another scream rips through the night air, closer this time, laced with pure terror. We exchange urgent glances.

"That's close, Ava," Luca says grimly, already moving. "Grab your sword. Let's go!"

I wrench open the car's rear door, snatch the sword from the floor where Rose placed it earlier, and slam the door shut. I quickly hand Sam the pistol loaded with wooden rounds from my tactical harness as we break into a run, heading towards the source of the screams. Behind us, I hear the remaining diner patrons spilling out onto the sidewalk, drawn by the sounds of distress, just as a third scream, abruptly cut off, chills me to the bone.

Luca and Rose, their shifter speed already kicking in, pull ahead rapidly, disappearing around a nearby corner into a narrow alleyway. Sam and I pound down the sidewalk after them. I hear a low, vicious growl as we round the corner.

The scene that greets me in the dimly lit alley freezes my blood for a split second. A man is savagely attacking a woman, forcing her back against the graffiti-covered brick wall. He looks crazed, feral, like someone in the grip of a violent drug-induced psychosis. But then I see his head dip towards her neck, jaws wide, fangs elongating, and I know instantly… vampire. My brain momentarily struggles to reconcile the clear view I have when I should be in an oppressive darkness, as we are away from the main streetlights. The ring. It's granting me perfect night vision. At the same moment, movement flickers above. Another figure watches from the rooftop of the building flanking the alley on our left.

"I *told* you fools to leave!" the figure on the roof bellows down at Luca and Rose, who are now engaging the vampire attacking the woman. His voice is distorted, filled with inhuman rage. "If you don't clear out now, I'll make you *both* our next victims! Sticking your nose where they don't belong!" He, too, is clearly not human. Even from this distance, my enhanced vision picks out the details, the burning crimson glow of his eyes, the elongated claws on his hands, the flash of sharp fangs as he snarls. Another vampire.

Without hesitation, I lift my sword as he spots me, his attention shifting towards me. He leaps gracefully down from the rooftop, landing silently on the alley floor, abandoning his initial intent, which I think is to flank Luca and Rose. Instead, he faces off with me, looking like a predator sizing up his prey. He sneers, taking a step towards me, clearly underestimating the threat I pose. Then, his gaze flicks back towards Luca and Rose, who are now fully engaged with his partner further down the alley. Recognition, or perhaps scent, finally dawns on him. "*Shifter*," he hisses, the word filled with a mixture of hatred and sudden apprehension. He immediately abandons his approach towards me, turning back towards the sounds of the struggle, concern for his partner overriding his initial aggression towards us *humans*.

"Incoming!" is all I shout, breaking into a dead sprint, chasing after him down the alley, my sword held ready. Then I realise something else astonishing – I can *track* his movements. Even though he's moving with supernatural speed, he should be a blur to normal human eyes, except I seem to be able to follow his trajectory, anticipate his path. The ring isn't just granting me night vision; it's enhancing my perception, slowing the world down just enough.

Rose spins at my warning shout, reacting instantly, intercepting the second vampire just as he reaches her. Her hands have already shifted, lethal claws extended. I see them flash, slashing downwards across the vampire's chest and face. He hisses in pain and fury, managing to grab her arm, using his strength to slam her hard against the brick wall, the impact sickeningly loud, just like I was flung into the wall in the factory. But unlike me, Rose isn't stunned; she bounces back immediately, launching herself at him again, a whirlwind of claws and fury.

Meanwhile, further down the alley, Luca has dragged the first vampire off the woman. She lies slumped against the wall, unnervingly still, silent. Dead? Or just unconscious? "Sam!" I yell over my shoulder, not breaking stride. "Get the girl! Get her out of here! Now!"

"On it!" he replies immediately from just behind me. Good. At least one innocent might survive this tonight.

I keep pushing, pumping my legs harder, racing towards the frenetic melee where Rose and the second vampire trade vicious blows, claws tearing at clothing and flesh. Luca is still occupied with the first vampire further down, too far away to assist Rose directly. My heart pounds a steady rhythm against my ribs, the familiar battle calm descending, sharpening my focus. I watch their deadly dance, assessing angles, waiting for an opening. Rose, perhaps sensing my approach, or maybe through sheer tactical brilliance, suddenly ducks under a wild swing, grabs the vampire's arm, and uses his momentum to spin him around, forcefully shoving him directly into my path.

A savage grin splits my face. Perfect. Without conscious thought, I adjust my stride, swing the sword high in a glittering arc, leap forward, and bring the blade down with all my strength and momentum in a clean, decisive swing, aiming for the juncture of neck and shoulder just as Rose positions him flawlessly for the killing blow. He sees me coming at the last possible second, his red eyes widening in shock and disbelief as the blade bites deep into his unnatural flesh.

I land lightly on the balls of my feet as the vampire's head separates cleanly from his shoulders, tumbling away with a wet thud. Simultaneously, his body begins to dissolve, crumbling inwards, turning to black ash before my eyes. My forward momentum carries me directly into the disintegrating form. I stumble slightly, crashing through the exploding cloud of ash, the fine, acrid powder instantly coating me from head to foot, filling my mouth, my nostrils, making me gag and cough violently, fighting the urge to vomit up my recently consumed dinner.

Through my watering eyes, I hear another strange, high-pitched screaming hiss from further down the alley. I look towards Luca just in time to see the first vampire dissolving into a similar cloud of ash. Luca must have capitalised on the distraction of his partner's demise. He curses, clutching at his chest, which is now slick with an alarming amount of dark blood, looking more like a scene from a slasher film than a tactical engagement. He staggers slightly, then heads towards us. Seeing me covered head-to-toe in vampire dust, a brief, grim smile touches his lips before his expression sobers, likely contemplating the difficulty of explaining my current state and his.

Rose, however, seems less concerned with explanations. "Well, well," she remarks dryly, shaking her head as she looks me over, picking a fleck of ash from her cheek. "Looks like Ava finally got her wish after all. Saw one go 'poof'," she mimics my earlier hand gesture with theatrical flair, "up close and personal."

"Hilarious," I retort, still coughing, trying to spit out the vile taste of vampire ash. "You are *so* funny right now." Luca can't help but let out a short, sharp chuckle at Rose's dark humour. Rose turns back to me, her amusement fading, replaced by an expression of fierce pride that makes my heart give an unsteady lurch.

Luca reaches us, leaning heavily against the alley wall for support, clearly weakened by blood loss. "Ava," he manages, his voice strained, "you… and I… will need to take the car. Get ourselves cleaned up. Now." He glances towards the mouth of the alley where Sam disappeared with the victim. "Rose, get Sam on the comms. Tell him to call the backup team immediately. Have them dispatch medical for the woman and secure the scene before the locals arrive. We need containment."

I nod in agreement but add my own instruction, "Tell Sam to inform dispatch that we apprehended two suspects, involved in the assault. State we're transporting them immediately to the nearest FBI field office for interrogation under the Domestic Terrorism Act. That should buy us some time, keep local PD off our backs for a while." I turn back to Luca, concern overriding protocol. "I should stay here. Can you drive in your condition?"

"I'll manage," he grits out, pushing himself away from the wall, though he sways slightly. "Rose and Sam can handle things here. You need to get out of here and get cleaned up; you look like you wrestled a chimney sweep, which will be hard to explain."

Rose heads quickly towards the alley entrance, intercepting Sam, who is just returning, his face grim. Even from here, I can tell the woman didn't make it; my stomach clenches. Despite the victory, the cost feels heavy. Luca, though visibly injured and covered in blood, is at least mobile. My current state – coated in incriminating paranormal ash – is far harder to explain away. I wait in the shadows, listening to the distant wail of approaching sirens, until Rose returns with the Tahoe. She pulls up beside me, the passenger door swinging open. I slide in quickly, sinking into the seat, the lingering scent of Rose a strange comfort amidst the peculiar stench of the ash, then Luca replaces Rose in the driver's seat.

"Well done, Ava," Luca says quietly as he pulls away smoothly, expertly navigating the backstreets away from the converging emergency vehicles. "You got your first confirmed vampire kill. And," he adds, glancing over at me, a genuine smile finally reaching his eyes despite the pain evident in his posture, "in truly spectacular fashion, I might add. I saw the whole takedown just as I finished mine. Distracted the hell out of my opponent."

The adrenaline begins to fade as we drive back towards the motel, leaving the attack scene behind. The world outside the windows seems distant, unreal. All I can think about is getting clean, getting safe, and maybe, just maybe, collapsing into bed with Rose's warmth when we can. The thought of Rose is a distant comfort, a beacon I hope to reach soon. But first, the literal and bureaucratic filth has to be dealt with.

The immediate priority upon reaching our motel rooms, our supposed detour to a non-existent field office providing the perfect cover, to get cleaned up. The vampire ash feels like a second skin, gritty and vile. I stand under the scalding spray of the shower for what feels like an eternity, scrubbing until my skin is raw, willing every last particle of the creature down the drain. Stepping out, wrapped in a clean towel, a new curiosity strikes me. My harness and weapons. They'd been as coated in that disgusting ash as I was. Yet, as I inspect them, they seem pristine. Not a speck. Not a trace. Clean. Like I had never been covered in the ash of the vampire. How? The only explanation, as improbable as it seems, has to be the ring. Papa Legba's gift continues to surprise, its magic apparently extending to my accessories.

Once dressed in fresh clothes, the sense of normalcy feels deceptive. To maintain our cover story, I quickly look up the location of the *actual* nearest FBI field office. Close by, thankfully. Always good to have your alibis straight, just in case anyone, like our charming Chief Thornton, decides to get pedantic. Just then, my phone buzzes. A message from Sam. *'At police HQ. Thornton's on a tear. Meet us here. He's already asked about the field office transfer and confirmed the one you'd use.'* So much for a quiet debrief.

Luca, patched up as best as he can be for now but still looking paler than I like, drives us to the police headquarters. The usual swarm of media vultures hasn't descended yet – a small mercy. Still, caution dictates parking a block away and approaching the station on foot to remain inconspicuous. The moment we step inside the familiar, dreary building, the sound of Chief Thornton's voice rises in its customary belligerent bellow, assaults our ears. He's, predictably, already laying into Sam. As we pass the front desk, snippets of his tirade are impossible to miss.

"…want those prisoners here, Agent Miller! Here! So, *my* detectives can question them! You feds had no damn right to spirit them away! This is *my* city, my jurisdiction!" Thornton roars, his face flushed a dangerous shade of puce. I barely suppress a groan; the man is a broken record of territorial bullshit. His eyes, bulging slightly, swivel and lock onto me as I approach with Luca. Like a bull spotting a new red cape, he redirects his venom. "Agent Bekke! Finally! Where are my prisoners? The ones your team supposedly apprehended?" His tone is dripping with sarcasm and accusation.

I meet his glare with my practised, cool composure, the one that always seems to infuriate him further. "Chief Thornton," I begin, my voice even, professional, "The individuals involved in tonight's violent assault, which, I remind you, targeted federal agents as well as a civilian, were apprehended under suspicion of activities falling under the Domestic Terrorism Act. As such, their custody and interrogation fall squarely within federal jurisdiction. My agents are currently conducting those interrogations at a secure FBI facility. We will, of course, notify your department of any actionable intelligence that pertains directly to local statutes and does not compromise the ongoing federal investigation."

Thornton's jaw clenches, and he opens his mouth, undoubtedly to repeat his 'this is my city' mantra. I'm not in the mood for an encore. "Chief Thornton," I cut in smoothly, my voice dropping slightly, hardening just enough to carry an unmistakable edge of authority, "with all due respect, we've had this discussion before. Multiple times. I am the lead agent of this joint task force, vested with the authority to conduct this investigation as my team and I deem appropriate to ensure its success and the safety of this city's inhabitants. Your involvement, while potentially valuable, is contingent on cooperation, not obstruction. Frankly, your current approach is counterproductive. We are here to help *your* city, to protect *your* people. It would be far more efficient if you stopped working *against* us and started working *with* us. Until I see a genuine willingness to do that, your direct involvement will remain limited."

He stares, his eyes narrow, clearly trying for intimidation. The usual power play. And, as usual, it bounces right off me. I hold his gaze, unwavering, until he is the one to break contact, spinning on his heel with a frustrated snort. He stomps into his office, the door slamming shut behind him with a reverberating crack that speaks volumes of his impotent fury.

I let out a slow breath I hadn't realised I was holding, turning to my team. Luca is sporting a small, impressed smile, though he still leans subtly against the wall for support. Sam, on the other hand, looks like he'd just swallowed a particularly sour lemon, his brow furrowed with worry.

"What is it, Sam?" I ask, though I have a pretty good idea.

"Ava, do you *have* to keep poking the bear like that?" he asks, his voice a low, anxious murmur. "He's the Chief of Police, for crying out loud!"

A flash of irritation sparks through me, not just at Thornton, but now at Sam's timidity. "I don't 'poke bears,' Sam. I refuse to be bullied or to let an inflated ego impede a critical investigation. Especially not his. He's a liability when he's like this." Frankly, dealing with local political bullshit is supposed to be *his* forte, not mine. His current failure to manage Thornton is just adding to my frustration.

Without waiting for a response, I turn and head back towards the station exit, my patience officially depleted. I feel an exhaustion wash over me, more mentally than physically, the thought of sleep – and Rose – is an increasingly urgent siren song. As I walk through the main bullpen, however, several of the uniformed officers look up. I receive a few subtle nods, a couple of quiet, almost grateful 'Agent Bekke's.

Small acknowledgements, but they are enough to slightly lift the weight of annoyance, a reminder that not everyone in this building is an obstacle. I offer a curt nod in return before pushing through the doors and back out into the relative calm of the night.

CHAPTER 20

JUMPING TO CONCLUSIONS AND ALMOST OFF A
RELATIONSHIP CLIFF

I reach our car first, just before news crews start to turn up. Not long after, Luca and Rose reach the car and get in. Both look worried. "Are you okay, Ava?" Luca asks, turning around in the front passenger seat to look back at me.

"I'm fine," I say, my tone sharper than I intend. "It's just that guy's attitude is getting on my last nerve, so is Sam. He is supposed to be dealing with this crap, not me." My frustration is evident.

"Sam says the Chief won't deal with him as you're the head of the task force," Luca explains, his expression serious. "And he clearly has an issue with you, which I believe has something to do with his digging into your background." He's not wrong; I'm sure that's a big part of it. The thought just sours my mood further.

"Maybe Agent Moore should have thought about this and removed my military records, or at least the more sensitive stuff," I shoot back, still on edge. The whole situation is a mess.

"Um… I believe he did," Luca says sheepishly, avoiding my gaze for a second. "He thought about removing parts, but then said there was so much, he wiped it all and replaced it with something more suited for the FBI."

My head snaps up. I gape at him. "Then how did he find out about my past?" The question hangs heavy in the air.

"Sam thinks his contact knows of you, and that's how he got the details," Luca says, his voice low. "Sam mentioned this while I was training him. He says he's looking into who his contact might be so he can get Adam onto it." That's at least something, though the idea of my past being so easily accessible is unsettling.

"Where is Sam anyway?" I ask, needing to change the subject before I dwell on it too much.

"He told us he was going to give a press release," Rose explains from beside Luca, her voice calm as ever. "Saying that while we were eating out in a local establishment, we heard screams, so we investigated and saved a woman from an attack, capturing two suspects. The FBI has taken them into custody under the terrorism act." I just nod, not saying anything as I try to push down the knot of irritation and anxiety in my gut, even though that's a lie, as the woman died anyway.

"Ava, we don't have enough time right now." I lift my head to face Luca as he speaks, his tone ominous. "I need to talk to you concerning your relationship with Rose, how it will affect you, and things you need to know about." When he finishes, it causes me to frown; I turn my head to Rose for answers, a new wave of apprehension washing over me.

"Luca! Is now really the time for this?" Rose says, evident frustration etching lines on her face. "Ava has had a lot to deal with, and adding to it this soon isn't going to help. I was going to slowly bring up some of the subjects when I felt the time was right." She reaches over and grabs my hand, offering comfort, but the gesture does little to ease the sudden tension.

I look between them as they stare at each other, a silent battle of wills passing between them, effectively ignoring me. "What do I need to know?" I say through gritted teeth, my frustration and anger bubbling up again, I'm not going to get my answer now, though. Sam walks up and gets in the car, oblivious to the charged atmosphere.

Luca just manages a terse, "We will talk."

I shake my head, turning to look out of the window as we pull away. Rose gives my hand another quick, reassuring squeeze before she lets go, a subtle movement Sam won't notice.

As we pull away, I put my frustration to one side and ask Luca, "Are you going to be okay? You got some injuries back there?"

"Yeah, I'll be fine; I'll be healed by morning. It looks worse than it is," Luca says as he looks at me through the rearview mirror.

"Really, that's so unfair," I say and turn back to looking out the window. My comment makes everyone chuckle.

We drive back to the motel in a strained silence, at least on my part. Sam explains the press release he gave, but I don't pay attention, nor do I say anything. I just sit there, stewing. When we park, I get out immediately, head straight to my room, and let myself in, needing space. Rose follows me shortly after, murmuring a goodnight to the others before closing the door behind her. She pauses near the door, looking at me briefly as I methodically remove all my weapons, laying them out on the cheap motel dresser. Then, she approaches and hugs me. I fight the embrace for a split second, my body rigid, but then I give in, the tension draining out of me with a sigh.

Rose whispers in my ear, "Sorry, honey."

I wrap my arms around her waist, pulling her closer. The heat radiating from her body soaks into me, instantly relaxing my coiled muscles. "It's okay," I murmur into her shoulder. "What is it I need to know? Also, why are you so hot? I've been meaning to ask."

Rose chuckles, a soft sound against my ear. "Thanks, I'm glad you think I'm hot."

I give her a light, playful slap on her arm before responding, "You know what I mean. Why do you give off so much heat? Don't get me wrong; I like it—I love it, actually—but I'm just wondering." It's a genuine curiosity.

"It's hard to explain," Rose says, her voice thoughtful as she pulls back slightly to look at me. "It has something to do with being a shifter. Our animals generate heat. It's great in winter, as we never get cold, and it helps regulate our temperature better in the summer. I'm actually surprised you're able to fall asleep on top of me during these summer months, because I'm even hotter than usual." As she explains this, I listen, intrigued by the mechanics of it all. However, the way she says *her animal* sparks another question.

"Why do you call it *your animal*?" I ask, burying my head into her shoulder, trying to absorb more of her comforting heat. "It's you, isn't it? You're the animal as well?" My understanding of shifters is clearly still very basic. Her answer isn't what I expect and makes me pull back to look at her.

"Well… yes and no," she says, a slight hesitation in her voice. "Our animals are a part of us. However, they have their own instincts and thoughts, which I can guide, but they also have their own minds in a way. Nevertheless, we share the same brain and memories. When I shift, I let her take over."

"What!" The word escapes me, my voice more like a mouse's squeak than anything human. My mind struggles to process this new information.

"Yeah, this is part of what Luca wants to talk to you about," Rose explains, and I feel her body shift, stiffening slightly as if she's worried about my reaction. My high-pitched squeak probably didn't help matters. "There is a lot you still don't know. We have a lot of customs you may feel very awkward about, and will probably find very uncomfortable taking part in, especially being human." As she speaks, another thought pops into my mind, a more pressing concern.

"If… the animal in you has its own mind," I begin slowly, trying to piece it together, "does it have an opinion about you falling for a human? And when I pet you in animal form, is it *you* I'm petting, or her?"

Rose doesn't answer immediately. She goes ramrod straight, her expression unreadable. I am now properly worried, a cold dread seeping into me. *Her animal side doesn't like her falling for a weak human like me. I knew things were too good to be true. Maybe this is why Luca wants to talk to me; Rose is scared to tell me herself.* As usual, my mouth engages before my brain has a chance to fully process the implications. "Your animal side doesn't like you falling for a weak human, and it's causing you problems, isn't it?" I say the words, they tumble out, my voice flat as I try to keep my emotions in check. I try to pull away from her, intending to finish getting undressed and climb into bed alone, hoping I can keep the inevitable tears from falling in front of her.

"Ava." Her voice is soft but firm.

"No, it's fine. I understand," I interrupt, pushing down the lump forming in my throat. "Maybe this wasn't a good idea anyway." I try to push her away again, but she holds onto me, her grip surprisingly strong.

"Rose, please, just let me go," I say, my eyes starting to get watery. I curse myself internally for this emotional fragility. *What is wrong with me? Since I met Rose, it's like the lock on my emotions has rusted and broken, letting everything out all at once, leaving me with no chance of keeping them under control.* An idea, a desperate one, comes to mind. Rose mentioned how to break a bond, you have to look your other half in the eyes and say you reject them. I'm not sure it will work since we've already accepted the bond, but it's worth a try if it will allow her to make peace with her panther.

I'm about to turn and face her, to utter the words I already regret, when Rose takes me completely by surprise. She starts to growl, a low, guttural sound rumbling in her chest, and at the same time, I feel her hands begin to shift against my back, nails elongating, pressing into my skin.

Her panther must be furious with her, forcing the shift. My eyes go wide, my head shooting up to look at her face, trying to see if she's losing control, if her panther is about to take over completely. As I look her in the eyes, I see my chance to fix this, to free her. I find anger in her eyes, yes, but also something else I can't quite decipher. The set of her jaw is hard as it, too, starts to shift. I try to push her away again, a surge of panic lending me strength, but she still won't let me go.

I'm about to say, '*I reject you,*' the words burning my tongue, when Rose speaks, her voice tight, teeth gritted. "Ava, if you had just let me explain, you wouldn't be saying such ridiculous things that are making me incredibly mad right now. I want to let you keep thinking your stupid thoughts are correct, just to teach you a lesson, but I'm not that cruel. And my panther wouldn't let me be, either."

I hold off on the rejection phrase, her words cutting through my panic. I run through what she just said, trying to hold back the tears that are now almost impossible to contain. "Fine," I manage, my voice cracked with emotion, betraying how close I am to crying. "Explain."

Rose pulls me back against her body, her strength easily overwhelming mine. She sighs, a profound, long exhalation that seems to carry a world of frustration.

"Oh, Ava," she murmurs, her voice softer now. "She has nothing against you. In fact, you've pissed *her* off more than you've pissed *me* off, because she's the one that *causes* the bond. In our history, it's said that the gods granted shifters the bond so our animal side can recognise when they find their perfect mate. This bond is also said to be an indicator that your prime mate will allow you to strengthen the bloodlines."

Rose takes a calming breath, her chest rising and falling against me. "I don't see how that would work for me, with you being human, but clearly, the gods have decided we are meant to be together, that you are mine and my pantheress's perfect mate. As I said before, I never expected it to happen to me, but it did. The way I feel about you is genuine, Ava, and so are my panther's feelings for you. They're the same as mine. She is so happy that we found you. She loved it when you accepted her, when you rubbed your face against hers and then ran your hands through her fur."

I don't know what to say. Here I am, moments from trying to break the bond because I jumped to the idiotic conclusion that her panther was rejecting me. I might be good at my job, a competent soldier, but I clearly don't know the first thing about emotions and relationships. The control I usually maintain over my feelings shatters, and the tears finally start to fall, not running down my cheeks but soaking directly into Rose's top as I press my face against her. My crying isn't quiet, either; it's a series of ragged, hiccupping sobs. Rose just holds me, rocking me slightly in her arms.

CHAPTER 21

BEDTIME BANTER, BIZARRE BONDING RITUALS (HELLO, PUPPY PILES!),
AND BARGAINING (BADLY) WITH BONE-CLAD BAR PATRONS FROM MY
NIGHTMARES

It takes a while before I can speak again. I hate how I've become so… *girly* recently. I've cried more since I met Rose than I have in all the years since I was a teenager, back when I locked down my emotions upon enlisting.

"Are you sure?" I finally choked out, my voice muffled against her shirt. "There are no issues. Everything is okay?"

"Ava, everything between us is great," she says, her voice firm but gentle, though I can hear a hint of lingering annoyance towards the end. "There is nothing wrong with us. Unless you keep saying stupid stuff like that, *then* we will have a problem."

"Then what problem does Luca need to talk to me about?" I ask, pulling back just enough to see her face.

"Ava, there are rules about dating within the pack, and even when dating outside of it. Normally, the Alpha would have to agree to me dating outside the pack, but with the bond, he lost his right to give or deny permission. However, there are still other rules and customs he needs to ensure you're aware of. Then… there are times when, as a pack, we kind of…." She hesitates, a blush creeping up her neck.

I look at her, sensing her discomfort. "What?"

"I'm not sure how to explain it without it sounding… sordid, to a human," she says, her voice getting quieter. "But it's a normal shifter thing. I guess the best way to describe it to you is… we have times when we sleep as a… you would call it a puppy pile or a bundle." She explains this, her gaze dropping for a moment.

"Oh," is all I manage to say as her words sink in. They all sleep together as a pack sometimes. She's trying to explain that it isn't a sexual thing, but still, the thought of it makes me feel incredibly awkward.

"Ava, you don't have to take part," she quickly adds, sensing my unease. "But it's something our animal side needs, so I stay in animal form, like everyone else, and we just bundle in together. We do it in human form sometimes too, as nudity isn't really an issue with us, but humans who have joined our pack in the past have sometimes had issues with it. You'll notice I touch you a lot, whenever I can. We *need* to touch. Our animal side needs that physical contact to feel part of the pack, to feel secure. So, you'll notice it a lot when you finally meet what's left of Luca's pack. It's one of the main things he wanted to talk to you about, so you wouldn't react badly when the others touch you a lot. Luca is trying to stop himself from doing it with you at the moment, until we are able to explain things."

"Okay," I say slowly, processing this. "I guess I can get used to that. I wouldn't call myself a prude, so… we will have to see how I do." I start to calm down, the earlier panic receding. "Sorry for jumping to conclusions again, and if I upset you both. Also," a new, slightly awkward thought occurs to me, "does this mean I'm dating two people? Erm, beings? I don't know what to call it." I feel my cheeks heat up.

Rose chuckles, the tension finally breaking. "Ava, yes, you have technically got two girlfriends. Live with it."

"Okay," I say, a small smile playing on my lips despite myself. "I feel… special, lucky. But don't you get jealous? What if I enjoy running my hands over your animal's fur so much that I want you to always shift for me?" I ask, a little worried about what she might say.

"Honey, it wouldn't bother me in the slightest," Rose says, her smile widening. "I'm one with my animal side. When you stroke her, you are stroking me too. I feel it, too, so don't worry. And on the flip side, she feels everything I feel. She even… poked her head out, so to speak, when you screamed and caused those issues with next door,"

Rose finishes with the dirtiest, most suggestive smile I have ever seen on her face.

My jaw drops at the admission. "I did not scream!" I protest, with a fake annoyance I don't entirely feel. "I would remember if I screamed." I deliberately don't respond to the part about her animal side 'poking its head out,' because I had kind of already guessed something like that, given the faint claw marks on my back that, surprisingly, still don't itch or hurt.

After my emotional rollercoaster, where I very nearly destroyed something incredibly good and special, we finally get ready for bed. Rose gets into bed first, sliding under the covers. I hesitate, feeling awkward, suddenly unsure if she will even want me to join her after I let my paranoid brain run wild. But when Rose sees me hesitating, she pats the other side of the bed, a clear invitation. Relief washes over me, and I quickly slide into bed beside her. As soon as I slip under the covers, Rose wraps an arm around my waist and tugs me into her side, ensuring my head is resting comfortably on her shoulder. I sigh in contentment as the incredible heat coming off her starts to soak into my skin, chasing away the last vestiges of my earlier chill. I'm not having any issues with the heat radiating from her; I've spent most of my career in hot countries, so this is nothing new. In fact, I hate winters now because the cold always seems to get right into my bones. Maybe the winters won't be so bad from now on, at least until I have to return to my usual, solitary job.

I fall asleep pretty quickly, nestled against her warmth. I'm not sure how long I have been asleep, when I have the distinct sensation that I am starting to wake up. It seems far too soon. When I open my eyes, I know instantly I'm not in the motel room anymore. I suddenly find myself sitting in a rustic, dimly lit bar. I look around, my heart beginning to pound with panic. The place is completely empty, apart from the sound of soft jazz music playing in the background. Then, a voice makes me jump, because it comes from right next to me, where no one was a second ago. I spin around and find someone—well, *something*—sitting close to me in the booth I now realise I'm occupying.

He looks like a skeleton, but one wrapped in a tight, leathery layer of skin, like old parchment. He's wearing an old-fashioned, somewhat dapper suit, complete with a top hat, and he holds a cane in one bony hand. Even though he doesn't look remotely human, there's still an odd look about him that isn't wholly horrifying; in fact, it's somehow… almost appealing, which immediately makes me feel grossed out by my reaction. *Maybe he has some kind of magic that makes him seem appealing. Whatever it is, I feel distinctly yucky.*

"Hello there, Ava," he says, his voice a deep, smooth southern drawl that seems to echo in the silence of the strange bar.

"Who are you?" I demand, my voice coming out a little shakier than I'd like. "What do you want?" My hand instinctively goes to where my sidearm would normally be, but of course, it's not there.

"Well now, I'm just lookin' to see if you take a likin' to my little gift," he says, his gaze flickering down to my hand. When I follow his line of sight, I see the ring, the one Madi gave me, still on my finger. I try to touch it with my other hand, but my fingers pass straight through it, making contact only with my skin beneath. It's there, but not physically tangible in this place.

I look back up at him, a flicker of understanding dawning. "Do you mean this ring?" I ask, raising my hand. It's still a beautiful, if unsettling, piece of jewellery.

That's when it clicks. I realise who I must be sitting with. I gasp, taking him in again, this time with dawning recognition. I manage to pull my jaw off the metaphorical table, and he chuckles lightly, a dry, rustling sound. "You're Papa Legba," I state, more than ask.

He tips his hat slightly in my direction. "At your service, child," he responds, a slow smile spreading across his leathery face. "Yes, I surely did mean that ring."

"Why am I here?" I ask, my mind racing. "In this… dream bar?

Is this a dream, or have you somehow kidnapped me?" The panic is still there, a cold knot in my stomach.

"I sensed it when you went and put that ring on, darlin'," he says, his voice calm and unhurried. "I do believe you've already taken out your first vampire with its help. Good job. You are, indeed, still asleep in your bed. I just took advantage of you havin' no mental defences right now to come and pay you a little visit. You surely oughta work on that, y'know. Need to be thinkin' of a sturdy wall all 'round your mind, picture it strong, unbreachable. You don't have magic, not like some others do, though, truth be told, all humans possess a little spark, in their own way, so it ain't gonna be easy for you. But if you train yourself at it, real diligent and for a good long stretch, you'll start to build up some proper defences. Never can tell, that little ol' ring there might even help things along."

"Thanks… I think," I say, trying to absorb his advice even as a thousand other questions vie for attention. "I'll get on that. But again, why am I here? Why visit me?"

"I do find myself mighty intrigued by you, child," he says, his dark eyes fixing on me with an unnerving intensity. "I gave you that ring because, you bein' the first human ever linked to a shifter through a true mate bond, I was wantin' to see if I could sense anythin'… out of the ordinary from you in person. Perhaps a little trace of shifter in your bloodline from way back yonder, somethin' like that. There is somethin' 'bout you that feels… familiar, and I do believe I know what it is. Makes you right special. So, I gave you the ring to help keep you safe, to make certain you stay alive long enough for us all to see what interestin' paths your future might take you down." He says this as his intense eyes bore into me, making me feel like I'm a specimen being studied for some arcane psychological experiment. Then he says something that throws me completely off balance. "She ain't goin' to be none too pleased when she finds out I gave you that ring, mind. But she will come 'round to seein' it's a good idea, in the long run."

"Who?" I ask immediately. "Who are you talking about?"

"Ah, now that particular thing, I can't be tellin' you her real name, I'm afraid," he says, with a look that almost seems like genuine apology. "She needs to keep what she's doin' a real close-guarded secret for as long as humanly—or otherwise—can be managed, so they can't put a stop to her. Otherwise, this whole grand notion might just fall apart somethin' awful."

"Has this plan got something to do with me?" I ask, a fresh wave of worry washing over me. I don't like the idea of my life being manipulated by unseen forces.

"No, as it happens, that plan itself has nothin' directly to do with you, child. Truth is, she ain't entirely certain 'bout you at all. She was shown a vision, y'see, but she doesn't recall seein' your particular face in it."

"Luca said he heard a female voice tell him to seek out Agent Moore," I say, connecting the dots, or trying to. "So, her plan, whoever she is, was to involve Luca from the start. What does that mean for Rose and me? Were we just… an accident?"

As things usually go with me, my mouth engages before my brain has fully caught up. "So, I have nothing to do with any of this? What about Rose?"

He steeples his long, bony fingers and leans forward slightly, his eyes glinting in the dim light. "We ain't entirely sure 'bout that part just yet, darlin'. It wasn't meant to be Rose accompanyin' him, y'understand. Supposed to be his other beta comin' along with Luca. Elijah. She was fully countin' on Luca to bring him, not Rose. But then, o' course, we didn't figure on Agent Moore pickin' you for this assignment, and then Luca decidin' not to crowd you with so much… testosterone, as you might say. She ain't one bit pleased her carefully laid plans aren't rollin' out quite as smooth as she'd hoped," he explains, a hint of amusement in his tone.

I think about what he's saying, and I can feel myself getting annoyed. He carries on, oblivious or indifferent to my rising irritation. "She was mighty set on Elijah and Reya, gettin' themselves involved romantically. But it seems what she hoped for there can't happen now, 'cause young Reya has gone and formed a bond with somethin' else entirely unexpected. Now that *there* is somethin' that piques my interest even more than your own unique spot of bother," he says, his eyes taking on a distant, far-off look for a moment.

I am really getting annoyed now. Whoever this mysterious 'she' is, she's actively trying to mess with people's lives to get her own way, and that, in turn, has directly affected my life as well. Though I have to admit, it also brought Rose and me together. I can never truly be sorry for meeting Rose. "Why is she doing all this?" I demand. "Why is it so important for her to mess with things and people like she is?"

"Ah, well, that there's the heart of it, ain't it, child?" Papa Legba says, his gaze returning to me. "I told her, plain as the nose on your face, that the vision she was shown might still happen even *with* her considerable meddlin'. She set certain… events in motion some thirty years back, when she first caught wind of nefarious plans to attack the four main realms, but she couldn't rightly pinpoint who was behind it all, or exactly when it was all gonna go down. And everythin' she tried to do to stop it, well, it didn't halt things, not really. So, she gathered a few of us influential types to cook up a sort of fallback plan, somethin' to give the world a fightin' chance, a little glimmer of hope. Even tho' that doesn't seem to be panin' out entirely as she planned, I do confess. Bottom line is, darlin', H…Cat saw a horrific vision of the world bein' completely overrun by all sorts of paranormals, and countless humans bein'… slaughtered." He says this last part slowly, watching my reaction intently. He gets one. I gasp, my jaw dropping as a visceral panic starts to rise in me at the sheer horror of what he's describing.

"How do we stop that?" I ask, my voice barely a whisper, my heart starting to race uncontrollably. I can feel myself fidgeting in distress in the real world, a vague awareness of Rose shifting beside me, and the bar around me begins to blur at the edges. Papa Legba reaches over with surprising speed and grabs my wrist, his touch shockingly warm but firm. The bar snaps back into sharp focus just as I feel Rose stroke my hair in my sleep, a distant attempt to calm whatever nightmare she thinks I'm having.

"Not just yet, child," Papa Legba says, his voice a little softer now. "My apologies if that's overly distressin' for you to take in. She's particularly… vexed, you might say, on account of a certain book just now. The amusin' part is, she doesn't yet realise I'm the one behind that book, well, diary, to be exact. Anyway, I figured you, of all folks, deserve some manner of explanation, seein' as you ain't truly part of this paranormal world and by rights oughta choose how your own life unfolds. I have this powerful feelin', y'see, that you're far more important than anyone's yet grasped. I don't rightly know just how important you'll end up bein', or whether your part will be to help us or stand against us. I confess, I'm mighty keen to find out. What I am sure of, however, is that they, all of 'em—might very well need your own special kind of help with what's undoubtedly on its way." He says this as he stares deep into my eyes, as if he's trying to see something hidden in the very depths of my soul.

I relax, just a little, as I listen to him, though the fear is still a cold weight inside me. Fear of him, this ancient demon, god, and fear of his apocalyptic pronouncements about the human race being slaughtered. "I wish you had kept all of that to yourself," I say, my voice weak, a tone I despise in myself.

After I take a deep, steadying breath to try and calm myself, I continue, a new resolve hardening within me. "Right now, a part of me wants to run for the hills and become some sort of doomsday prepper, waiting for the end of the world. But that's not me. I am a fighter, not a runner. I just… I need to work out how I'm going to explain all of this to Rose," I say, already trying to figure out the best, least terrifying way to do it.

"I'd much rather you kept this little talk between us, if that's at all possible, child," Papa Legba says, his tone becoming serious again. "So that the wrong people don't find out before the time is right."

I baulk at that immediately, shaking my head firmly. No way

am I going to keep something this monumental from Rose. That wouldn't go well at all if I started our relationship by keeping secrets of this magnitude from her, by lying through omission. I'm upfront with things; it's who I am. "I won't keep anything from Rose," I state unequivocally, staring him down, hoping he gets the message that I am absolutely serious about this. "Sorry, but if you didn't want me to say anything to anyone, especially her, you shouldn't have told me in the first place."

Papa Legba watches me for what feels like an uncomfortably long amount of time, his expression unreadable. Then, he finally speaks, a sigh escaping his lips that sounds like dry leaves skittering across pavement. "Figured as much. Very well, child. Fine. But you best remember this, you owe me a favour now. I've managed, through a power of effort, to keep my beloved New Orleans mostly clear of this growin' war. But as the enemy keeps buildin' their strength, they'll come for me and my city sooner or later, once more. When that fateful day comes 'round, I surely hope you'll come and repay the debt you now owe me. I'll send Madiya to fetch you when it happens, should you prove… hesitant, or perhaps forgetful, in payin' what you owe. And you had best hope, for your own sake, that I'm destroyed right along with Madiya if it comes to that. Because she *will* come for you if I can't claim my due. Also, you keep this in mind, Madiya ain't necessarily your enemy, Ava. She can be a powerful friend to you, if you let her."

Before I can protest that I didn't actually agree to any kind of deal, that I owe him nothing, that I'm not at all sure I could ever trust Madi, he waves his bony hand in front of my face in a dismissive gesture. As he does, I feel myself sinking back, the rustic bar and its strange occupant receding into the welcoming darkness of deep sleep.

"It was… right illuminatin' seein' you, Ava," I hear his voice say, fading as he and the bar vanish completely into the blackness. "I surely do hope you impress me, child, just like I reckon you will. I will also be looking for a weapon for you to use, that will help you just as much as the ring has." He's gone before I can protest.

CHAPTER 22

I wake abruptly, surfacing from the depths of sleep, not gently, but wrenched back into consciousness. For a baffling moment, the dim light filtering through the motel room curtains battles with the lingering images of the dream bar – Papa Legba's intense gaze. My heart gives a nervous flutter. I find myself cradled securely in Rose's arms, her steady breathing a warm rhythm against my back. Her scent is a comforting anchor, dispelling the unsettling echoes of the dream encounter.

My voice is thick, scratchy from sleep and disuse when I finally manage to speak. "What's wrong?" I mumble, my head still fuzzy. A moment of déjà vu washes over me – the sensation of being calmed, Rose's hand stroking my hair. Then the memory slams into me with full force. "Papa Legba," I blurt out, the name escaping before I can think, jolting upright so fast my head swims.

Rose tightens her grip, pulling me back against her solid warmth. "Ava, what's wrong?" she asks, her voice husky with sleep but laced with immediate concern. "You were thrashing about earlier, crying out in your sleep. You said his name then, too."

"He paid me a visit," I say, the words tumbling out as the dream's reality solidifies in my mind. "In a dream."

"Honey, it was just a dream, that's all," she murmurs soothingly, trying to calm me. But I shake my head against her shoulder, the movement small but insistent.

"No, Rose, I don't think it was," I insist, the certainty chilling despite the warmth of her embrace. "I think it was real." I quickly recount the conversation, the details sharp and vivid in my memory – the bar, his appearance, the cryptic warnings, the favour owed, the mention of Elijah and Reya.

As I speak, I feel Rose stiffen when I mention Elijah's name, her breath catches. "So, this Cat, the voice you heard at the ranch," she clarifies, her tone sharpening with focus, "she was hoping for Elijah to meet someone named Reya, whom she's protecting? But that plan's kaput because this Reya has now bonded with *something* else, not *someone* else?"

Her focus narrows to that one detail, momentarily baffling me. "Yes," I confirm, slightly exasperated. "He specifically said *something* else. Why? Does that detail matter so much compared to, you know, the visions of human slaughter?"

Rose shifts, pulling back slightly so she can look at me, her brow furrowed in concentration. "Because I've heard old tales… stories about witches forming bonds with creatures, familiars, using them as sentries, weapons, spies… but that doesn't quite fit." She shakes her head, dismissing the thought. "Then there's the other… Daemons. I can't quite recall the specifics of those legends…"

"Daemons?" I echo. "Not demons like Madi?"

"Yes, exactly," Rose confirms, nodding slowly. "The original Daemons, who were known as the fallen angels, created the lesser demons, that's what the legends claim anyway. It's all tangled history, hard to know what's true anymore."

"I still can't believe angels and everything else you and Luca have told me about are real. I don't think I will truly believe it until I see them for myself," I say as I shake my head and smile at Rose.

"They are, I've never seen one though," Rose sighs. The weight of this ever-expanding paranormal world is starting to press down on me. "Reapers, which are lesser angels, apparently can shroud themselves, making them invisible. Luca once mentioned to me that you might feel a chill wash over you if one passes close by while collecting a soul."

The memory of unexplained cold spots from past missions sends an involuntary shudder through me. I mentally shove the image of a Grim Reaper lurking nearby firmly away. "Okay, enough about reapers and daemons before I freak myself out completely," I say, forcing a lighter tone. "Tell me about Elijah. Why would Cat be so interested in him?"

Rose considers this, her gaze thoughtful. "I'm honestly not sure what makes him so special to her plans," she admits. "The main thing about Elijah is that he's a dual shifter. It's rare, but it usually happens when both parents are different types of shifters. Most offspring take after only one parent. But," she adds, anticipating my next question, "it means both his forms are slightly weaker than a single-form shifter. That's the trade-off."

"Weaker? But he's still a beta?" I ask, confused. That doesn't track with the pack hierarchy Luca described back at the ranch.

"He might not have the raw strength of, say, Luca or me in panther form," Rose clarifies, "but he compensates. He's incredibly fast and agile, and he can shift between his two forms – a large eagle and a standard-sized cheetah – quicker than anyone I've ever seen. It's disorienting in a fight."

"Wow," I breathe, imagining it – talons and beak replaced by claws and teeth in a dizzying blur. "Okay, I can see how that combination would be effective."

"He's definitely impressive to watch," Rose agrees. "But still… special enough to hinge a world-saving plan on? Why would bonding with this Reya be the key?"

"Maybe we'll find out eventually," I say, then pause as another memory surfaces. Rose has moved closer again, her face nuzzling the back of my head, and I hear her take a long, slow inhale through her nose. The action feels strangely intimate. "Hey," I begin, shifting slightly, "what was that?" The earlier memory of her breathing me in returns. "Are you… smelling me again? Do I need a shower?"

She chuckles softly against my hair. "You do smell," she confirms, and I tense, mortified, before she continues, her voice turning warm, almost reverent. "You smell like home, Ava. Like a forest on a summer evening after rain, cool and clean, with just a hint of vanilla underneath." She takes another deep breath, her eyes closing briefly. "It took you long enough to notice. I've been doing it since we met. Your scent… it drew me in from the start, but now," she nuzzles closer, "it's even stronger. Perfect. There's nothing better."

Her words make me feel both awkward and incredibly cherished. *Perfect? Me? Smelling like a forest?* It's bizarre, yet undeniably appealing. "Pervert," I murmur, nudging her gently, although there's no heat behind the word. How can a person smell like that? Then again, how can a person turn into a panther? I decide firmly that some shifter mysteries are best left unexplored, especially those involving scents and arousal.

We start to get ready, the easy domesticity a stark contrast to the danger and revelations swirling around us. I pull on my usual black jeans and a dark grey T-shirt, adding my worn leather jacket over my body harness as the air holds a surprising coolness for June, the familiar weight settling against me. Then, I slide the sword into its sheath. As I do, I catch Rose watching me, an appreciative glint in her eyes.

"What's up?" I ask, instinctively checking my reflection for anything amiss. Even in the mirror, the weapons are plainly visible to me, a phantom weight no one else can perceive.

"It's just… amazing," Rose says, shaking her head slightly. "Watching them vanish the moment you let go. One second, I see a formidable arsenal, the next… just you. I can't even feel them when I touch you. It's incredible, Ava. You're literally our secret weapon."

A thrill shoots through me at her words. *Secret weapon.* I like the sound of that. A flicker of the future crosses my mind – returning to my old life, this ring making my solitary work lethally efficient. But then... what about Rose? The thought brings a sharp pang, a complication I immediately shelve. We have this mission that might be a long fight first.

"I love this sword," I say, changing the subject, running a hand almost reverently over the hilt that juts out over my shoulder. "Still surprised the CIA had something like this just lying around."

"Oh, they didn't make it," Rose clarifies. "Turns out, after the attacks back in 2000, the FBI collected a load of strange artefacts left behind at various scenes. Apparently, it's all stored in some secret evidence warehouse. Adam took us there initially, hoping we'd find useful weapons. Most of it was junk, but then we saw the swords... he said someone tried to destroy a lot of the evidence back then, incinerate it, but some things, like your sword, survived."

"Wow," I breathe, fascinated. "A warehouse full of potentially magical artefacts? I'd love to see that sometime."

"Maybe Adam will take you, if you ask nicely and we ever get a day off," Rose replies with a smile.

I make a mental note to do just that. We then meet the guys outside; the air is still cool and carries the scent of damp earth from an earlier drizzle. We pile into the Tahoe and set off for our now-customary late breakfast, seeking out the diner where Mel works, hoping for more local gossip, unfortunately, it's too early to ask Mel herself.

This time, however, the diner feels different. As Luca pushes the door open and steps inside, an unnatural hush descends over the place. Chatter ceases, cutlery clatters against plates, then falls silent. Every single patron slowly turns, their eyes fixed on us. It's unnervingly silent, the only sound being the low hum of the refrigerators and the distant sizzle from the kitchen. It feels just like that scene in old horror films, the one where outsiders enter the creepy small-town pub, and everything simply... stops, and the patrons all stare at the newcomers.

"Not creepy at all," I whisper, mostly to myself, the words

barely audible. Rose snorts softly beside me. My skin prickles, an inexplicable chill running down my spine despite the diner's warmth. What the hell is going on?

Just as I'm about to suggest we beat a hasty retreat, Chen, the waitress who's served us the past few days as Mel only works evenings, emerges from the kitchen, wiping her hands on her apron. A wide smile breaks across her face when she sees us.

"Afternoon!" she calls out cheerfully, seemingly oblivious to the eerie silence. "Your booth's ready for you. Another late night chasing bad guys after the attack?" She gestures towards our usual corner booth, somehow miraculously empty despite the packed room. We follow her, bewildered, acutely aware of every eye still tracking our movements. Even Luca looks flummoxed.

"Um… kind of," I manage, forcing a smile. "We did have a late night, but we can't really talk about it. Thank you for… keeping a table for us? We didn't know you'd expect us."

Chen snorts, a sound remarkably similar to Rose's earlier reaction, then schools her features. "Sorry," she says, though her eyes are twinkling. "You've been coming in regularly the last few days, always around the same time, usually twice daily. Figured we'd keep the booth open just in case."

"But… why?" I ask, genuinely baffled.

Chen turns, her expression softening, her gaze encompassing all four of us. "Because you tried to save Rachel the other night, right after you left here," she explains, her voice lowering slightly but carrying easily in the still-quiet diner. "She's a friend. Was good people. And," she gestures around the crowded room, "after that attack happened so close, folks were scared. But seeing you guys around, knowing you caught those responsible… well, it gave people confidence to come back out. Our esteemed Police Chief hasn't done squat for years. You've been here a short time and have already made a real difference. So… thank you."

Luca glances around, taking in the now nodding, smiling faces.

"I… I'm lost for words," he admits, looking genuinely taken aback. "For the first time in my life."

As Chen takes our orders, my mind whirls. This public support… it's unexpected. And potentially useful. An idea sparks, audacious and risky, but perfectly suited to the situation. When Chen leaves, I lean forward. "Okay, new idea regarding Thornton…"

Opportunity knocks. "Thank you," I say sincerely to Chen when she returns with our drinks, then, projecting my voice slightly so others can hear, I add, "It's very kind of you all. We're just doing our job. However, I know what you mean about your Police Chief. He actually called me into his office, threatening to have us removed from his city if we didn't do things his way."

The diner instantly erupts into angry chatter, the previous silence shattered. Rose leans closer, whispering in my ear as the noise level rises, "What are you up to now, Destroyer?"

"Leverage," I whisper back, keeping my face neutral. "If the Chief feels enough heat from his own constituents, maybe he'll back off complaining to the FBI about me."

"Ahh, clever girl," Rose murmurs, though her eyes hold a hint of concern. "But I think Sam's about to have kittens."

We glance across at Sam. Sure enough, he's scowling, his disapproval radiating across the table. Looks like my plan might work on the Chief, but Sam's another story. I discreetly nudge Rose under the table. "I better tell Luca why I did it, too," I mutter, keeping my voice low.

"Don't worry, he heard you," Rose replies almost silently, a smirk playing on her lips.

I glance at Luca. He catches my eye and gives a subtle, almost imperceptible wink. Damn their hearing. A sudden, mortifying thought strikes me – if he heard *that* whispered exchange, what else might he have overheard from his adjoining motel room? I feel my cheeks heat up and quickly focus on the menu as Chen waits for our food orders but looks too pissed to care right now.

The angry buzz about the Chief continues around us. Chen, looking furious, loudly announces to a nearby table, "That man is officially banned from this diner! Effective immediately!" She then takes our food orders. Before leaving, she leans in conspiratorially. "Don't you worry about him," she assures us, her voice fierce. "He's up for re-election next year. After this? He won't be Chief much longer, not if we have anything to say about it."

The moment Chen walks away, Sam leans forward, his voice low but vibrating with anger. "What the hell are you playing at, Ava? First, you antagonise the Chief in his own station, and now this. You're deliberately stirring up trouble!"

Before I can formulate a response, Rose explodes, her earlier amusement vanished, replaced by fierce loyalty. "She's trying to fix the mess you were worried about, you idiot!" she snaps, her voice sharp enough to cut glass. "She's hoping the locals pressure him so he backs off complaining to the FBI and getting us all recalled!" Her chest heaves, her eyes flashing as she glares at Sam. I place a calming hand on her thigh under the table, giving it a warning squeeze. She needs to let me handle this.

Realisation dawns on Rose's face, followed by a worried glance at me. "Sorry," she whispers, the sound barely audible even to me. Though inwardly annoyed that she jumped in, I take pity on her. It wouldn't look good if Sam thought I needed her to fight my battles.

"Don't worry about it," I murmur back, then turn to face Sam directly. "What Rose said is correct. And yes, maybe I didn't handle the Chief perfectly yesterday, but he threatened me at the wrong time. This opportunity presented itself. His position is elected; public pressure might make him reconsider escalating things. Sam," My voice hardens slightly. "You need to either get on board with how we sometimes have to operate outside the standard rulebook, or you need to request a transfer. This isn't a normal mission. This is… something else. If you've truly read my file, you know I bend rules to get the job done. There's a reason I was chosen to lead this, and it wasn't for my adherence to protocol."

Sam shakes his head, looking unconvinced but seemingly willing to drop it for now. "How did you know the locals would react like this?" he asks, still frowning.

"He's clearly rubbed people the wrong way for a long time," I reply simply. "And I'm generally good at reading a room, assessing potential reactions."

"I just hope you're right and this doesn't backfire," Sam mutters, still looking troubled. "But… I'll think about what you said."

After our food arrives, we eat mostly in silence, the background chatter slowly returning to normal levels. As we eat, I remember the dream visitor I haven't told the guys about yet. Should I tell Sam? Luca definitely needs to know. I debate internally, weighing the need for transparency against Sam's already fragile state.

As usual, Rose seems to sense my internal conflict and takes the choice away from me. "By the way," she announces casually, looking pointedly at Luca and Sam, "Ava had a visitor in her dreams last night. It's a real doozy."

CHAPTER 23

SOUL SEARCHING, AFTERLIFE POLITICS, AND SAM'S

EXISTENTIAL CRISIS IN THE BACKSEAT

I sigh inwardly and shoot Rose a look, which she, of course, meets with an expression of pure, wide-eyed innocence. Right. Fine. Might as well get it over with. Keeping my voice low enough not to carry beyond the dubious confines of our diner booth, I give them the redacted version of Papa Legba's little dream-visit, ending with the part where he mentioned needing to find a weapon I can actually use against these new… *adversaries*.

Do you know who this Cat might be? She must be the voice we have been hearing, right? Can we actually find her?" I ask.

Luca shakes his head, and that momentary flicker of excitement I felt dies a quick death. "Sorry, Ava. No idea who she is specifically, but the way she has contacted us both, I think she might be dead or a god, possibly both, I know of no other beings who can contact someone in this way."

"What do you mean, dead? How can someone dead contact us?" Sam finally echoes my unspoken question, his voice a little shaky.

"Think about it," Luca explains, his patience a stark contrast to the bombshell he just dropped. He keeps his voice low, a conspiratorial murmur. "That kind of mental projection, reaching across realms without physical proximity… it's typically an ability associated with powerful entities no longer bound by physical limitations. Ghosts, powerful spirits… dead gods or live." He pauses, anticipating my next thought. "I know you'll bring up Papa Legba. But he's different. He straddles the realms, a Loa of the crossroads between life and death. His abilities are unique, and he is still a type of god in a way."

"Okay," Sam concedes slowly, the gears visibly turning in his head. "But what if Cat is some kind of death god, too?"

Another thought, colder and sharper this time, slices through my own confusion. "Are you really saying ghosts are real!!!" The words are out before I can stop them, the sudden, desperate hope of seeing my parents again making my voice tremble. *Damn it, Bekke. Get a grip.*

"Yes, Ava, ghosts are real," Luca confirms, his eyes softening with a sympathy that makes me want to look away. "Unfortunately, shifters generally don't have the Sight needed to perceive them. Maybe you do, because of the ring?" He glances at my hand. "It's also possible that the attacks wiped out many Reapers. We might see an increase in spirits, ghosts sticking around because there aren't enough Reapers to collect all the souls now. So, they'll continue to linger here." He studies me carefully, his gaze unnervingly perceptive. "You might have even seen one already and just… not realised it."

Gobsmacked doesn't even begin to cover it. My mind reels, a confusing mess of grief and disbelief. The image of my parents, so long suppressed, floods back with painful clarity. I'm desperately trying not to cry. Not here. Not in front of them. "How… how can ghosts be real?" I manage the words thick with emotion. "Does it mean… I could see my parents again?"

The sympathy on their faces is almost unbearable. I hadn't meant to voice that last part aloud, the raw, childish longing slipping past my carefully constructed defences. Luca's expression falls, and I know the answer before he even speaks. It's written all over his face.

"Let's finish eating," he says gently, his voice laced with a pity I don't want, can't stand. "We can talk more about this in the car or back at the motel. This isn't really… diner conversation."

I nod numbly, forcing myself to pick at the rapidly cooling eggs. They taste like cardboard, tasteless suddenly. The fragile hope that flared so brightly just moments ago gutters and dies, leaving behind only the familiar, hollow ache of loss.

After leaving Chen a generous tip—more out of habit than actual appreciation for the meal at this point—we head back out into the bright Pittsburgh sunshine. The city's normal hustle and bustle feels distant, alien, overshadowed by the weight of unseen worlds pressing down on me.

As soon as I climb into the back of the Tahoe, the door slamming shut with a heavy thud that echoes the sudden weight in my chest, I turn towards the front seats, a desperate need for answers I'm pretty sure I won't like. Luca is settling into the driver's seat, his usual fluid grace momentarily replaced by a thoughtful, almost sombre stillness. Sam gets in beside him, looking pale and distinctly preoccupied. Rose slides in next to me, her thigh brushing mine, a small, grounding point of contact in the swirling chaos of my thoughts. I don't give Luca time to even start the engine. "Tell me," I demand, my voice tighter than I intend, the soldier taking over. "What I need to know. About ghosts. About my parents."

Luca twists in his seat, his dark eyes meeting mine, a complicated mixture of reluctance and sympathy in their depths. He sighs, a heavy sound that seems to carry the weight of centuries. "Ava…" he begins, his voice low, hesitant.

"No, Luca." My patience is non-existent. "Please. Just… tell me, I need to know."

He holds my gaze for a long moment, then nods slowly, a hint of resignation in the movement. "Alright." He takes a breath, visibly gathering his thoughts. "When your parents were killed… when any human dies, through violence or natural causes… their essence, their soul, departs the physical body. Typically, entities known as Reapers are tasked with guiding these souls. They would have collected your parents' souls shortly after their deaths and escorted them… elsewhere. To the other side."

The words hang in the air, clinical, precise, and utterly devastating. "Elsewhere? Other side?" My tactically trained mind feels lost, but I latch onto the phrasing, desperate for an answer to give me a route, a destination I can somehow reach. "What are you saying? A ghost *is* the soul. So, they're not just… gone? And this *other side* – what is it? Where is it? Can I go there?" The questions tumble out, a torrent of sudden, fierce hope warring with a decade of carefully managed grief.

Luca holds up a hand gently, a silent plea for patience. "Slow down, Ava. This… this isn't common shifter knowledge, not the specifics. Most of what I know comes from stories, ancient lore passed down, sometimes fragmented, sometimes contradictory." He pauses, a nostalgic, almost sad flicker in his eyes. "When I was very young, before the attacks… a Mage visited our pack lands." Beside me, Rose shifts slightly; she looks intrigued to hear this as well. Luca continues, his voice tinged with a respect that borders on awe. "She stayed with us for a season. A powerful, ancient being, steeped in history, the likes of which few remember now. During the evenings, she would share tales, fragments of cosmic history, creation myths, the wars between the gods… things most shifters barely comprehend. I don't know how much literal truth is and how much allegory is, but I'll tell you what I recall as accurately as possible."

He takes another deep, contemplative breath, his gaze distant, as if searching the landscapes of his memory. The silence in the car feels thick, charged, heavy with unspoken possibilities. I find myself holding my breath, waiting. Rose subtly shifts closer, her shoulder pressing lightly against mine, a silent offering of support I hadn't realised I needed until I felt it.

"The Mage spoke of the beginning," Luca begins, his voice taking on a slightly different cadence, more formal, almost storyteller-like. "Of the first deities, beings of immense power – light and darkness, life and death. There was… a schism. A fundamental disagreement that fractured their unity. The gods aligned with light and life, fearing corruption or perhaps seeking isolation, created—or perhaps merely opened a doorway to—another plane of existence, a separate realm. To this place, they banished their children, their first creations, perhaps to protect them, perhaps to contain them. The gods of darkness and death, mirroring their counterparts, did the same, carving out their own realm."

He pauses again, frowning slightly as he tries to piece the fragmented narrative together. "The timeline gets muddled here in my memory… but at some point, the original goddess of Life, perhaps disappointed by the actions of her celestial offspring, performed an act of profound creation. Using powerful, primal magic, she forged the human race, in her own image, the Mage said. But intentionally without the inherent powers of the gods – perhaps as an experiment, perhaps as a statement. Then," Luca continues, his voice regaining momentum, "centuries passed. Humans spread across the world. Eventually, the banished children of the gods, along with *their* children, found their way back to this plane. Another war erupted, fiercer than the first, that caused the gods to banish their children in the first place. This conflict, the Mage claimed, resulted in the death of most of the original gods themselves."

My mind struggles to grasp the scale of it – gods warring, dying. It's a concept so far beyond my tactical understanding that it's almost laughable. Almost. Luca continues his story, "The subsequent generations of gods, the children and grandchildren, then began to interact directly with humanity. They displayed their powers, demanded worship, and gathered followers among the mortals who were scattered across the now-vastly populated earth."

I lean forward, utterly captivated, the earlier anxiety momentarily forgotten, replaced by a strange mix of awe and an unsettling sense of… connection? This isn't just shifter lore; it feels like *our* hidden history, buried beneath layers of myth and conveniently edited religion.

"I don't know how much time passed," Luca admits, shaking his head, "generations, certainly. But inevitably, conflict arose again amongst these younger gods. This time, tragically, they used their human worshippers as pawns, as armies, pitting mortals against mortals in divine proxy wars. The devastation was immense. And when the dust settled, the world was haunted. The souls of the slain lingered, unable or unwilling to move on. To the surviving gods, these souls were visible, tangible entities, almost as real as the living. They could perceive them and interact with them. But they also realised something profound, the soul, the essence of that original divine spark given by the goddess of Life, persisted even after the physical body decayed. It didn't age, though it retained the image of its vessel at the moment of death. The soul was… eternal, in a sense."

My breath catches. "Interact? How? Could they… touch them? Feel them?" The image of hugging my parents again, even as spectral forms, floods my mind with a raw, painful intensity.

Luca gives me a sad, knowing smile. A punch to the gut would have been kinder. "The Mage said the gods could, yes. Using their inherent magic, they could bridge the gap, interact with the souls almost as if they were still physically present." His gaze softens with pity, a look I despise. "But that interaction required divine power, Ava. Something mortals lack."

The fragile flicker of hope dies, leaving behind the familiar ache of absence. No hugs. Maybe not even sight, unless the ring… I brutally shove the thought away. *Later. Focus, Bekke.* "So… souls are leftover magic?" I clarify, trying to anchor the overwhelming concept in something tangible, something I can categorise.

"In essence, yes. The spark of creation persists." He offers a faint, almost wistful smile. "The Mage even spoke of shifter souls retaining the ability to shift in the afterlife. Imagine seeing a spectral panther…" Luca trails off, a distant look in his eyes. He shakes his head slightly, refocusing on the grim lesson. "The remaining gods on the side of light and life, perhaps moved by compassion or guilt over the wars they'd instigated, began to perceive something else – the souls had auras. Colours reflecting their mortal lives. All humans, the Mage claimed, were born with pure white auras, a reflection of their divine origin. But mortal choices, acts of cruelty, selfishness, violence… these actions tainted the soul, darkened the aura over time. The original goddess, having been betrayed by her children, supposedly imbued humanity with these auras as a way to gauge trustworthiness, maybe because their children betrayed their parents, so they wanted a way to see if they could trust their new creation."

Auras. Madi, the Crossroads Demon, mentioned my aura. *What colour is mine now?* The question slams into me. After years as a soldier, an assassin… is it irrevocably grey? Or black? The thought sends a cold, unwelcome chill down my spine.

Luca continues, oblivious to my sudden internal turmoil. "The light-aligned gods began gathering the souls with the brightest auras – the pure white ones, and those only slightly dimmed. These souls are the ones who lived predominantly good lives. They took these souls to their own realm, the one humans eventually called Heaven. The gods of darkness and death, seeing this, grew suspicious. They feared the light gods were assembling an army of souls for a future conflict. So, they retaliated, gathering *all* the remaining souls-the darkened, the corrupted, the malevolent-and dragging them to *their* realm, the plane they named the Underworld. Hell." He pauses, letting the weight of those final words settle in the stifling air of the Tahoe. "Then, driven by paranoia and perhaps a twisted curiosity, the dark gods began to experiment on the souls they'd collected. They warped them, twisted their magic, and mutated their forms. Thus," his voice drops, taking on a graver, almost chilling tone, "the first demons were created, shaped by their creators, the Daemons, as they called themselves. They didn't stop there. They spawned Wraiths, Succubi, myriad other horrors designed to feed on mortal fear and life force, or to harvest souls directly from the living. They unleashed these abominations upon our world, seeking to diminish the number of *pure* souls the light gods could claim."

"Eventually," Luca adds, each word heavy with grim finality, "the most powerful Daemon god cast a permanent spell upon the Underworld itself, ensuring that *all* souls arriving there would automatically mutate over time, twisting into demonic forms without direct intervention. A self-perpetuating engine of corruption. Later generations of gods, the Mage said, lacked the power to undo this curse."

The implications crash down on me, a suffocating weight of cosmic horror. "Wait," I choke out, my voice trembling, the carefully constructed walls around my emotions starting to crumble. "Are you telling me… my parents… if their souls weren't perfectly white… they could have been taken to the Underworld? Turned into…... into *demons*?" The horror of the thought is absolute, a cold fist clenching around my heart. "And me?" The question rips from my throat before I can stop it, raw with a sudden, visceral terror. "My job… the things I've done… Does that mean *I'm* destined for the Underworld? To become one of those… things?"

Beside me, Rose lets out a low, guttural growl, a sound of pure, protective fury directed not at me, but at the sheer, cosmic injustice Luca is describing. I barely register it, consumed by my rising panic, the professional soldier side of me momentarily lost in the terrified child part of my brain.

Luca looks stricken, clearly realising the personal devastation his ancient history lesson has unleashed. "Ava, I… I am so sorry," he stammers, his usual composure fractured, looking genuinely distressed. "I wasn't thinking… I didn't consider… regarding your parents, I cannot know the state of their souls. Only the Reapers and the gods could judge. As for you…" He hesitates, searching for reassuring words that probably don't exist in any language, mortal or divine. "Your work… it's complex. You eliminate threats, protect others… does that darken a soul, or is it judged by intent? I don't know. Witches or Mages, those attuned to such things, might be able to perceive an aura's colour, but… we shifters cannot. I believe… I *hope*… that actions taken in defence, or to prevent greater harm, are viewed differently. Killing an innocent civilian is one thing; eliminating a terrorist or a monster targeting innocents…" he trails off, unable to offer any concrete certainty. "I just don't remember the specifics the Mage might have shared about intent versus action."

His uncertainty offers little comfort, but I appreciate the attempt. I manage a shaky breath, forcing the raw panic down. Compartmentalise. *Focus, Bekke. You can't change the past, or the potential future judgement of your damn soul. Focus on the present. On the mission.* I give Luca a tight, jerky nod, indicating he should continue, needing the distraction of the narrative, anything to pull me back from the abyss of that horrifying possibility.

He looks hesitant, clearly worried about causing further distress, but after a moment, he resumes, his voice subdued, tinged with a sadness that mirrors my own. "There isn't much more to the core story, Ava, though I'm certain I'm missing vast swathes of detail. The gods of light and life refused to engage in the same soul-twisting horrors as the Daemons. Instead, they focused on empowering humans, teaching them rudimentary defences against the demonic incursions, ways to fight back, and methods to potentially kill some of the lesser creatures. The Mage did mention one other possibility," Luca adds, a touch of wonder, almost reverence, entering his voice, "a belief that a human soul which remained truly pure, untouched by darkness throughout its entire mortal life, could undergo a different kind of transformation upon entering the realm of angels. Not mutation, but… ascension. They called them Eternal Angels. These souls spontaneously grew white wings, becoming guardians within that realm, welcoming and guiding the other souls arriving."

Eternal Angels. The concept is almost beautiful, a stark, luminous contrast to the grotesque horrors of the Underworld. A tiny, fragile seed of hope sprouts within the wreckage of my earlier despair – maybe my parents… maybe they were pure enough.

"As the divine lineages continued," Luca presses on, his narrative bringing the ancient history closer to our chaotic present, "intermingling occurred. Gods procreated with humans. Their offspring, demigods, possessed diluted powers. Those demigods, in turn, sometimes paired with mortals, further diluting the magic, giving rise to beings like witches, mages, warlocks – mortals capable of channelling magic, but far removed from the power of the original deities. My own shifter race likely originated from similar dilutions, a specific type of magic that manifests as shapeshifting. Beings like Angels and Reapers also arose from these divine bloodlines, their power tied to their heritage. And their allegiance, their origin," he adds significantly, his gaze pointed, "could often be discerned by the colour of their wings."

My mind immediately flashes to Madi, the Crossroads Demon, her vast, leathery black wings blotting out the mundane reality of the motel parking lot lights. An unwelcome shiver traces down my spine.

"White wings signify alignment with light and life, originating from that realm," Luca confirms, clearly anticipating my thoughts. "Black wings denote allegiance to darkness, death, the Underworld."

I frown, the connection still feeling tenuous, abstract. "Okay, interesting cosmic trivia, but I still don't see how wing colour relates to my parents, or seeing them again?" My impatience, my raw need for a tangible answer, leaks into my tone.

Luca offers a small, patient smile, though it doesn't quite reach his eyes. "Because, Ava, access between the realms seems to be keyed to that alignment. The Daemons discovered their dark-winged angels and demons couldn't physically enter the realm of angels. Conversely, a white-winged angel couldn't enter the Underworld. Souls, too, seemed bound – a dark soul couldn't be forced into the light realm. Whether the original gods erected these barriers or it is a fundamental law of these alternate dimensions, the Mage didn't know. The practical reality is that passage requires the correct *key*, which seems to be symbolised by wing colour." He leans forward slightly, his expression earnest, almost pleading for me to understand. "What that means for you, Ava, is that even if you could find your parents' souls – assuming they reside in the realm of angels – *you* likely couldn't enter. And finding a being with white wings willing and *able* to escort a living mortal across that threshold… the risks, the unknowns… It might not even be possible. The transition itself could destroy a physical form." His words, delivered with a quiet finality, finally extinguish the last, stubborn ember of my desperate hope of reunion.

The weight of it all – the cosmic wars, the divided afterlife, the potential damnation of my soul, the crushing impossibility of ever seeing my parents again – settles on me, heavy and suffocating. Rose puts a comforting arm around my shoulders, pulling me gently against her side, her warmth a fragile shield against the sudden, overwhelming cold. I turn my gaze towards Sam, expecting to see shared confusion, perhaps curiosity. Instead, his face is ashen, his eyes wide with a dawning horror that mirrors my initial reaction, only magnified a hundredfold. He looks utterly lost, adrift in the face of these soul-shattering revelations. Existential dread, it seems, is a human universal.

"Sam?" I ask softly, my own grief momentarily overshadowed by a wave of concern for him. "Are you okay?"

He turns his head towards me with an unnerving slowness, his movements stiff, almost robotic, like a marionette whose strings are too thick and stiff from age. His eyes seem unfocused, staring *through* me rather than at me. He looks physically ill, pale and clammy, with a sheen of cold sweat on his brow.

"I'm… fine, Ava," he rasps, his voice thin and strained, utterly unconvincing. "It's just… a lot. To process." He swallows hard, his gaze flickering around the confines of the car as if seeing it, and perhaps his entire life, for the very first time. "Makes you re-evaluate… everything. Every choice." He shakes his head slightly, a tremor running through him that has nothing to do with the vehicle's suspension. "Can we… can we just go back to the motel, please? I think… I need some time alone."

His distress is palpable, far more profound than just intellectual shock or morbid curiosity. He's confronting his mortality, his past actions, his entire belief system, through this terrifying new lens of cosmic judgement. I feel a pang of empathy, understanding his sudden, acute existential dread all too well. "Sure, Sam," I agree quietly, my voice still a little shaky. "Sure. Let's head back."

The drive back to the motel is shrouded in a heavy silence, thick with unspoken thoughts, unasked questions, and a universe of anxieties. When we pull into the familiar, slightly depressing motel parking lot, Sam practically bolts from the car before Luca even cuts the engine. He heads straight for his room without a backwards glance, his shoulders slumped, the weight of the newly revealed cosmos clearly crushing him.

I make a move to follow, a residual sense of team responsibility, wanting to check on him, but Rose's hand on my arm, gentle but firm, stops me. Luca turns in his seat, his expression a mixture of compassion and resignation. "Let him go, Ava," he advises gently, his voice low. "He needs to process this in his own way. Hearing about the tangible consequences of morality, the reality of souls and afterlives… it hits humans differently, harder sometimes. Especially those trained in logic and evidence, those who rely on the seen and proven." He sighs, the sound weary. "I didn't intend to cause such distress. Growing up surrounded by these stories, even fragmented ones, perhaps desensitises us shifters to the raw impact. I didn't anticipate how it would affect him… or you."

"It's not your fault, Luca," I reassure him, though my mind is still reeling, trying to recalibrate my entire understanding of existence. "You're right, we humans… we grow up with diluted versions, religious doctrines, philosophical debates… We compartmentalise death, the afterlife. It's all theoretical. But to hear it laid out like that… cosmic laws, divine judgements, souls being mutated into demons…" I shudder, a visceral reaction I can't suppress. "It forces a confrontation with choices made, paths taken. Even those of us who aren't religious, who operate on a more… pragmatic moral code, grapple with the implications. To learn there might be a literal Heaven and Hell, judged by the colour of your soul… that's… profound. And frankly, terrifying." I pause, another thought, another layer of this impossible reality, striking me. "You're basically telling us everyone is immortal, in one form or another."

Luca considers this, tilting his head, his expression thoughtful. "In a way, perhaps. As I tried to explain, the soul – the magic – persists after physical death. Unless," he adds, his tone turning grim, "it's consumed or destroyed by certain entities. Demons, Wraiths… they feed on that essence. Vampires drain the life force, the magic within the blood, but typically the soul itself remains intact, capable of regeneration, unless the victim is drained completely, unto death. So, true, absolute immortality? Probably not attainable. Even the gods apparently died. But yes, barring soul-destruction, the essence endures beyond the body's demise. Physical immortality, like that of vampires, means not dying of age or disease, making one harder to kill. Ethereal immortality is… different. Less substantial, perhaps, but no less real."

CHAPTER 24

PRETTY SURE 'VAMPIRE COMPULSION' WASN'T COVERED
IN BASIC TRAINING

We trail back to our room with Luca in tow, only to find Sam already hunched over the plans, barely registering our entrance. The air in their room is thick with the cloying scent of stale coffee and the focused energy of a man wrestling with hard truths. Luca initially gestures towards grabbing our notes to take to Rose's and my room, but seeing Sam so engrossed, a silent agreement passes between us, and we shuffle into the guys' cramped space instead, finding spots to join his silent scrutiny of the gathered intelligence. The cheap, patterned carpet does little to absorb the sound of our movements, but Sam remains oblivious, lost in the stark realities spread before him.

"You okay, Sam?" I ask, keeping my tone even, my voice carefully neutral. The story Luca shared earlier about souls and the afterlife clearly hit him with the force of a freight train. He just shrugs, a dismissive wave of his hand encompassing the scattered papers on the cheap motel desk – a clear signal he's buried in thought and not up for conversation. My gut tightens a little; I recognise the look of a man grappling with concepts far bigger and more terrifying than bullets and bad guys. I let him be. Forcing him to talk now won't help anyone. So, we settle in, a strange quartet in a dim motel room, the only sounds the rustle of papers and the distant hum of traffic, as we immerse ourselves in the grim task of finalising tonight's strategy.

We spend our time completing our plan. Eventually, a fragile consensus is reached, the words hanging in the air like brittle threads. A plan, as solid as we can make it given the multitude of unknowns, is in place. With precious little time before we're due to head out, Rose and I break away from the guys, seeking the relative sanctuary of our room for a few moments of… preparation. And yes, the first thing we do is share a shower. Ensuring we are economical with water! My skin tingles under the spray, the steam a temporary veil against the harsh realities waiting outside. And if our *water conservation* efforts involve a little more than just soap and shampoo, well, a girl's got to find her comforts where she can, especially when facing down a nest of vampires. *Especially* when it might be the last chance we get. The thought, cold and unwelcome, slithers into my mind, a chill that has nothing to do with the cooling water. I push it away, focusing on the heat of Rose's skin against mine.

"Have I told you today that you are beautiful?" Rose asks, her voice a soft murmur against my hair, the words a gentle caress. I manage a small smile, the muscles in my face feeling stiff.

"I don't think so. But you're the beautiful one, not me." It's an old argument, one I'm surprisingly happy to lose these days.

"Let's not argue about it, because I *will* win," she says, a playful warmth in her tone that almost makes me believe it. "Let's just say we're beautiful together."

A comfortable silence settles for a moment, a rare pocket of peace, before I break it. "I thought you were the tough one, not the schmaltzy one?" I tease, lifting my head to see the side of her face, the gentle curve of her smile in the dim light filtering through the cheap curtains. My reward is a soft, lingering kiss as she turns fully towards me, her lips warm and sure against mine. The motel room, the impending danger, it all fades for a precious second, lost in the simple sensation of her.

"I think we're very much alike, honey," she whispers, her lips brushing mine, sending a shiver down my spine despite the warmth of her body. "We're both tough *and* schmaltzy. Except," a mischievous glint dances in her green eyes, a spark of her usual fire, "you're a bit of a pervert as well, after what you did in the shower."

"Hey!" I feign offence, giving her side a light pinch. My heart does a little flutter, a ridiculous, teenage reaction. It's this teasing, this intimacy, that makes everything else bearable, that grounds me.

"Ow!" she yelps, though her smirk tells me she's far from hurt. "You don't have to be mean just because you're a pervert. I *like* that you're a pervert."

I prop myself up on an elbow, looking down at her, my mouth agape in mock shock. "Well, if I'm a pervert, then you're a sadist. You like it rough, which," I lean closer, my voice dropping to a conspiratorial whisper, the words meant only for her, "I happen to like it too, but that's just between us." I seal the confession with another kiss, crawling on top of her, the cheap motel bedspread crinkling beneath us, a soundtrack to our stolen moment.

Her muffled protests of "P-er-vert" are lost against my lips as we kiss for a long moment, a tangle of limbs and shared warmth, the world outside ceasing to exist. Eventually, breathless, I settle back into her side, my head returning to its favourite spot on her shoulder, the faint scent of her soap and something uniquely *Rose* filling my senses, a comforting perfume I can't help but enjoy breathing in.

It *is* strange, I reflect, my cheek resting against the steady beat of her heart, how quickly Rose and I have settled into this easy intimacy, like we've been orbiting each other for years instead of mere days. The bond, I suppose, that inexplicable tether I'm still trying to understand. The thought is both terrifying and exhilarating.

"Are you confident about our plan this afternoon?" I ask, the question hanging heavy in the air between us, puncturing the quiet. My own confidence feels like a badly worn tyre, slowly losing air.

Rose swivels her head, her gaze, sharp and perceptive, meeting mine from the corner of her eye. She studies me for a moment, a flicker of something unreadable in their depths, before responding. "I was going to ask you that. After the revelations from Luca's story earlier, I wondered if you were okay." Her voice is laced with genuine concern, the green of her eyes soft, a stark contrast to the shifter's lethal power I know she possesses. "Sam was clearly having issues, and that's why we assigned him the role we have. We haven't had a chance to talk about it, but I've been worried about you. Wondered if you were coping with it all?"

I knew these questions were coming; a part of me dreaded them. But there's no avoiding it, not with her looking at me like that, her concern a palpable thing. Lying, especially this early, feels like poisoning a well I've only just discovered. Besides, I've always prided myself on being direct, even if it ruffles feathers. At least people know where they stand. It's a habit forged in a world where misunderstanding can get you killed.

"I was upset at first," I admit, the words feeling small and inadequate against the enormity of it all. My gaze drifts to the faded wallpaper, anywhere but her too-knowing eyes. "It's… my parents." The admission tastes like ash in my mouth. "I hadn't thought about them in a long time, not like *that*. What Luca said… it all came flooding back." My breath hitches slightly, an involuntary betrayal of the turmoil inside. "I had this moment of sheer panic, Rose. Thinking they could be… demons now. Wondering if we'd come across them, and if I'd even recognise them. Or if they'd know me." The vulnerability hangs in the air, raw and exposed, making my skin prickle.

Rose pulls me tighter, her embrace a silent reassurance, her strength a comforting pressure against my back. "It was clear you were upset about what might have happened to them, where they might have ended up," she says softly, her cheek against my temple, her breath warm against my skin. "I'm sorry you had to hear about what really happens after someone dies like that. I didn't think about your situation before Luca started his story."

I run my fingers over her cheek, the skin smooth and warm beneath my touch, as I study the delicate curve of her jaw and the faint lines of concern etched around her eyes. "You don't have to apologise,

Rose. You can't be expected to think of everything." A humourless laugh escapes me. "Yes, I was shocked about finding out what could have happened to my parents. It freaked me out so much, the thought of them being turned into demons… Right at that moment, if I knew someone who could take me there, I would have stormed the underworld and laid siege to it to find them." The image, ludicrous and desperate, flashes through my mind. "Then it started to sink in. I was being stupid. I know my parents. They weren't bad people. There's no way they were taken to the underworld." My voice gains a surprising firmness. "I believe they're happy, together, in the other place." The conviction in my voice surprises even me. It's a fragile hope, a lifeline in a sea of uncertainty, but it's mine.

"I'm sure they are," Rose murmurs, her voice a balm against the raw edges of my grief. "They had to be good people to have a daughter as… remarkable as you." She pulls back slightly, her gaze intense, the first truly serious look I've seen from her since we met, a look that demands honesty. "Please don't dwell on it now. I don't want you distracted. If you think you are, even a small amount, tell me. We can delay things until tomorrow." Her earnestness is a tangible thing, a weight of responsibility I don't want her to bear alone.

"Rose, I promise, I'm good," I say, and I mean it, the words tasting true on my tongue. The storm in my head has passed, leaving a clearer, if somewhat battered, sky. "I had a moment, but I'm good. All that's on my mind right now is you, and how good this feels." I give her a pointed look, a silent promise. "Later, all that will be on my mind is getting justice for the victims of this city." The shift in my tone is automatic, the familiar steel of mission focus settling into place, a welcome, well-worn cloak.

A slow smile spreads across Rose's face, chasing away the last of the shadows in her eyes. "Wow. I do *not* want to ever play poker with you. I feel sorry for all your enemies out there if they have to deal with you when you give *that* look." She rests her head against mine, a comfortable weight, her hair still smells faintly of the cheap motel shampoo and something uniquely her. "Anyway, good. I would hate to think something bad would happen because I didn't make sure." Her voice lightens, the teasing note returning. "We ought to start getting ready, though, before we lose track of time and the guys find us playing… naughty nurses."

Once we return to the guys' room, we confirm our plan, but a complication has arisen with the plan we made. Given that Sam has now been publicly identified after participating in the press conferences and being recognised by the locals in the diner, his face is too well-known. "With Sam being recognised, it's too risky for him to place the cameras," Luca states, voicing the obvious. "He's the public face, however inadvertently."

Sam looks uncomfortable but nods in agreement. "He's right. It's too hazardous." He still seems to be mulling over what Luca told us, his expression unreadable. "I can talk you through the setup, Ava. They're solar-powered for a slightly extended life, but the placement needs to be discreet yet allow for sunlight if possible." He outlines the specifics of the miniature cameras, his tone is strictly professional, but I can see he is still struggling. I listen intently, but I'm eager to get this underway. The sooner we have intel, the better. My patience for sitting idle is already wearing thin, and the lingering effects of the diner conversation make me crave action.

Once Sam has finished his explanation and I've familiarised myself with the devices, Rose voices her concern. "Are you sure you want to do this, Ava? You'll be out there alone, essentially. Sam will be on overwatch, but…" She trails off, but her worry is clear.

"I'll be fine," I reassure her, though the thought of Sam as my only immediate backup isn't exactly comforting, given his current mood and my lingering doubts about his field readiness. "I'm the only one who can get close without raising alarms if these vamps are in there."

I quickly went and changed into workout clothes – sweat pants and a tank top. I really do need to find time for a proper run; the urge to pound the pavement and clear my head is strong, but there's been no opportunity. I strap on the body harness, but this time, I only load the sword on my back. Jogging with a full complement of daggers and guns would be more than awkward. One significant advantage of the ring becomes immediately apparent when I slip the small cameras into a pouch on the strap around my waist; they vanish along with the harness and sword.

We head out in the Tahoe. First, we drop Sam off at a tall apartment building a couple of blocks from the church. Its height offers a perfect, unobstructed view. Then Luca drives another block over before pulling to the kerb. This is where he and Rose will wait. Before I get out, I fit an earpiece, checking the connection with a quick sound check. "Comms good," I confirm. "Wish me luck."

"Always," Rose says, her voice tight with concern. Luca gives a curt nod, his eyes watchful.

I start jogging, settling into an easy rhythm, taking in everything. The streets are quieter than I'd expect for this time of day, even with the recent attacks being nocturnal. This might be trickier than I anticipated. My first pass by the church is purely reconnaissance. There aren't many ideal spots for camera placement. I do, however, spot him – a figure lurking in the deep shadows near the main entrance, partially obscured by the church's large sign and the surrounding trees. He's definitely watching the street.

On my second lap, I have a stroke of luck, a car turns onto the street, heading towards the church. The watcher, who had tracked my first pass with unnerving stillness, shifts his attention to the approaching vehicle, his posture tensing as if expecting trouble. Seizing the moment as I draw level with a sturdy tree across the street from the church, I retrieve a camera from my pouch. With a small, almost imperceptible hop, I place it high on a branch, ensuring it's aimed correctly. The car drives past just as I resume my jog, and the watcher's gaze returns to me. I offer a slight, neutral smile, acknowledging his scrutiny, and continue on. Once I round the corner, I murmur into the comms, "First camera is up. In a tree, street-side."

I don't give them a chance to respond or, more likely, to question what I'm about to do. If they knew, Rose would be shouting, and Luca would be issuing calm but firm orders to abort. The other ideal spot is far more audacious, on the church sign itself, right out front where the watcher stands. The sign has a small, broken lip underneath, seemingly unused.

This means getting close. Very close. Before turning the corner for my next approach, I deliberately loosen one of my shoelaces. As I come back into view of the church, I cross the road, now on the same side as the shadowy figure, which I'm sure is a vampire. I maintain a steady pace. By the time I reach the church grounds, my lace is conveniently undone and flapping around my feet. I pull out the second camera, activating it with a discreet click of the button on it as it rests in my palm. He is definitely watching me more intently now, his head tilted slightly as I approach. Just before I reach the path leading to the church doors, I look down at my shoe with an exaggerated frown and a sigh.

I slow my pace, stopping near the end of the short path. I glance around, feigning a search for a place to sit, and *notice* the bench conveniently located right next to the church sign. Perfect. I head for it, positioning myself so the man can't quite see my hands as I sit down. I stick the camera onto the underside of the sign's lip, then lean over and retie my lace, my movements economical and quick. I notice as I place the camera that there are letters stacked in the lip; these must have been used once to change the message on the main sign.

"Hey, beautiful," a voice says, smooth as velvet, startlingly close. I hadn't heard him move. I finish tying my lace and sit up, schooling my features into neutrality. He's standing right there. My body tenses, every instinct screaming to draw a weapon, but I only have the sword, and that would be a dead giveaway. I have to hope he didn't register my minute flinch. I look up, and my breath catches.

He's easily one of the most handsome men I've ever seen,

enough to give Luca a serious run for his money. Dark, captivating eyes that seem to have a faint reddish tint in the shadows of his hood – so, definitely one of the bitten. A perfect jawline, a charming smile complete with dimples. Pre-Rose, pre-all-this, he'd have been exactly the type I'd seek out for a no-strings hook-up. Now, though beautiful, he stirs nothing in me beyond a professional assessment of a threat. All I care about, all I *feel* for, is Rose. Still, I can play the game. "Back at ya, handsome."

A predatory smile spreads across his face. "Saw you running. New around here? I'd have noticed you before." His voice is like a caress, and I feel a faint, almost imperceptible brush against my mind. My thoughts race. *Vampires. Compulsion.* It's a common trope in movies, but if that mental touch was real, I need to be careful.

"Yeah, just moved in down the road. First chance I've had to get out for a run. Are you with the church?" I ask, gesturing vaguely towards the building.

"I am," he confirms, edging closer. "You should join us. We're holding extra prayer services, given what's happening. There could be a place for you here."

There it is again, stronger this time – that mental nudge. I find my gaze drawn to his, a strange lassitude creeping over me. His eyes are like deep pools, and his suggestion starts to sound… appealing. *Too* appealing.

"The situation isn't great, so it's nice you're trying to help," I hear myself say, my voice sounding distant, sleepy. Then, another sensation washes over my mind, this one sharp, clear, and fiercely familiar. *Rose.* The feeling of her presence, her concern, her… possessiveness, cuts through the fog like a beacon. I snap back to full alertness instantly.

"When I'm more settled, I'll drop by," I say, getting to my feet. The vampire looks momentarily confused, then becomes concerned.

He reaches for my arm. "You really should. I can promise you a life you've only dreamed of." His frown deepens when I don't respond immediately to his touch or his words as he places a hand on my arm just below my shoulder.

I sidestep his hand, easily breaking his contact. "Like I said, maybe another day. Lots to do. Have a good one," I say, moving back towards the sidewalk. His deepening frown is my cue. I break into a jog as soon as my feet hit the pavement, heading back towards where Luca and Rose are waiting.

When I reach our car and jump into the back, I'm immediately hit with a barrage of angry questions. "What in the seven hells were you thinking?" Rose growls, her eyes blazing.

"That was incredibly reckless, Ava," Luca adds, his voice tight with controlled anger. "He could have taken you."

"Are you finished?" I snap, cutting them off. The adrenaline is still pumping, mixed with annoyance. "It might have been nice to know that compulsion was a real thing."

"What!!!" Rose exclaims, her anger momentarily forgotten.

"Yeah. Felt like something brushing against my mind. His voice was too smooth, almost hypnotic." They exchange a look before Luca responds,

"Apologies, Ava. We should have been more thorough. Compulsion is a rare gift among vampires, usually only seen in older, more powerful ones. They can't typically use it effectively in a fight, as it requires focus. If he were attempting it on you, he's likely quite old. The more pressing question is, how did you break free?"

I shrug, still irritated by the omission of critical intel. I replay the encounter in my mind. "When I looked into his eyes, it felt like I was sinking. Then, it was like… like a jolt. It came with a feeling of Rose," I say, looking at her. Her anger has softened, replaced by a complex mix of emotions.

"Interesting," Luca murmurs, his gaze flicking between us.

"What is?" I demand.

"There are many stories and rumours about truly bonded pairs," Luca explains, his analytical curiosity piqued. "One persistent rumour is that they can share senses, or at least strong emotional impressions, especially when one is in danger or under duress." It's intriguing, what I felt, it was like Rose was *there*.

I look directly at Rose. "What were you thinking, exactly, when you saw what was happening on the camera feed?"

"What? I was furious, that's for sure," she says, a lingering sharpness in her tone.

"What are you getting at, Ava?" Luca asks, leaning back to watch us both.

"I felt something specific. I want to know if *you* were thinking something specific, Rose," I press, watching her face for any sign of recognition.

Rose starts to speak, then pauses, her mouth closing. She seems to be searching her memory, then her eyes widen in a classic lightbulb moment. "I was… I was beyond pissed. My first thought was how I was going to punish you for being so reckless. Then I wanted to tear down that street and rip his head off. A few other… less charitable things. But underneath all that, in the back of my mind, there was this… this encroaching darkness, like you were drifting away from me. All I wanted, all I could think, was that I needed to get to you, to be with you, to grab you and pull you back to me." A slow smile spreads across my face as she finishes.

"That means something to you, doesn't it, Ava?" Luca observes. I nod.

"It does," I confirm. "When I felt like I was sinking into his eyes, what washed over me, what snapped me out of it, was the distinct sensation of Rose suddenly being *with* me, wrapping her arms around me, pulling me back. It cleared my head instantly. That's when I got out of there. It might have made him suspicious, but we'll have to see." I pause, another piece clicking into place. "Something similar happened the other day, too. I'd almost forgotten. When we were with the Chief and that crossroads demon, I thought I was getting incredibly angry, but then it felt like it was *Rose's* anger, not mine, bleeding over."

"So, the old stories are true," Luca says, clearly fascinated by this confirmation. "A truly bonded pair develops a mental link."

Rose gets a decidedly mischievous glint in her eyes at this news. Luca notices it too and chuckles. "Ava, I think you might be in for some interesting times. Rose looks like she's already plotting how to use this new development to her advantage." He starts the car, pulling away from the kerb to go pick up Sam.

I just shake my head at Rose, a small smile playing on my lips. He's probably right. But right now, all I feel is a renewed sense of connection, a tether in the swirling chaos of our new reality.

CHAPTER 25

We arrive back at the motel; Sam says he can set up our tablets so we can watch the feeds from the church anywhere, which is a small mercy. I was worried that if we all had to bundle around one screen, we would all start to get on each other's nerves. I bypass our room, heading straight for theirs, the echo of my footsteps feeling unnaturally loud in the corridor, my mind still feels a bit off after my encounter with the vampire which I'm going to keep to myself as Rose will freak out if I tell her I'm still feeling off, I'm sure I will feel better soon enough.

Going into their room feels… foreign. I've become so accustomed to the shared space with Rose, her scent filling our room, making me feel at home, so the sterile motel smell here assaults my senses. It feels wrong, out of place. I gravitate towards one of the two chairs by the window, needing the stability, the solid feel of wood beneath my hands as I watch Rose murmur something to Luca. Her profile is etched against the dim light filtering through the window, the curve of her jaw, the line of her neck… It's bizarre, this magnetic pull towards her, this woman who represents everything I never knew existed until days ago.

My life has always been compartmentalised, mission, downtime, training, and survival. Emotions were weaknesses, distractions I couldn't afford. Since my parents… since that night, loneliness has been a constant, unwelcome shadow, punctuated only by fleeting, meaningless encounters after missions, a way to blow off steam, to feel something other than the cold steel of a rifle or the grit of sand. My few friendships are built on shared danger and long absences, comfortable silences understood across continents.

And now… now there's this. A world ripped open, revealing monsters and magic, shifters and demons. Things that should only exist in hushed whispers or crackling campfires are suddenly my reality. Missions I thought were straightforward might have involved targets vanishing not through skill, but through *other* means. Tangled in the centre of it all is Rose. Beautiful, infuriating, terrifying. My perfect mate, destiny's choice, a universe's gift. The thought is ludicrous, yet the pull I felt towards her from the moment we met, that inexplicable draw that made me choose the seat beside her over any other, feels undeniable now. Was that the bond, even then? A subtle thread tightening before I even knew what it was. Maybe my human senses dampened it initially, needing time, proximity, *contact* to recognise its strength.

Doesn't matter now. Since my encounter with the vampire and the feeling of Rose in the back of my mind, I now have a constant awareness of her, as my eyes unconsciously track her movements. Is this right? Can I trust this feeling, this fate thrust upon me? A corner of my mind, the cold, logical part honed by years of survival, whispers warnings, but the rest… the rest feels irrevocably tethered to her. The memory of my distress when I thought her panther would reject me broke through defences I didn't know could crumble. That pain, that fear of loss… it mirrored the desolation after my parents died, a terrifying echo of love and potential heartbreak.

"Ava, you okay?" Rose's voice pulls me from the depths, looking concerned.

My head snaps up. "What? … Sorry, I was a million miles away. What's up?" My voice sounds distant, even to my ears.

Rose chuckles, a low, warm sound that soothes some raw edge inside me. "I was asking if you were ready; you look deep in thought.

Anything interesting?" Her gaze is searching, knowing.

A smile plays on my lips despite myself. "Um… I'm not sure. It'll cost ya, but I can't say here." My eyes flick instinctively towards Sam, hunched over his laptop, pretending not to listen but radiating suspicion like cheap cologne.

Rose's eyes light up with curiosity. "I'm interested in finding out now, but as you said! Anyway, I came over to say we got the feeds up. Are you coming over to see what we got?"

The thought of crowding around a single screen, as Sam hasn't set up the others yet, the forced proximity with Sam's distrustful energy, makes my skin crawl. "Maybe in a bit. It'll feel a bit claustrophobic for me with all four of us crammed together. I'm going to go change out of these clothes. You can catch me up when I return," I say, needing space, needing distance. I stand abruptly, heading for the door, aware of Rose's concerned gaze following me. I know she wants to follow, but Sam's presence pins her in place.

Back in the relative sanctuary of our room, I peel off my workout gear, the fabric clinging uncomfortably. Jeans, T-shirt – my usual armour. I leave the harness, with the sword which is oddly comforting now, resting on the now spare bed. Stretching out on our now shared bed, the cheap motel mattress groaning beneath me, I stare at the stained ceiling, the patterns swirling like the chaos in my head. The vampire's compulsion… that chilling brush against my mind, the seductive pull towards oblivion… it still feels unsettling. And this mental link with Rose, feeling her anger, her presence snapping me back from the brink… it's another layer of complexity I don't know how to navigate. How can I be a soldier, an assassin, relying on sharp edges and emotional detachment, when I'm this exposed, this vulnerable? I'm just human, surrounded by beings of immense power, ancient histories, and complicated pack rules. Doubt gnaws at me. Am I enough?

A sharp rap on the door jolts me. My hand instinctively goes to where a dagger *should* be – of course, I have none on me right now.

Annoyed at the interruption, wanting only solitude, I drag myself off the bed. Swinging the door open reveals Luca, not Sam, not Rose, I'd expected one of them, except Rose would have just let herself in. His expression is serious, a careful mixture of worry and something unreadable.

"Can we talk for a bit?" he inquires, his voice low, steady.

Wordlessly, I step back, holding the door wider. He enters and closes the door softly behind him when I move away, then takes the chair by the window, settling himself with a quiet intensity. I perch on the end of the bed, muscles tense, waiting.

His dark eyes meet mine, concern etched around them. "Are you alright after what the vampire attempted?" he asks.

A humourless laugh escapes me. "Define, *alright*. Yeah, I'm fine. What's up?" The words sound clipped, harsher than intended.

"I want to use this time to have a quick chat. We haven't really spoken much since the ranch, so I want to make sure you are happy with everything. We also have the situation between you and Rose to talk about, too."

The mention of Rose sends a complicated mix of warmth and anxiety through me. "The vampire thing… yeah, it caught me off guard, I still feel slightly off after what he tried to do," I admit, the words tumbling out before I can stop them. "It has made me wonder why I am here. I'm just a human being with some trained abilities. They are nothing compared to what you and Rose have and can do, let alone the vampires and whatever else we will have to go up against," I take a deep breath.

Luca looks surprised at my response, as if it isn't what he expected me to say. Before I let him respond, I continue, "Then I apparently have a bond with a woman who is a shifter. A bond between us shouldn't be possible at all, especially as I'm human and shouldn't happen between same-sex partners. Then I have Papa Legba paying me a visit in my dreams."

At those final words, Luca's expression shifts. "That's

something else I wanted to talk to you about. We couldn't really talk in the diner, so I wanted to hear more about his visit in more detail," he says in a more demanding way than you would expect for a typical chat. "Let's start with him. Please tell me again what he said in more detail."

I gather myself and try to remember everything he said, "He told me about this woman who's trying to bring one of your people together with a woman called Reya to bond with or something, but you chose Rose to bring instead. Apparently, the woman she wants your guy to meet has bonded with someone else or something else, so her plans have gone out the window. Legba is also very interested in the bond between Rose and me and wanted to see what I thought about his gift."

Luca looks speechless at first, but he finally pulls himself together, "I was going to bring someone else, but at the last minute, I chose Rose when I heard Agent Moore was going to put you in charge of this team, I thought having an even team would make things more comfortable for you, but I have come to realise I wasn't being fair to you, watching you deal with the police Chief and how you have dealt with everything so far and the environment you usually work in, has shown me you can deal with anything and anyone so that you wouldn't have had an issue with your team consisting of all men."

"I'm used to being surrounded only by men in the special forces, so you're right. I would have been fine with a team of only men, but it has been nice to have Rose on the team, even with all this bond stuff." I say, wishing I didn't have to do this right now.

"Yes, when Rose told me about what she was experiencing, I recognised it as the bond. I had hoped to talk to you both before anything happened between you, but it was too late. We need to talk about the rules of pack life. I'm not happy, Rose let things progress without you knowing what it means to be mated to a shifter and be part of my pack," Luca said, looking very determined.

"Rose did mention something about pack rules, and normally, you would have to agree to it if someone in your pack wants to date someone outside of your pack. I don't see why you get to decide on something like that, to be honest."

Luca doesn't look happy with what I've said, but doesn't react. "The rules are there to keep the pack safe. They could destroy us if we let the wrong person into the pack. What do you think would happen if we let someone in? We told them and showed them who we really were, but they couldn't handle it. What do you think they might do with that information?"

I thought about it. He's right in a way. It could be bad for them. I didn't exactly react well to start with, and Agent Moore said he didn't either. "Sure, I can understand it a little. They could go and tell the wrong people, and then the wrong kind of attention can be drawn to you."

"Exactly. I have heard of a small pack being wiped out because a female shifter fell in love with a local man. After she told him the truth and showed him that same truth, turning into a tiger, he ran from the pack, returning with a group of men with guns and killed them all in a surprise attack, as the men all had military backgrounds."

I sat there in shock at what he was saying. I know people can be evil, but that is just wrong. I also know men aren't as good as women at accepting someone who is different and can do stupid things in response, but that is just wrong, so wrong. "Yeah, okay, I can understand your rules, but how can you tell if someone is going to react badly or not?"

"That's the question, isn't it? It's hard, so we have to do little tests to see how they will react to other things, then we start to build up a picture of their state of mind; nine times out of ten, we get it right, but now and then we do get it wrong."

"What do you do if it goes badly, and they can't accept the truth and run?" I ask, worried about the answer.

Luca takes a few seconds studying me before he gives me his answer, "We send someone to follow them. We have to deal with it if they plan to put us in danger. Sometimes, a threat is enough, but sometimes, we have to take drastic measures. When possible, my father got a witch to make the person forget everything about us. We don't take that kind of action lightly, but now we find ourselves in a difficult situation. After all the attacks, we no longer have enough pack members to find our mates within the pack, although my pack is pretty even right now with regard to sexes. What it means, though, is that they are forced to look outside of the pack now more than ever."

I understood what he's saying, but I'm unsure how to take it that he is telling me they might have to kill those who don't accept them, but I understand wanting to protect themselves. I don't know what life is like as a shifter, so maybe I shouldn't judge them, especially me. I'm special forces and an assassin when needed. "I understand, so what else do I need to know about pack life?"

Luca gives me a small smile before he responds. He looks relieved. "Well, you have a choice to make. You either agree to join my pack and follow the rules and the orders of the pack leaders, which is, of course, me as alpha. Then there are Rose and Elijah, my betas; even though I became alpha as a child after the attacks happened, there was a beta who had been leading us for years, as I was too young. When the attack on our pack happened, I was out on a diplomatic mission with one of the betas to learn the ropes. This kind of thing started when I was five. On the way back from the pack we were having talks with, we always had a scout behind us to see if we were going to be followed and attacked. On this occasion, our scout caught up with us much sooner than we expected, so we thought he was going to tell us they were following us." Luca pauses a second, taking a deep breath, then continues, "He informed us the pack we just left were attacked and wiped out. They were so surprised they couldn't mount a defence. We increased our speed to get back home, and when we arrived, we found local authorities in our community and bodies everywhere. We thought they were the ones who had killed our friends and family, but as we watched on and listened to the conversations taking place, we heard that there were attacks all around the country and the world, so we realised the police weren't responsible for our people being killed. We waited for the police and the FBI to leave, then we searched for survivors who could be hiding. We found only three children, three of my friends."

Luca closes his eyes and sighs before he continues, "Sorry, I got sidetracked, but I thought you might like to know what happened so you can understand things better. Anyway, as I started to say, you have to choose if you are willing to follow the rules and orders. Otherwise, Rose and you have to leave the pack and either find another pack to join or create your own; that's your first choice. If you decide to join, you must take on a role within the pack. You will either take turns helping in different areas each week so you don't get bored and unhappy with doing something you don't like or if you are exceptional at something and it's something you enjoy doing, then you can stay in that position till you tell us otherwise, most packs follow the same lifestyle, it has been found it helps to keep pack life a happy one for most, of course at present those of us that are left are basically on the run now, so no one is happy anymore, that's why I agreed to this mission, hoping we can find who is behind it all and eliminate them to restore order, so we can get back to our normal pack life."

I think about what he's saying, my mind goes to Rose and what she told me. She was on the streets, and when she finally accepted Luca's help, she found a place she could call home. I wouldn't make her give that up. "Well, to start with, I would never ask Rose to leave your pack. How would your normal pack life work for someone like me who has a career that takes me away to places around the world?"

"That's not an issue. As long as you help even in a small way when you are around, then no one will have an issue. Some of us still need to earn money to help the pack. You will find that a normal pack life is a simple one, most of the time, and hopefully, you will experience it in the future. Maybe you will change your mind about your career after we finish this mission," he said with a clear hint that's what he was hoping for.

"Why would I change my mind about my career? It's all I've ever wanted to do. I don't see that changing," I say, confused about why he thought I might consider leaving the forces.

"I take it, then, Agent Moore didn't talk to you about his plans for the future?"

I shake my head before I say anything. "No, he didn't. Would you care to enlighten me?"

"I'm not sure I should mention it," Luca says, looking worried like he has just put his foot in it.

"Just tell me, now I know something is being kept from me. It will bug me, I will pester you nonstop," I say, making sure Luca understands what would happen if he didn't tell me.

Luca sighs and says, "Depending on how this went, I know he was going to talk to you about a new role. I thought he might have talked about it before we left, so you could think about it while we were on this mission," Luca looks extremely worried, I'm guessing about what my reaction is going to be.

"Just spill it, Luca; if you don't, I'm going to call Agent Moore about it to get answers and tell him it's all your fault," I say with a smirk.

Luca doesn't look impressed with my statement and looks even more worried about telling me, but looks resigned to having to tell me. Then he looks into my eyes and says, "After we are done, Agent Moore plans to set up a new agency to deal with Paranormal issues. His current department doesn't have a name within the CIA, and he said he wouldn't be able to run this new agency from within the CIA. He mentioned calling it the PBI. Paranormal Bureau of Investigation, but he isn't sure that would be accepted unless the truth comes out to the public, so he's going to think of a name that doesn't mention the paranormal, hoping it's not treated as a joke by those not in the know. This department, with no name within the CIA and FBI, is the only department that is aware of the paranormal world to an extent, but only has a handful of people." he said, triggering something in the back of my mind when I turned up at CIA headquarters and the departments you can't just go to on your own; now I knew the department with no name was real.

"Okay, but how does that affect me?"

"He mentioned hoping you will run the first team if this goes well, even though he is part of this department with no name. They don't have a team out in the field yet; well, that's what Agent Moore told us, and even though he works for that department, he still didn't react well when he saw us shift," Luca said, chuckling to himself, thinking back to that moment.

I wasn't sure what to say about that. I love my job, of course. Like every job, not everything is perfect, but I can't see myself doing anything else. If I did return to my usual missions, I wouldn't see Rose often. I still don't understand why they would want a normal human to deal with paranormal issues, unless they want me because they don't fully trust a paranormal individual to run things. As a human, I am one of the most highly skilled individuals who has a small chance against these beings. "Well, for now, it's not worth considering as we have a mission, and that is all that matters."

"Of course, to finish off for now about pack life, if you challenge me or a beta about our authority, it will be a challenge to the death in the case of challenging myself. If you challenge a beta, it's either to death or until someone submits, so you have to be careful, as a challenge can't be taken back."

"Are you serious? If I don't agree with something, I either have to keep my mouth shut or challenge you. Let's say I challenged you and somehow managed to win. Then what?"

"Nothing. You are human. Only a shifter can be an alpha of a pack. There is a kind of magical transference that happens to make someone alpha. You can tell if someone is an alpha or beta by eye colour, so if you did manage to beat me, you would be allowed to keep your life and leave, then the betas will fight to see who becomes the new alpha."

"Eye colour, what do you mean? Does it change or something?" Luca stares at me, and then his eyes start to change to red around the outside of the pupil. It's like a neon light has been switched on. They glow, then fade and vanish. I have just one question, "I've seen you flash your eyes at Rose. Do betas have a different colour?"

"Blue" is all he says.

I have another question, "So if I manage to beat an alpha or beta of another pack, would I have to join that pack?" Luca smiles at my question and then says, "No, you would only have to join if you were challenging them to join. Normally, you would challenge a normal pack member to join. Let's say you challenge a beta of another pack and beat them, and the transference was to work for you; you would then have a choice to become a beta and move up within my pack or join the other pack and replace the beta you beat. As a new beta and you stayed in my pack, then for some reason you were to challenge and beat me, you would have another choice. Take over my pack as it was to the death, or you start a new pack, taking with you those who would prefer to follow you from my pack."

I just sit there trying to absorb all these rules, but I can't see how most of them affect me. I'm human, so this magical transference wouldn't work on me; otherwise, Luca would have heard about it if it did. That leads me to another question, "Okay, I understand, but it does make me wonder about something else."

"I think I know what you are about to ask," Luca says with a knowing smile.

"Not sure you do, but go on, what am I about to ask?" I say, crossing my arms over my chest, waiting to see how smart he thinks he is.

"You want to know if you can be turned into one of us? It is something you and Rose are going to have to be careful about, as I can tell Rose has broken your skin," Luca said, looking concerned.

I'm gobsmacked that he guessed what I'm going to ask. I also start to blush a little as he knows Rose has bitten me, "How?"

"I could smell the blood on you after Rose had her chat with you!" he says with a smirk, knowing we hadn't just had a chat. "Also, everyone asks if they can be turned. The answer to that one is yes, but it can only happen on a full moon. Rose would have to bite you on the neck after midnight of a full moon and keep you in that position for at least twenty minutes for the change to happen. If it happens, there is a chance the change will be rejected. If that happens, you will die."

"What! Why would anyone want to risk it?" I ask as my voice rises at the end.

"Sometimes, when a human joins a pack, they want to join us fully and are willing to take the risk. It's very rare for someone to die, but it does happen; for some reason, the animal rejects the host. Also, we live a lot longer than humans, so they want to take the risk to be with their partner longer."

I just shake my head. I can't believe anyone would want to risk it, but I suppose love has driven people to do all sorts of things, even in the human world. The part about living longer catches me off guard, though. "Exactly how long do shifters live for?"

"Up to 250 years, the average is 200 to 220 for the born; for the bitten, it's more like 150 to 200; some shifters species only have a range from 120 to 180; it all depends on the type of animal they shift into," Luca says, watching me closely to see how I react.

"Wow, that's long. Why would the universe give us this bond thing, then, when I will die while Rose is still in her prime? That makes me sad, knowing she will go on and have another relationship or two. What about when I get old? It will look ridiculous; she will have to help me walk to the bathroom at some point. I wouldn't let it get that far; I would make sure she left me by then," I went off on one; I'm talking to myself in the end and not to Luca. When I look at him, he seems dumbfounded.

"Now it's my turn to say, wow! I have never had this conversation with someone, or listened as my father had when someone new joined his pack, they never went there so quickly. Normally, those kinds of questions crop up years later. You have an amazing mind, Ava. It's truly amazing. I wouldn't say that to Rose if I were you," Luca says, shaking his head, still looking dumbfounded.

"I'm not stupid; of course, I wouldn't, but it is something I won't be able to stop thinking about now. I do have one other question, though, and I feel a little awkward about asking it," I say, averting my eyes and looking down towards the floor.

"Just ask and get it over with," Luca says.

"Well….erm…" I feel like a child as I try to ask my question. I get there in the end, though. I watch Luca smirk like he already knows, "So…Rose bit me, well, a couple of times. I thought I was going to have a nasty wound on my neck on full display, like the scratch marks on my back, but my neck healed like it never happened, and the scratches on my back are pretty much gone now," I say, feeling like I'm going to blush again, its something I seem to be doing a lot since meeting Rose.

"Arrh, it's a shifter thing and a bond thing. When we bite for the first time with a new partner, it connects our souls. It's hard to explain to someone with almost no knowledge of our world. After the first time, it heals instantly, but from now on, it won't be as powerful as the first time and won't heal as fast. But it will heal faster than normal human healing. Maybe for you and Rose, it will be different. There are rumours that the bond increases those abilities so that you could heal faster after the first time, but I'm not sure, as you're human, and I don't know what's real or not. The fact that you healed instantly suggests it works even for humans," Luca explains. I'm just lost with how much there is to know.

CHAPTER 26

OTHERWORLDLY MEETINGS, URGENT AGENDAS, AND CAT MUTTERING
ABOUT MEDDLESOME LOAS

Luca and I chat for a bit longer after he explains the pack rules and the implications of the bond. The conversation eventually shifts from the complexities of pack life back to the immediate, chilling reality of Papa Legba's visit. His concern is a palpable thing in the small motel room, a heavy cloak settling over his usual alpha confidence. He requests, his voice tight, that I run through everything again – every word, every nuance, every subtle shift in Legba's demeanour and not just my edited version I previously gave him. I oblige, recounting the strange dreamscape bar, the skeletal figure in the top hat, his unsettlingly familiar yet alien presence, the southern drawl thick as molasses dripping strange prophecies and veiled warnings. As I detail the conversation, the interest in our bond, the mention of the woman going by the name Cat, which I'm not sure he meant to tell me, but I'm unsure if that is the real name of the woman's voice we have both heard, as it seemed like he was going to say another name I think begins with an 'H'. Also, Cat's thwarted plans involving Elijah and this Reya, the favour Legba expects in return for his *gift* – Luca's frown deepens, etching lines of worry around his eyes.

"I'm troubled by the thought that he's interested in you and Rose," he finally admits, rubbing a hand over his jaw, a gesture of deep unease. "Deeply troubled. Based on everything I've ever heard, every scrap of lore passed down, Legba doesn't involve himself without a steep price, a twist in the bargain. His gifts are never free, Ava, no matter what Madi claimed. Sure enough, after the fact, you find out there is a price. His interest… it rarely brings good tidings." He paces the small space between the bed and the window, restless energy coiling within him. "I'm also worried that this other individual," he spits the words out, "I trusted the voice I heard," his distrust for this Cat is now evident, "she might be manipulating things, influencing my pack members for her own agenda. I didn't challenge the voice when I first heard it, when it led me to Moore. Back then… I allowed myself to hope it represented guidance from one of our own deities, a sign we weren't forgotten in this fight." He stops, turning to face me, his expression grim. "But given Legba's interference now, his sudden, vested interest… I have to question everything. Reconsider their true motives entirely."

I listen patiently, absorbing his distrust, his caution born from a lifetime navigating a world far more treacherous than the battlefields I know. His perspective is valid, grounded in experience I lack. Yet, my gut, that primal instinct honed sharp by countless life-or-death situations, screams a different message. "I don't think so, Luca," I counter, the certainty in my voice surprising even myself. "Think about it. If they – Cat, Legba, whoever – were truly adversaries, why guide us at all? Why give me the ring? Why warn us? They've had ample opportunity to betray us, to lead us straight into an ambush. Instead, they've offered cryptic help, pieces of a puzzle. I believe they *are* here to aid us, in their convoluted way. We should trust them, cautiously perhaps, but trust them nonetheless. For now."

Luca studies me for a long moment, surprise warring with ingrained suspicion in his dark eyes. He eventually lowers his gaze slightly, a reluctant concession. "Maybe you're correct," he murmurs, the admission seemingly costing him a measure of pride. "It's… difficult. Following orders from a disembodied voice, placing faith in beings known for deception… it goes against every instinct I have. And," he adds, a familiar spark of alpha irritation returning, "I also don't usually follow other people's orders."

That last comment, delivered with a hint of challenge, raises my hackles. My own ingrained defiance surfaces. I meet his gaze squarely, my voice level. "Do you have a problem with me leading this task force?"

A fleeting, almost imperceptible smile touches his lips before vanishing. It's enough to irritate me, but before I can formulate a sharp retort, he holds up a hand, forestalling me. "Your case is unique," he clarifies, his tone shifting back to serious consideration. "Normally, if you were another shifter, perhaps from a rival pack or even unaligned, my own panther nature would resist submitting to your authority. It's pack dynamics, pure instinct. But because you're human…" he shrugs slightly, "that instinct doesn't trigger in the same way. It's… different. So, no, your leadership isn't the issue," he pauses, a calculating glint entering his eyes, "At least for now."

I narrow my eyes, catching the underlying tease but also the implied condition. He confirms it before I can ask. "The only time I *would* have an issue," he states plainly, meeting my gaze without flinching, "the only time my nature would likely rebel against your command, is if you ever decide to accept the bite. To *become* one of us. *Then*," he emphasises the word, "my panther wouldn't take orders from you."

It's a clear boundary, rooted in primal pack law. I nod slowly, accepting it. Fair enough. Satisfied the point is made, Luca leaves, heading back to the other room to presumably take over monitoring the camera feeds from Sam. The door clicks shut behind him, leaving me enveloped in the sudden, heavy silence of the motel room. The air still hums faintly with the intensity of our conversation, thick with unspoken fears and the weight of ancient rules clashing with this new reality I live in.

I need to process. To think. But my mind feels like a tangled knot – Papa Legba's cryptic pronouncements, Luca's pack laws, Moore's potential plans for my future, the impossible reality of the bond with Rose. It's too much. My carefully constructed mental compartments are overflowing, the walls crumbling under the pressure.

Exhaustion, bone-deep and relentless, starts to drag me under. I collapse back onto the bed, the worn mattress dipping beneath my weight. Closing my eyes, I try to do what Legba said to focus on that mental wall, picturing sturdy bricks rising stone by stone, mortar sealing the gaps, a fortress against the intrusions plaguing my sleep. *Defence. Control. Discipline.* The mantras loop, a familiar litany from years of training, but they feel inadequate now, like trying to hold back the ocean with a bucket. Sleep claims me before the imaginary wall gains any height in my mind, pulling me down into a welcome, albeit temporary, oblivion.

But the peace is fleeting. The blackness behind my eyelids shifts, lightens, and resolves into rock, grey, unforgiving stone that towers and surrounds me. I'm standing, though I don't remember getting up, in a desolate valley. Jagged peaks stab at a turbulent sky, bruised purple and angry grey clouds swirling overhead. The air is thin and cold; there are no smells in the air, which feels off-putting, as I'm unable to smell anything except a metallic tang that coats the back of my throat. There's a profound silence here too, deeper than any absence of noise I've ever known, the kind of quiet that presses in on your eardrums. Disorientation washes over me. *Dream? Memory? Another intrusion?*

"Hello, Ava."

The voice materialises behind me, soft as velvet, yet carrying an undeniable resonance. It's the voice from the ranch, the whisper on the wind. Cat's voice. I pivot, the movement strangely effortless, like I weigh nothing. There she is, standing a few paces away, radiating a soft, internal luminescence that pushes back the gloom of the valley. She is undeniably, breathtakingly beautiful, her features possessing a symmetry and grace that seems sculpted rather than born. A simple, unadorned robe flows around her, its fabric rippling softly despite the utter stillness of the air. The word forms unbidden in my mind, *Goddess.*

"Thank you," she says with a faint, knowing smile playing on her lips.

My cheeks warm instantly. Damn it. "You can hear my thoughts?" I stammer, feeling exposed.

"In this place, yes," she confirms calmly. "This space exists… between moments. Between worlds. Thoughts resonate clearly here."

"So, this isn't a dream?" I cling to the possibility, needing some anchor to the reality I understand.

"No," she replies, a hint of weariness entering her tone. "I pulled your consciousness here; It requires… effort. An expenditure I can ill afford." She gestures vaguely at the desolate surroundings. "I needed to speak with you, away from prying ears, both mundane and magical."

Her confirmation solidifies the strangeness, the sheer impossibility of it all. "You're Cat? The voice?"

"I am the one who has guided you, yes," she affirms. Her gaze becomes intense, searching. "Papa Legba paid you a visit and let slip the name I use; he's a menace." It's a statement, not a question.

"He did. In my dreams. How did you…?"

"He leaves ripples," she dismisses the question with a wave of her hand. "His energy is distinctive, disruptive. What did he tell you? What does he want? He is interfering again, deviating from the agreed path." Frustration tightens her serene features.

Hesitantly, I relay the conversation, the focus on my bond with Rose and Legba's fascination with this *impossible* connection, the mention of her plans involving Elijah and Reya being disrupted,

Cat listens, her expression hardening into sharp annoyance as I speak. "That meddling Loa! He knows the stakes, the delicacy of the balance! We agreed—*I* laid out the strategy after the visions showed what was necessary. His interference, his… games…" She trails off, visibly reining in her temper. "He needs to trust the path, trust *my* guidance. This isn't the time for his tricks or bargains." She takes a deep, centring breath, the ambient light around her pulsing faintly. "His interest in your bond with Rose… that is… unexpected. Potentially complicating. But," a thoughtful, almost calculating look enters her eyes, "perhaps also… useful."

Before I can ask what she means, she continues, "But his mention of Reya, of Elijah… He revealed too much. Some threads are best left untouched until the proper time." She shakes her head, muttering, "He always did enjoy stirring the pot."

"He also said you were hoping Elijah would bond with Reya, but she bonded with something else instead?" I venture, recalling the odd phrasing.

Cat's eyes narrow slightly. "Legba speaks in riddles when it suits him. Reya's path is… complex. Her allegiances are still forming. The entity she has connected with…" Cat hesitates, choosing her words carefully. "It is a powerful, ancient being, and not entirely predictable. It complicates matters significantly."

"What kind of entity?" My mind flashes back to Rose's speculation – familiars, daemons, and whatever else she mentioned at the time. There is so much to remember; I'm having issues recalling it all.

"Not now, Ava," Cat cuts me off gently but firmly. "That knowledge is not yet necessary for your part in this. Focus on what is immediate. Papa Legba gave you the ring." Again, a statement.

"Yes. He said it would help me." I touch my finger instinctively, though the ring remains invisible even here. "It lets me see in the dark, track movement I shouldn't be able to see, and… it hides my weapons."

"As I suspected," she nods slowly. "He recognised the potential in you, the faint echo of my bloodline. He seeks to protect his investment, perhaps? Or maybe," a flicker of something unreadable crosses her face, "he simply enjoys the game. Regardless, the ring is powerful; it was created for a human a long time ago. Use it wisely." Her expression turns grave, urgent. "But the ring is not enough. Listen to me, Ava. You *must* get to Chicago. Now. The path I set for you begins there in earnest. What you need to find, the next step… it awaits you in that city. Do not delay."

"But why? What's there? What am I looking for?" The questions burst out, frustration mixing with a growing sense of dread.

"Understanding," she replies cryptically. "And the beginning of the answer to stopping the slaughter, Legba undoubtedly warned you about." Her gaze holds mine, filled with an ancient sorrow and fierce determination. "I will find a way to deliver a weapon to you. Something forged for this war, something that resonates with… who you are becoming. But first, Chicago. Trust me, please. Trust your instincts. You are running out of time." The edges of the valley begin to blur, the rocky peaks dissolving like smoke. "You are being woken."

"Wait! Who *are* you? Also, did you just hint that I am of your bloodline?" I shout into the dissolving scene, desperation clawing at me.

Her voice echoes, fading as the vision collapses into darkness, "You will find out… eventually."

CHAPTER 27

OF TEARFUL CONFESSIONS, TENTATIVE THEORIES, AND TELEVISED TERRORS

I jolt awake, sitting upright abruptly as arms wrap around my shoulders. Fear, sharp and cold, pierces through me – a vampire, here in our room, about to bite. I flinch, attempting to hit whoever holds me, but their grip is too powerful. "It's okay, Ava. It's me, Rose."

Although her words don't immediately register through my panic, her familiar voice and the warmth emanating from her begin to soothe the frantic thumping in my chest. My heart gradually slows as I lean back into Rose's embrace, a strange discomfort settling in with this unwelcome vulnerability. If only these supernatural beings would stop invading my sleep, I could avoid waking up in such a state of terror.

"Did you have a nightmare, honey?" Rose asks, her voice soft as she tries to comfort me.

I sigh, still catching my breath, willing my heart to return to a normal rhythm before I can respond. "Not really," I say sheepishly, hating to admit fear, especially to her.

"Ava, you can tell me. Even if it's silly, or maybe you just don't want to admit what you see as a weakness."

I turn towards Rose, my mouth dropping open. She *guesses* why I hesitate. "How?"

"I'm starting to get to know you," she explains, a gentle smile in her voice. "But I also felt your emotions as you slept, which tipped me off; it's why I came back, because I could feel how worried you were."

I already suspect this bond between Rose and me is going to be a pain, but I *really* don't like that it gives her a window into my emotions. I know I've felt her anger before, but I've always been a fiercely private person. Perhaps Papa Legba's advice about my mental weaknesses prompted me to start thinking of a wall around my mind, but I fell asleep before I made much progress with it. Maybe it's something I need to take more seriously. I decide right here and now that it's something I'm going to work on every day. I start to imagine a wall around my mind subconsciously. Instead of thinking about forming the wall brick by brick, I imagine a complete wall around my mind as Rose comforts me. If it can at least stop these dream invasions, I'll be grateful.

Frustration bubbles up, but I reluctantly tell Rose what flashed through my mind when I woke – the fear of a vampire attack. I can see the effort it takes for her to keep a straight face, a slight twitch at the corner of her lips betraying her amusement.

"I would sense them from next door and come running to protect you," she says, her voice firm with conviction. Then she kisses my cheek and pulls me tighter against her body, her arms a secure shield around me. It does make me feel better, safer. My heart, which had just calmed, picks up its pace again, but this time for a completely different reason, a warmth spreading through me from being wrapped so securely in her arms.

While I enjoy this moment, cocooned in her embrace, I tell her about Cat's visit in my sleep, ending with her last comment about being of her bloodline. When I finish, she looks shocked, then worried, and says something I'm not expecting. "She must be a god, like Luca guessed. I haven't heard of any other magical being able to project themselves like that without being in direct contact with you. If she is, and you are from her bloodline… Ava, this is amazing! It explains how we can have a bond."

I frown, pulling back slightly to look at her. "Why is this amazing? Does this change things with us or something?"

Rose shakes her head, a flicker of annoyance in her eyes. "No, silly. I'm just saying I always knew you were magical because of how I feel about you, but now it seems you're even *more* magical. I'm so glad we might finally have an answer for how we share this bond. It doesn't change how I feel about you, not at all. It's just… it's really been bugging Luca because he's so adamant that this kind of bond can't happen with a human. Papa Legba is regarded as a kind of god, but I don't think he is the type of god I think this Cat is. He's a kind of minor god, a Loa. They say he wasn't descended from the original gods, like I think Cat must be; he apparently came into being through a ceremony performed by enslaved Africans who prayed to Vodou spirits during a burial, asking to be saved. The stories claim he manifested in Haiti and followed his people to New Orleans, then never leaving. He's one of many Loa who came to be. To be honest, I don't know how much of what I've heard is true."

Now *I'm* pissed. I need to set aside the Legba lore and the possibility that Cat is descended from the original gods for a moment, because something more pressing keeps nagging at me. "So, you had an issue with me being human?"

Rose looks flabbergasted, then genuinely hurt by my accusation. "What are you talking about? I have no issues with you being human. No shifter worth their salt has issues with that. Why would you even think that?"

"It just feels like you and Luca wouldn't be happy if I were *just* human," I say, agitation rising in my voice. "Like there has to be something extraordinary or magical about me for you to accept me, to accept this bloody bond thing that you're both so obsessed with."

Rose pulls away from me, and the raw hurt in her eyes is like a punch to my gut. I didn't expect my words to land so hard. Contrition washes over me instantly. "Sorry," I mumble. "It's just… all I've been hearing is *bond this, bond that*. I accept it, okay? But the more everyone goes on about it, the more obsessed you all seem, the more I start to wonder if my feelings are even my own. I'm wondering if they're being forced on me. I *know* how I feel, Rose, and I'm desperately hoping these feelings are real because… because I've fallen for you. Big time."

I watch Rose, bracing for her reaction. For a moment, her expression remains unreadable, and a knot of anxiety tightens in my stomach. Then, slowly, her face softens. "I'm sorry," she says, her voice soft and laced with a fearful tremor that worries me – did I take it too far?

"Why are *you* sorry?" I ask, confused. "I was expecting you to lose it with me."

"I'm sorry because we *have* been going on and on about the bond," she admits. "You're even being hassled in your sleep by gods because of it. I'm sorry because I wasn't seeing this from your perspective. For shifters, we're told stories all our lives about how special the bond is, how rare. For me… I feel like everything I've gone through has been worth it because there was a reason I had to endure it all – to get to you. I couldn't be happier. In fact, I've never been this happy before in my entire life. So, yes, I'm sorry we've been so caught up in it." She averts her eyes, but not before I see the tell-tale shimmer she's trying to hide.

I place my hand under her chin and gently try to guide her face back to mine. She resists at first, but I persist, and she finally relents. As I draw her face towards me, my suspicion is confirmed. She's crying. Not big, heaving sobs, but the silent, emotional tears of someone overwhelmed by happiness, perhaps afraid of losing it. I study her face for a second as the tears trace slow paths down her cheeks. She briefly tries to turn away again, I understand why, but I refuse to let her hide. I move closer, my lips finding hers in a gentle kiss.

"Rose," I say softly, pulling back just enough to look into her eyes, "it may be too soon to say this, but I've always been someone who speaks her mind. So, Rose… I love you."

I catch her completely off guard. She just stares at me, her mouth slightly agape. Slowly, the tears intensify, flowing more freely. Then, in a blur of motion, she takes me by surprise, her arms repositioning around me in seconds. She pulls me against her so tightly that the scratch marks on my back, a souvenir from our first time together, finally flare with pain as Rose's embrace stretches the scratch marks that are barely visible now. I can't help but wince, but she doesn't notice, her head buried in my hair. When she speaks, her voice is muffled against my scalp. "I-I love you too," Rose says, her words punctuated by soft sobs.

We stay locked in that embrace for what feels like an eternity, *maybe ten minutes*, before Rose finally pulls away enough to look me in the face. "Sorry," she sniffles, a watery smile appearing. "I must look a mess right now."

I can't help but smile back. Here I am, wrapped in the arms of the strongest, most powerful, and undeniably beautiful woman I've ever met, and she's as endearingly emotional as any human. "I should be the one saying sorry. I got a little arsey back there. I like being human, and the thought that I might not be… it got to me. Thinking about it, though, this Cat woman said I'm of her blood. It has to be incredibly distant, so I'm probably just human. Nothing more, nothing less."

"Ava, I don't care if you're *only* human," Rose insists, her gaze earnest. "I got obsessed with the whole bond thing and didn't think about your feelings. It won't happen again. What I care about is how I feel about *you*, not… not the other thing." She clearly avoids saying the word *bond* again.

"Rose, don't worry about it," I reassure her. "I do understand your side. I probably would have acted like you and Luca if I'd grown up in your world. But honestly, I don't believe this Cat is a god and I'm somehow related to her, even if she was born thousands of years ago. I know I'm human, and that's it." I rest my head on her shoulder.

"Whoever she is, she's clearly trying to manipulate this Reya person. I wonder what's so special about her! Maybe we'll meet her at some point," Rose muses. "I'm also intrigued about this weapon she also wants to get for you. I already think you look hot as hell when you use that sword. I could watch you all day wielding it against our enemies."

I feel her heart rate increase through my arm resting across her chest, my left hand on her other shoulder.

I decide to let Rose and Luca think what they want about who Cat is. I'm not going to speculate further. I'll wait until I find out the truth, if ever. I can't risk being distracted by it right now.

Rose stays with me, and we manage to get a little more sleep, both of us emotionally spent. We need to ensure we're well-rested for the fight ahead, which I'm sure will be the toughest I've faced to date.

We wake a few hours later, feeling more refreshed and with no more dream interruptions. Once we've freshened up, Rose pops next door to coordinate watching the camera feeds. She returns carrying two large tablets and writing pads. "Sam has set up the feeds on these, so we don't have to sit next door. We can relax while we watch," Rose says with a cheeky smile.

We make ourselves comfortable on the bed, propped against the pillows, and settle in for the long hours of observing the church. We need to determine what the vampires are up to and how many are inside. We've already taken out four, which must have them worried about their missing comrades; there also can't be many more in the city, or there would be a lot more violence. I just hope they don't escalate their plans and kill or turn more people while we sit here watching.

It's very strange for me to watch them. They act… normal. Like anyone would, I find it hard to reconcile the image of these men and the lone woman I've seen with my ingrained concept of vampires. Growing up in a world rich with entertainment – books, movies, Tv shows – you're conditioned to see vampires act a certain way. Of course, there are exceptions where vampires fight on the side of good. My mind starts to wander. Is there a slim chance that one of these vampires we're watching could be on the side of good, perhaps infiltrated this group to bring them down, or is merely trying to hide because anyone on the side of good is now their enemy? I don't know if it's my training that makes me think this way, but it's certainly a tactic I would consider to survive.

"Ava, what's up? You look worried," Rose says, her voice pulling me from my thoughts. I jump slightly, which seems to be happening a lot lately when I'm lost in thought.

"Okay, now I'm definitely worried with how you just reacted," she says, looking concerned. "Come on, what's on your mind, honey?"

"Sorry," I say as I shake my head. "I was in my own little world. Didn't mean to worry you. I think my training is making me wonder if we might take out someone innocent – someone who's just using this group, this nest, to hide in, to survive. I see it all the time in my line of work." I avoid looking directly at Rose, half-expecting her to think I'm being ridiculous.

I can feel Rose staring at me. She's quiet for what feels like an eternity before she finally offers her opinion. "The only vampires that can genuinely be on the side of good are born vampires. They're the ones with pale skin and pale pink eyes. We haven't seen any born vampires while we've been watching. The ones we've seen so far are turned; they have no souls to speak of, and all they care about is draining victims and turning others when they're strong enough to help protect themselves from their enemies."

I let out a breath I was holding, relieved. I was expecting Rose to call me stupid or something, but instead, she reminds me of details I've already forgotten, my brain still rattling with so much new information. "You're right," I concede, watching the feed from the camera I placed under the church sign. "I forgot that detail. I'm overwhelmed with all the new information. I'm being silly."

"No, you're not," Rose says firmly. "You've dealt with an incredible amount since we met at that ranch. You can't be expected to remember every single detail. I'm here to help you learn as quickly as possible, with everything you need to know. Just ask me if you need anything clarified, okay?" She leans over and kisses me on the cheek. I can't help but smile in response.

I turn to face her and return the kiss, aiming for the side of her mouth as she's still partly facing the tablet. I rest my forehead against hers, immediately soaking in the comforting heat radiating from her skin. "Thanks," I say softly. "I am a little overwhelmed right now, but I'll deal with it. This isn't something I'm used to. Normally, I'm always in control, on top of everything – it's why I'm so good at my job. I'll get back there as I get more used to this new world I didn't know I was living in, and once we start taking action."

"It's fine, honey, I understand," she says, her voice full of warmth. "You're dealing with everything so much better than we expected. I'm impressed, and so is Luca. It's not easy to impress him, but he is. This is your first mission dealing with paranormals, so of course, it's going to be one of the hardest beings to go up against for your first time out. Once we've taken out these vamps, you'll feel so much better. Believe me, you'll be back in control and kicking arse like never before."

She's right, of course. "I know. Thank you." I pull back slightly. "We'd better get back to watching. I want these vampires gone. I don't think I've ever hated anything as much as I hate them already." "Vampires are our mortal enemy," Rose sneers, her eyes fixed on the screen with renewed intensity. "I know exactly how you feel."

CHAPTER 28

Inter-Agency Cooperation? More Like Inter-Agency
Consternation

For two long days, we hole up in our motel rooms. The air has grown thick with the smell of stale coffee and takeout containers. We have been meticulously watching the church feeds that Sam managed to set up on our tablets before the tiny camera batteries finally die, which Sam believes will be by the morning. The flickering images reveal a disquieting normalcy – figures moving inside the old building, coming and going occasionally, their movements mundane and almost human. It's chillingly deceptive. We pore over the footage, analysing patterns, counting heads, trying to gauge the number of vampires we're truly up against. The initial count appears low – just four distinct individuals have been consistently identified. Too low, Luca insists, his brow furrowed in concentration as he replays a clip for the tenth time.

We are all bundled in Rose's and my room today, we have taken breaks over these two days, Luca and Sam would head out and do more sword training and Rose and I would go to the park so she could continue my training with going up against shifters, it also helped to see just how much the ring is helping me being able to track her movements as she is faster than a human can move.

"It doesn't add up," he murmurs, more to himself than anyone else, tracing a figure on the screen with his finger. "For a nest established long enough to account for the attacks spanning back years… four is not enough. Barely a fledgling group." He leans back, crossing his arms, his alpha instincts clearly troubled. "My gut tells me this isn't the primary nest. It's too small, too… sloppy, almost. Like the vampire we encountered attacking that woman, I'm sure he was recently turned."

His first theory – that this is a very new nest – feels wrong, clashing directly with the twenty-three-year timeline of escalating incidents outlined back in the police files. It doesn't fit the pattern.

His second theory resonates more deeply, chilling me despite the warmth radiating from Rose beside me on the cramped motel bed. "Maybe," Luca continues, his voice low and thoughtful, "they operate like a virus, spreading slowly, deliberately. The attacks over the decades were calculated, kept below the threshold of major alarm. Low numbers initially, ensuring they didn't skew crime statistics too drastically, allowing them to operate under the radar." He looks around at us, his gaze intense. "Then, once their numbers reach a certain point in one city, strong enough to sustain themselves and defend territory, they split. Half stay, half move on to infest a new city, repeating the process. A slow, insidious takeover."

The implications are staggering. If Luca's right, we aren't just dealing with isolated pockets of evil; we're facing a coordinated, continent-spanning infestation. "So, this group," I clarify, my voice tight, "they might just be the latest offshoot? Tasked with seeding a new nest, turning humans, expanding their reach?" The thought is terrifying in its scale.

"It's plausible," Luca concedes, his expression grim. "It fits the slow burn, the gradual escalation over two decades. It explains the relatively small number we've observed here."

We identify two of the vampires on the footage – cross-referencing their faces with missing person reports from the Pittsburgh files reveals they vanished last year—two more victims consumed by this creeping darkness. The weight of it settles heavily in the room.

It's now the second night since we set the cameras, it will be the last. The camera I set under the church sign has already died because it wasn't getting much sun, so we are just watching the feed from the camera in the tree across the road, deep into the early hours of the morning. The tablet screens glow dimly, casting long shadows. Rose and I are on watch again, the silence punctuated only by the hum of the air conditioner and the distant sounds of the city starting to wake up filtering through our open window. Sam and Luca are attempting to sleep in the adjoining room, although I doubt either is truly getting rest. Suddenly, a sharp knock echoes through our room, making both Rose and I jump; someone is at our door.

Rose untangles herself from beside me and pads silently to the door, pausing for a moment, likely listening or scenting who's there. "It's the guys," she confirms as she opens it.

Sam enters first, his face etched with urgency, followed closely by Luca, who looks equally tense. "We have a situation," Sam announces without preamble, his voice clipped. He strides towards the bed where I'm sitting up, tablet forgotten in my lap. "Chief Thornton has been blowing up my phone for the last hour. Non-stop calls, increasingly abusive voicemails." My stomach clenches. "Someone was killed not long ago – another brutal attack, hallmarks match. And worse, another person was abducted. There was a witness this time, who saw the victim being dragged away. Thornton is demanding answers, wants to know what the hell we're doing, and insists on seeing us immediately."

Just as the weight of Sam's words sinks in, Rose, who had moved back to watch the live feed on her tablet while Sam was speaking, lets out a sharp hiss. "Hey! You need to see this!" She swivels the tablet, angling it so we can all see the feed.

"What is it, Rose?" Luca asks, instantly alert, moving closer.

"The church feed… look." Her finger taps the screen as she rewinds the feed a few minutes. "The vamps… they just carried someone inside. Looks unconscious… or worse."

We crowd around the small screen, the grainy footage playing out a scene of horror. Two of the vampires we recognise effortlessly carry a limp human form through the main entrance of the darkened church before disappearing inside. A wave of cold fury washes over me. I surge off the bed, my immediate instinct to gear up, to go *now*. I start towards my clothes, piled on a chair.

"Ava, wait." Luca's voice is calm but firm, stopping me in my tracks. He places a restraining hand gently on my arm. "It's too late."

"Too late?" I whirl on him, disbelief and rage warring within me. "What are you talking about? They *just* took them in! It hasn't been long! If we move now, get there fast, we might still be able to save them! Isn't that why we're bloody here?" My voice rises, frustration making it sharp. Why are they just standing there?

Rose moves to stand in front of me, her hands coming up to rest gently but firmly on my shoulders, forcing me to meet her gaze. Her eyes are filled with a pained understanding that chills me more than Luca's calm statement. "Ava, listen to me," she says softly but with undeniable conviction. "It *is* too late for that person. As soon as they got them inside that church, behind closed doors… they would have drained them. Immediately. Either to feed, or," her voice drops slightly, "to begin the turning process. They don't take prisoners, Ava. They don't wait. I promise you, with absolute certainty, there is *nothing* we can do to help that specific individual right now." The finality in her tone is like a physical blow.

My shoulders slump, the fight draining out of me, replaced by a sickening wave of helplessness and anger. Powerless. Again.

"All we *can* do now," Rose continues, her grip tightening slightly, grounding me, "is finalise our plan to take *them* out. All of them. That's the only way to potentially save the victim now – if they *are* being turned, stopping the process before it completes, though even that…" she trails off, the unspoken *is unlikely* hanging heavy in the air. "We hit them hard, we hit them fast, and we don't stop until every last one of them is ash."

The raw fury returns, cold and focused this time. She's right. Rescue is impossible. Retribution is all that's left. I nod mutely, sinking back onto the edge of the bed as Luca and Rose begin discussing tactical approaches, entry points, lines of fire. Their voices become a low murmur, the technical details of orchestrating death a familiar, almost comforting backdrop to the turmoil inside me. The planning should be my domain, but right now, my head feels too full, too heavy with the weight of failure.

My CIA-issued mobile buzzes insistently on the bedside table, shattering the tense quiet. I glance at the caller ID – blocked number, but it can only be one person. With a sigh laced with irritation, already anticipating the onslaught, I pick up, bracing myself. "Bekke."

"*Agent Bekke!*" Thornton's voice explodes through the receiver, tight with barely suppressed rage. "Are you and your so-called *task force* actually *doing* anything constructive, or just enjoying the local hospitality? Because while you've been… *investigating*… we've had *another* murder and an abduction! We have a witness this time! If you don't start pulling your weight and addressing this escalating situation now, I will be contacting your superiors directly. Make no mistake, I *will* ensure they are fully apprised of your staggering incompetence!" His litany of threats continues, fuelled by bruised ego and impotent fury.

Something inside me snaps. The simmering anger from Rose's earlier confirmation of the victim's fate, combined with Thornton's blustering arrogance, boils over. All attempts at diplomacy, at playing the political game, evaporate. "Chief," I interrupt, my voice dangerously calm, laced with ice, "we are *aware* of the abduction. Thank you for confirming the additional homicide. We have, in fact, located the primary operational base of the gang responsible, something you seem to have been utterly incapable of finding yourself. We are currently finalising our assault plan to neutralise the threat with minimal risk to *my* team, something I'm sure you wouldn't do with regard to your officers. We anticipate executing the operation by tonight." I pause, letting the silence stretch, imagining his face turning a deep shade of puce. "I *was* going to request local support, standard inter-agency cooperation. However, given your persistently obstructive attitude, your unprofessional attempts at intimidation, and your clear inability to grasp the severity of this situation, I've decided against it. My team and I will handle this ourselves. You can read about it in the papers… assuming we choose not to release a statement through your department at all." I don't wait for a response. I end the call, the silence in the room is profound.

I look up to see three pairs of eyes staring at me – Luca's impressed, Rose's concerned but approving, and Sam's… horrified.

"Ava!" Sam sputters, running a hand through his hair distractedly. "Please, let me try to handle him from now on! You can't just… hang up on a Chief of Police like that! If he complains to the wrong people at the Bureau, people who don't know the full context, they could impose oversight! Send someone out to *supervise* us! We'd be hamstrung, unable to operate effectively! You know the protocols!" His voice is agitated, laced with genuine fear for the mission's integrity.

I take a deep breath, forcing the anger down, recognising the validity of his concern, even if his approach grates. "Sorry, Sam," I say, my voice tight but controlled. "Bad timing. Being told we were too late to save that woman… it pushed me over the edge. He caught the brunt of it."

"I understand the frustration, Ava, believe me," Luca interjects, his tone placating but firm. "But we *do* need to try and maintain a semblance of cooperation with local forces where possible. If word gets out that we're unprofessional, confrontational… other cities might shut us out before we even arrive. We need access, information, and local knowledge. Burning bridges, even with asses like Thornton, isn't strategically sound long-term."

"Luca's right, Ava," Sam adds, looking genuinely worried now. "This… aggressive side… it wasn't in your file. I'm trained for standard inter-agency friction, bureaucratic runarounds… not this level of open conflict. I'm… frankly, I'm not sure how to manage this aspect of your leadership style."

His words sting, another reminder of how far outside my normal operational parameters this mission is pushing me. I close my eyes briefly, gathering myself. "Okay," I say, meeting their gazes evenly. "Apologies. Both of you. You're right. I let my frustration get the better of me. It won't happen again." I focus on Sam. "I understand the need for diplomacy. But you also need to understand, Sam, that appeasing bullies like Thornton doesn't work. It emboldens them. He saw you as weak, someone he could take advantage of, and that reflects poorly on the entire team. We *have* to project strength, competence, and absolute authority. Otherwise, Luca's right – we'll be dismissed, stonewalled everywhere we go." I pause, letting the words sink in. "The message leaving Pittsburgh needs to be unequivocal. This task force gets the job done, and we don't tolerate interference or disrespect. We already made him look foolish on live Tv. The next press conference needs to reinforce that *we* succeeded where he failed, *despite* his lack of cooperation. If that message isn't delivered clearly, if we appear subservient to local egos…" I trail off, letting the unspoken threat hang in the air. "Then maybe I *am* the wrong person for this job."

The room is silent for a long moment. Finally, Sam nods slowly, reluctantly. "Okay, Ava. I… I see your point. We project strength."

"Good." I stand up, the decision made. "Right. It's late, nearly morning. We hit the church tonight. Get some sleep. Now, please leave. I need some rack time." I turn towards the bathroom, dismissing them, needing the solitude to wrestle with my own conflicting emotions before facing the vampires again.

I hear muffled whispers behind me, then the soft click of the door closing. Alone at last, turning on the shower, hoping the rush of hot water would sluice away some of the tension. Just as I step under the spray, the bathroom door opens again. I tense instinctively, then relax as Rose's silhouette appears through the frosted glass. She doesn't speak, simply undresses quickly and slides into the shower stall with me, her presence solid and reassuring in the small space. She closes the glass door, pinning me gently against the cool tiles with her body.

"That," she murmurs against my wet skin, her voice a low purr, "was unbelievably hot. Standing up to them like that… taking charge." Her hands begin a slow exploration, tracing patterns on my back. "You might be right about needing to project strength." A wicked glint enters her eyes. "Right now, though… I have a lot of pent-up energy I desperately need an outlet for. If," she adds, her voice dropping to a husky whisper that sends shivers down my spine despite the steam, "you're amenable?"

A slow smile spreads across my face. The exhaustion, the anger, the guilt… they momentarily recede, replaced by a different kind of heat. "Show me what ya got, shifter," is all I manage before her mouth finds mine. She does. Gloriously.

Later, curled together in bed, the aftermath of passionate release leaving us languid and sated, sleep finally claims me. As my head rests on Rose's shoulder, her steady warmth a comforting anchor in the darkness, my last conscious thought is that tonight, ash will fall.

CHAPTER 29

OF COMMS, COUSINS, AND KITTY CATS: A STAKEOUT

SHIFTER STORYTIME

We arrive later that day at the exact location we used the other day when we dropped off Sam, allowing him to establish overwatch like he did when I set up the cameras. Unfortunately, they are now useless; the batteries are completely drained, even with the tiny solar panels. Sam explained that the constant Wi-Fi signal they used quickly consumed the power. Since the signal couldn't reach our motel directly, he set up a Wi-Fi relay router on the roof, which he hid carefully. Apparently, this relay employs advanced battery technology designed to last significantly longer, transmitting the video signal via a mobile network connection.

We hope nothing significant has changed since the last grainy images the camera transmitted. The air in the Tahoe feels thick with anticipation as we review the mission parameters we established. Sam is being dropped off first to play Overwatch at the church. I value this role immensely; it's vital when working in a team. A key task is preventing ambushes, stopping anyone from sneaking up on us, while also keeping track of our targets moving through the urban landscape. Experience has taught me it's worth; the overwatch position saved my life a few years back during a hairy engagement in hostile territory. An enemy combatant attempted a flanking manoeuvre, trying to sneak up behind our group. My senses prickled, and I spotted them just in time, but there was no guarantee I would have reacted quickly enough without the warning from above. Since then, I have always insisted on having someone in that role when operating with a team; it feels even more critical now, facing opponents whose capabilities I'm still struggling to comprehend fully, but he won't actually be watching over us, his main role is to watch the church, to pass on intel when he can.

Sam climbs out of our vehicle; he retrieves a nondescript duffle bag from the trunk. Inside, I know, rests his preferred rifle, alongside a few other weapons selected for potential close-quarters combat, should his position be compromised. He circles around to the rear passenger-side window where I'm sitting, the window slightly fogged from my breath.

"Are you all set, Sam?" I ask, my voice low, studying his face for any lingering doubt.

"Yep, I'm all good." He leans casually against the door, projecting confidence, though I sense a flicker of unease beneath the surface. "I'll make contact as soon as I see any movement from the church," Sam confirms.

"Good. As we observed, they tend to head out at different times, staggering their departures. It'll start getting properly dark within the hour, so there might be a bit of a wait. Hope you're prepared for the boredom," I say, trying to inject some normalcy into the situation.

"I am, don't worry; it's not my first stakeout." A hint of annoyance creeps into his tone. "I know you don't know my background, Ava, but I *am* good at my job," Sam asserts, a defensive edge sharpening his words.

"Sorry, Sam." I offer a conciliatory nod, feeling a pang of guilt. "I'm used to having full intel on everyone I work with, knowing their strengths, weaknesses, trigger points. It helps build trust and anticipate reactions. Hopefully, the more time we spend working together, the better we'll synchronise as a unit. I'm sure you have your concerns about me, about all of us, as well," I concede, acknowledging the strangeness of our forced alliance.

"Actually, when it comes to your field abilities, I have zero issues. Your reputation precedes you, *Destroyer*. I know exactly how good you are," Sam replies, the compliment slightly undermined by the way his gaze drifts towards the front seats, a silent question hanging in the air about Luca and Rose.

"Keep yourself safe up there, Sam. Eyes open, no unnecessary risks. We're planning to spread out initially until we regroup here later to take down the church and eliminate any remaining vampires," I reiterate the plan, meeting his gaze firmly.

We watch him melt into the urban shadows, his movements economical and practised. Once he's out of sight, I signal for Luca to proceed to my designated drop-off point. From the limited camera views, we could discern the general direction the vampires favoured when leaving the church. Our strategy involves positioning ourselves along their anticipated route. I'll then track them on foot, maintaining distance while relaying their movements, as we remain uncertain about their final destination within the sprawling city. It has to be just me following; Luca was adamant about minimising the risk of them detecting the distinct shifter scent. He explained there's a chance the newer vampires might not recognise the scent immediately, but vampiric turning often imparts a kind of residual, genetic memory. The risk is too high; most vampires instinctively recognise shifters as ancient enemies.

Luca finds a parking space offering good access routes, allowing us to move in any direction swiftly if needed. The spot is ideal, tucked behind an empty store plastered with *'For Sale'* signs, ensuring minimal foot traffic and prying eyes. After parking, the silence inside the Tahoe feels heavy again. We settle in, preparing for what could be a long, tedious wait.

The agreed-upon plan avoids a direct, mass confrontation at the church. Instead, we'll wait for some vampires to depart on their nightly hunt. I'll shadow them discreetly on foot, watching for an opportune moment—an isolated alley, a deserted stretch of road—to strike when they're away from public view. The biggest risk, besides getting ambushed myself, is a bystander witnessing the attack. I shudder, imagining someone filming the takedown on their phone, capturing the unnatural sight of a vampire crumbling to ash instead of collapsing like a normal… well, corpse. That kind of evidence hitting the internet would unleash chaos.

I had meticulously marked the locations of all recorded attacks over the past twenty-three years onto a city map. Sam's initial assessment was spot-on, the attacks were overwhelmingly concentrated in the city's poorer, more neglected districts. Even the cluster of evening hotspots where we intervened the other night was situated in a comparatively run-down area. This pattern gives us a strong indication of their likely hunting grounds tonight.

It's currently just past 8pm the sky outside is beginning to deepen, transitioning from late afternoon gold to the bruised purples of early evening. Full darkness won't settle for another hour and a half, maybe longer at this time of year. We came out this early as a precaution; one night, bafflingly, two vampires had emerged from the church during twilight hours. We can't afford to take chances. I need this mission to be concluded successfully tonight. I need to shut down the antagonistic Chief of Police, maybe even embarrass him publicly again if the opportunity arises. More importantly, I need to regain my equilibrium, that internal sense of control. There's no better way for me to achieve that than being immersed in a mission, focused and lethal.

Not long after we settle into our observation post, Sam's voice crackles clinically in our earpieces, devoid of any unnecessary inflexion, "At home, over." The military brevity feels strangely comforting, a piece of my old world intruding on this new, bizarre reality.

I press the small activation button hidden in the collar of my tactical top. It has two settings, push-to-talk for brief transmissions and an open comms channel for continuous communication during active engagement. "Roger," I respond, confirming his message. He's in position, eyes on the church, our silent guardian angel armed with high-velocity rounds.

"Perhaps we should establish our own communication protocols for the team, simpler phrases, or maybe just stick to straightforward language over the radios," Luca suggests from the driver's seat, his voice thoughtful.

I turn towards him, slightly surprised. "Why the change?"

"Rose and I aren't military personnel or trained agents," he explains patiently. "It would take too long for us to learn all the standard military or agency call signs and jargon. We need communication that's simple, unambiguous, and easy to understand instantly under pressure. There's no room for mistakes or confusion when things go sideways."

I groan inwardly and lightly slap my forehead with my hand, feeling foolish. Rose chuckles softly from the front passenger seat. How could I have overlooked something so basic? Sam, too. We're so ingrained in our respective training protocols. "You're absolutely right. My apologies. That should have occurred to us sooner. I'll message Sam immediately and instruct him to keep all communications simple and clear—no jargon, no codes," I say, leaning forward slightly between the front seats to address both Luca and Rose directly.

"Thank you," they reply in unison, a hint of relief in their voices.

Feeling the need to break the renewed tension, I pull out my phone and quickly text Sam about the comms adjustment. I don't expect a reply; he needs to remain focused on his surveillance, and this isn't critical right now. As I look up from my phone, my gaze lands on Rose. She catches my eye and blows me a playful kiss across the confined space of the car. Heat instantly floods my cheeks. I automatically glance towards Luca, half-expecting some reaction, but he just sits there, a faint, knowing smirk playing on his lips; I feel awkward and understand why couples weren't allowed to work together because, right at this moment, I'm distracted.

Trying to regain composure and shift the atmosphere, I decide to pursue a thread from our earlier conversation, something sparked by Luca's storytelling. "Luca?"

He turns his head slightly, that infuriatingly attractive smirk still lingering. Rose shifts, too, to look at me.

"Yes, Ava, what's on your mind, cousin?"

The term catches me entirely off guard. "Why did you just call me that? We are definitely *not* cousins, not at all."

Luca merely shrugs, while Rose beside him erupts into another soft chuckle. "I told you it would freak her out if you used that term," Rose said teasingly.

Luca's smile widens slightly before he responds, seemingly enjoying my discomfort. "Well, I have a theory, it was hinted that this Cat is of your bloodline, and if she is dead, then her best possibility for contacting someone would be through her blood, as it would give her a better connection. So, if you look at it from that point of view, the fact that she contacted us both the same way, then maybe we are related, and I mean *very* distantly related, I thought it was nice."

I'm momentarily speechless. He has a twisted sort of logic, I suppose, but it feels absurd. Now I knew what to say, "I don't think that is how it works, even if she is possibly thousands of years old, there is no way *we* are related. Otherwise, you could say half this country was related to me."

Both Rose and Luca chuckle again, this time louder. It makes me frown. "What's so amusing now, kitty cat?" I direct the jab at Luca, primarily out of mild irritation.

"You," Rose said and then burst out laughing again. I'm sure because I called Luca a kitty cat. However, Luca doesn't look amused and has stopped his chuckle.

"Me," I say as I scowl at them both.

"Ava, I was teasing you. I thought it might loosen you up a little. You seem tense, which I understand, and please don't call me that. My panther doesn't like it," Luca said, flashing red-rimmed eyes at me.

I couldn't stop myself. I joined Rose and laughed, trying to answer him as I did, "Y-yes, ki-kitty."

Rose cracks up so badly in the front passenger seat that she doubles over, sounding like a heavy smoker. Luca was right. I am tense, and this moment really has helped me. "You're right. I am a little. After all, it is the first vampires I've had to go up against."

Rose is starting to pull herself together, but she looks like she'd been crying—happy tears, so she doesn't look upset, and she is able to talk again.

"Well, technically, it's not. You have already faced up against a vampire and won," Rose says, looking proud of me.

"I guess, anyway, before the pair of you decide to tease me again, I want to ask you something," I say.

"Go ahead," Luca says with an amused smile.

"The story you told us, you said it was a mage who was visiting your pack. Well, what is a mage, and why did she tell you the stories in the first place?" I ask, intrigued to find out what a mage is.

Luca seems impressed that I'm asking the question, "As far as I know, a mage is like a witch but is strong in all elements, whereas a witch is only strong in one element, she was also unique because mages are usually men, unless I've remembered wrong and she was just a witch maybe. They usually also fight on the side of good, so I'm hoping there are still mages out there we can find to help, but last I heard, they were very rare these days. Mages also travel a lot, where witches set up covens and stay in the same place."

"Why are they rare? And what do you mean by elements?" I ask.

He gives me a small smile and says, "I technically just gave you the answer to your first question. There are two reasons, really, why they are rare. Basically, if a mage mates with a human, the children will end up being only witches at best. A mage would have to mate with another mage to have a child who is a mage, but even then, they will probably be weaker so if they are travelling all the time, they are likely to end up with a human as a mate, as for the elements, there is fire, earth, air and water; each element gives a witch different abilities sometimes they have similar ones, but that's really all I know as my training was cut off and my father didn't know much about witches, I do remember he went to see a coven but any knowledge he gained wasn't passed on to me at the time."

I cringe at the word mate. Before I say anything, Luca continues, "The only other thing I know about witches is when they setup a coven, they bind their powers to the land to create, I think it is called a nexus or something, and if they feed their power into that land every month on the full moon their power can increase and can increase the power of the next generation, I think I heard it can be hit and miss sometimes, where one generation is born with very weak powers, also when a witch creates a coven the power they put into the land draws in other magical beings even shifters sometimes as they want to gain that power or seek it's protection, this can be dangerous for witches."

I'm so intrigued by it all that I could sit here all night listening to Luca tell stories. "With regard to why she stayed with us, I don't know because I was so young, but one thing I do remember is just before she left, she came to me and said, I hope my stories help you one day. I'm not sure, but now, thinking back, I wonder if she knew what was coming because the attacks happened two days later. Normally, shifter packs don't teach details of other magical beings. They teach the basics, so we know what to expect and how to fight or defend ourselves or when to run, which is very rare for a shifter to do, but there are things in the world you just run from," he said.

"Wait a second, are you telling me a mage can see the future?" I ask.

Rose shrugs, "We might never know. It's possible, as I've heard that anything to do with visions is an air witch ability, so maybe a mage can have that ability, as they should be able to read minds and things like that, or she met a witch or something else on her travels. Maybe she recognised Luca from possible future images she might have seen, so she told him the tales. That's all the extra information I know, as my teaching was cut off, too, as I ended up on the streets."

I hated hearing about what her family did to her. I reached in front and squeezed her hand in comfort. "Wow, I hope we find someone with the gift. It could help us find out who is behind everything or even help us find others who are in hiding," I say as my brain races with possibilities. Then I noticed the look Luca and Rose share.

"What?" I ask, feeling slightly annoyed by how they share looks and keep me in the dark.

Luca is the one who answers me, but Rose places her hand on my shoulder and squeezes, "Whoever is behind the attacks back in 2000 did their research. They managed to take out everyone who had the ability to stand up against them. Rose and I were lucky because we weren't with our packs at the time. Being a child of the alpha, I was destined to take over eventually unless my father was challenged, so I had to accompany pack members when they visited other packs, but when we returned to our pack lands, all the adults of our group but one headed out to find those responsible, we never saw them again, as I said before we managed to find a few other kids who had managed to hide, then we ran; eventually we lost the only adult in our group a few years later when he tried to protect us, but helped us get away."

I'm fascinated with it all and slowly realising they have both gone through so much compared to me. I know watching my parents die is one of the worst things you can experience as a child, but they have been going through shit for years since they were children.

CHAPTER 30

IN WHICH I FOLLOW VAMPIRES AND ROSE TRIES (AND FAILS)
TO KEEP A COVER STORY DECENT OVER COMMS

We settle into a comfortable silence, the low thrum of the engine and the aircon the only sounds for a few minutes. We sit, cocooned in the darkness, waiting. The air feels thick, charged with unspoken anticipation. Luca remains focused behind the wheel, his profile stoic, while Rose, beside him, occasionally glances back; her concern is a tangible presence even in the dim light filtering in from the distant streetlights. I run through the intercept plan for the tenth time, mapping the streets in my head, visualising the vampires' likely path, calculating distances and potential obstacles. Despite years of training, despite the unnatural edge the ring gives me, a knot of cold uncertainty coils in my gut. This isn't Colombia or any of the other countries I've operated in. This isn't a human target I can track through familiar patterns. These are predators from a world I'm only beginning to comprehend, operating by rules I don't fully understand. My usual pre-mission calm feels distant, replaced by a feeling of anxiety I haven't felt since… well, since the days after my parents were killed.

The digital clock on the dash clicks over silently, each minute stretching thin. Just after 9pm, the quiet is broken, Sam's voice, sharp and clear in our earpieces, snaps me to full alert.

"Three targets on course, twenty."

Twenty minutes. Not kilometres. Military brevity. Plenty of

time to get into position, but also ample time for the unpredictable to happen. My breath catches, a small hitch I quickly suppress. *Focus, Bekke. Control the controllable.*

"Confirm; I will head to intercept; stay frosty," I reply, my voice steady, practised, masking the slight tremor deep inside. I don't need to ask what they're wearing; their dedication to the dramatic trench-coat-and-hood ensemble is almost comical, if they weren't so deadly.

"Right, here we go," I murmur, the words a familiar ritual, a way to settle my nerves. My gaze meets Rose's in the rearview mirror. "I'd better head out so I don't miss them. I will update you when I am in the intercept location." I hesitate, the vulnerability feeling raw. "Are you sure you need to keep your distance for this part?" The thought of facing the unknown alone, relying only on my augmented human senses, feels like stepping off a cliff.

"It's best we do. You can get close to them without being detected, so we need to stick to our plan, Ava," Luca states firmly, his voice the calm, unwavering anchor of the alpha. He's right, tactically. My lack of a distinct shifter scent is my greatest advantage for stealth. Their presence, reassuring as it might be, would ring alarm bells in the vampires' sensitive noses.

Rose leans over the seat back slightly, her green eyes finding mine in the dimness. The warmth and worry in her gaze are almost physical. "You will be okay, Ava, you got this. Don't think about what they are. Think of them as humans high on drugs," she advises softly, offering a fleeting, encouraging smile. She reaches back, squeezing my shoulder briefly, a firm pressure that sends a wave of borrowed strength through me, grounding the fluttering anxiety. The connection, the bond, flares momentarily – a silent promise. I want to reach for her, hold her hand, absorb that warmth for a moment longer before stepping out into the cold uncertainty, but the mission clock is ticking. I manage a tight smile in return and push the door open, the relatively warm June air washing over me as I step out.

The night feels heavy, expectant. The usual city symphony – distant sirens, traffic hum, indefinable urban noise – seems muted tonight. I leave my leather jacket folded on the seat; the air is close, and the ring makes concealment redundant. My arsenal feels like phantom limbs strapped to my body, invisible yet undeniably present. A final, habitual check by touch, sword snug in its back sheath, the custom Glock secure at my side – the modified gun with its wooden-tipped rounds on my left hip – the four daggers nestled firmly in their designated spots. Muscle memory confirms readiness.

I glance up. The sky is a deep, clear indigo, sprinkled with faint stars barely visible through the city's light pollution. The moon is a pale silver, offering negligible illumination. Usually, I'd prefer an overcast night, thick cloud cover to deepen the shadows, aids concealment. Tonight, it hardly matters. The ring continues to cast the world in its strange, perpetual twilight, sharpening edges, brightening colours, granting me sight beyond human limits. *Okay, Bekke. Time to move.*

I pull the hood of my top over my head, the soft fabric settling around my face, helping me blend into the urban landscape as I step away from the Tahoe and onto the pavement.

"On foot, over," I whisper into the comms, the activation click startlingly loud in the perceived quiet.

"Roger, out," Sam's prompt reply is a distant point of contact in the encroaching isolation.

My boots make soft sounds on the pavement as I walk casually along Dunlop Avenue, heading towards the intersection with Russell Street. The air smells faintly of asphalt, dust, and something vaguely floral from a nearby neglected planter box. Each footstep feels deliberate, measured. The streets are quieter than I'd like, fewer pedestrians than usual, even for this time of night. This emptiness makes me feel exposed and conspicuous, despite my ordinary appearance. It also raises the tactical concern – will the lack of available prey force the vampires to deviate from their expected route?

I reach the crosswalk and wait for a passing car before jogging across Russell Street. The school building on the corner looms large, its darkened windows reflecting the streetlights like vacant stares. A shiver traces its way down my spine – superstition, or maybe just nerves? I push the feeling down. Focus on the objective.

At the end of Russell Street lies the gas station, its fluorescent lights casting a harsh, sterile glow over the concrete forecourt. It feels too bright, too exposed. My destination is the scraggly patch of bushes bordering the rear of the lot, near the air pump and vacuum station. According to our intel and last night's reconnaissance, the vampires typically pass this way, using Pendle Avenue as their main thoroughfare.

I scan the area quickly – a lone car filling up at a pump, no one else visible – before hanging around behind the bushes. The leaves are dry and scratchy, releasing a dusty, green scent as I disturb them. I settle against the trunk of the only tree next to the bushes, concealed from the street but with a clear view of the intersection.

"At target location, over," I transmit, keeping my voice hushed. Two clicks acknowledge my position. Right, phase two. Establish the plausible reason for lurking. I pull out my phone, dialling Rose, the screen illuminating my face momentarily in the gloom. Cover story. Argument with girlfriend. Simple. Effective. Except Rose rarely sticks to simple when she can make things complicated… and embarrassing.

She answers, and immediately, her voice drops into that infuriatingly distracting, breathy whisper. No trace of argument, just pure seduction aimed straight down the phone line. *"I will watch you across the office…"*

"Rose, the *argument*, remember?" I hiss, trying to inject annoyance, but my voice comes out tighter than intended. Heat starts to creep up my neck. This is ridiculous.

She completely ignores my attempt to steer the conversation back to the plan. Her words weave a scenario that has my skin prickling and my focus fracturing. *"…copy room… lock the door… push my body against yours…"* Images flash behind my eyes – Rose, the scent of her skin, the heat… *No! Focus! "…run my hands over your hips… short skirt… contact with your skin… goosebumps… heart rate starts to increase…"* Damn her, she knows exactly the effect she has. My own heart rate is definitely increasing, partly from sheer frustration.

"…back of your knees… up the back of your legs…" I shift my weight, the rough ground uncomfortable beneath my boots. *"…lifting it up… revealing your knickers, pale pink… bottom looks good enough to bite…"* I squeeze my eyes shut for a second, trying to block out the mental images. *"…cup your right cheek… kiss your neck… little bite…"* A phantom tingle ghosts across my neck where her teeth have marked me before. *"…cup my favourite part to play with… feel your pussy getting hotter…"*

"Oh my god, Rose, you need to stop," I plead again, my voice strained, barely audible even to myself. Is that movement down Pendle? Or just a trick of the light?

She continues, her voice a low, hypnotic murmur. *"…claw comes out to play… slices right through the material… underwear starts to drop down… cups and squeezes your left breast… breathing increase… cup your naked pussy… spread your legs… red hot… feel your pulse in the palm of my hand…"* My breath catches. My skin feels flushed. This is torture. *"…claws come out to play again, which cuts your bra straps… falls out down the front of you… hand over your left breast again… firm squeeze, I slide a finger into…."*

Movement. Sharp, distinct. Three dark figures turning the corner onto Pendle, moving with purpose. *Targets.*

"Rose!" The shout rips out of me, louder than intended, sharp in the night air.

"Targets here," I add instantly, snapping the phone shut, my face flaming, pulse hammering a frantic rhythm against my ribs. *Get a grip, Bekke! Mission time!* I force deep, measured breaths, pushing down the distracting heat Rose ignited. Key the mic. Keep the voice steady. "T-targets l-located," – damn it, still shaky – "confirm it's a go."

"Confirm go," Sam's voice replies, blessedly professional.

"Confirm go," Rose adds, pure, unadulterated amusement colouring her tone. *Oh, she is SO much trouble and SO going to die.*

I peer through the leaves as the three vampires glide past the gas station entrance. Their movements are unnervingly fluid, lacking the slight hesitations and shifts of human locomotion. They didn't react to my shout, seemingly oblivious. I give them a thirty-second lead, a buffer zone, then melt out from behind the bushes, keeping to the deepest shadows along the building walls.

Once they turn left onto Pendle Avenue, I follow, matching my pace to maintain the distance Luca recommended – just within the enhanced visual range provided by the ring.

"Heading west on Pendle," I report softly into the comms.

The street is lined with a mix of closed shops and darkened apartment buildings. The air is cooler here, away from the gas station's lights. Following them requires constant vigilance, predicting their path, using parked cars and darkened doorways as intermittent cover. They move like wraiths, silent and purposeful.

After several blocks, they make an unexpected left turn, heading south onto Ebbs Street. This deviates from the pattern we observed last night. My pulse quickens. Where are they going? I pick up my pace slightly, the gap widening faster than I like. Reaching the corner, I scan quickly before turning.

"Heading south on Ebbs," I relay, double-checking the street sign, my mind racing through the map Luca showed us. Ahead lies Lancaster Avenue, and beyond that, the dark span of Ebbs Bridge crossing the river. This route leads towards quieter, more residential zones.

"Possible residential," Luca's voice confirms my fears, sounding grim in my ear.

A cold dread settles in my stomach. No. They wouldn't. Not a house. Not families. The potential change in target makes my blood run cold. The operational parameters just shifted dramatically. The urge to abandon stealth and engage them *now*, right here on the street, is a physical ache, a desperate need to prevent them from reaching potential victims. But the street, though quiet, is still too unpredictable.

They reach Lancaster and turn south again, their dark forms moving inexorably towards the bridge—my training wars with my rising panic. *Maintain discipline. Observe. Wait for the optimal moment.* However, the image of unsuspecting families asleep in their beds fuels a desperate sense of urgency.

"South, Ebbs bridge," I whisper, my voice tight.

The bridge stretches ahead, an exposed crossing over the dark, slow-moving water. Tracking them across it without being seen will be nearly impossible. I hang back, letting them get a significant lead, hoping the distance and the bridge's structure will offer enough concealment. Once they are about halfway across, I start my crossing, staying low, using the concrete barrier between the sidewalk and the road as meagre cover. The air here smells damp, carrying the faint, earthy scent of the river below.

They are pulling further ahead, nearing the opposite bank. The area beyond the bridge appears less developed, darker, and features a dense stand of trees bordering the road, possibly better terrain for an ambush.

"Start to move in," I breathe into the comms, signalling Luca and Rose to close the distance.

Just as the thought forms, the lead vampire halts abruptly at the far end of the bridge. The others stop instantly, a synchronised freeze that screams *alert*. My reaction is pure instinct. I dive flat onto the sidewalk, the impact jarring my teeth, the rough concrete scraping against my cheek. My heart slams against my ribs like a trapped thing. Slowly, cautiously, I raise my head just enough to peer over the concrete lip. The bridge's gentle arch provides a narrow sightline. They stand clustered, motionless, their heads slowly turning as they scan the darkness behind them and the bridge. *Did they hear me? See me? Sense me?* That predatory stillness sends a shiver down my spine.

Headlights lance through the darkness from behind. A car approaches, crossing the bridge. I hug the concrete, making myself as small as possible, praying the driver is oblivious, just focused on the road ahead. The car passes without slowing. The vampires don't react to it, but they remain alert, poised.

After an agonising minute that stretches into an eternity, they finally relax, turning and resuming their walk, continuing straight down the road away from the river. I release a shaky breath, the tension easing slightly. I push myself up cautiously, checking they haven't glanced back, then start walking again, trying to close the distance they gained while I was pinned down.

They move quickly now, their pace eating up the pavement. They are nearing the edge of even my enhanced vision, approaching a sharp bend in the road ahead. I'm losing them. Just as I'm about to radio Luca to fall back, they stop again, just shy of the bend.

No more waiting. I sprint the remaining length of the bridge, vaulting the barrier at the end and launching myself down the short, steep embankment towards the shadowed river path below, the loose earth sliding under my boots. From this lower vantage point, crouched in the darkness where the path forks, I can just make out their silhouettes against the dimly lit road. They're moving sideways now, towards a small, overgrown hill that rises steeply from the edge of the sidewalk, dense with tangled bushes and small trees.

Attack now? The terrain is better here, more cover, less chance of witnesses. But are they leading me into a trap? Before I can fully weigh the options, they move again, a sudden, impossible burst of speed. They don't run *around* the hill; they seem to run *into* it, vanishing into the thick foliage in the blink of an eye.

My decision is made. "First bend after the bridge, we are go," I gasp into the comms, pushing off the ground, sprinting towards the spot where they disappeared, my lungs burning, adrenaline singing in my veins.

It takes a couple of minutes of hard running to reach the location, my breath coming in short, sharp gasps. My fitness level needs work; this paranormal hunting is demanding, also I haven't done much working out since I returned to the states, well, apart from my workouts with Rose, *does that count?* I scan the dense wall of vegetation covering the hill. Where did they go? Doubt flickers. Did I imagine it? Then, partly concealed by overhanging branches and thick ivy, I spot it. A narrow, almost invisible path, barely more than a deer trail, wound steeply up the hillside. I follow its ascent with my eyes. At the top, nestled amongst the trees, sit three houses, dark and isolated, overlooking the river valley. Three houses. Three vampires? My stomach churns. This just got infinitely more complicated.

The silent arrival of the Tahoe next to me makes me jump. Luca and Rose are out instantly, their heightened senses already processing the scene. A quick sniff of the air, a shared glance, and their focus locks onto the hidden path. Confirmation.

While they verify the trail, I send the coded alert: "Charlie, go." Backup mobilises. Six elite operators are heading to reinforce us, another six establishing a perimeter around the church, with Sam ready to lead the assault there if necessary. State police will be looped in for containment once the primary threats are neutralised.

Luca gestures, a silent command. *Follow*. He takes point, moving up the path with the inherent stealth of a predator. This time, Luca has left the sword he's been using behind as he plans to use his claws from now on. We follow, Rose moving fluidly behind him, I'm bringing up the rear, sword now in hand, the polished silver feeling cold and reassuring in my grip. The path is steep, uneven, littered with loose stones and tangled roots. The air is heavy with the scent of damp earth and decaying leaves.

At the summit, the three houses emerge fully from the trees, stark and silent under the silver of the moon. They look deserted, with windows that are dark, empty voids. Luca pauses, scanning, sniffing the air again. He holds up three fingers, points to his nose, then indicates each house in turn. *One in each?* The thought sends a fresh wave of dread through me. Splitting up against vampires in unfamiliar territory… tactically unsound, but unavoidable if they've dispersed.

He confirms the assessment with curt hand signals. Rose gets the house on the far right. Luca and I take the leftmost one. I instinctively want to argue, to keep Rose with me, the protective urge flaring unexpectedly strong. But this isn't about feelings; it's about survival, about neutralising the threat as efficiently as possible. The memory of battlefield axioms – *don't bunch up, cover all angles* – overrides the personal connection. I give a stiff, reluctant nod. Rose meets my gaze across the small clearing, a silent acknowledgement passing between us – worry, resolve, trust – before she turns and vanishes soundlessly towards her objective.

Luca taps my shoulder, pulling my attention sharply back to our target. We circle around to the rear of the leftmost house, sticking to the dense shadows cast by the trees. The darkness here is profound, almost absolute; the ring's twilight vision struggles against the lack of ambient light, confirming my theory that it needs *some* light source, perhaps the moon. I retrieve the night-vision sunglasses and slip them on. The world shifts back into familiar green and black relief. Luca notices, frowning slightly, but says nothing.

He halts near the back door, which hangs slightly ajar, a dark slit promising entry. He tests the air again, then gives me a sharp, affirmative nod. *Target acquired. Inside.* Showtime.

CHAPTER 31

KITCHEN NIGHTMARES: VAMPIRE EDITION, AND WHY

CREAKY HINGES ARE THE TRUE ENEMY

I gently push the heavy, ancient wooden door open, the protesting groan of its hinges echoing like a death rattle in the sudden, oppressive silence that falls around us. My senses scream into overdrive; Luca's earlier warning about the need for a calm and slow approach reverberates in my mind. He's right; that was until the hinges let out a death squeak. Hesitation is no longer a luxury we can afford. My heart hammers against my ribs, a frantic, almost painful drumbeat, as a low, guttural groaning drifts from the shadowed depths of the house. The sound twists something cold and sharp in my gut – adrenaline mixed with a heavy dose of dread. Every instinct screams at me to charge in, to find the source of that suffering, but years of hard-won discipline clamp down hard on the impulse. Recklessness is the fastest way to join the ranks of the dead.

The doorway reveals a cramped laundry room, starkly utilitarian, even shrouded in the gloom filtering from some unseen source. The air hangs thick and heavy, smelling faintly of mildew and the cloying sweetness of old detergent. We move like wraiths through it, our combat boots making barely a whisper on the cracked linoleum floor. Another door looms ahead, this one also slightly ajar, another dark slit promising further unknowns. I reach for it, my fingers brushing the cool, peeling paint, easing it wider with excruciating slowness. Beyond lies the kitchen, as expected. Faint light glints off stainless steel appliances, their surfaces reflecting distorted shapes in the dimness. Just as Luca tenses beside me, preparing to move through the opening I'm creating, the top door hinge lets out a piercing, drawn-out shriek, loud enough, it feels, to alert anyone within a mile radius. We both freeze mid-motion, every muscle locking rigid. Luca reacts with inhuman speed, a dark blur launching himself forward and diving behind a large, solid-looking kitchen island, seeking immediate cover.

He gestures frantically, urgently – *right!* – while he slides left, hugging the island's protective bulk. My sword feels like a natural extension of my arm, cold and reassuringly solid, as I keep it tucked into my side, making sure it doesn't catch on anything. My grip tightens on the hilt instinctively, my knuckles turning white against the dark wrap. I slide into the position he indicated, pressing myself against the cool, smooth surface of the island's end panel, making myself as small a target as possible—the smell of stale cooking oil and something vaguely metallic taints the air here.

Then, a voice, smooth as poisoned silk and chillingly casual, cuts through the thick tension. It slides from the shadows deeper within the house, laced with unmistakable malice. "Dex, I think we have company," it drawls, the sound seeming to curl around us. Despite the warmth radiating from Luca's proximity, a wave of goosebumps ripples across my skin. "There's a hint of something… *interesting* in the air. Different. Be careful." A low, cruel chuckle follows, humourless and predatory. "Maybe someone came to visit one of the households and heard our new family member groan in pain? Decided to be a hero and check it out?" Another chuckle, dryer this time. "Dex, hurry up. I don't like dealing with little blood bags myself, but it's going to be a nice treat for when *they* wake up."

Rage, cold and sharp and utterly focused, spears through me. *Treats.* They're turning someone, using innocents like cattle. The desire to inflict pain, to make them suffer slowly, is a visceral, burning thing low in my gut. But I wrestle it down, locking it behind the icy wall of professional detachment. Control is everything. My mission is elimination, not vengeance. I force my breathing to even out, straining my ears, listening intently. No footsteps, no sound beyond the rhythmic *drip... drip... drip* of a leaky tap somewhere in the kitchen and the frantic thumping of my own heart against my ribs. Luca remains utterly still beside me, a coiled predator radiating barely suppressed power.

Suddenly, the air shifts, a subtle displacement, a *feeling* of presence drawing near. He's here in the kitchen with us. My eyes dart to Luca, waiting, needing his signal, my sword held low and ready. The weight feels balanced, familiar.

"I know you are here, little hero," the silken voice purrs, much closer now, seeming to originate just beyond the island's corner. My muscles tense further. "You smell funny as well. Different. I'm not sure why, but I'm going to find out." The voice itself is still unsettlingly pleasant, almost sweet, a horrifying counterpoint to the menace radiating from the unseen speaker. It's the kind of voice designed to lure prey into a false sense of security before the strike.

Luca signals – a quick, decisive point to my sword, followed by a sharp swinging motion, then a gesture low to the right, around *the island*. He shifts beside me, and I hear the soft *snikt* as his claws extend, wicked points of darkness against his skin. Then, he launches himself from cover, a silent explosion of contained power. I count two frantic heartbeats, the sound deafening in the enclosed space, then I explode into motion, staying low, hugging the contour of the island as I round the end.

The kitchen erupts in violence. Snarls, guttural and inhuman, rip through the air, punctuated by the sickening crunch of impact as bodies slam against cabinets and countertops. Dishes rattle precariously on unseen shelves. I rise from my crouch, sword held high in a two-handed grip, just as the combatants whirl into my line of sight. It's a chaotic, terrifying dance of blurs, Luca and the vampire locked in a deadly, intimate embrace. Luca hisses sharply as obsidian claws rake across his chest, dark blood welling instantly, staining his tactical gear.

But even as the blow lands, he reacts, shoving the vampire hard in the chest with raw, shifter strength. The creature staggers backwards, unbalanced, stumbling directly into my prepared strike zone.

There's no time for hesitation, no space for doubt, only action honed by years of lethal practice. My blade arcs down, a precise silver flash cutting through the gloom. I feel the impact resonate up my arms – a jarring thud against something solid, followed immediately by a sickening lack of resistance as the razor-sharp edge bites deep into flesh and bone. The vampire sees me at the last possible fraction of a second, his head snapping around as my sword descends. Shock flares in his eyes, wide and red-tinged, just before the blade makes contact with his neck.

Then it's over. I look him directly in the eyes as his form begins to dissolve, his expression frozen in that final moment of stunned realisation. Recognition hits me like a physical blow – it's the vampire from outside the church, the one who tried the compulsion, the one with the deceptively handsome face and the smile full of lies. A grim, cold satisfaction settles deep within me as I watch his features contort and turn black, crumbling into fine, dark ash that whispers like dry leaves as it floats gently to the linoleum floor. This time, thankfully, the foul dust settles harmlessly, sparing me another disgusting, cloying coating.

Luca doesn't pause, doesn't look back, already moving with predatory focus towards the doorway from which the now-disintegrated vampire emerged. His trust in my ability is absolute, almost unnerving. The confidence is flattering, but the adrenaline still sings a high, frantic tune in my veins. I shake off the momentary trance induced by the kill, the lingering image of dissolving features fading, and move swiftly to follow, falling into position beside him at the threshold.

"Dex, who was it?" the second voice calls again from deeper within the house, the tone sharpening with impatience and a dawning suspicion. Silence answers him. I desperately hope Dex was the only other vampire in this immediate vicinity. But Luca's earlier assessment of three houses, three targets… my stomach clenches again. Did they split up after all? Or are they all converging here?

"Dex, what's going on? Answer me now!" the voice demands again, louder this time, tinged with anger. Still, nothing answers him but the oppressive silence of the house. Dex is dust beneath my boots.

Luca gestures forward, a silent command, and we advance cautiously down the narrow hallway, a tightly coordinated two-person unit moving through the encroaching darkness. He moves with a fluid grace that still catches me off guard, reminding me again of seasoned spec-ops soldiers I've worked alongside. How did he learn this? The first door on our right reveals a formal dining room, swallowed by shadows. Dust motes dance in the faint beams of moonlight piercing through grimy windows. Luca clears it with swift, economical movements, shakes his head – empty – and we press on.

Then, the sound I've been dreading rips through the silence from upstairs – a child's terrified cry, high-pitched and desperate, followed immediately by the sharp, ugly crack of a slap. The crying cuts off abruptly, choked into silence. A sickening thud echoes down the stairwell, like a small, fragile body hitting the floor hard. Bile rises, hot and acrid, in my throat. "Please… don't hurt my brother… he can't help himself," a girl's trembling voice pleads, barely audible but carrying clearly in the charged silence. Rage, white-hot and fierce, simmers dangerously beneath my enforced calm. I want to sprint up those stairs, sword first.

We check the next door – a small downstairs bathroom, also clear. The final door on this level is situated at the foot of the stairs. Luca nods towards it, indicating for me to clear it while he covers the stairwell, the most likely point of attack now. I take a deep, steadying breath, push the door open, and sweep the living room quickly with my eyes and weapon. Couch pushed against the far wall, the ubiquitous flat-screen Tv dark and silent, a bookcase overflowing with titles I can't read in the gloom, a low coffee table. No immediate threats, no obvious hiding spots. I shake my head slightly at Luca and take position beside him at the base of the stairs, sword held ready.

He points to himself, then gestures upward. He's taking point going up. My stomach tightens. Stairs are always a tactical nightmare, the defender's advantage, a prime spot for deadly ambushes. Just as Luca places his boot silently on the bottom step, the vampire upstairs speaks again, his voice echoing slightly in the narrow stairwell, attempting to sound reasonable, conversational even.

"I think I know what you are," he begins, letting a calculated pause hang heavy in the air. We remain silent, refusing to give away our exact position. "Shifter," he continues, confirming his guess. "But I don't understand your actions. The council assigned us this area. The closest designated shifter territory should be in Michigan and Wisconsin. Pennsylvania was given to *me*. If you've taken out Dex, why? We're all supposed to be on the same side now, aren't we? Did Dex perhaps hurt someone you care about before we took over this territory? If it's simple payback you wanted with him, consider it done. I'll let you go." His voice drips with false magnanimity. "But I find myself asking… what happened to the four others of mine who have gone missing recently? I was just about ready to send out another recruitment group, but now I have to start all over again. I'm beginning to wonder if *you* are responsible for their disappearance."

Council? Assigned areas? Recruitment groups? My mind races, frantically cataloguing the slivers of crucial intel embedded in his monologue, even as the tension coils tighter and tighter in my gut. Luca expertly uses the vampire's ongoing speech to cover his ascent, moving with incredible stealth up the stairs. I follow suit, trying to emulate his silence, placing my feet carefully on the side edges of each step. I'm halfway up when a tread groans loudly under my weight. *Damn it!* I freeze, cursing silently. Luca pauses above me, glancing back fleetingly. He'd used the walls, leveraging his strength to minimise his weight on the creaky structure. I don't have that option. No choice but to push onward. Another agonising creak escapes as I reach the landing, broadcasting my position.

Luca's already moving down the upper hallway, melting into

the shadows. The ambient light is marginally better here; pale moonlight streams through a large window at the top of the stairs, illuminating dust motes dancing in the air. I gratefully ditch the night-vision glasses, blinking rapidly as my eyes adjust. The ring's twilight vision seems dependent on some level of existing light, completely useless in the pitch blackness downstairs. My right hand is aching again; a quick glance reveals my knuckles are bone-white, strangling the sword hilt. I consciously relax my grip, flexing my fingers.

Four doors line this upper hallway. Following the typical layout, I deduce three bedrooms and a main bathroom. The two doors nearest us are open, the two further down are closed. The master bedroom, where the voices, I'm guessing, originated, has to be the one at the far end. Luca is already clearing the first open room with silent efficiency. By the time I reach his position, he's finished—no time to waste. I move to the next open doorway, peek cautiously inside – a child's bedroom, decorated with cartoon characters I don't recognise. The bed is empty, and toys are scattered across the floor. I do a quick sweep, clear, and move back into the hallway. That leaves the two closed doors. The nearest must be the bathroom, the end door, the master.

My hand is just reaching for the handle of the closest door when another muffled noise drifts from the room at the end of the hall—a soft thump, then silence. I freeze again, every nerve ending alight. I *have* to check this room and clear every space. I push the door open quickly – it's the bathroom, as suspected, complete with a large, old-fashioned claw-foot bathtub. Clear. I rejoin Luca outside the master bedroom door. We flank it, pressing ourselves flat against the wall on either side, preparing for entry, anticipating potential gunfire or an immediate attack.

Before we can finalise our breach plan, the vampire speaks again, his voice carrying clearly through the thin wood of the door. "I know you're just outside the door, shifter. You can enter. I would like to know what you're playing at. I want to see if it's *me* that has wronged you; to do that, I need to see your face."

I look at Luca, searching his expression for a plan. He meets my gaze, then decisively reaches for the doorknob, turns it slowly, silently, and pushes the door open just a crack, putting a finger to his lips for absolute silence. I can't see anything from my position, shielded by the wall. Luca remains partially hidden behind the doorframe, only a sliver of his body exposed, his eyes fixed intently on the room's interior.

"There you are, shifter. I'm going to take it, Dex is… gone," the vampire says conversationally, followed by that grating, creepy chuckle that makes my skin crawl. "So, shifter, I don't recognise you. Why are you here? Why are you screwing up the plan?"

Luca remains silent for a tense moment, clearly weighing his options. Then, he asks coolly, "What plan is that?" It's not the approach I would have taken, too direct perhaps, but maybe he's trying to gauge the vampire's reaction, probe for weaknesses.

The vampire tuts audibly. "I'm not stupid, shifter," he replies, his tone laced with condescending amusement, still spitting the word 'shifter' like it's a curse. "I'm starting to think you're not with us after all. That you somehow escaped the cleansing, the purge. Now, how did you manage that? Did you run away with your tail tucked between your legs?"

Luca growls, low and menacing, a dangerous sound in the confined space. "I'm just special and awesome. What can I say?" The unexpected humour throws me for a loop. I fight back a surprised chuckle. Luca is full of surprises.

"You may have escaped the cleansing, shifter, but your time has most definitely come," the vampire snarls, his amusement evaporating, replaced by cold fury.

"As I see it," Luca retorts, his voice dangerously smooth now, "I've already removed four of your little fang buddies… oh, wait, I forgot about poor Dex. Make that *five* fangers down. So, frankly, I like my odds."

A furious hiss answers him from inside the room. "I wondered what happened to them! These two and the ones next door," – he must mean the parents – "will start to replace them nicely. Now I just need to replace Dex to get back on track with the recruitment schedule. Oh, I'm going to enjoy this… *very* much."

I watch Luca's face intently, searching for his next move. His eyes flick briefly towards the floor inside the room – are the parents there? The children? Then snap back to where the vampire must be positioned. I see his teeth grind, his visible claws extend a fraction more, bunching the muscles in his forearm. He's coiling, preparing for battle.

"Are you saying," Luca asks, his voice deceptively calm, masking the undercurrent of rage, "that you have already started the turning process with the parents?"

"Yes," the vampire confirms, his voice dripping with sadistic pleasure that makes my stomach churn violently. "They are currently… indisposed… enjoying the transition to glorious immortality. Once they're ready to move, probably by tomorrow night once we've finished feeding them, we'll take them back to the nest. Then, when they awaken, hungry and confused… their darling little children will be there waiting. A first meal. I think I will particularly enjoy the fear on the little blood bags' faces when their own parents drain them dry."

Nausea, potent and overwhelming, claws its way up my throat. My fault. All my fault. I waited too long, hesitated on the bridge. These children… they're going to suffer a fate worse than anything I endured. The thought, the sickening image it conjures, almost makes me collapse right there in the hallway, wanting to sob, to scream. But the knowledge that the children are still alive, still potentially salvageable, keeps me upright, keeps the cold fury focused. I start to reach for the gun holstered at my side, the one loaded with the blessed wooden bullets. My plan crystallises – shoot the bastard while Luca keeps him talking. End this nightmare. But just as my fingers brush the weapon's grip, everything dissolves into instant, terrifying chaos. All hell breaks loose.

CHAPTER 32

FANGS FOR NOTHING, AND WHY I'M A TERRIBLE

WINGMAN IN A SHIFTER FIGHT

Darkness shatters, not into light, but into a kaleidoscope of colours that envelopes my vision, as agony and confusion hit me. One moment, I am poised, ready to breach; the next, a freight train slams into me from behind. The impact is a brutal, crushing weight, my sword clattering uselessly away, skittering across the hallway floor. Fear, cold and absolute, grips me as I see Luca's head whip towards me, his face a mask of raw surprise that twists into stark fear in the space of a heartbeat. Then, searing pain explodes in my neck.

My vision swims. Agony continues to rip through my neck, draining my strength, leaving me weak and trembling as an iron grip clamps onto the crown of my head, yanking it sideways, forcing my gaze towards Luca. He is turning, reacting, but that split-second distraction is all it takes. A dark blur, impossibly fast, launches itself from the master bedroom, a streak of condensed violence that takes Luca clean off his feet. He disappears from my narrow field of vision with a sickening thud.

The pain in my neck is a roaring inferno, each throb a fresh wave of debilitating weakness. *Rose.* The thought rips through the fog. *This vampire… must have bested Rose, taken her out at the other house.* It's the only explanation that makes sense. The bitter irony is a cruel twist of the knife. Overwatch. We always need overwatch. Sam is at the church, though, not watching over us. Again, my fault.

Through the encroaching darkness that clouds my vision, I watch the chaotic blur of Luca battling the vampire as they reappear in my line of sight. Blood, dark and slick, already stains his clothes, painting grotesque patterns on the vampire's equally frenzied form. *The ring,* a desperate, useless thought, surfaces. *I wish I didn't have the ring on.* Then I wouldn't have to witness this, wouldn't have to see Luca possibly dying, his life ebbing away while I am helpless. He can't win. The vampire took him by surprise, even if he does win, it won't be in time. Not before this thing drains me.

I'm pinned, a rag doll beneath an unyielding force. My arms are trapped, another hand viciously securing them. I can feel their claws, needle-sharp, digging into my skin, a prelude to the tearing I know is coming. The pain, however, is already starting to fade, a terrifying numbness creeping in. The kind of sedative vampires produce that makes you stop fighting, that Luca warned me about. It begins its insidious creep through my veins, dulling the pain but dragging me further into helplessness. Is this it? Will I die here, watching Luca fall, knowing Rose is already gone? It's working with chilling efficiency. My chances of survival are plummeting with every stolen breath, then a distinct female voice chuckles in my ear, "Thought you could sneak up on us, did you!" Then I feel a pull on my neck again as she continues to drain me.

A strange, detached daydream starts to form – *Will I see Rose again?* For a fleeting, mad moment, hope flickers. Even if my body dies, my soul will live on, thanks to what Luca told me in his story. Then, the cold reality crashes back in. Vampires don't just drink blood; they drain life force, essence. My soul will not be sticking around. It will be… consumed. Hope flutters and dies, and my mind, exhausted and battered, begins to surrender.

Then, everything changes.

The crushing weight vanishes. My head lolls free; my hands are released. A new sound rips through the house, echoing from the hallway behind me – a deep roar, the sound of a very large, very angry predator.

The kind of sound you hear in the wild, when it's feeding time, only a thousand times more menacing.

I crane my neck, desperate to see, wincing as fresh agony shoots through my neck. My heart, which has been slowing, is still struggling against the sedative, gives a violent lurch, then begins to hammer a frantic, unsteady rhythm. It feels like it is trying to tear its way out of my chest, a bizarre thought flashes – *can you have a heart attack from sheer relief?*

It's Rose, she is in her magnificent, terrifying panther form, a sleek black nightmare of muscle and fury, launching herself at the female vampire who was seconds from ending me. *She isn't dead!* That single, overwhelming realisation is a jolt of pure adrenaline, a shockwave of hope that gives me the strength to fight, to stay alive.

The vampire is off me. My head is clearing, the fog of the sedative receding slightly. I have to help. Getting to my feet is out of the question; the blood loss and the lingering drug make my limbs feel like lead. But my training, the years spent fighting off the effects of various incapacitating agents, gives me a sliver of an edge. *Thank God for brutal instructors.*

Rose is fresh to this fight, a whirlwind of black fur and flashing claws. Luca, though, was at a disadvantage from the start. I have to help him—my hands, clumsy and uncoordinated, fumble over my tactical harness, searching for a weapon. Disoriented, I'm not even sure where my hands are until they brush against something familiar. *Yes.* The grip of a pistol. My thumb, shaking, fumbles with the retention strap. Hope surges again as I pull the weapon free. Wooden bullets. *Thank Christ.*

With trembling hands, I raise the gun, trying to train it on the chaotic dance of Luca and his attacker. My vision keeps blurring, focusing, then blurring again. It's hard to track them, two blurs of desperate violence. Then, a clear shot. A big, dark back, exposed for a split second. No time to hesitate. I squeeze the trigger three times, the reports deafening in the narrow hallway, praying I don't hit Luca.

"No!" A scream, sharp and furious, echoes from behind me.

My head whips around, well, more like a snail's pace really than lightning speed. *Rose.* The vampire has Rose pinned in the corner, blood matting her dark fur. Fear grips me at the sight of Rose hurt and in immediate danger, I have no option but to act quickly. I raise my gun again, sighting on the vampire's back—three more shots.

The panther turns to me, a low, menacing growl rumbling in her chest. I flinch, surprised, wondering what I've done wrong. She chuffs, a sound like a dry cough, glances back at the rapidly dissolving pile of ash on the floor, then snorts. Turning back to me, she pads closer, the anger in her eyes seeming to melt away. As she reaches me, she drops to her belly, crawling the last few feet, and pushes her massive head into my side. I finally let out a breath I was holding.

A grunt from the other end of the hall. *Luca.* I twist, relief washing over me as I see him standing amidst a cloud of his own vampire ash, which is already starting to soak into the blood covering him. He looks like hell, but he is alive.

"Thanks, Ava," he gasps, slumping against the wall. He looks utterly spent. "You saved my life."

I probably look just as bad, but at least I've avoided another dusting of vampire remains. The adrenaline begins to recede, and the true extent of my weakness hits me. I don't think I can stay conscious much longer. My hand reaches out, finding a patch of Rose's fur miraculously free of blood. The feel of it, the impossible softness, it's too much in my current state; her warmth radiates through my hand and into my body, making me slip into the darkness more quickly.

My eyes start to close as I'm about to pass out, then the feel of Rose's fur in my hand vanishes, causing a tiny jolt of adrenaline, a last flicker of awareness. Has another vampire dragged Rose away? Panic flares, but when I manage to force my heavy eyelids open again, it's not a panther or vampire I see. It's Rose. Beautiful, naked Rose, crouched in front of me. Okay, maybe a slightly yucky naked Rose right now, given the blood, but definitely still beautiful. I expect thanks, perhaps a relieved kiss. What I get makes me chuckle; well, I try to chuckle, but I sound more like someone dying as they start to cough up blood, so I end up gurgling instead of chuckling.

"Ava, you stole my kill!" she rants, though a smile plays on her lips. "Let me guess, you got the one downstairs, too? So that means you're on three, Luca is on two now, while I'm on zero. This has *not* been my week." Her smile starts to fade as she takes in my condition, her eyes widening with concern as I struggle to keep my eyes open, my eyelids beginning to close again as the small adrenaline rush recedes.

I know I'm going to pass out any second, as the darkness has almost fully encroached on my vision now. "Rose," I manage, my voice a thread. "Help Sam… breach the church. Luca… sort things here… unless you stay…" The words slur. "…blacking out now." The sea of darkness finally swallows me whole.

I have no idea how long I am out. As I start to regain consciousness, the first thing I hear is a faint, rhythmic beeping. Then memories, sharp and brutal, flood back. I try to bolt upright, convinced I'm still in that hallway, surrounded. A hand, firm but gentle, presses me back down. A voice, achingly familiar, makes my heart sing, or at least attempt a slightly less erratic rhythm.

"Ava, honey, you need to lie still, or you might pull your stitches," Rose says, her face swimming into view.

I can't help but stare up into her eyes, wondering if I'm dreaming. Cuts and bruises mar her perfect skin. An animal has attacked her. A different kind of animal. I raise a hand, my fingers gently tracing the lines.

Rose smiles. "I was thinking you might find me ugly with all the cuts and bruises. Looks like I was being a silly, vain girl to think you wouldn't find me attractive looking like this."

"Are you okay?" I rasp.

"I will be fine, honey. Once I get some sleep, I heal fast, so most of what you see now will be gone by tomorrow. You will be able to check out my body and find nothing wrong," she says, and winks.

There is only one adequate response. "Bitch."

Rose chuckles, then leans down and gives me a gentle kiss.

Panic flares again as I take in the unfamiliar room. It looks like a house, not a hospital, but as I look around the room, I see that it has all the equipment of a hospital room, as it all blinks and beeps next to the bed I'm in. However, that's not what I'm looking for. "Luca? Where's Luca?" I beg, my voice cracking.

"He's okay, Ava. He's helping Sam with the cleanup," Rose reassures me.

I slump back against the pillows, relief making me weak. Another worry surfaces. "The children? Please tell me the children are alright?"

"Yeah, they are fine. They were taken to the hospital. We also made sure they didn't see anything; the vampires had knocked them out, so we were lucky in a way."

"What about their parents? Were you able to save them? Stop the process, I mean?" I whisper, glancing around.

Rose's face falls, her head dropping slightly, eyes closing for a brief, painful moment. A sinking feeling washes over me. "Ava, when the process is started to turn someone into a vampire, you can't stop it." Her voice is low, heavy with regret. "I got the kids out of there before I headed to the church. Well, after I got dressed. I didn't want to scare them any more than they already were. Then Luca dealt with the parents. It needed to be done. They were suffering during the change, so it was best for them. We couldn't let them complete the change; they would have been out of control and vicious without a master to try and keep them in check," Rose explains, her fingers gently brushing my hair back from my face.

The memories of my parents, watching them die from my hiding spot… these children, even younger than I was. My control shatters. I start to cry, not loud, sobbing cries, but silent, hot tears that soak into the pillow. Rose sits on the edge of the bed and gives me a gentle hug.

When I finally trust my voice not to break, I ask, "What about the church? Do we need to get over there?"

Rose pulls back slightly, her eyes meeting mine. "We did as you ordered, Ava. We notified Sam to breach the church; I went over there to help once our backup team took charge of securing the area. You and Luca needed help; I wasn't going to leave until I knew you were both going to get medical help first. We breached the church and found just one vampire inside. Sam was positive no one else left after the others did." She takes a breath, hesitating.

"Just say it, Rose," I prompt, a new fear for Sam twisting in my gut.

"Sam jumped the gun and went in before I arrived, so he went in with just the backup team. He lost one of the men before I got there. The vampire managed to slip in behind and took the agent out. Luckily, Sam saw me approach and stopped the shooting. Thankfully, the vampire was distracted from all the shooting, so I managed to take him out with ease. We found two dead victims inside; Sam mentioned something about covering up how they died. That's not my business. Anyway, when Luca felt better, he headed over there after a short nap so that his body sped up the healing process," Rose says.

I feel a pang of guilt for the lost agent and team member. Again, it was my fault, as we should have all been there. Sam... not waiting for Rose, I'm going to have to have words about it. We either need to work as a team, or this isn't going to work.

"Ava, what's wrong? You don't look happy."

I can't stop the words. "It's all my fault. If I had acted sooner, they wouldn't have killed the parents, and then we could have dealt with the church as planned."

"Ava, none of it is your fault, so don't beat yourself up about it," Rose says, her expression serious. I know she is annoyed by my tone. "Let's say you had tried to deal with the vampires sooner, and out in public. In the midst of the takedown, a pedestrian appeared and distracted us. They could have got the upper hand and killed us all." She has a point. I try to suppress the guilt, but it's not an easy thing to do when I still feel guilty. I don't say this to Rose, so I let her think she has helped me.

"I do have one question, though," I say.

"That is?"

"Why do I still have the harness on and all my weapons, but I've been stripped out of my clothes and put into a hospital gown? Why and how? Also, if it wasn't you who did that, then someone is in trouble and going to lose their eyes." I try for a confused and serious face; I probably look demented.

Rose surprises me by bursting out laughing. It takes her a moment to compose herself. "Ava, no one can see the harness or touch it, not to mention the weapons, which again, no one can see or touch. The medical team put together by the CIA removed your top in the unmarked ambulance. When I got here, I stripped you out of your other clothes and put you in the gown. The only weapon we could touch was your sword, which I put in our vehicle when I headed to the church."

I look down at myself, frowning. "I don't understand. If no one can see the harness or touch it, how did you get me into the hospital gown?"

Rose laughs again. "As I said, we can't see or touch it. Your clothes came off like you weren't wearing it, so it was easy to get the gown on. It's like the harness is out of phase or something."

That seems impossible. I will have to test it later. For now, I unclip it and try to get it off. As soon as I unclip it, Rose is able to see it, so she grabs it, helping me out of it, and then places it on the chair next to the bed.

"So where are we?" I ask, relaxing back down on the bed.

"We are in an FBI safe house. The Doctor will be in soon to check on you. You needed a couple of bags of blood; he also gave you something to counter the sedative, so you didn't get that high after effect as it started to break down in your system. It has affected how you smell to me. I don't like it." She pauses for a second, then adds, changing the subject, "I was scared there for a moment, Ava." I know what she means. "When you blacked out on me, I thought you were dying for a moment from blood loss. I froze for a moment as I looked at you, covered in blood. I was scared to check for a pulse, but I had to do it no matter what. The relief I felt when I found a pulse made me cry. Don't do that to me again, you hear!"

I cup Rose's face, gently run my thumb over her cheek, then lean up and kiss her. I'm not about to tell her I thought *she* was dead for a moment and hoped to see her once I had died and become a ghost. Before I can say anything, we are interrupted as the door to the room opens. Rose pulls away. It hurts my feelings momentarily, but I understand why she did it; I know how she must have felt when I pulled my hand out of hers when she opened the door to find Sam standing there when we first got together.

"Agent Bekke, I see you are back with us. That's good. I'm Doctor Stevens," the man says as he walks up to the monitor next to the bed. He has a standard hospital chart and makes some notes, then feels my pulse and frowns. "Your pulse is a little high, but it's acceptable."

I can't help but smile as I look at Rose. She's grinning. I want to laugh, but manage to hold it in and distract myself by asking, "So I can go, right? I would prefer to rest in my motel room."

"All of you agents are the same. I'm afraid not. But if everything is still good by morning, I will let you go as long as you promise to rest for a few days to let your neck start to heal."

I groan at his response. He's a typical doctor. He checks the bandage on my neck, turning to a nurse who has followed him into the room. "Would you mind changing the bandage? That should be fine until morning." He then turns back to me and says, "Sleep well, agent. See you in the morning."

The nurse nods. The doctor then leaves the room while the nurse grabs a clean bandage and everything else she needs, then carefully removes the bandage on my neck and gently cleans my skin around the wound, making pain shoot through my neck as she works under the watchful eyes of Rose. Once the nurse is finished and has left the room, I ask Rose, "Did you follow my plan and call in the state police to help instead of the Chief?"

A smirk spreads across Rose's face before she answers. "We did. The state police were more than happy to help with the cleanup and be seen as helping the city sort out the gang issue." Rose chuckles before she speaks again. "The Chief has been calling us all non-stop, leaving nasty voicemails. Luca said Sam finally answered one of his calls and lost it, just like you did. He told him we would speak to him about everything when we can; right now, we are dealing with some injuries, and we lost an agent. Then he hung up. Looks like you are having an effect on Sam." Rose then can't help but laugh, then says, "I know you are having an effect on me."

I give her my best smile. I think I even blush a little. I have no idea how I can blush with blood loss, but I feel it all the same.

We talk for a bit longer, but I start to get tired. It doesn't help that Rose is running her hands over my leg nearest her as we talk. It has the effect of lulling me to sleep.

CHAPTER 33

WAKING UP IN A SAFE HOUSE, BANDAGED, AND SLIGHTLY

DISAPPOINTED ROSE ISN'T MY PILLOW

I'm abruptly woken by the morning sunlight streaming through a gap in the curtains, hitting my face with intrusive brightness. My eyes struggle to crack open against the brightness, stinging in protest. A groan escapes my lips as I attempt to turn away, burying my face deeper into what I hope is Rose's shoulder, but as I grip it, I realise it's just a pillow.

"Morning."

The voice, deep and unfamiliar, startles me. It doesn't belong to Rose. My eyes snap open, scanning the room, searching for her, but she's not here. A strange, hollow ache clenches in my chest, an unfamiliar sensation that makes me instinctively press a hand over my heart. From a chair tucked in the corner of the room, I see Luca watching me, a curious expression on his face.

"Rose went down to freshen up and grab us some breakfast. She hoped to make it back before you woke. She is going to be disappointed she wasn't here when you did," Luca states, his usual tone back to normal. The instant he speaks, that odd tightness in my chest dissolves, leaving me puzzled but relieved.

"Are you okay?" I ask, my voice raspy. Concern replaces my confusion as I remember the state he was in last night. "You looked badly injured when I... when I passed out."

"I'm good, Ava. Healing up fast, just like shifters do. Rose is the same. Afraid it's going to take a little longer for you, being human and all," he reassures me, though a flicker of something–maybe pain, maybe a memory–crosses his features. "Although I do believe you are healing quicker than you should be, it seems what we talked about is true about the healing thing due to the bond. Anyway, thank you, by the way, for saving me. That vampire took me by surprise when you were attacked; if you hadn't shot him, I think he might have won," Luca said with the most grateful look I had ever seen from someone.

I manage a small shrug, trying to downplay it, though my neck twinges in protest. "Not the first time I've woken up feeling like I've gone ten rounds with a truck, though usually it involves a hospital bed, not a… safe house?" I glance around the unfamiliar room again. "Good to know the bond comes with perks like faster healing. I already feel pretty good."

"I guess in your line of work, you are going to get some injuries."

"More times than I'd like," I admit. "Actually, while we're waiting for Rose… can I ask you something?"

Luca nods with a smile, "Sure, go ahead."

"I noticed the way you moved last night. Did you get military training?"

He seems thoughtful for a moment. "Not exactly," he says slowly. "Many shifters go into private security, some do go into the services, but it's a risk to do so. They then bring the things they learn back to the pack and teach others. The beta I was with as a kid when the attacks happened used to be in private security. The company he worked for had ex-military personnel conducting the training, so while we were on the run, he began teaching those skills to me and the other kids who had survived. You could look at it that way, I suppose, as I did receive military training, but nothing like you have been trained over the years," Luca explains.

"Oh, okay, I just wondered," I say. "It felt like I was working with one of the guys I sometimes work with; I thought it would be awkward and clumsy, but I'm glad it wasn't," I say.

"Thank you," Luca replies. "I expected you to ask us questions about our training and stuff, but you didn't."

"I was distracted by all the paranormal stuff. My brain hasn't stopped wondering about many things," I say.

"Like what?"

"I won't keep asking questions because I may not stop," I shake my head. "I also might not remember everything if you tell me in such a short space of time. I'm going to let it happen more naturally, so I'm learning what I need at the time instead of loads of random stuff for which I may never need the answers."

"Good point; that's probably for the best. It's also the complete opposite of what Sam and Agent Moore were like," Luca says with a cocky smile. If I hadn't had this thing with Rose, I would be so interested in him, but since I got together with Rose, I've lost all interest in him or anyone else.

I'm about to ask Luca a question and go back on what I just said when the door of my room opened. It's Rose, as she enters the room, she's facing Luca and hasn't noticed I'm awake.

"I'm sorry it took longer at the diner. Everyone heard rumours about last night, so I got bombarded with questions; I'm glad my face has fully healed, or I might not have gotten out of there."

"That's okay, Rose. I kept your girl company while we waited for you," Luca said, cool as a cucumber.

Rose freezes, looking confused for a second just before she reaches Luca. She shoots her head in my direction. When she sees I'm awake with a big grin on my face, she holds out the bags of food absentmindedly, "Here, take these, please," then heads for me when Luca takes the bags.

"You're awake. I thought you were going to sleep all day," Rose says, beaming at me.

"No chance," I grin back. "I want to get out of here as soon as possible, which better happen right after we have eaten. If you got me anything, that is, which you might not have if you thought I was going to sleep all day."

Rose gave me a cuddle and a quick kiss on the lips, "I got your usual. Like, I wouldn't get you anything. If the doctor doesn't let you go this morning, I will break you out," Rose says with her usual cheeky smile.

"Very good answer, Rose; you might be my favourite person today," I say, smirking at Rose's reaction.

"Today? Just today? I better be your favourite person today and every day from now on," she says, lavishing a kiss on me.

We ate the food Rose got for us and discussed last night about what we could have done differently. The only thing we could have done, really, was to attack the church head-on with all the vampires present. If we had done that, we would have needed more cameras, including one inside, to pull off the operation successfully. It would have also increased the risk of more people getting injured or killed; on top of that, the whole mission would have taken much longer, so more innocent people would have been killed; the vampires could have also turned more, increasing the number of vampires we had to go up against making things much harder and possibly impossible for just the four of us.

I realise what Rose and Luca are doing. It's working as well. As we review the other ways we could have played things out, my guilt starts to wane. By the time the doctor turns up, my guilt is almost gone. I've never felt guilt like this before, yes some of my missions involved innocent people, and some died but not by my hand, but I never felt like this, the way I see it, even if a few innocents did die, I was saving so many more once I completed the mission. Especially those missions dealing in the worst kind of crime, the trafficking of women and children.

"Good morning, everyone. Agent Bekke, how are you feeling after some sleep? Looks like you have managed to eat?" the doctor asks in the cheery way most doctors are when they enjoy their work, unlike some I have met who are grumpy and keep you waiting and don't care if you decide to leave early. It's the doctor's cheery demeanour that keeps me in this bed, for now! Otherwise, I would have left and taken the risk if he were the grumpy kind, hoping I wouldn't pull any stitches, or I would have been forced to return with my tail between my legs. That being said, I do need to leave today.

"I'm very good, Doc. I had a good night's rest and a good breakfast, so if you give me the go-ahead, I will thank you and then get out of your hair; I will rest after we sort out the press conference for today."

The doctor ignores me, gently removes the bandage on my neck, studies it for a moment, then turns to the same nurse from last night and says, "Can you please give it a good clean and put on a new dressing? I will sort out some painkillers and paperwork for the agency. Once they have been signed, the agent can go."

I'm gobsmacked by what the doctor said. I turn to Rose and Luca to see if I heard right, and both smile in response. "Doctor Stevens, I like you. You can fix me up again anytime, so thank you," I say, not believing my luck.

"Just rest, please. I'm sure I will see you again. I am technically working for your team right now; I like you too, as you haven't been a pain like most agents are when they get hurt. Have a good day, and I hope the press conference is as good as the last one," he says with a big grin on his face.

"It should be better than the last one. Again, thanks," I say and wait for him to leave. The nurse then changes my bandage and leaves. Once she walks out the door, I turn to Rose and Luca and say, "Let's do this."

We arrive back at the motel and find Sam waiting for us. "I'm glad to see you're okay, Ava; when you're ready, we need to deal with the police Chief and hold the press conference. I've also given our mission report to Agent Moore, so you don't have to worry about that."

I guess there's no rest for the wicked. "Thank you, Sam. You did well. I'm sorry about the agent you lost. I wish things had turned out better, but it is our first mission like this, and we will learn from each one."

"Thank you. We were sure there was only one left. I thought we could handle it, so I didn't wait for Rose. I'm sorry, I won't make that mistake again. At least we succeeded and helped our first city," Sam says, looking lost and guilty.

"That's good. Now we need to deal with the Chief and the Press, then we can get out of here and have a break. I'm going to need a few days off to heal up, so I'm ready for the next fight. Unless we come across something easy, we have been lucky and managed to gather some small pieces of intel, but nothing major can be acted upon. There aren't any other enemies in this city, and with what we learned last night, I can't wait to hit the road," I say, feeling relieved.

Sam's smile returns, "Yes, the Chief is getting on my last nerve. I think if we don't hold a press conference soon, he is going to hold one and just state he has dealt with everything and take the credit, stating he can't give details because of the domestic terrorism act," Sam says, his face turning from a smile to one of anger.

"I'm going to get cleaned up. Give me an hour, arrange the press conference, make it known we are holding it, not the Chief. There's that small park area across the road from police headquarters; let's hold it there again. Did you let the State Police Commander know we wanted him there or a representative?" I ask as I watch Sam's facial expression change again to one of joy.

"Erm, Ava, you promised the doctor you would rest; this isn't resting," Rose says, concerned.

I turn to look at her. "I'm going to rest, but we need to do this press conference so that when we arrive in different cities, we aren't treated like we have been here. Then, we can leave this city tomorrow and rest as we head for Chicago. I promise I will rest then. All I'm going to be doing is talking to that sexist bear of a man."

Rose nods, then Sam speaks again, "I have worked on the press release; I can't wait to see the Chief's face."

"Sam, you have started to show a side of yourself I didn't expect. I was sure you were a by-the-book man, but I like this side of you a lot. It's one of the reasons I turned down the offer to become a full-time CIA agent. I'm not the by-the-book kind of girl."

"Yes, well, I like my job, but I am starting to enjoy this freedom a lot. Anyway, you'd better go get cleaned up so we can get this over with," Sam says, looking happier than I've seen him since we arrived here.

"Yes, sir." I salute with a cheeky grin, then leave the guys' room and go into mine. I start to strip out of my clothes when Rose closes the door behind her.

"Do you need my help so you don't get your bandage wet?" Rose asks.

"I didn't think I needed to ask," I say as I continue towards the bathroom.

Rose's face lights up like a Christmas tree. She starts to strip off her clothes before joining me. My shower takes longer than planned. It wasn't what you were thinking. It was hard trying not to get my wound and bandage wet. Fine…okay, it was partly what you were thinking. We end up being twenty minutes late.

We all head to the police headquarters. I'm starting to regain my old confidence now that we have succeeded in our first mission against paranormals. I'll admit that for the first time since joining the military, I've been a little nervous. Now, I'm starting to feel like myself again, knowing it's possible to go up against what's out there trying to wipe us out, even though I did get injured again.

As we approach the station, the news crews are already starting to arrive, but not at the station itself, but across the road, as we had requested in the small park area; even the state police are already present. I can't help but smile when I see Chief Thornton standing at the top of the steps in front of the building entrance, looking angry and confused. He also appears to be trying to call out to the press and points to the front of the building. That is, until he sees our vehicle passing by and turns towards the side parking area. The last thing I notice is him heading back into the building.

We enter the building through the side entrance, just like we have before. I don't expect the welcome we get as we reach the bullpen. I think the officers and detectives of this city will be upset with us because we didn't involve them; however, as soon as they see us enter the area, they all start clapping and nodding. I feel confused and taken aback as my pace slows in response.

Luca places a hand on my shoulder before speaking. "They see you as one of them, you helped their city and got injured in the process." Luca is right. Even though they don't really know who we are, we are all on the same side, no matter what, so I nod in thanks as we move through the floor; it doesn't take long for the Chief to show up.

"What is going on out here?" the Chief bellows. Then he sees us. "You four, in my office now."

We stop in the middle of the bullpen. Some people are still clapping or nodding while the Chief gives them dirty looks. Then he shouts at us again, "I said I want you in my office NOW!!!"

Everyone realises something is about to happen when we don't move or react, so they stop clapping. Now, it's my turn to speak. "Chief Thornton, you are not our boss. We are only here out of courtesy to give you an update." The Chief's face turns bright red with anger. A few of his men snicker, which causes the Chief to look at his men to see who's responsible.

"Everyone, we managed to track one of the gang members after a tip we heard in a diner; we checked out the tip and found a gang member entering an abandoned factory where we tried to capture him; he attacked us and was killed in the attempt. We searched the area and found intel that led us to a church."

I was rudely interrupted by the Chief, "Are you telling me you kept vital details from me when we could have raided this church the day after, you have just admitted to a mistake that is going to get you relieved of your duties if I have anything to do with it."

"I don't think so, it's more likely you are going to be losing your position. Even the state police will be issuing complaints about your ineffectiveness. This task force was established to identify the individuals responsible for the events occurring in our country and gather intelligence. Like any task force that is put together, they keep what they learn to themselves and only pass on information at the right time."

I take a deep breath and quickly continue before he can say anything else. "We are now here to tell you and your men and women what happened last night," Chief Thornton gets all flustered as he knows what I said is right. "As I said, the intel led us to a church east of the city. It could have been nothing, but the literature we found and a map indicated areas they were targeting, which matched the reported attacks, proving we were on the right track. I pretended to be a jogger and planted a few cameras near the church. I came in contact with a member of the gang who was a guard at the main entrance. He tried to get me to enter, but I made my excuses and planted the last camera right under his nose. We watched the church for two nights and devised a plan, as we couldn't confirm final numbers. Last night, we followed three members as they left the church and headed towards the lower-end nightspots. We planned to wait till they were away from the innocent public, but they changed their routine last night and headed for a residential area. We did lose track of them briefly because of this sudden pattern change, from what they had been doing the previous nights. By the time we tracked them to three houses, there was evidence they had entered all three, so we split up. When Marshal Cole and I entered a house, we heard children crying and a gang member talking; we engaged, two were killed, and one captured; we arrested him under the domestic terrorism act, and he was questioned by my men and revealed some intel we will be following tomorrow taking us out of this lovely city," I take another deep breath and have a quick look around the room to see everyone's reaction, so far it looks like I'm holding their attention and no one seems to be angry with us.

"In the engagement, I was injured slightly. I'm afraid we were too late to save Mr and Mrs Norris. What we understand is that they planned to start taking children to brainwash them to join them. The children are being well looked after, and I will make sure they are given everything they need. Our second team, led by Agent Miller, breached the church with Marshal Peyton and the second half of our backup team and found only one more gang member inside; he managed to kill one of our agents before he was taken out as they saw no sign he planned to give up, so we had no choice. We found two of the reported missing inside the church. From everything we have learned, the gang we engaged are the only ones in the city responsible for the attacks. Agent Miller is going to give a press conference. Thank you to those who supported us, and we hope your city remains safe."

I then turn and head back out of the building. Again, I'm taken by surprise when everyone starts to clap and cheer. This time, officers approach us and start to shake our hands while the Chief tries again to regain control of the narrative, but is drowned out by all the cheering.

When we exit the building, I wish Sam good luck and head for our vehicle while Sam heads for the park area, where the news crews wait for him, so he can explain to the people of this city that their Chief kept working against us and continued to threaten us to get us disbanded because he didn't want anyone coming into his city and getting the job done where he had failed for years.

CHAPTER 34

DINER DIPLOMACY, ALIEN PROBING THEORIES, AND THE

CASE FILE THAT SCREAMS "WOLVES!"

During the day, we have lunch and dinner, and then breakfast the next morning at the diner we have been using since we arrived in this city. The initial warmth we received seems to have solidified; everyone greets us with enthusiastic cheers of congratulations each time we visit, as they have either seen Sam's press conference or heard about it from word of mouth. It's a strange feeling, being hailed as heroes when the reality of our fight is so hidden and messy, as they have no idea of the truth of the matter; if they really knew the situation, they wouldn't be cheering us as heroes.

After our final breakfast there, we finally hit the road. The journey is slow; my neck injury protests sharply whenever I stay in one position for too long, forcing us to take frequent breaks. The dull ache is a constant reminder of the fight, of the vampire's fangs, of how close I came. Each stop is a necessary evil, delaying our arrival but allowing the throbbing to subside just enough to continue. Rose hovers protectively during these stops, her concern an unmistakable warmth that both soothes and slightly embarrasses me. Luca remains watchful, his gaze scanning our surroundings, ever the alpha, ensuring the temporary halt doesn't become a vulnerability. Sam uses the time to keep Agent Moore updated, while Agent Moore updates him on any changes around the country, especially any attacks that have gained more publicity than usual, in case we might need to divert resources as a situation requires our immediate attention. his efficiency is a stark contrast to my forced inactivity.

We finally roll into Chicago well after the evening rush hour has dissipated, the city lights painting streaks across the car windows. We could have pushed harder, arrived sooner, but the thought of navigating downtown traffic after the long, painful drive held zero appeal. We find a decent hotel overlooking the quiet ribbon of the Little Calumet River, the water reflecting the bruised twilight sky. We check in, and the hotel's anonymity provides a brief respite; we settle in for the night.

We take the next couple of days at a slower pace, partly to allow my neck to heal, partly to gather our bearings in this new city. We use mealtimes as opportunities for reconnaissance, trying different diners around the city, listening to local chatter, trying to gauge the atmosphere. The stories we hear about the strange disappearances are bizarre, ranging from cult abductions to alien probing – outlandish theories that mask a terrifying reality we're beginning to grasp. One man adamantly blames a cult, adding with a lecherous wink that they're "probably perverts doin' pervert things." Another insists that aliens are responsible, complete with detailed descriptions of probing procedures that leave us struggling to maintain a straight face. It's a surreal experience, laughing at these wild guesses while knowing the truth is far more monstrous.

Everything changes the next morning. We're having breakfast in yet another diner, the coffee weak and the toast slightly burnt, when we receive the call. We head straight for the main municipal police building downtown. Having researched beforehand, we know the city's police force is headed by a superintendent, which hopefully means a more centralised system and not fragmented districts. Sam contacted the superintendent's office yesterday, securing an appointment and hoping to avoid the friction we encountered with Chief Thornton. I hope she's not his golfing buddy or something.

Inside the imposing building, I approach the main reception desk, the cool marble floor silencing my boots as I walk. "Morning," I say, offering a professional smile. "Agent Bekke. My colleagues and I have a ten-thirty meeting with the superintendent."

The receptionist, a woman with sharp eyes and an efficient air, taps a few keys on her computer. "Yes, Agent Bekke. I have you right here," she confirms, glancing up at our group. She hands us visitor passes. "You'll need these for the elevators – new security feature."

"Thank you," I reply, clipping the pass to my jacket.

We ride the elevator up, the silence punctuated only by the soft hum of the machinery. Exiting onto the correct floor, we face another reception desk, this one guarding the executive offices. "Agent Bekke, here to see the superintendent," I repeat.

"Yes, I was just informed you'd arrived," this receptionist replies, already standing. "Please follow me." She then leads us down a carpeted hallway towards a large corner office, its glass walls offering panoramic city views, though the blinds are currently angled for privacy. She knocks softly, opens the door, and announces, "Your ten-thirty is here, ma'am."

A voice from within responds, warm but firm, "Send them in, Sarah. Thank you. And please check if they'd like refreshments."

"Yes, ma'am," Sarah confirms, turning back to us. "Would any of you like coffee? Water?"

We all decline politely. Sarah ushers us into the spacious office where four chairs are arranged opposite a large, tidy desk. Behind the desk sits a woman who radiates quiet authority.

"Superintendent, thank you for seeing us on short notice," I say, stepping forward.

She rises smoothly and extends her hand. Her handshake is firm, her gaze direct. "Happy I could accommodate you. Welcome to

Chicago. Please, have a seat."

We arrange ourselves in the chairs. I take the one directly opposite her, with Rose settling immediately to my left. Sam, perhaps wanting to project importance or simply taking the next available seat, sits beside me, leaving Luca to take the final chair on Sam's right.

"Superintendent," I begin.

She holds up a hand, a small smile playing on her lips. "Please, call me Annmarie."

"Thank you, Annmarie. I'm Agent Bekke, or Ava if you so choose," I reply, nodding. "This is Agent Miller, or Sam," I gesture beside me. "Deputy Marshal Cole, Luca," indicating Luca on Sam's right. "And Deputy Marshal Peyton, Rose," I finish, glancing at Rose beside me.

Annmarie acknowledges each introduction with a nod, her sharp eyes assessing us individually. "A pleasure to meet you all," she says, her tone professional but not unfriendly. "I must admit, I was surprised to hear your task force was heading to Chicago. We pride ourselves on having one of the lower crime rates for major cities right now." Her gaze lingers, clearly expecting an explanation.

"We received some intelligence during our investigation in Pittsburgh that pointed us in this direction," I explain carefully, mindful of my neck bandage, which she subtly clocks. "We understand your reported crime rates are lower, but we are aware of one particularly brutal killing here that shares concerning similarities with cases we encountered there. Additionally, you have several unusual missing persons reports – individuals disappearing and reappearing weeks later with complete amnesia. Our intel suggests a connection, which is why we're here – primarily to follow those leads while I recover from an injury sustained during the Pittsburgh operation."

Her expression remains neutral, but her eyes sharpen. "I saw the press conference Agent Miller gave," she states. "Quite… impactful. Impressive work taking down that gang on your first assignment, especially while dealing with the… *personal* style of Pittsburgh's Chief of Police." A hint of dry amusement enters her voice. "I've never cared for Thornton myself. Always trying to steal the spotlight. I also saw some local Pittsburgh news interviews afterwards; citizens praising your team, mentioning you tried to save a woman right outside a diner you frequented. You were certainly unlucky drawing Thornton first, but rest assured, you won't have those kinds of issues here. I'm happy to cooperate."

Relief washes over me, loosening a knot of tension I hadn't realised I was holding. "That's good to hear, Annmarie. Thank you."

"So," she leans forward slightly, getting down to business. "What exactly do you need from my police force?"

Sam fields this one, stepping smoothly into his liaison role. "We'd appreciate access to any case files involving strange or unexplained crimes," he says. "Particularly missing persons cases with unusual circumstances, or assaults and homicides with bizarre elements – anything that deviates significantly from the norm."

Annmarie considers this, tapping a pen against her desk blotter. "Basically, your *weird shit* files," she translates bluntly, a ghost of a smile touching her lips. "Understood. While I don't quite see the connection yet, you have my full cooperation. I can arrange for you to use a secure conference room here. They do lock, and you can change the code to whatever you want for security."

"Thank you for the offer, superintendent, but we've been instructed to maintain strict operational security," Sam replies smoothly. "We have access to a designated safe house for handling sensitive materials but we are unable to disclose the details of it, if at all possible can the files be delivered to our hotel then we can take the files to the safe house or we can pick them up from wherever is convenient for you, but we appreciate the gesture to use your conference room."

"Fair enough. Just remember those files are confidential police records," Annmarie reminds him firmly and doesn't look too happy that the files will be leaving her building.

"Understood completely," Sam assures her. "Any files will be reviewed securely and returned or stored appropriately at the safe house. Nothing will fall into the wrong hands; we have other agents who will guard them when we aren't there."

"That's all I need to hear," Annmarie nods, satisfied. "I'll assign a liaison officer to your team. If you require anything further – resources, local intel, backup – contact them directly. And I'd appreciate periodic updates, within the bounds of your operational security, of course."

"Thank you, superintendent," I say, rising from my chair and extending my hand again. "We'll keep you informed as much as we can. Hopefully, this will just be an intelligence-gathering stop for us. We appreciate your cooperation."

———————

It's been a whole day since we requested the files to be collated and delivered, so far we haven't heard anything. In the meantime, we continue our low-key exploration of the city, using mealtimes as an opportunity to ask locals about the strange occurrences. The theories remain wild, but the underlying fear is palpable.

Yesterday, however, something threw a wrench in the works. As we headed towards a promising-looking diner, both Rose and Luca froze mid-stride, their bodies instantly tensing. A shared look passed between them, laden with a meaning I couldn't decipher but immediately recognised as danger.

"Shifter," they breathed in unison, the word hanging heavy in the air.

We beat a hasty retreat; the near-encounter left a sour taste in my mouth. Finding a different, more secluded diner, I demanded answers as soon as we slid into a booth tucked away in the corner.

"What's going on?" I ask, keeping my voice low.

Rose exchanges another glance with Luca before answering,

her usual confidence slightly dimmed. "We think... we think shifters might be responsible for the missing persons here, Ava. The scent... it was wolf. Strong. And recent."

"Okay," I process this new, alarming possibility. "So, how do we handle this? How do we confirm it and deal with them?"

"Ava," Rose begins, looking down at the table, a rare hint of shame colouring her cheeks, "This changes things. If there's an established wolf pack here, turning humans... this isn't something we can just walk into right now. We're not equipped. We need backup, *real* backup, other paranormals."

"We can't just leave, Rose!" I insist, frustration bubbling up. "Cat, the voice, guided us here for a reason. There must be something we're meant to find, something important."

"Let's confirm the theory first," Sam interjects, ever the pragmatist. "We need to know for sure if shifters are involved. We can gather intel, assess the situation, *then* decide on the next step. Is there a chance you might be mistaken, and the scent you picked up on was just a shifter passing through the city?" Luca and Rose exchange dubious looks but eventually concede, albeit reluctantly.

The tension remains thick as we eat. Luca then explains the necessity of moving hotels daily now. "If shifters are active, especially wolves, they'll pick up our scent eventually. They're territorial. They won't take kindly to other shifters, especially panthers, on their turf. We need to keep moving, make it harder for them to track us. We also need to go through the files and check to see if any hotel workers have been involved in the disappearances." We agree that as soon as we receive the files, we will review them to check. The thought that any random hotel employee could be a shifter hiding in plain sight sends a fresh chill down my spine. I also can't help but look around the diner, wondering if any of the patrons could be shifters too, then I realise I'm being silly as Luca and Rose would have picked up on them before we even entered the building.

Back in the guys' room at the current hotel, discussing our next move, a sharp knock echoes on the door. Luca moves towards it cautiously, sniffing the air almost imperceptibly. He opens it to reveal a uniformed police officer, looking crisp and professional.

"Afternoon," the officer says politely. "Looking for Agent Bekke? Tried her room, no answer. Reception said her colleagues were in this one."

I'm sitting near the window, slightly out of his direct line of sight. "I'm Agent Bekke," I call out, standing up. "Come on in."

Luca steps aside, allowing the officer to enter. He carries a large, expandable file box. He approaches me directly, and I offer my hand, deciding that politeness is the best approach. "Thanks for coming," I say.

He shakes my hand firmly. "Lieutenant Parker, ma'am," he introduces himself. "Superintendent Cleveland asked me to compile these files you requested. Went around the districts myself. Pulled everything that looks remotely strange or out of the ordinary. Not entirely sure what you're looking for, so apologies if some of these aren't relevant."

"We appreciate the effort, Lieutenant. I'm sure this will be very helpful," I reply, accepting the heavy box.

"Is there anything else I can assist with? The Superintendent assigned me as your direct liaison while you're in Chicago."

"Thank you, Lieutenant Parker, that's very helpful to know," I say sincerely. "This is all we need for now. We'll need some time to go through these. We'll be in touch if anything comes up we need help with."

"Understood. My contact details are inside the box," he informs me. "Call anytime. And enjoy your stay in Chicago, hopefully under better circumstances than you had in your last city."

"Thank you," I repeat, shaking his hand once more.

After Parker leaves, I heft the box onto the small table by the window and open the lid. My breath catches. It's crammed full of files, way more than I was expecting for a city with one of the lowest crime rates. "Wow," I breathe, stunned by the volume. "I didn't expect nearly this many."

Luca comes over, peering into the box, his expression grim. "Twenty-three years, Ava," he says quietly, worry etching his face. "If our theory that it might be shifters here, then the disappearances make more sense, as it could indicate the wolves have been recruiting and expanding, they've had a long time to build their numbers undetected."

"Right," I straighten up, pushing down the sudden wave of unease. "Looks like we'd better get started. Are we taking these to the safe house?"

Luca shakes his head, his gaze distant. "Too risky now, knowing shifters are likely active here. We can't risk leading them to the safe house. We'll review them here, then stash them in the Tahoe's hidden compartment before we move hotels tonight." He sighs. "This just got potentially a lot more complicated."

We each grab a stack of files, the weight of the city's hidden horrors settling upon us as we begin the daunting task of sifting through years of mystery, hoping to find a single thread to pull.

CHAPTER 35

The air in the hotel room grows stale, thick with the scent of cheap paper and photocopier toner mingling with the lingering smell of yesterday's takeaway. We've spent the entire day hunched over these case files, trying to tease some sense out of the disjointed reports of disappearances and strange occurrences that plague Chicago. Room service replaces diner trips, a necessary evil to avoid drawing attention now that we know shifters – *wolves* – are active in this city. My muscles ache from sitting, my eyes burn from scanning endless lines of text, and a restless energy thrums under my skin. I'm getting antsy, feeling trapped, needing a break from the oppressive weight of these files, when Luca suddenly slams a hand down on the table, making us all jump nearly out of our skin.

"We are right," he states, his voice tight with a grim certainty that chills me more than the air conditioning. "The shifters here *are* increasing their numbers. Significantly."

"What did you find?" Sam asks, pushing his own stack of files aside. I'm still trying to coax my heart rate back down from the ceiling after Luca's sudden outburst.

Luca points a finger at a pattern he's laid out across several files. "Look. Every single one of these missing persons? Taken just before the full moon. They return, almost without fail, just before the *next* full moon." His finger traces a timeline. "A few come back later, sure – probably took them longer to get control, to integrate after the change. And a few… a few don't come back at all." He looks up, his dark eyes meeting mine, heavy with implication. "It's shifters, Ava. No doubt in my mind. But look at the frequency – they're only actively taking people for about half the year. Even so…" he trails off, shaking his head. "The potential numbers are staggering, far higher than I ever anticipated. They can't possibly keep this level of activity sustainable without exposing themselves." He pulls up something on his tablet. "And I've been doing some digging online. There is a corresponding spike in people officially *leaving* the city – moving away, changing addresses – that almost perfectly matches the number of disappearances during those active months. They're doing exactly what the vampires did in Pittsburgh – building an army, then dispersing them to other cities to set up new cells, new packs." The way he says it, flat and devoid of hope, makes my stomach clench.

"There has to be a plan," I insist, refusing to accept the bleakness settling over the room. My voice sounds firmer than I feel. "We can figure out a way to deal with them." I'm trying to keep positive but Luca's defeatist tone grates on my nerves.

"Ava, I don't think you're grasping the scale here," Rose says softly, her usual confidence replaced by a weary gravity. "Even if we called in our backup team, even if we somehow convinced the entire Chicago PD to believe us and fight alongside us… based on these numbers, we would *still* be outnumbered."

I stare at them, my mind struggling to comprehend. Hundreds? Thousands? An army of shifters hidden in plain sight. "That… that can't be right," I stammer, shaking my head. The logistics seem impossible. "Someone would notice. You can't hide that many."

"Why do you think they send the bitten back home after only a month?" Luca counters, his voice low. "They integrate them back into society, hiding them in plain sight. They look human, act human most of the time. Just waiting. Waiting for the call, for the orders to activate."

"Large packs, truly established ones, can number in the hundreds, Ava," Rose adds, her green eyes pleading for me to understand. "Especially if they've been around a long time and haven't faced significant opposition. Normally, inter-pack warfare keeps numbers down, creates a balance. But most other packs were wiped out in the Purge, as they call it. These wolves have had over two decades to grow unchecked. Historically, once a pack reaches a certain size, others stop challenging them altogether. It becomes too dangerous."

The full weight of it finally hits me, a suffocating pressure in my chest. This isn't just a mission; it's a war. How do we face an entrenched, potentially overwhelming force? My earlier confidence feels naive and foolish. "So," I swallow hard, my throat suddenly dry, "what do we do?"

Luca sighs, running a hand through his already messy hair. "This is why I wanted to head south first," he admits. "Most of the known shifter territories, especially wolf packs, are concentrated in the north – Michigan, Wisconsin, the Dakotas. They favour the wide-open spaces, the forests." He meets my gaze directly. "We need help, Ava. Serious help. Allies. We can't take on packs of this size alone."

A cold dread seeps into me. "And what if there's no one left to find?" The words slip out before I can stop them, tinged with a frustration that borders on despair. The high from our success in Pittsburgh evaporates, replaced by the chilling reality of our situation. "What if *we're* all that's left?"

"I don't know, Ava," Luca replies honestly, the uncertainty heavy in his voice. "I truly don't know."

Rose reaches over, her hand covering mine briefly, a silent offering of support. "I have to believe there are others," she says, her voice regaining a flicker of its usual strength. "We survived. Others must have too. We have to find them."

"I hope you're right," I say, forcing the despair back down. Focus. We need intel. "Maybe… maybe we can still use this situation. Turn it to our advantage somehow. Gather intelligence that will help us later, when we *do* have backup."

The room falls silent for a moment, each of us lost in the grim possibilities. It's Sam, surprisingly, who breaks the silence, his voice cutting through the gloom. "We still need confirmation," he says, tapping a file. "We need to verify your theory, Luca. See if at least a couple of these returned missing persons *are* actually shifters. Then," he pauses, glancing at me, "maybe we consider capturing one. See what information we can extract."

Luca immediately shakes his head. "Too dangerous. If we go anywhere near one of their homes, especially a newly bitten one who might not have full control yet, they could lash out and hurt innocent members of their family. They'll also know shifters are nearby immediately, then could track our scent back here, or wherever we move to next."

"We'll need to move again tonight, probably every night we remain in this city. Did anyone notice hotel workers listed among the missing or returned?"

We all shake our heads—a small mercy, at least. The thought of a seemingly harmless concierge or cleaner being a hidden wolf is deeply unsettling.

"Alright, new plan," I say, trying to regain control of the situation, pushing down the image of wolves hiding behind friendly smiles. "If you two," I nod towards Luca and Rose, "can't get close without tipping them off, then it falls to Sam and me again. How do we identify one? What do we look for?"

Luca and Rose exchange that familiar, weighted look. A wave of unease washes over me – no, not mine, it's Rose's. Sharp and cold, like a sudden draft. It prickles against my skin, a foreign anxiety bleeding through the bond. I quickly try to erect the mental wall Papa Legba mentioned, picturing a solid brick wall, mortared tight, to shield myself from her fear, needing my head to be clear right now. It doesn't seem to work immediately, her apprehension still a faint static in the back of my mind, but as I keep imagining the wall, her fears start to leave me, I'm shocked it seems to be working.

While they share looks about how to answer me I decide on a different tactic, okay, low-risk approach. Recon first. "What if Sam and I talk to a couple of the *wives*?" I suggest focusing on the practical. "The cases where the husband disappeared and returned. We pose as local detectives, follow up, and ask if the husbands remember anything new. Wives notice changes. They'll know if something's off, more than the men might admit." I add a pointed look towards Luca and Sam, a slight jab I can't resist.

Luca considers it. "It could work," he concedes slowly. "Targeting the spouse means you avoid direct contact with the potential shifter initially. Less risk of immediate detection if they *can* somehow sense you're not who you say you are."

"What?" I frown. "Sense we're not...."

Luca and Rose share another look, this time Luca sighs, looking distinctly uncomfortable. Rose avoids my gaze entirely. "Shifters... we have certain, uh, heightened senses," Luca explains hesitantly. "Beyond hearing and smell."

"Like what?" I press, suspicion coiling in my gut.

He takes a deep breath, like he's bracing himself. "Emotions," he admits quietly.

"Excuse me?" I echo, baffled.

"Emotions... they have distinct scents," Luca elaborates, watching me warily, clearly expecting an explosion. "We can... smell deception. Fear. Other strong emotions. It helps us read intent, gauge threats."

The air crackles with unspoken tension. He's admitting they can smell lies. They've known *all along* when we've been scared, uncertain, maybe even dishonest. My voice climbs, sharp with disbelief and a sudden, stinging sense of betrayal. "What the hell? Seriously? You can *smell* lies? And you didn't think that was important information to share?"

"It was for protection, Ava," Luca says quickly, holding up his hands defensively. "Ours. We've seen how humans react to things they don't understand, things that make them feel vulnerable or threatened. We needed to know if… if we could trust you. In case we needed to leave to protect ourselves."

Rose finally speaks, her voice pleading. "We wanted to tell you, Ava, truly, especially after… well, *after*. But there just wasn't the right moment. We didn't want to overwhelm you even more."

Their explanations, however logical, feel like flimsy excuses. The trust I thought we were building suddenly feels fragile, undermined by this deliberate omission. A coldness settles in my chest. "Sure," I say flatly, the word devoid of emotion. I stand up abruptly. "Sam and I will go talk to one of the wives. Then we figure out how to capture one of these walking *lie* detectors. Let's pick one and get on with it."

I turn away, ignoring Rose's attempt to catch my eye, needing space. We spend the next hour selecting a suitable target – a husband who went missing six months ago and returned a month later, whose wife reported significant personality changes to the police. His work schedule means he'll be out this afternoon, giving us a window of opportunity.

We drive towards the address, parking two streets over as planned. The files are secured in the Tahoe's hidden compartment. As Sam and I prepare to get out, Rose reaches for my arm. "Not now, Rose," I say curtly, pulling away and exiting the vehicle without looking back.

The walk to the house is tense. Sam, sensing the chill, tries to bridge the gap. "You can't hold it against them, Ava," he says quietly as we walk. "Yeah, it pissed me off too, but I get why they kept quiet."

"I understand, too, Sam," I reply tightly. "Can we just focus on the task at hand, please?"

"Sure," he agrees easily, then pauses. "But I don't get why you're being so cold towards them. Especially Rose." He waits, but I keep walking, eyes fixed ahead. He sighs. "Look, Ava… I know something's going on between you two. It's pretty obvious."

I stop dead, groaning inwardly. Great. Just perfect. I turn to face him, bracing myself. "What are you going to do about it, Sam? Run crying to Agent Moore?" The aggression in my voice surprises even me.

He holds his ground, his expression serious but calm. "No. I'm not going to report it," he says evenly. "As long as you make the right calls. As long as your decisions are based on logic, on the mission, not… emotion. Not personal feelings."

The relief is instantaneous, a physical release of tension I didn't know I was carrying. "Okay," I breathe, the fight draining out of me. "Okay. When we have time, when things aren't so… *critical*, I'll explain. It's complicated. Shifter lore and stuff." I meet his gaze. "I didn't want to hide it, Sam, but I was worried. Worried you'd insist Rose had to leave the team."

"Don't worry about it," he reassures me. "As long as the mission comes first, we won't have a problem. But," he adds, a slight smile touching his lips, "I *am* curious to hear this explanation. Just… keep the perverted details to yourself, okay?"

I manage a small chuckle despite myself, the shared joke easing the remaining tension. "No promises," I say, turning back towards our destination. "But it's not like that."

We reach the house, a neat suburban home with a well-tended front garden. Taking a breath, I press the doorbell. Less than a minute later, the door opens, revealing a woman in her late thirties, her eyes wary, shadowed with suspicion.

"Hello," she says cautiously. "Can I help you?"

"Mrs Cunningham?" I confirm, offering a badge and a hopefully reassuring smile. "Detective Bekke, Chicago PD. This is my partner, Detective Miller." Sam flashes his badge, too. "We were hoping we could ask you a few follow-up questions about your husband's disappearance at the end of last year? We promise we won't take up much of your time."

Her eyes narrow slightly. "Can I see those badges again,

please?" she asks, her voice tight. "We've had reporters trying to trick their way in, pretending to be officials."

We hold out our authentically looking police department credentials, provided by the CIA. They have provided us with a range of credentials that we can use if needed, but not all have backgrounds that can be verified, so we must exercise caution when using them. She studies them intently for a long moment before finally nodding, seeming satisfied. "Okay," she sighs, stepping back. "Come in."

She leads us through a tidy hallway into the kitchen. "Please, sit down," she gestures towards the kitchen table. "Can I get you anything to drink?"

"No, thank you, we're fine," Sam replies for both of us. We take seats opposite her. She sits down heavily, the weariness I saw at the door settling deeper into her features. She waits, her hands clasped tightly on the tabletop.

"Mrs Cunningham," I begin gently, "we're sorry to bring this up again, but we were wondering if your husband has recalled anything at all about the time he was missing? Any fragments, any details, however small?"

She lets out a short, bitter huff. The sound is raw with frustration. "No," she says flatly. "He refuses to talk about it. He swears up and down that he remembers absolutely nothing. Acts like spending nearly a month vanished off the face of the earth is no big deal."

"Really?" Sam leans forward slightly. "He just... acts like nothing happened?"

"Pretty much," she confirms, her voice laced with resentment. "And I barely see him anymore."

This confirms our suspicions more easily than I expected. "What do you mean, you hardly see him?" I ask, keeping my tone neutral. "Is he disappearing again?"

"Not like *before*," she clarifies quickly. "But he's just... out. All the time. He used to be such a homebody, you know? Loved his shows, his Xbox... Now? He's always going out. Says he's with the lads," she scoffs. "Guys, I've never even seen before, just show up for him. His old friends? Dropped them completely. Like they never existed."

A wave of sympathy washes over me. This woman's life has been completely upended, and she has no idea why. At least I knew *why* my world shattered. She's just left floundering in the wreckage.

"So, you'd say his personality has undergone a complete change since his return?" Sam probes gently.

"Oh, absolutely," she nods emphatically. "He's irritable, snaps at me over nothing. He never used to be like that." Her voice drops, fear creeping into her eyes. "Sometimes… sometimes I feel like he might actually hurt me if I push him too hard for answers." She looks down at her hands. "My friends keep saying maybe he hit his head, that the memory loss explains the changes… but…" she trails off, clearly unconvinced.

"Maybe," I agree softly, ignoring Sam's warning glance. "But if you ever feel unsafe, Mrs Cunningham, please, reach out to family, friends. Don't stay if you feel threatened."

She gives a tired nod. "I've thought about it," she admits quietly. "Believe me." She glances at the clock. "Is there anything else? I really need to get on with things."

"No, that's everything. Thank you for your time, Mrs Cunningham," Sam says, rising smoothly. "We appreciate you talking to us. We are still actively investigating these disappearances."

As we stand to leave, she hesitates, then adds, almost as an afterthought, "There is one other thing… it's probably nothing, just… weird." She frowns. "He has to shave *so much* now. Like, sometimes twice a day. I swear, sometimes in the morning, it looks like he's grown a full beard overnight. It's… bizarre."

Bingo.

We thank her again, offer our condolences for her situation, and make our exit. Walking back towards the car, the confirmation hangs heavy between Sam and me. Her husband isn't just changed; he's *been* changed. He's a bitten wolf shifter. And now we know for sure.

CHAPTER 36

The One With Shaving Secrets, Relationship Repairs, a Dead Wolf, and a Very Bad Feeling About Luna Falls

We moved to a new hotel yesterday, a necessary precaution after confirming the shifter's presence after visiting Mrs Cunningham. The conversation about her husband, the rapid hair growth – textbook signs of a bitten wolf shifter, according to Luca, solidified the danger. It also brought up uncomfortable questions.

"Do you grow facial hair that quickly?" I ask Luca the question popping out before I can stop it, picturing him having to shave multiple times a day.

He grins, clearly anticipating the query. "Afraid so," he confirms. "It's a shifter thing – accelerated hair growth. A lot of shifter guys grow beards; less hassle than shaving twice a day to stay smooth like I prefer." He shrugs. "Comes with the territory."

My gaze flicks involuntarily to Rose. Suddenly, her longer stints in the bathroom make sense. It wasn't just primping; she was dealing with the same accelerated growth, likely shaving her legs or dealing with other unwanted hair. A small detail, but another layer of their hidden reality.

The evening is spent huddled in the guys' room again, strategising amidst takeout containers and lukewarm coffee. The air is thick with tension and the smell of greasy food. I find myself withdrawing slightly, the earlier revelation about shifters being able to smell lies still stinging. It feels like a breach of trust, a secret deliberately kept that makes me question every interaction, every shared confidence. Rose keeps casting worried glances my way, her hurt radiating across the room, almost palpable thanks to this damned bond. I ignore her, focusing on the files, on the mission, burying the hurt under layers of ingrained professionalism.

"Ava," Rose finally says later, her voice soft, tentative, as we return to our new, sterile room. The awkwardness between us is a tangible thing. "How long are you going to stay mad at me? I… I don't like this." She looks genuinely miserable, and despite my wounded feelings, seeing her unhappy twists something inside me.

I sigh, collapsing onto the edge of the unfamiliar bed—the bedframe squeaks in protest. "I'm not mad, Rose," I say, my voice flat, trying to keep the hurt from bleeding through. "I understand *why* you kept it secret. Logically, I get it. But…" I hesitate, searching for the right words. "You've had chances since… since *us*. Why didn't you tell me then? It feels… dishonest. My feelings are hurt right now, that's all."

She flinches as if struck, her gaze dropping to the cheap carpet. "I was scared, Ava," she whispers, her voice barely audible. "You've been dealing with so much, learning about this world, the bond… everything. I was worried that if I added one more thing, one more layer of… *us* being different, you might decide it was all too much. That *I* wasn't worth it."

"Not worth it?" The words echo my earlier confusion. "Rose, what are you talking about?"

She finally looks up, her beautiful green eyes shimmering with unshed tears. "That you might think *I* wasn't worth the trouble," she repeats, vulnerability laid bare.

My own hurt evaporates instantly, replaced by a fierce surge of protectiveness. I move towards her, pulling her into a hug. She resists for only a fraction of a second before melting against me. "Don't be ridiculous," I murmur into her hair, inhaling her unique scent. "Rose, I love you. Nothing is going to make me change my mind about that.

Unless," I pull back just enough to meet her gaze, my tone firm, "you keep secrets from me again. Deal?"

A watery smile touches her lips. "Deal," she whispers, relief washing over her features. "I won't. I promise. I love you, too."

I kiss her, sealing the promise, the lingering awkwardness dissolving in the renewed connection. We get ready for bed, the earlier tension replaced by a comfortable intimacy. As we settle under the covers, I tuck myself against her side, my head resting on her shoulder in what's quickly becoming my favourite position—the heat radiating from her sinks into my bones, a comforting, living warmth. I drift off easily, feeling safe for the first time in what feels like forever, even knowing the dangers lurking just outside our door.

The next morning, we reconvene over breakfast – another diner, another city block explored. The topic inevitably turns back to the shifters. Do we try to capture one? Do we gather more intel? Or do we cut our losses in Chicago for now? The only question left unanswered is why Cat wanted us to come here; was it just to see the extent of what the wolves are up to, so we know we need to work harder to find others to help us?

Before we can make a decision, my phone starts to ring, I'm confused for a moment as the only people who know the number are right here, unless its Agent Moore, but when I finally pull it out I see it's actually Lieutenant Parker. "Agent Bekke," I answer crisply.

"Agent, it's Lieutenant Parker," the familiar voice comes through the line. "Sorry to disturb you, but I stumbled across another case file. It didn't come up in my initial search, but something the detective involved mentioned made me think of your request for *strange* cases."

"We're just finishing breakfast, Lieutenant. What have you got?" My interest piqued.

"I can meet you to drop it off, I'm already out and about," he offers.

Ten minutes later, Parker meets us in the diner's car park, handing over a slim file. "This was filed as a standard home invasion," he explains, looking slightly uncomfortable. "Nothing in the official report flags it as unusual."

My internal alarms begin to chime softly—home invasion. The words echo with a chilling familiarity. Parker continues, oblivious to my sudden tension, "But the lead detective contacted me after hearing I was pulling odd cases for you. He admitted he left certain details out of the report because… well, because they sounded unbelievable."

"Go on," Sam prompts, leaning forward slightly.

"You might think this is crazy," Parker says then hesitates, "but a neighbour, the one right next door, swears she saw a massive wolf running *from* the house moments after the estimated time of the attack, disappearing into the woods behind the properties." My blood runs cold. *Wolf.* "The victim – the mother – her injuries were consistent with a large animal attack. The official conclusion was the intruder had an attack dog, maybe a Husky or similar breed."

A tight knot forms in my stomach. I force the words out, needing to know. "Were… were children involved?"

Parker nods grimly. "Yes, well, they are young women, actually, they are the daughters."

I have to look away, bile rising in my throat. Images flash – broken door, shadows, stillness, the metallic tang of blood. *Please don't say they saw it happen.*

"The woman had three daughters," Parker continues, his voice dropping slightly. "I think triplets. It was their birthday, actually. They were out at the mall. Came home to find the emergency services swarming their house." Thank God for Small mercies. "The detective drove them to the hospital himself, but their mother… she didn't make it. Died from her injuries shortly after arriving." He sighs. "Apparently, the girls haunted the station for nearly a month, demanding answers, updates. Then, suddenly, after the case was officially closed as an unsolved home invasion and their mother's body was released, they just… stopped coming."

He hesitates, then adds, "There was one other odd detail the detective mentioned, wasn't sure if it was connected. Decided it was probably just grief-stricken vandalism, let it slide. Seems the night their mother died at the hospital, nurses reported hearing glass shatter. Found the lights in their mothers room smashed. No witnesses. And earlier that evening, around the time the girls would have been heading home from the mall, dispatch got two separate calls about three young women smashing streetlights along the route, acting erratically. The callers specifically mentioned the girls didn't seem to have any weapons or tools to break the lamps…."

Smashing lights with no tools? Magic? My mind races. We thank Parker profusely for the information. As soon as he drives away, Sam flips open the file.

"He's right," Sam confirms after scanning the first few pages. "Cleaned up nicely. No mention of wolves or unexplained phenomena. Standard home invasion, victim deceased, case closed pending new evidence."

"What about the father? Husband?" Luca asks, voicing the thought forming in my own mind. Could the wolf have been him? He lost control and killed his wife?

Sam reads further. "File says the father died before the girls were even born. Car accident back in 2000."

2000. The year of the Purge. The year Luca's and Rose's lives were shattered. This isn't just a random attack.

"Could this be it?" Rose asks, her voice filled with a sudden, breathless hope. "The reason Cat sent us here. Are these sisters what Cat wants us to find?"

"It's possible," Luca concedes, his expression thoughtful. "We need to talk to these women. Immediately. Sam, the address?"

Sam reads it out. "But Luca, if their father died in 2000… they could be paranormal, meaning either the wolf came for them, or maybe the wolf wasn't the attacker, but a *protector*"

"Maybe," Rose adds grimly, "the wolves might have already got to them?"

Luca's eyes narrow. "There's another possibility," he says slowly, drawing our attention. "My father… he spoke once of legends, rumours among the packs. About the wolves trying to create hybrids. Shifters who could also wield magic. It was considered extremely difficult, almost impossible." He looks at the file Sam is holding. "If these girls survived, if their father *was* killed in the Purge because he was magical… maybe they *are* magical too. Maybe that's what the wolves were really after."

Magic. Hybrids. My head swims. "How old are the girls?" I ask, needing concrete facts amidst the swirling possibilities.

Sam consults the file again. "Twenty-three," he replies.

"Okay, but why were they still living at home? All three of them? Statistically, at least one of them should have moved out, or maybe gotten married by now. It doesn't add up."

"They were hiding," Sam says quietly, a certainty in his voice that speaks of experience. "Laying low."

"Maybe," Luca agrees. "What date was the attack?"

"Just a few months ago," Sam confirms. "They could still be in danger."

A sense of urgency grips us. We pile back into the Tahoe, the address punched into the satnav. It's close by, worryingly so. As we turn onto the quiet, tree-lined street, my stomach plummets. The houses are large, affluent, and situated on spacious lots. The address we seek is at the very end, nestled against the edge of dense woods. And hammered into the perfectly manicured lawn is a realtor's sign. Bright, cheerful, proclaiming the property as 'SOLD'. The house itself looks vacant, curtains wide open, a subtle air of emptiness clinging to it. They're gone.

"Looks like they moved," Sam states the obvious, disappointment heavy in his voice.

"Or they were taken," Rose counters darkly, "and forced to

sell." The thought makes me clench my fists. If the wolves have them…

We get out, approaching the empty house almost hesitantly. "Which neighbour saw the wolf?" I ask Sam. He points to the house on the right. As if summoned, a curtain twitches in the window, and an elderly woman emerges, sharp-eyed and moving with surprising speed towards us. "Can I help you?" she demands, her voice raspy but strong.

Sam takes the lead, recognising her from the file description. "Mrs Harris? We are detectives from the CPD," he says, flashing his badge again, we all flash our badges too as she scrutinises the credentials with narrowed eyes.

"Detectives? What are you doing back here? Isn't this case closed?" she asks suspiciously.

"Officially, yes, ma'am," Sam confirms smoothly. "But we're following up on some similar cases in other jurisdictions. We were hoping to speak with the Wilks sisters again, see if they remembered anything new."

Mrs Harris sighs, her shoulders slumping slightly. "Afraid you're too late, Detectives. The girls left right after Elspeth's funeral," she says sadly. "Haven't heard a peep from them since. Worries me sick, it does. Lovely girls, all of them." Her gaze drifts towards the empty house. "Heartbreaking, what happened to their mother. They just… vanished. Posted the house keys through my letterbox with a little note saying sorry, and that a realtor would be in touch to collect them."

While Sam continues to gently question Mrs Harris, my attention drifts. Luca and Rose aren't looking at the house; their focus is entirely on the dense woods bordering the property, their bodies subtly tense, nostrils flaring almost imperceptibly.

"Did they happen to leave a forwarding address, Mrs Harris? Any idea where they might have gone?" Sam asks.

"No, dear, not a word," she shakes her head regretfully. "Maybe the realtor knows?" She looks back at the house, her expression pained. "It was just awful, the police… useless. Tried to tell me I didn't see what I saw." Her voice trembles with indignation. "Told the girls it was probably just a big dog. Searched the woods, found nothing, case closed." She shakes her head again. "The poor girls were devastated, shut down completely for weeks. Took all my effort to get them eating again." She lowers her voice conspiratorially. "But I *know* what I saw, Detective. That wasn't any dog. The thing was huge! Big as my little hatchback! Haven't set foot near those woods since."

"The official file just lists it as a home invasion, ma'am," Sam confirms gently.

"I knew it!" she exclaims, vindicated. "Knew they lied to those poor girls! Probably to get young Reya to stop pestering them down at the station every day!"

Reya. The name hangs in the air, heavy with significance. The same name Papa Legba mentioned. The one Cat planned for Elijah to meet. I exchange a wide-eyed look with Sam. It *has* to be her.

"Mrs Harris, do you happen to remember the name of the specific realtor the sisters used?" Sam asks, recovering quickly. "I see the company sign, of course, but the agent's name?"

"Oh, yes, dear, let me see," she thinks for a moment. "Think I kept her card… Indoors. Let me fetch it for you," she says, bustling back towards her own house.

The moment she's out of earshot, I turn to Luca and Rose. "What is it? What's in the woods?"

Luca's voice is low, urgent. "We've got company," he confirms, his eyes fixed on the treeline. "Watching us. Wolf scent. Strong."

My gut clenches. "Okay," I say, my mind racing. "New plan. Get the realtor's details, act normal, and leave. Circle back, take them out. We can't let them report back to the pack."

Luca nods grimly. "They know we're asking about the sisters now. If they figure out who we really are, they'll hunt *us;* luckily, the wind direction is in our favour, so the wolf can't scent us right now."

Mrs Harris returns, pressing a business card into Sam's hand.

We thank her again, make plausible excuses about checking other leads, and walk calmly back to the Tahoe. As we drive away, turning the corner out of sight, Luca gives the order.

"Sam, Ava, when we get there, please stay put," he commands as he pulls over several blocks away, positioning the car for a quick getaway but hidden from the main road. "Prepare yourselves, but don't engage unless absolutely necessary. We'll handle this. You won't be able to keep up once we shift." He glances at Rose, a silent communication passing between them. "If they survive, we'll drag them back here."

Sam and I exchange a look but nod our understanding. We watch as Luca and Rose quickly strip off their clothes, their movements economical and practised. I avert my gaze, giving them privacy, though a part of me-the part now irrevocably tied to Rose—wants to watch the transformation again. A moment later, a soft warmth brushes against my hand. I look down, startled, into the intense green eyes of Rose in her panther form. She nudges my hand gently, a silent reassurance. Hesitantly, I reach out, stroking the unbelievably soft fur behind her ear. A deep purr vibrates through her body and up my arm. Luca makes a low sound, a signal, and Rose pulls away, melting into the shadows alongside him as they disappear into the woods bordering the quiet street.

"Incredible, isn't it?" Sam murmurs beside me, his voice filled with awe as we both stare at the spot where they vanished. "Seeing them… like that. Makes you feel small."

"It's definitely… something," I agree, grabbing my sword hilt, the cool metal a familiar anchor in this increasingly bizarre reality. "But remember, Sam, beautiful things can be deadly. And whatever's in those woods… it's likely terrifying." My thoughts drift to the thought of this hidden world, the possibility that the fairy tales and horror stories humans created were just distorted echoes of the truth, perhaps even planted seeds to prepare us.

"Do you think Reya is the same one? The one Papa Legba

mentioned?" Sam asks, pulling me back to the present.

"The coincidence is too great," I reply grimly. "It has to be."

Before Sam can respond, the quiet afternoon erupts. Savage roars, deeper and more guttural than any zoo animal, echo from the trees, punctuated by the sharp crack of splintering wood. We freeze, weapons ready, straining to hear, every muscle taut. The snarls and growls continue, a brutal symphony of violence hidden just beyond the veil of leaves. Then, abrupt silence. It stretches, heavy and unnerving—my pulse pounds in my ears. We wait, barely breathing, scanning the treeline, wondering who-or what-will emerge.

Minutes crawl by like hours. Then, movement. Bushes rustle violently, and the sleek black form of Luca bursts from the undergrowth. Rose follows a second later, effortlessly dragging the massive, limp form of a grey wolf behind her.

I quickly grab their discarded clothes from the Tahoe, laying them out on the hood. Rose approaches, transforms back with a ripple of muscle and fur, and quickly dresses. I can't help but stare at the wolf she dropped unceremoniously on the ground near us. It's huge, far larger than any natural wolf; it looks brutish, ugly compared to the fluid grace of the panthers.

Keeping my sword ready as Rose finishes dressing. I move to stand guard over the downed wolf while Luca shifts back. The wolf lies utterly still, its breathing shallow, ragged. "Do we need restraints? Somewhere to secure it?" I ask, keeping my voice low.

Luca shakes his head as he pulls on his jeans, his breathing still heavy from the fight. "No point. He's dying," he states flatly. "He'll shift back any second now."

"He wouldn't submit?" Sam asks, understanding dawning in his eyes. Luca shakes his head as he finishes dressing. We all stand watching the dying wolf.

"Sam, call backup," Luca instructs quietly. "Standard cleanup crew. Body disposal."

As Sam makes the call, I move closer to Rose. "Are you okay?

You've got some new injuries," I murmur, noticing angry red lines welling with blood on her arm.

She glances down, then dismisses it with a wave of her hand. "Nothing serious. He was outmatched, two against one. Didn't land anything solid. They'll be gone in a few hours," she assures me, running a comforting hand over my arm.

"What happened in there?" Sam asks, pocketing his phone.

"He wouldn't yield," Rose repeats. "Wouldn't surrender. Shifter pride. Left us no choice."

Just then, the wolf's body twitches violently. Rose grabs a blanket from the Tahoe, tossing it over the shifting form just as the transformation reverses. Fur recedes, bones crack and reshape, and in seconds, a battered, bleeding human man lies where the wolf was. I find the process both grotesque and utterly fascinating.

He groans, eyelids fluttering open. Pain etches deep lines around his eyes and mouth. He's a mess, covered in deep gashes, blood staining the blanket dark red.

"I thought you said he was dying?" I whisper, startled he's still conscious.

"I am," the man rasps, his voice weak, watery. He coughs, a wet, rattling sound.

Luca steps forward, looming over him. "Why were you watching the house, wolf?" he demands, his voice hard, devoid of pity.

The dying shifter manages a weak, bloody smirk. "Alpha… Alpha will return… with the prize…" he gasps, struggling for breath. "Then… we will be… most powerful… pack… take out the council… rule…" His eyes glaze over slightly.

"What prize? Where is your Alpha?" Luca presses, leaning closer.

The man's breathing hitches. He seems to be fading fast, coherence slipping away. "Alpha… small town… east… east of Jackson…" he mumbles, his words slurring. "Prize… in his hands… new generation… plan… action… hidden… army… hundreds…

waiting….” His eyes roll back, and his body goes limp, the last breath rattling from his chest. Silence falls, heavy and final.

“East of Jackson,” Luca repeats thoughtfully, staring down at the dead shifter. “Whatever this prize is… it’s not our primary concern. Not yet. We need to find the sisters.”

“We need to wait for the cleanup crew,” I state, pulling my gaze away from the body.

“I can wait,” Sam offers immediately.

“No,” I counter instantly. “If another wolf shows up, you’re vulnerable alone.”

“Ava’s right,” Luca agrees. He looks between Rose and Sam. “Rose, you took more hits. You stay with Sam. Wait for the team. Ava and I will check out that realtor. We need to find those sisters. Then we can find out why the wolf’s alpha is heading somewhere east of Jackson.”

Rose opens her mouth to protest, but a sharp look from Luca silences her. She nods curtly. I hate leaving her, especially knowing she’s injured, but Luca’s logic is sound, as it would raise questions about why an officer turns up with fresh injuries that are still bleeding. And maybe Sam is right – we can’t let personal feelings compromise the mission.

Luca and I get in the Tahoe. As we drive away, I watch Rose in the side-view mirror until she disappears from sight, a pang of worry echoing in my chest.

“She’ll be fine, Ava,” Luca says quietly, noticing my distraction. “She’s a beta for a reason. Strong, capable. Probably Alpha material herself. I expect her to take over the pack if anything ever happens to me.”

“I know,” I sigh, leaning my head back against the seat. “It’s just… complicated. Dealing with my family stuff, then the bond, the mission… it’s a lot.”

He glances over, his expression softening slightly. “I understand. You’ve handled more than most could, Ava. Honestly? You really are doing better than I expected."

"Yeah, well, some days it feels impossible," I admit. "But after Pittsburgh… taking down those vamps… it felt like maybe, just maybe, we have a chance."

"Confidence is key," Luca advises as he parallel parks neatly outside a modern office building with 'Anderson Realty' etched on the glass door. "Let doubt creep in, and it'll eat you alive. You start second-guessing, hesitating… that's when you get beaten."

"Point taken," I say, climbing out. "Let's hope that doesn't happen."

We enter the realty office, Luca holding the door. It's small, minimalist, with only one woman visible behind a sleek desk. She looks up as the bell chimes, pasting on a bright smile. "Welcome to Anderson Realty! How can I help you today?" Her cheerfulness feels jarringly out of place.

"Special Agent Bekke, FBI," I state, flashing my badge quickly, deciding to use my official badge this time, Luca showing his Marshal credentials beside me. "We're looking for Gail Anderson. We need to ask her about a property she handled recently."

The woman's smile falters, replaced by wary defensiveness. "*I'm* Gail Anderson," she confirms. "And I haven't broken any laws, agents. I don't understand why the FBI and the Marshals Service are interested in my business."

"We're not suggesting you have, Ms Anderson," I say, adopting my most diplomatic tone. "We're trying to locate three sisters, last name Wilks. Their mother's death is potentially linked to other cases we're investigating across state lines. We believe they may be in danger. We need to find them urgently. Do you have any information on where they moved?"

She eyes us suspiciously, tapping a perfectly manicured nail on her desk. "I don't know… client confidentiality… don't you need a warrant for that kind of information?" she stalls, clearly reluctant.

"We can obtain one within the hour," I reply, letting a hint of urgency colour my voice, "but time is critical. Every minute we waste potentially puts these women at greater risk. Please, Ms Anderson, if you have anything that can help us ensure their safety…." I let the plea hang in the air, trying to gauge her reaction, annoyance simmering beneath my calm exterior.

She sighs dramatically, finally capitulating. "Okay, okay, fine. Honestly, the hassle…" she mutters, turning to her computer and clicking through screens before swivelling it slightly towards us. "They moved to a place called Luna Falls. That's all I have. No specific address; all the closing paperwork was handled electronically by email, but the bank account provided by their mother a few years back, in case she wanted the property to be sold, is located in Luna Falls."

"Luna Falls. Thank you, Ms Anderson. You've been very helpful," I say, turning to leave, relief mixing with apprehension.

"Wait," she calls out suddenly, stopping us at the door. "There was one thing… it struck me as odd at the time."

We turn back expectantly. "What was that?" Luca asks.

"The bank account details the mother provided for the funds transfer from the house sale…" she frowns, pulling up another screen. "It wasn't under Wilks. The account name was Reya *Harper*." She shrugs. "Maybe they knew they were in trouble, using an alias?"

Harper. I see Luca stiffen beside me, a flicker of recognition, or perhaps alarm, crossing his face. I file the name away, waiting until we're back in the privacy of the car.

"What is it, Luca?" I demand as soon as the doors are closed. "You reacted to the name Harper. Why?"

He stares out the windscreen for a long moment, his brow furrowed in thought. "I'm not sure," he begins slowly. "We're assuming the sisters are potentially magical, right? Maybe witches, so that the wolves could use them, like my father once told me about how they are always looking to add magic back into their bloodlines, so my thought about the situation might be correct, except, if they were, why would the wolves just let them leave after killing the mother? Unless…" he trails off, then continues, thinking aloud, "Unless the daughters *didn't* inherit any gifts. Maybe the wolves realised they were useless, killed the mother because *she* was the target, or maybe she fought back and died protecting them? Maybe the wolves are only watching the sisters now, waiting to see if *their* children manifest any abilities?" He shakes his head. "But the name… Harper… when I was young, before the Purge, I remember my father mentioning meetings with the Harper coven. He said they were one of the oldest, largest, most powerful witch covens in the country. Based near… damn, I can't recall where exactly, but Harper is a significant name in witch circles." He looks at me, confusion warring with concern. "It makes no sense. If the sisters are tied to the Harper coven, why hide under the name Wilks all these years? And why switch back *now*? Unless… unless the wolves weren't after magic at all? Maybe they just wanted the mother for some other reason?"

He's spiralling, trying to connect disparate, confusing pieces. We pick up Rose and Sam, quickly briefing them on the realtor's information and Luca's Harper Coven theory. Sam immediately starts tapping Luna Falls into his laptop, searching for its location. We watch as his face pales, his eyes widening in alarm.

"Sam? What is it?" I ask, a knot tightening in my stomach.

He looks up, his expression grim. "Luca… where did that wolf say his Alpha went again?"

Luca frowns. "East of Jackson. A small town out there. Why?"

Sam swallows hard. "Luna Falls," he says, his voice barely a whisper, "is a small town, just east of Jackson, Mississippi."

A collective intake of breath fills the car. "Crap," I curse, the pieces slamming together with sickening clarity. "He's going after the sisters. We have to get there. Now!" Panic claws at my throat. Those women have been through hell; we can't let the wolves get to them.

"Ava, wait," Luca cautions, his voice tight with urgency. "We could be too late already. And even if we're not, we are *not* equipped to take on a pack, let alone an army, potentially hundreds strong, according to that dying wolf."

"So, what? We just let him take them?" I retort, anger flaring alongside the fear. "We were guided here, Luca! To them! We have to do something!"

"I think we have to find out," Sam suggests hesitantly. "Ava and I can go in and do the same as we did here, say we are just checking up, see if they remember anything, then we can get a feel for the sisters and see if we can pick up on anything strange."

"I like that, using the mother's case to get close. Assess the situation. See if there are any hints that the alpha is actually there, if the sisters are okay? If everything seems… *normal*, or if the threat is clearly too big, we pull back. Regroup. Get Agent Moore involved. But we have to *see*." I say, looking at Luca pleading he agrees with me. "By the time we get there, my neck will be fully healed."

Luca rubs his temples, torn. "It's a massive risk," he murmurs, glancing at Rose, who looks equally apprehensive. "The wolves could be everywhere. Watching the town, watching the sisters. We don't know what we're walking into. But…" he meets my gaze, determination hardening his expression, "we have to know. We have to see if these sisters are who Cat sent us to find." One by one, nodding grimly, they agree.

"Okay," I say, taking charge again, pushing down my own fear. "Sam, call Lieutenant Parker. Arrange to drop off the files. Please inform him that we appreciate the superintendent's help, but we have an urgent lead that is taking us out of state. Ask him if they can keep compiling a list of any further missing persons who return, just in case. Then," I take a steadying breath, "plot the fastest route to Luna Falls, Mississippi. Let's move."

The End

You will next see Ava and her team in:

Dark Intentions – The Harper Legacy Book 2